The Player & the Game

Also by Shelly Ellis

Can't Stand the Heat
Another Woman's Man
The Best She Ever Had

Published by Dafina Books

The Player
& the Game

SHELLY
ELLIS

Kensington Publishing Corp.
http://www.kensingtonbooks.com

DAFINA BOOKS are published by

Kensington Publishing Corp.
119 West 40th Street
New York, NY 10018

All Kensington Titles, Imprints, and Distributed Lines are available at special quantity discounts for bulk purchases for sales
promotions, premiums, fund-raising, and educational or insti-
tutional use. Special book excerpts or customized printings can
also be created to fit specific needs. For details, write or phone
the office of the Kensington special sales manager: Kensington
Publishing Corp., 119 West 40th Street, New York, NY 10018,
attn: Special Sales Department, Phone: 1-800-221-2647.

Dafina and the Dafina logo Reg. U.S. Pat & TM Off.

ISBN-13: 978-0-7582-9094-6
ISBN-10: 0-7582-9094-2
First Kensington Trade Edition: September 2013
First Kensington Mass Market Edition: August 2015

eISBN-13: 978-0-7582-9095-3
eISBN-10: 0-7582-9095-0
Kensington Electronic Edition: August 2015

10 9 8 7 6 5 4 3 2 1

Printed in the United States of America

To Andrew, for making me laugh—even when I don't want to laugh.

To Chloe, for making Mommy push herself and get out there and hustle. Those diapers aren't going to pay for themselves!

Acknowledgments

The Gibbons Gold Digger book series has been a whirlwind ride for me. For months, I was biting my nails, waiting to hear whether the book I submitted had a chance after hearing rejections from both agents and other publishers, and pretty much concluding that it didn't. Then my soon-to-be editor Mercedes Fernandez e-mailed me saying, "Hey, can you send me the second book?" Then I heard a few months later that Kensington would be moving forward with the entire series . . . and the clouds parted!

So as always, I have to say thanks to Mercedes for being a champion for the series and taking a chance on me and my work. I'm glad you believed in the Gibbons sisters and my writing. I am forever grateful.

Next, I have to say thanks to my hubby, Andrew. You're not a women's fiction or a romance fan, but you've had faith in my writing from day one. You love me and support me without hesitation. There is no substitute for having a partner who's willing to listen to your neurotic ramblings in bed in the wee hours of the morning and bring you ice cream when you're depressed.

The Internet has helped me to reach out to other authors who I greatly admire and who have been very encouraging. Though I know she won't remember this, I appreciate the sweet note of congratulations from the talented Ms. Beverly Jenkins. I'm a huge fan of her work so to get any note from her was amazing.

See you on Facebook for book club night, Ms. Jenkins! Thanks to authors Cheris Hodges, Phyllis Bourne, Cydney Rax, and Daamiah Poole for retweets and book blurbs. Having successful authors reach out to say something nice is refreshing. I hope I can repay the favor to you guys and other burgeoning authors like myself some day.

I also want to say thanks the to romance authors in Washington Romance Writers. You guys have been a treasure trove of information, resources, and support. One day, I will not be pregnant and will finally make it to our author retreat.

Thanks to Jamie at the coolest web site online, Black GirlsNerds.com, for spreading the word about my work and for bonding with a fellow black nerdette. Thanks to blogs like Romance University, Romance Cooks, and others for letting me blog on your sites. And thanks to all the review sites and book clubs that have given my books a chance.

Finally, I have to give a big thanks to my parents, extended family, and friends for your lifelong support.

her shoulders and raised her already dangerously short skirt even higher.

She adjusted the realtor name tag near her suit jacket lapel, casually ran her fingers through her long tresses, and reached into her purse. She pulled out her cell phone and quickly dialed her assistant's number. Thankfully, the young woman picked up on the second ring.

"Carrie, honey, I'm running late . . . Yes, I know . . . Are you already at the open house?" Stephanie asked distractedly as she dug for her keys in her purse's depths. "Are any buyers there yet? . . . OK, OK, don't freak out. . . . Yes, just take over for now. Put out a plate of cookies and set the music on low. I'll be there in fifteen minutes . . . I know . . . I have every confidence in you. See you soon."

She hung up.

With car keys finally retrieved, Stephanie pressed the remote button to open her car doors. The car beeped. The headlights flashed. She jogged to the driver's-side door and opened it. As she started to climb inside the vehicle, she had the distinct feeling of being watched.

Stephanie paused to look up, only to find a man standing twenty feet away from her. He casually leaned against the brick front of one of the many shops on Main Street. He was partially hidden by the shadows of an overhead awning.

He looked like one of many jobless men you would find wandering the streets midday, hanging out in front of stores because they had little else to do and nowhere else to go. Except this bored vagrant was a lot more attractive than the ones she was used to seeing. He also was distinct from the other vagrants in town because she had seen him several times today and earlier this week.

Stephanie had spotted him when she walked into the nail salon and again as she left, absently waving her nails as they dried. He had been sitting in the driver's seat of a tired-looking Ford Explorer in the lot across the street from the salon. Though he hadn't said anything to her or even looked up at her as she walked back to her car, she had the feeling he had been waiting for her.

She had seen him also on Wednesday, strolling along the sidewalk while she had been on her date with her new boyfriend, Isaac. The man had walked past the restaurant's storefront window where she and Isaac had been sitting and enjoying their candlelit dinner. When Stephanie looked up from her menu and glanced out the window, her eyes locked with the stroller's. The mystery man abruptly broke their mutual gaze and kept walking. He disappeared at the end of the block.

The mystery man had a face that was hard to forget—sensual, hooded dark eyes, a full mouth, and a rock-hard chin. He stood at about six feet with a muscular build. Today, he was wearing a plain white T-shirt and wrinkled jeans. Though his short hair was neatly trimmed, he had thick beard stubble on his chin and dark-skinned cheeks.

"Are you following me?" Stephanie called to him, her open house now forgotten.

He blinked in surprise. "What?" He pointed at his chest. "You mean me?"

"Yes, I mean you!" She placed a hand on her hip. "Are you following me? Why do I keep seeing you around?"

He chuckled softly. "Why would I be following you? Lady, I'm just standing here."

He wasn't just standing there. She sensed it.

"Well, this is a small town. Loitering is illegal in Chesterton. You could get arrested!"

"It's illegal to stand in front of a building?" Laughter was in his voice. He slowly shook his head. "We're still in America, right? Last time I checked, I was well within my rights to stand here, honey. Besides, I'm not panhandling. I'm just enjoying the warm sunshine." His face broke into a charming, dimpled smile that would have made most women's knees weak. "Is that a crime?"

Stephanie narrowed her eyes at him warily.

She didn't like him or his condescending tone. He was attractive, but something emanated from him that made her . . . uncomfortable. It made her heart-beat quicken and her palms sweat. She wasn't used to reacting to men this way. Usually her emotions were firmly in control around them, but they weren't around this guy. She didn't like him one bit.

"If . . . if I catch you standing here when I get back, I'll . . . I'll call the cops," she said weakly.

At that, he raised an eyebrow. "You do that," he challenged, casually licking his lips and shoving his hands into his jean pockets. Defiantly, he slumped against the brick building again.

Stephanie took a deep breath, willing her heart to slow its rapid pace. She climbed into her car and shut the driver's-side door behind her with a slam. She shifted the car into drive and pulled off, watching him in her rearview mirror until she reached the end of block. He was still standing in front of the building, still leaning under the shadows of the awning, still looking smug as she drove to the end of Main Street and made a right.

Finally, she lost sight of him.

"Shit," Keith Hendricks muttered through clenched teeth as he pushed himself away from the brick building once he saw the taillights of Stephanie Gibbons's BMW disappear.

"Shit," he uttered again as he strode across the street to his SUV, pausing to let a Volkswagen Beetle drive by.

Though he had played it cool in front of her, he had started to sweat the instant Stephanie's eyes had shifted toward him.

He was getting sloppy. He had decided to get out of his car and walk near her office to try to get a better vantage point, to see if her boyfriend, Isaac, was going to meet her here today. But Keith hadn't counted on her noticing him standing there. More importantly, she had noticed *and* recognized him from the other occasions that he thought he had been discreetly tailing her and Isaac. It had been a mistake, a rookie mistake that wasn't worthy of the four years he had spent as a private investigator.

"You messin' up, boy," he said to himself as he opened his car door, climbed inside, and plopped on the leather seat. He shut the door behind him and inserted his key into the ignition.

But he had to admit he was out of practice. This was his first real case in months.

He had been eager to accept this one, to sink his teeth into something meaty. He had been tired of the busy work that had filled his days for the past few months. Stokowski and Hendricks Private Investigators had been going through a bit of a dry spell lately. With the exception of this con artist case, they had been doing nothing but process serving for months, delivering summonses and subpoenas. When Keith left the ATF to start the PI business with retired cop and family friend Mike Stokowski four years ago, process serving wasn't exactly the exciting work he had had in mind. He had hoped things would pick up soon. Now they finally were, but this case had been complicated.

He had finally located Reggie Butler also known as Tony Walker *now* known as Isaac Beardan. The con artist and Casanova had left a trail of heartbreak and several empty bank accounts along the Eastern Seaboard. Each time Isaac moved on to his next con, he changed his name, his look slightly, and his story. It made him a hard guy to find.

One of the most recent victims from which Isaac had stolen thirty thousand dollars worth of jewelry had hired Stokowski and Hendricks PI to track him down. Keith had traced the smooth-talking bastard here, to the small town of Chesterton. Keith still wasn't sure though if Isaac worked alone on his cons. He didn't know what role his girlfriend, Stephanie Gibbons, played in it—if any. Hell, maybe Isaac had selected her as his next victim.

"Don't worry about her," a voice in Keith's head urged as he pulled onto the roadway. "You finished your part of the case. You found him. You've got photos . . . documentation. The police can track him down now and press charges. That's all that matters."

But was that all that mattered? Should he warn the new girlfriend about Isaac?

An image of her suddenly came to mind: her pretty cinnamon-hued face; the limber legs like a seasoned dancer that were on full display underneath her flowing, pleated skirt; and her full red glossy lips. He remembered the stubborn glare she had given him too, trying her best to intimidate him, but failing miserably.

"If you tell her the truth, she'll tell Isaac," a voice in his head warned. "It'll put him on the run again. The authorities will never be able to track him down."

Keith frowned as he started the drive back to his hotel. It was true. Isaac would know he had been found and only move on to the next place and start a new con. No, Keith couldn't tell her the truth about Isaac. He had worked too hard on the case to throw it all away now.

"Maybe she'll figure out he's full of shit by herself," Keith murmured as he gazed out the car's windshield.

But he knew that wasn't likely. Isaac was well practiced at this game. He was a champion player. Keith doubted Stephanie Gibbons would be any different than any of the other saps Isaac had swindled.

Chapter 2

"Open your eyes," Isaac whispered into her ear, making Stephanie's hair flutter along her temple, sending chills of anticipation up her spine.

"But I'm afraid to look, Isaac! Can't you just tell me what it is?"

"Trust me, baby. You'll like this surprise," he assured warmly. "Open them."

Stephanie held her hands over her eyes, feeling like a kid on Christmas morning, scared to discover that the Cabbage Patch doll or the Barbie doll palace she had asked Santa to bring her wasn't waiting for her under the Christmas tree.

It had been a long day. The open house had gone well, but she still hadn't been able to forget about the stalker guy from earlier. His face kept haunting her, making her feel off her game as she showed the three-thousand-square-foot colonial to buyers and other real estate agents, as she tried to turn on the charm. Stephanie had been looking forward to her date with Isaac to help her finally forget about the stalker, but Isaac had shown up an hour late for today's date, which was out of character for him. He assured her that there was a good reason for his tardiness, and that "good reason" happened to be waiting for her outside her home. He instantly had piqued her interest.

She was accustomed to men bringing her gifts—perfume, diamond bracelets, and the occasional Birkin bag—but not one that required her to step out of her front door. Stephanie just hoped she wouldn't be disappointed. She and Isaac had been dating for less than two months. They were still in that period when "complete honesty" was a dirty word. If the surprise turned out to be lackluster, she'd have to pretend amazement. She didn't want to hurt his feelings. After all, the very resourceful and very *rich* financial planner Isaac Beardan could be her next husband.

"*If* you play your cards right," her mother's warning voice whispered in her head.

Since her four daughters were old enough to wear lipstick and panty hose, Stephanie's mother, Yolanda Gibbons, had taught them that their goal in life was to sniff out a rich man and snag him when the opportunity came along. Stephanie planned to do that with Isaac, but she had to be cautious.

"Open your eyes," Isaac ordered again as they stood on the curb.

Behind her palms, Stephanie practiced her amazed expression one last time. She slowly lowered her hands to her sides. Her eyelashes fluttered open.

Isaac rubbed her slender brown shoulders and grinned. "Well? What do you think?"

She wouldn't have to put on an award-winning performance this time.

Parked along the curb was a glistening cherry red SL550 Mercedes-Benz two-seater roadster with a tan leather interior and sparkling rims. Stephanie instantly hopped off the sidewalk and ran toward it.

"Isaac," she gushed, "she's beautiful!"

"You like it?"

"I don't like her. I *love* her!" she corrected.

Anything that stunning *had* to be a "her." Stephanie lovingly ran her fingers over the car door and laid her hand on the buttery-smooth leather head cushion.

"When did you get her?"

"I've had it for months back at my place in South Carolina, under a tarp in my garage," he said casually, pushing back his suit jacket and shoving his hands into his pockets. "I finally had it delivered today."

"Well, she's *gor*geous," Stephanie whispered, ogling the car again.

She briefly envisioned herself in the passenger seat with the wind blowing through her hair as Isaac drove down I-495.

I have to take a ride in this bad girl—immediately, she thought.

"And you're gorgeous too." He then dangled his SmartKey. ". . . Which is why I'm giving the car to you; a gorgeous car for a gorgeous lady."

Stephanie had been leaning over to look more closely at the dashboard buttons and video screen. When he said those words, she snapped up her head so fast she almost got whiplash. She blinked in shock and pushed her long locks out of her eyes, spitting hair out of her mouth.

"You're . . . You're giving the car to *me*? Really?"

He nodded and jingled the key, holding it out to her.

"Oh, Isaac, *baaaaaby!*" She ran toward him and leaped into his arms. Stephanie looped a hand around his neck and gave him a searing hot kiss while ever so gently tugging the car key out of his hand.

Isaac eagerly kissed her back, cupping his hand at the base of her neck and tilting back her head. His other hand then slid from her waist to her ass. He squeezed the cheeks then gripped them firmly. He parted her lips with his tongue.

Stephanie suddenly pulled her mouth away and shooed his hands from her rear end. No need to put on a display for the neighbors. Most of the old biddies in her neighborhood could document her every move anyway.

She tugged him toward her house. If they were going to do this, she wanted to do it in the privacy of her own bedroom.

"Come with me," she said saucily as she led him up the concrete walk to her front door, making sure to put a little shimmy in her walk as she did so.

"But I thought I was taking you out to dinner?" He hopped slightly to dodge the spray of water coming from the sprinkler system on her pristine lawn.

"There's been a change of plans," Stephanie whispered seductively, putting her key in her front door. She closed the door behind him and led him down a darkened hallway to her bedroom. When they entered, she shoved Isaac back onto her bed. She then slowly lowered the zipper on the side of her dress before tugging the straps off her shoulders.

"Is somebody about to be my bad girl?" Isaac asked huskily, taking off his suit jacket then his gray tie.

"Your naughty girl, baby!" she assured.

He squirmed excitedly as she opened her night-table drawer and pulled out the fur-lined handcuffs. She twirled them around her index finger and grinned.

Sex wasn't about enjoyment for Stephanie or for most Gibbons women. Again, it was about putting on a performance. Like a stripper walking the stage, she knew what to do to "make it rain," how to get a man's blood pumping. Her pleasure wasn't important. What was more important was to become his fantasy, to leave him trembling in the beginning, and satiated in the end. At least Isaac didn't have any weird kinks that she had to work around. He liked hand-cuffs, the occasional blindfold, and ice cubes. She could handle that.

Tonight's performance was no different than any other. She undressed herself slowly, careful to leave on her high heels, letting Isaac take in the full view of her naked body in all its glory. Hours at the gym to maintain her size 6 frame were done for this very reason. When he gazed at her, she wanted everything to be taut, perky, and firm.

No cellulite dimples around here, Stephanie thought.

She bound his right hand to one of the headboard posts, using the handcuffs. She used his necktie to bind his other hand. She undressed him too, opening his shirt buttons eagerly, lowering his pants zipper with her teeth, expertly putting the condom on with her mouth—making him groan with excitement and need. From there, it was all teasing and nipping, grinding and moaning.

Stephanie rode him cowgirl style, squeezing her nipples as she did it, pretending that she was having the time of her life. When she finally pretended to come, she bucked her hips and threw back her head, making sure she shouted loud enough to make it believable, but not too loud to be over the top. When he fell back against the headboard, slack and slick with sweat, she smiled.

Mission accomplished, she thought.

Stephanie rolled onto her stomach and raised her wineglass to her lips, savoring the taste of the last bit of sauvignon blanc on her tongue. The handcuffs still dangled from one of the bedposts. Their clothes still littered the carpeted floor. She watched as Isaac slowly rose from the bed and enjoyed the view of his muscular backside in the orange glow of her desk lamp as he walked across the room and picked up his gray boxer briefs.

"Thank you for my gift," she murmured lazily, sitting her glass on her night table, "if I haven't said thank you already."

"You didn't have to say it." He tugged on his underwear. "You *showed* me how thankful you were—repeatedly."

She rose to her elbows and smirked. "And you liked every minute of it."

"You damn right I did."

He walked toward the bed and slapped her ass before leaning down to kiss her hungrily. She raised herself to meet his lips, putting all her charms into the kiss. For a split second, it seemed as if the kiss would deepen and Isaac would tug off the boxers he had just put on, but abruptly, he pulled his mouth away.

"Can't start that," he muttered, licking his lips. He wandered back to the other side of the bedroom, grabbed his white dress shirt, which had been tossed on a velvet settee in the corner, and put it on. "I'm sorry, but I've got to go."

"*Awww,* already?" she asked, poking out her bottom lip in an exaggerated pout.

"I'm afraid so, gorgeous." He buttoned the last shirt button then grabbed his pants.

Stephanie crisscrossed her bare legs. "But how are you going to get home if you're leaving your Mercedes here?" She paused. "You *are* leaving the car here, aren't you?"

"Don't worry. I told you, the car is yours. I'll just catch a cab."

Stephanie frowned. She felt her first pangs of guilt at those words. "Well, that doesn't seem right. Why don't you let me take a quick shower and get dressed? I could take you home."

"I said don't worry about it, baby," he assured, raising his zipper. "I've got it all covered."

Stephanie sat upright. She shook her head, bemused as she watched Isaac dress. "Why are you in such a hurry, Isaac?"

"I'm not. Wild horses couldn't drag me away from your fine ass." He was still smiling as he shrugged into his suit jacket. "Look, why don't we do this? Why don't we kiss each other good night and agree to meet up next week, say Thursday? We'll take a trip to one of the jewelers on Main Street and I'll let you pick out anything you want."

Jewelers? Stephanie instantly perked up and swung her legs over the edge of the bed. She cocked an eyebrow. "Anything I want?"

He nodded, raising his collar before tossing his silk tie around his neck. "Maybe even a gift of the solitaire diamond variety."

Stephanie's eyes widened. She practically leaped the distance from the mattress to eight feet across the room where Isaac stood. "*A solitaire diamond?* Do you mean an engagement ring?" She stood naked in front of him with her hands on her hips. "Isaac, you better not be playing with me! This isn't a joke, is it?"

He knotted his tie. "No, it isn't a joke, baby."

She grinned. "Are you asking me to marry you?"

"What do you think?"

Less than two months, Stephanie thought excitedly. This had to be a Gibbons family record. It was less than two months and she was already engaged!

Thank God he was dressed or she would have shoved him back onto the bed. Instead, she had to satisfy herself with wrapping her arms around his neck and giving him a long, soulful kiss.

"Gotta go, gorgeous," he murmured, prying her arms from around his neck and slapping her on the ass again.

"All right, honey." She adjusted his tie and tapped the tip of his nose. "I guess we'll just have to save the rest for next week."

Isaac kissed her hand, bidding her a gentlemanly farewell. He then turned and walked out of her bedroom, before giving a wink.

"See you Thursday," he called before turning around and striding down the hallway.

"See you Thursday," she sang after him.

When he shut her front door, she clasped her hands together and jumped up and down on the balls of her bare feet, barely able to contain her joy.

Chapter 3

"I have good news!" Stephanie exclaimed, tossing her linen napkin over her lap.

It was the day after Isaac's visit. She was in between scheduled showings, having a casual bistro lunch outside with her three sisters and enjoying the spring day. She had driven her new Mercedes roadster with the top down on the way there, basking in the warm sunshine and her good fortune. She had become engaged, gotten a new car, and made a bundle of money under Isaac's financial guidance, all in one week. She wanted to share the news with the world, but for now, she would settle for gloating to her sisters.

"Good news, huh?" Her eldest sister, Cynthia, drolly rolled her hazel eyes and sipped from her glass of raspberry iced tea. "Let me guess. Neiman Marcus is having a sale?"

Her second oldest sister, Dawn, giggled between chews of chicken, pesto, and sun-dried tomatoes. She pushed her tinted sunglasses to the crown of her head, revealing her comely ebony-hued face. "No, no! Her boyfriend broke down and bought her those

python Prada pumps she's been obsessing over for
the past month." Dawn turned to Stephanie and tilted
her head, sending her jet black, glossy bob swinging.
"We hope you and your shoes are very happy together,
Steph," she said patronizingly, patting Stephanie's bare
arm.

Their table erupted into laughter. Stephanie narrowed her eyes in response.

Her sisters were laughing now, but they wouldn't
be in a few minutes. In fact, they probably would be
speechless, gnashing their teeth and green with envy—
even greener than Stephanie's silk emerald halter
dress—when she told them that Isaac had proposed.

The only one who wouldn't be jealous was Lauren.
The youngest of all the sisters had already married
her millionaire—the entrepreneur and ex-football
star Crisanto Weaver—nearly four months ago in a
small private ceremony at his mansion in Chesterton.
Even more amazing, Lauren actually seemed to be in
love with her husband.

Well, I won't have love, Stephanie conceded, but
there were worse things. Money and a sense of security would do, and that was *exactly* what Isaac could
provide for her.

"If you all are finished cackling," Stephanie muttered, pushing what was left of her salmon around
her plate with her fork, "can I share my good news
now?"

Lauren grinned. "Go ahead, Steph. Tell us."

"Well, I just wanted to let you know that . . ."
Stephanie took a melodramatic pause. ". . . I'm *engaged!*"

The women around the table reacted simultaneously but in very different ways. Lauren's big doe-like

eyes widened in surprise. Dawn gaped in shock, looking horrified. Cynthia's face settled into a grimace.

"*Really?*" Lauren's smile tightened as she cleared her throat. "Well . . . uh . . . congratulations, Steph."

"How the hell are you engaged?" Dawn exclaimed. "Didn't you just meet him a little over a month ago?"

"So!" Stephanie said dismissively, waving her hand, sending her gold bangles jingling. "Less than two months is more than enough time to make a man fall in love with you . . . if you know what you're doing."

Dawn opened her mouth to reply, but Lauren gave her a warning glance. Dawn pursed her lips and kept silent, though she didn't look too happy about it.

"So, umm, when did he pop the question?" Lauren asked.

"Last night! And it was *so* wonderful. He showed such style and class."

Maybe she was exaggerating a little, but what did she care?

Stephanie clapped her hands and did a little dance in her chair, unable to contain her excitement.

"I'm engaged! I'm engaged! *I'm engaged!* And you all will be my bridesmaids—of course. Just like the last time I got married."

Cynthia snorted. "*Humph,* I don't see a ring on your finger. I'll believe it when you show us the evidence. Until then, I'm not convinced."

"I *am* engaged!" Stephanie argued, stomping her foot in frustration on the cobblestone sidewalk under their table. "He asked me! We're supposed to select the ring together at the jewelers next week!"

"Cynthia's just picking on you, Steph," Lauren assured, placing a hand over Stephanie's and giving it a squeeze. "We know that you're engaged. We believe you. It's just a little . . . sudden that's all. It did happen a little fast. You have to admit that."

"It's more than a little fast. You barely know the man!" Cynthia bellowed.

"You barely knew your first husband," Stephanie countered, making Cynthia grit her teeth.

Dawn sighed. "She does have a point, Cindy."

When Cynthia looked mad enough that steam would come out of her ears, Lauren intervened again, holding up her hands. "OK, OK, guys. There's no reason for us to start arguing. Stephanie just shared some good news. She's engaged. We should . . . We should be celebrating."

Stephanie eyed her little sister. "Yeah, we *should* celebrate, Laurie! Good suggestion!" She waved down a waiter who was passing their table on his way back inside the restaurant. "Excuse me. Can you bring us a bottle of champagne?"

He walked toward their table. "Sure, which one would you like?"

Stephanie reached for the leather-bound wine menu and flipped it open. She scanned the list and grinned. "We'll have the Perrier-Jouët."

"Will do," he said with a nod before turning around to get them a bottle.

"Oh, and bring four champagne glasses!" she called after him.

"Only three!" Lauren said.

The waiter nodded before disappearing behind the restaurant's front door.

"*Only three?*" Stephanie asked. "You aren't having any?"

Lauren shook her head. "No, my sparkling water is fine. I have to get back to the restaurant in a half an hour. I don't want to be tipsy with a butcher knife in my hand."

"Tipsy? But it's just *one* glass, Laurie! I know you're a lightweight," Stephanie said, alluding to her baby sister's petite size, "but you're not *that* light! Come on, have a drink with us. I'm paying! In fact, I'll cover the whole lunch!" She winked. "I've got extra cash now thanks to Isaac."

"No, really, it's ok."

"Oh, come on! *You* were the one who said we should be celebrating," Cynthia argued. "Just drink the damn glass of champagne, girl. It won't kill you!"

Lauren's smile withered. "I know it won't kill me, but I . . ."

"But *what?*" Stephanie asked.

Lauren glanced hesitantly at her sisters. She took a deep breath. "I'm pregnant," she suddenly blurted out.

"*What?*" they all cried in unison.

"I'm pregnant. That's why I don't want any champagne. The doc said I shouldn't drink anymore."

They started shouting questions then: *Why didn't you say anything? When did you find out? Have you told Cris yet? Does Mama know?*

For the first time, all of the sisters were smiling.

"No, I haven't told Mama yet," Lauren said. "I hadn't told anyone but Cris—until now. It's just I wanted to wait a week or so to officially get to the end of the first trimester before I shared the news. But, oh, well," she said with a laugh and a shrug, "so much for those plans."

"Oh, we haven't had a little one in the family in *so long!*" Dawn exclaimed, clapping her hands. "A baby! It's so exciting!"

Cynthia chuckled. "We haven't had any little ones, because you haven't given birth to any little ones. I've done my part." She pointed around the table. "It's the rest of you that keep dragging your feet when it comes to having babies."

"Well, not anymore," Stephanie announced. "Now Laurie has one on the way," she said, patting her sister's flat belly, making Lauren laugh. "And maybe I'll be next in line."

The rest of the lunch was filled with conversations about babies and weddings—well, mostly Stephanie talking about weddings and her sisters listening as she talked. When the check finally arrived, Stephanie instantly reached for it.

"Steph," Lauren said, "you don't have to pay for lunch. We can all chip in."

"Yes, I do," Stephanie insisted, tucking her debit card into the leather pocket. "I said I would. I told you I'm *flush* with cash now. It's no big deal."

"Hell, let her pay," Cynthia urged as Stephanie handed the bill and her card to the waiter. "It's her money."

Stephanie put on her sunglasses and grinned. "Thirty-percent return on investment," she said. "That's like . . . unheard of! I swear Isaac is a genius. He's like one of those supercomputers that tell you which stocks to pick. Cris should talk to him. He could take Cris from a millionaire to a *billionaire*, Laurie!"

"I don't know." Lauren pursed her lips. "Cris has

used the same investment advisor for years. He said he's wary of using someone he doesn't really know. He told me quite a few guys in the NFL got burned by advisors who swore they could make them bundles of money, but they turned out to not have a clue what they were doing. And that was in the best-case scenario. Many of those guys turned out to be pretty much conmen."

"But he *knows* Isaac," Stephanie argued. "Or at least he will. I'll make sure of that. They'll practically be related a few months from now when Isaac and I are married. They should talk!"

Lauren seemed to contemplate her sister's words. After some seconds, she shrugged. "Maybe. We'll see."

"No 'maybe,' " Stephanie urged, shaking her head. "He shouldn't let this opportunity get away! I swear to you, Isaac is—"

She was interrupted by the waiter who loudly cleared his throat. He hovered over her shoulder, near their restaurant table. Stephanie turned to stare up at him.

"Uh, ma'am, your card was declined. Would you like to use another one to pay for your meal?"

Stephanie pushed her gold-tinted sunglasses to the crown of her head. "*Declined?*" she asked, squinting up at him. "Are you sure?"

"Yes, I'm sure," the waiter said, nodding his blond head. "I ran it several times. I kept getting back 'insufficient funds.' I'd be happy to run another card though."

He then handed the debit card back to Stephanie. The table fell silent.

"Uh, why don't you use my card?" Lauren piped,

pulling her wallet from her handbag, opening it, and handing her credit card to the waiter. "That should cover it. Sorry for the trouble."

"No problem at all," the waiter said.

As he walked away with Lauren's card, Stephanie gazed at the card in her hand, transfixed.

"Maybe you just did a big charge and forgot," Dawn volunteered.

"Or knowing you, Steph, forgot to pay the damn bill," Cynthia said with a smirk. "Once you pay it, they should unfreeze the account."

Stephanie slowly shook her head, still staring down at the plastic in her hand. "No, this is my *debit* card, not one of my credit cards. It's connected to my checking account. I should have more than eighteen thousand dollars in there!"

"Then it was a mistake," Lauren reassured. "After lunch, just go to the bank and check it out. I'm sure there's some explanation."

Stephanie nodded. Lauren was right. It had to be a mistake. She sipped from her water glass, deciding to worry about it later.

Chapter 4

"I need to stop at an ATM," Cynthia called over her shoulder as they walked along Main Street. They were on their way to their cars that were parked in a lot at the end of the block.

The sisters drew a few admiring stares, grins, and murmurs of "Good afternoon" from the sundry men strolling along the boulevard. They were four beautiful women, after all—laughing and chatting as if they didn't have a care in the world. What man wouldn't stop to do a double take and look at them?

But the reaction was very different from the women they passed. The sisters drew eye rolls, sucked teeth, and the occasional sneer. The Gibbons girls had a well-established reputation in Chesterton as a family of gold diggers. The reputation extended back generations to their family matriarch, Grandmother Althea, who had used her pretty face and cunning ways to take her from the daughter of a poor sharecropper to the wife of a few millionaires. The female passersby wrongly assumed if the Gibbons girls were laughing, it was probably because of some rich man they had stolen or one they were *plotting* to steal.

"I should stop too to figure out what the hell is going on with my account," Stephanie said as they walked toward the bank.

Cynthia went to the ATM first, removing hundred dollar bills from the slot. She glanced down at her receipt afterward and her shoulders slumped. "I need to get a new man soon. Having a daughter in college has left me B-R-O-K-E."

"Or you could just get a second J-O-B." Lauren shook her head. "You don't want to depend on a man like that, Cindy. It's too unpredictable and self-reliance is good."

Cynthia glared at their youngest sister. "Is that so? Well, thanks for the helpful advice, Little Miss Married-to-a-Millionaire, but frankly it sounds hypocritical coming from you. *You'll* never have to take a second job to make ends meet thanks to that moneybags husband of yours."

Lauren glowered at Cynthia while Stephanie and Dawn exchanged a look.

Not this old argument again, the look silently conveyed.

Though they were all happy that Lauren had found love and happiness with Cris, Cynthia was still smarting from the fact that *she* had tried to come on to Cris when he first came into town almost a year ago. She had failed miserably though and he had chosen her little sister instead. Stephanie knew in the back of Cynthia's mind that Cynthia always wondered what her life would be like if *she* was Mrs. Crisanto Weaver. After all, he was the holy grail of what all of the Gibbons girls had been taught to look for in a man.

Lauren gritted her teeth. "Cris may be a millionaire, but that doesn't mean I'm reliant on him! I have a job, my *own* damn money, and—"

Stephanie loudly cleared her throat. "You done with the ATM, Cindy?" she asked, hoping to change the subject.

Cynthia nodded and stepped aside with Lauren still glowering at her.

Stephanie inserted her card and quickly punched her password into the ATM to check her balance. A receipt scrolled out of the slot. She read it and blinked in amazement at the numbers.

"That's not possible," she murmured.

"*One dollar and fourteen cents!*" Dawn declared, looking over Stephanie's shoulder at the receipt. "How the hell do you have only one dollar and fourteen cents in there? I thought you said you had closer to eighteen thousand dollars!"

"This . . . This has to be a mistake," Stephanie mumbled.

"It better be!" Cynthia cried. "Or you're B-R-O-K-E too!"

Stephanie was suddenly gripped with panic. She pushed her way past her sisters, who were huddled around her. She then ran to the bank doors as fast as her stilettos would allow.

The portly security guard grinned as he held the door open for her. Too busy to flirt, she didn't smile back. She stepped into the small, carpeted lobby with its potted plants and mundane office chairs before walking straight to the teller windows.

There was only one teller on duty and the line was seven people deep. It zigzagged around a navy velvet rope.

This can't wait, Stephanie thought desperately. *I need to talk to someone now!*

She walked past the LINE STARTS HERE sign and went straight to the teller window as an elderly black woman with glasses stepped away, clutching her bills and smiling.

"Hey!" shouted the middle-aged white woman in a gray business suit who was next in line. "We're all waiting here, lady! You can't just barge in!"

"Like hell I can't! This is an emergency!" Stephanie snapped back.

The woman gaped.

The young teller looked tiredly at Stephanie through the glass divider. "Ma'am, those people were in line."

"I know. I know," Stephanie said, holding up her hands. "I'm not doing a transaction. I just want to check my account balance. Please! That's all I need to know."

The teller pursed her lips. "Ma'am, you can check your account balance at the ATM outside or by phone. There's a 1-800-number that's—"

"Damn it, I know that!"

When the teller looked as if she was about to shift away from the counter to get the manager or press a panic button, Stephanie took a deep breath. "I know that. But . . . But I would like you to double-check, if you could. The ATM said my account is empty. *Please,* just check it . . . Then I'll be out of your hair."

The teller's nostril flared. She let out a long, slow

breath. "Fine. What's your account number? I'm also going to need some ID."

Stephanie quickly opened her wallet and handed the teller her driver's license. She then rattled off her checking account number.

After typing a few keys, the teller's eyes scanned the computer screen on her desktop. "Your account isn't empty."

At those words, Stephanie practically jumped for joy. She grinned. "Oh, thank God! I *knew* it had to be a mistake! It just didn't seem—"

"It says here that you have one dollar and fourteen cents available," the teller murmured.

Stephanie's grin disappeared. Her eyes almost popped out of her head. "*What?* How's that possible? What happened to the eighteen thousand dollars that was in there?"

"It says there was a transfer as of yesterday of seventeen thousand nine hundred and ninety-eight dollars to another account. It's not connected to this bank."

"Oh, my God," Stephanie uttered breathlessly.

"There was another transfer made from your savings account in the amount of thirty-eight thousand seven hundred and three dollars three days ago to the same account."

"Oh, my God!"

That was almost 80 percent of her savings!

Stephanie felt her knees buckle beneath her. She grabbed the counter to steady herself and to keep from collapsing to the floor.

The teller gazed up at Stephanie. "I can print a receipt if you'd like," she offered with syrupy sweetness.

"*A receipt?*" Stephanie squeaked as the blood drained from her head. "I don't want a damn receipt! I want to talk to the manager!"

"My money . . . What happened to all my money?" Stephanie muttered dully a half an hour later as her sisters steered her toward the parking lot.

The bank manager had confirmed the transactions had taken place last night and earlier that week. The funds were sent to some offshore bank in the Caribbean, according to the routing number.

"I can assure you that they were perfectly legal, ma'am," he had said with pinched lips in an officious tone.

When she had asked if the transfers could be returned, he said they probably could—but he couldn't say so for a fact. The bank would have to conduct a fraud investigation. She'd have to file a report with the police and sign an affidavit. After forty-five days, *perhaps* the fraud department would decide to give her money back. Meanwhile, she had a mortgage and several bills that would go unpaid.

With Lauren on one arm and Dawn on the other, Stephanie allowed herself to be blindly led to her car, not paying attention or caring where she was being taken. Cynthia brought up the rear, lugging Stephanie's purse.

Stephanie looked like a grief-stricken widow mourning the loss of her husband at a funeral. But instead, she was *really* mourning the loss of her beloved bank account.

All that money, she thought numbly. *All that money is gone. Gone!*

She wanted to weep but couldn't find the strength!

"Do you know who might have done it?" Dawn inquired, speaking carefully as if her sister was a recovering invalid. "Any idea?"

"No . . . not all," Stephanie mumbled.

"Maybe someone saw you type your password on your computer somewhere when you accessed your accounts online," Lauren suggested. ". . . Is there another way someone could have gained access?"

Stephanie shook her head. "No, no one else had access to my . . ."

Her words faded. She stopped in her tracks as a thought suddenly dawned in her addled brain. Her sisters slowed their pace with her.

"What?" Cynthia asked. "*What?*"

"Someone . . . Someone else had access to my accounts."

All her sisters gazed at her in astonishment.

"*Who?*" they asked in unison.

"Isaac."

Lauren slowly closed her eyes. "Oh, Steph, you didn't."

"He said he needed it so I could make money on this big IPO he had just heard about!" Stephanie shouted hysterically. "He called me in the car one day last week when I was with a client. He said I was going to make lots of money! We had to do it *now* or I'd miss out! He was looking out for me! He wanted me to buy shares myself, but I reminded him I was busy showing houses all day. I didn't know how long it would take! So I . . . So I gave him the password to my online shareholder trade account," she stuttered. Even as she explained it, she realized how ridiculous it sounded. But it seemed totally plausible at the time. "I made five thousand dollars on that investment! But I . . . But I forgot that it also gave him access to one of my online bank accounts and all the accounts connected to it."

"And you just *handed* that stuff over to him?" Cynthia cried. "What the hell is wrong with you, Steph? Are you insane?"

Dawn gave a rueful shake of the head. Her bob flapped in the breeze as she gazed sadly at her sister. "Never give a man the key to your financial security," Dawn murmured, iterating one of the many Gibbons family golden rules on gold digging. "Stephanie, you know better!"

"But isn't it like . . . encrypted?" Stephanie asked weakly. "I thought they don't show the full account numbers."

"I guess not encrypted enough," Lauren replied. "*He* managed to get it."

"But we don't know that for sure!" Stephanie argued. "It couldn't have been Isaac. It could easily have been someone else! He could be completely innocent!"

"Oh, come on!" Cynthia shouted, her hazel eyes blazing. "*Wake up!* You don't know this guy from Adam! He could be innocent . . . but he also could be the biggest hustler that ever lived! Besides, don't you think it's an odd damn coincidence that your money suddenly disappears when he gets access to your accounts?"

"But he's rich! He doesn't need my money! Plus, he made me five thousand dollars!" Stephanie countered, stomping her foot. "Why would he give me money just to take it back three days later? Why would he give me a car? Ask me to *marry him?* It doesn't make any—"

"Oh, my Lord!" Dawn shouted, cutting them off. "Look!"

They all turned their heads, following the direction that Dawn pointed. The sisters gawked, watching the scene unfold.

A red tow truck detailed with flames and the sign HENRY'S TOW 1-800-TRUK-YOU on its doors was in the parking lot. Isaac's roadster was hitched to the back and being raised into the air. A burly man whom Stephanie presumed to be "Henry" stood beside the tow truck as Isaac's one-hundred-thousand-dollar car was loaded onboard. The driver wore a crew cut and a ripped tank top that revealed a massive hairy chest and about twenty tattoos.

Stephanie's strength suddenly returned. She pulled her arms from her sisters' grasp and bolted the last half block, running toward the truck.

"What . . . What are you doing?" she yelled at the driver, fighting to be heard above the grating mechanical noise as the roadster was lifted. "Why are you taking that car?"

He looked at her and gave a smile that was anything but friendly. "This your car, honey?" he drawled as he popped his gum, jabbing his fat thumb over his shoulder at the glistening roadster.

"Well, yes, kinda . . . it's my . . . my car now. My fiancé gave it to me!"

"Is that right? Well, your car is bein' repo'd for nonpayment." He then shifted a few levers on the back of the tow truck, walked around the side, and opened the driver's-side door. He hopped behind the wheel. "And if you know what's good for you, don't try anything. Just let your fiancé work it out with the loan company. You don't wanna tango with me, baby!"

He then shut the truck's door and cranked the engine.

Stephanie took a step back as the tow truck suddenly pulled off with a lurch. She watched, stunned, while Isaac's roadster was carried off, drawing curious onlookers who milled about Main Street.

Stéphanie's sisters gathered around her on the sidewalk.

"Did that really just happen?" Dawn asked, still gaping.

"Yes, it did," Lauren answered quietly. "Isaac's car was repossessed."

"Oh, hell, no!" Cynthia shouted. "Enough of this bullshit! Get Isaac on the phone, Steph! If you don't track him down and beat the hell out of him, I sure as hell will!"

Stephanie shook her head. "I'm not calling him. I'm going to his house . . . and he better explain what the hell is going on!"

Chapter 5

Lauren and Dawn winced at the sound of screeching tires as they watched Stephanie and Cynthia hurtle down Main Street in Cynthia's black SUV. A postal courier with boxes in his arms who had been idly ambling through the crosswalk suddenly jumped onto the curb to escape being sideswiped by the speeding vehicle. He turned around and yelled a few choice four-letter words at Cynthia. She beeped her horn in reply before disappearing around a corner, sending a few more pedestrians running for their lives. It looked like the sister duo was headed toward Isaac's home.

Isaac might stand a chance of survival with Stephanie alone, but if Cynthia got her hands on him, he certainly was a dead man.

Dawn couldn't believe Stephanie had let this happen. *Hoodwinked by a conman?* How could she possibly have been so naïve . . . so trusting . . . so *stupid?*

"Well, this is a complete and utter travesty," Dawn said as she stood beside Lauren with her hand on her hip. "A.k.a. hot mess."

"Tell me about it," Lauren muttered.

Dawn turned to her sister. "I wonder what they're going to do. Hopefully nothing that lands them in jail." She threw up her hands. "Oh, who am I kidding? They know we'll bail them out."

"I've got my checkbook ready when the time comes." Lauren held up her purse to demonstrate.

Now that the show was over, both women turned around and walked toward their cars. Dawn took out her keys, pushed the loose strands of hair out of her eyes, and clicked the button on her remote to open the door to her cobalt blue Mercedes-Benz convertible.

"Well, I have to get back to the gallery. Gotta zip up the beltway to get into the city and who knows what the traffic will be like. A nightmare, I would imagine," she mumbled then fluttered her fingers in good-bye at Lauren as she climbed inside. "I'll catch you later. You take care of that little bun you've got in that oven, girl. And let me know if you hear any updates from Steph or Cindy, OK?"

"I will. Don't worry," Lauren said, smiling as she walked toward her car. "Keep your phone nearby."

Dawn nodded, put on her purple-tinted aviator sunglasses, and closed her car door behind her. She pulled off.

After enduring forty-five minutes of bumper-to-bumper traffic, Dawn finally arrived a little after two o'clock at Templeton Gallery. It was nestled on a street block in the newly gentrified part of the U Street Corridor in DC, bordered to the right and left by coffee shops, boutiques, and an upscale French restaurant. Dawn tiredly tugged off her sunglasses as she stepped through the revolving doors into the ceramic-tiled lobby then onto the hardwood floors of the gallery itself. A few men were on a ladder, carefully hanging one of the gallery's new artworks—a twenty-four-by-thirty-inch abstract painting—on one of the exposed brick walls. Dawn's assistant stood off to the side, watching carefully as they worked.

Dawn always liked to say that her assistant, Kevin, dressed the way she would if she were a gay man. Today he was dressed smartly in a leather vest, slim dove-gray slacks, and suede ankle boots. Horn-rimmed glasses were perched on his blond head. He lowered those glasses to his nose as he assessed the painting now dangling precariously on the wall.

"Drop it about a couple of inches lower . . . lower . . . Yes, that's it! Perfect!" Kevin said before turning his focus toward Dawn. "Hey! You're back already?"

"I told you I was only leaving for lunch," Dawn answered breezily, striding down a hallway toward her office. Kevin trailed behind her. "I would have been back sooner if it wasn't for the damn backup on the Woodrow Wilson Bridge."

She glanced down at her iPhone. There was still no call or text message from any of her sisters. She supposed it was still a little bit early for updates on the latest drama. Maybe she'd get a message by the end of the day.

"Did I miss anything while I was out?" Dawn called over her shoulder to Kevin as she opened her office door.

They both walked into the understated eight-by-eight-foot space. Dawn wanted the artwork to be the showcase so she kept her furniture in her office clean and minimal. A glass-top industrial table sat in the center with a leather swivel chair behind it. Stainless steel bookshelves were along the walls. But the room was filled with as many vibrant colors as the silk wrap dress Dawn wore thanks to the paintings and sculptures that dotted the space. A few of the paintings were even her works.

Kevin shrugged. "No, you didn't miss anything. I reviewed the proofs for the invitations that are supposed to go out next week. They looked fine. I spoke to Vince Loy also. He swears that he's going to have his final work finished in enough time for the exhibit in two months."

Dawn chuckled as she dropped her purse onto her desk. "Fingers crossed."

"Yes, fingers crossed," Kevin repeated, holding up his crossed fingers for illustration. "The installation for the show in two weeks seems to be going well. Besides all that . . . things have been pretty quiet around here."

Dawn flopped back into her desk chair. She adjusted the front of her dress, smoothing the collar. "Good. I'm glad to hear it. Let's hope it stays that way."

"My eyes have been opened!" someone shouted in the gallery foyer.

At the sound, Dawn and Kevin let out a collective groan.

So much for things staying quiet, Dawn thought.

The voice was all too familiar. It belonged to the gallery owner, Percy Templeton. The eccentric Brit burst into Dawn's office a few seconds later, holding up his hands toward the ceiling. He was wearing virtually the same outfit as Kevin today, though his vest was red, not gray. Unfortunately, the look didn't seem quite as polished or as flattering on Percy as it did on Kevin. That wasn't surprising, considering Percy's tall, paunchy build, and the fact that he was more than thirty years older than Kevin.

"Good afternoon, Percy," Dawn said flatly. "How can we help you?"

Dawn loved her job, but if there was one thing that made her hesitate about taking the director position at Templeton Gallery, it had been the knowledge that she would have to work for Percy. Not only did the man have "delusions of grandeur," but he was a total letch: he kept a harem of young playthings around him at all times and had even tried to add Dawn to the list on more than one occasion. But each time she had politely fended off his advances. Of course, Percy fit the profile of the guys she usually dated: rich men with bloated egos who were willing to throw money around. But Dawn approached her life a lot more cautiously than her sisters. She followed the Gibbons family rules and didn't believe in mixing business with pleasure.

"Have you *seen* the *New York Times* this morning?" Percy asked. His blue eyes were wide. His skin was flushed pink. He looked almost frantic.

Dawn shook her head. "No, the morning's been kind of . . . umm . . . hectic," she said, thinking back to Stephanie's whole conman catastrophe. "I haven't had a chance to look at it yet. Why?"

"The Arts section . . . It featured new and up-and-coming artists and one, I simply must have in my gallery," Percy said, pacing in front of her desk. "We *have* to have him, darling! I don't care what we have to do to get him . . . throw bags of money at him, offer him women . . ." Percy paused mid-stride. ". . . Or *men*, if that's more his style. I don't care if we have to kidnap him! I want him here! He's a . . . a visionary!"

Visionary? She looked up at Kevin. She could see the same skeptical look on the young man's face.

"Hey, Kev, can you get me a copy of the *Times?* We should have it in the waiting area up front."

"Sure. No problem," Kevin said before walking around Percy and heading out of the office.

"You have to see his work!" Percy continued. "It's evocative! Sensual! Thought-provoking! It's . . . It's . . ."

Percy closed his eyes and started to shake, then swivel his hips rhythmically, making Dawn raise her brows. She was going to have to hose Percy down if he continued to hump the air like that.

Definitely not proper office behavior, she thought, stifling a laugh.

Percy finally went limp and sighed, holding his chest. "I cannot . . . I cannot put it into words, darling!"

"Obviously," she murmured dryly just as Kevin walked back into her office. He handed her the Arts section, then quickly exited, preferring to remain scarce whenever Percy was around. She couldn't blame him. There were days when she really didn't want to deal with her boss either.

Dawn flipped open the paper and spread the broadsheet on her desk. Just beneath the fold was the photograph of a young man with white paint splatter on his tan, muscular chest and what looked like an orange sari wrapped around his waist. A wall covered with halogen bulbs was behind him, creating a halo effect. He looked to be in his early- to mid-twenties and certainly was handsome. He also looked like he knew how handsome he was, judging from the arrogant smirk on his bearded face.

Dawn read a few paragraphs in the article while Percy walked around her desk and stood over her shoulder, breathing down her neck. The artist's name was Razor, though he was born with the name Trent Horowitz. He had a strong pedigree, being the son of a Yale art professor and the grandson of a family of tycoons who routinely had college buildings and household products named after them. Trent/Razor had studied at one of the best art institutes in the country before quitting his junior year to move to Brooklyn to "live among the people." He started with a group of guerilla artists who would spray-paint obscene pictures on public buildings, but now he was on his own, doing art pieces with light and movement.

He had been flagged by quite a few in New York's art scene as "the artist to watch" this year. So far, he hadn't exhibited in any of the major galleries in Manhattan, but everyone assumed it wouldn't be long before he did.

Dawn let her eyes scan over some of the pictures of his work, including photos of his guerilla art. She looked up from the newspaper and sat back in her chair.

"He's fantastic, isn't he, darling?" Percy asked, rounding her desk, facing her again.

"He's certainly . . . interesting, but I don't know how we could get him for the gallery, Percy. If everyone is fawning over him in New York, why would he want to exhibit down here in DC?"

Percy stared at her, looking taken aback. "What . . . What do you mean?"

"Well, we're not exactly a prime art market. There's so much more this Razor guy could do up there than he could ever do—"

"Oh, please!" Percy scoffed. "You read yourself that he wants to be one with the people! Why would he waste his time with a bunch of Upper West Side snobs when he could be here elbow to elbow with those who love art and life just like he does? We are the pulse of this city, darling!"

"Yeah, I get that, but—"

"I'm glad you agree," Percy said, cutting her off again. He braced his hands against her desk and leaned forward. "So you also should agree that we need to start wooing him as soon as possible. I want his work in my gallery this season."

"*This season?*" Dawn cringed. "But we've already booked exhibits for the next several months! We have artists that we've promised—"

"So we'll rearrange some things!" Percy said dismissively with a wave of his hand. "Darling, I'm sure Razor will outsell any of those little exhibits you already have lined up. An artist like him could put our gallery on the map!" He grinned and rubbed his hands together eagerly. "So you'll go to New York then? He has a studio in Williamsburg. I heard he throws parties there every weekend. You should attend."

Oh, wonderful, she thought. Now she would have to trek all the way to Brooklyn to go to some twenty-something, hipster party and to try to win over a pretentious artist who probably had no intention of showing his work in a place like D.C.

"Sure, I'll . . . I'll do it, Percy."

Percy almost did a jig in response.

"All right, then, darling." He turned toward her office door. "You let me know when. I'm off to a meeting. I'll follow up with you in a few days."

Percy then strode out of her office and Dawn sank further back into her chair and moaned.

This was turning out to be quite a day. Dawn hoped Stephanie was having a better afternoon than she was. Maybe Stephanie had found Isaac and was finally getting some answers.

Chapter 6

Thank God she didn't carry a gun! If she did, Isaac would be in a dump-truck load of trouble right now. Stephanie was ready to rain more vengeance upon him than a multi-armed Hindu goddess. She was ready to release a tirade of curses that would have had any minister or priest clutching for his Bible, prepared to start the exorcism to rid her of her demons.

Man, I wish I had a gun, Stephanie thought morosely.

A 9mm would feel just perfect in her delicate, manicured hands—that's how downright furious at Isaac she was. Even her can of Mace would have sufficed.

"Should have brought that with me too," she muttered under her breath.

But her Mace was tucked in one of the deep pockets of her snakeskin hobo bag, which was sitting on the floor in front of the passenger seat of her locked BMW. Her sedan was double-parked at the other end of the subdivision's neatly ordered lot with its black-

and-white numbered parking spaces and crisp white lines. She wasn't about to head back there now.

No, all she had was her fury and her clenched empty fists. Well, her fury, clenched empty fists, and her stilettos. In a pinch those spiked heels could serve as weapons too. Isaac still stood a chance of death by Louboutin when he opened his front door if he didn't immediately start talking and giving her answers.

She marched up the brick front steps to Isaac's rental home and planted her feet on the tan WELCOME mat. Stephanie could have rung the doorbell, but she didn't. She could had tapped the brass knocker, but she didn't do that either. Instead, she pounded her fists on the front door, making the frame rattle.

"Isaac! Isaac! Open up the door, goddamn it!" she shouted. When her hands started to throb, she stopped pounding. She didn't hear the telltale sound of a deadbolt being unlocked or hear his feet shuffling on the other side of the front door.

Is he home?

She banged again and waited. There was still no response.

Stephanie raced down the steps and crossed the front lawn, feeling her heels sink into the plush turf as she went. She then walked to the front windows and stood on the balls of her feet, gripping the window frame for balance as she peered inside.

A quick scan showed that he wasn't there, and not only was *he* not there, but his cat, furniture, and window treatments were also missing. All she saw was the living room's stained carpet, a few bare lightbulbs, and an empty kitty litter box.

"See you Thursday," Stephanie angrily muttered, slowly shaking her head as she gazed at the vacant home, recalling the last thing he said to her. "That son of a *bitch!*"

Stephanie had initially tried to give Isaac the benefit of the doubt. She had even asked her sister Cynthia to drop her off at home so she could get her car and drive to Isaac's house and confront him alone. If Cynthia got her hands on him, he wouldn't have lasted long. Stephanie wanted to talk to him alone on the fleeting chance there was a possible explanation for all this.

But she couldn't give him the benefit of the doubt anymore. Though she hated to admit it . . . though it humiliated her to come to the final conclusion, she had to accept that Isaac had conned her. He had skipped town with her money—and her pride. He had pretended to fall in love with her and had gained her trust. Worse, he had managed to do it in a matter of weeks!

Dawn was right; Stephanie should have known better. Though they had never outright *stolen* money from men, all the Gibbons girls were tutored in the skills of deceit and manipulation. They had been taught by their mother and her mother before her. Running a scam like this was part of their basic education! She should have seen this one coming! But she hadn't, because she never considered that she'd one day be the prey, not the hunter.

"Doesn't feel good when it happens to you, does it?" a little voice in her head whispered as she walked back to her car to start her drive to the Sheriff's Office to file charges against Isaac. "You don't like it when the shoe is on the other foot, huh?"

Stephanie frowned. *Where had that come from?* She was the victim here! What she had done in the past was irrelevant.

"Sure it is," the voice mocked.

Stephanie shoved that chastising voice aside and instead chose to focus on the one that called for revenge.

She wanted Isaac arrested! She wanted him Tased over and over again until he was a twitching, frothy-mouthed mass on the Sheriff's Office floor! She wanted him to become the sex slave of some big hulking prison cellmate with bad breath and a big libido! In short, she wanted Isaac to feel sheer agony for what he had done to her.

Stephanie made an emergency call to her assistant and told her to handle the rest of today's showings as she pulled into one of the few empty spaces in front of the one-story brick building that was the Chesterton Sheriff's Office. When she hung up her cell phone, ending the call, she was certain she would get justice now. The cops would track down Isaac for sure.

Stephanie walked across the parking lot toward the double doors with efficient strides and pushed one of the doors open. She strode over the scuffed linoleum tiles in the Sheriff's Office lobby to the front desk where a short white woman in a tan police uniform stood in a cutout window.

The dispatcher's desk was visible behind her. The woman stared over the top of her glasses at a small book on the desk in front of her with pen in hand. When Stephanie drew closer, she saw the woman was playing a game of sudoku. The nametag on her chest read "Deputy Mitchell."

"I want to file charges!" Stephanie proclaimed, tossing her hair over her shoulder, putting her hand on her hip.

The deputy slowly raised her gaze from her sudoku square, squinted, and gave a patronizing smirk. "You want to file charges, huh? Against who?"

"My fian—" But Stephanie stopped herself. Isaac wasn't her fiancé. He never was! "I want to file charges against my . . . my ex!"

The deputy's smirk disappeared. She leaned forward and stared at Stephanie with concern. "Are they assault charges, ma'am?" she asked quietly. "We can have someone from victim services come out to talk to you if—"

"No . . . no, not assault," Stephanie hastily clarified. "Theft charges! Fraud!" She shrugged. "You know, stuff like that."

The deputy's shoulders slumped. "Oh," she murmured, sitting back in her chair.

Oh? What did she mean by "oh"?

The deputy turned around and grabbed a manila folder from a tiered rack on her desk. She flipped the folder open. "Well, I'm gonna have you fill out this form. I want you to list what—"

"*Form?* My ex stole nearly sixty thousand dollars from me, skipped town, and left me with almost nothing, and you want me to fill out a *form?*" She pointed down at the desk. "I want him tracked down now! I've seen those detective shows. Pull his cell phone records! See what was the last cell phone tower his calls pinged off of. *Whatever!* I'm not filling out a damn form! I want this taken care of *now!*"

The deputy narrowed her eyes. "Ma'am, you fill out the form with basic information, then—"

"Now," Stephanie said firmly, letting the deputy know that she meant business.

The deputy pursed her thin, wrinkled lips. "All righty then," she muttered, taking the form back and dropping it into her manila folder. "If you could have a seat over there," she said, pointing across the lobby. "I'll have one of the detectives come out to speak with you."

"Thank you," Stephanie said haughtily, before strutting to one of the leather chairs shoved against the lobby's left wall. She wiped at a speck of dust on the seat fabric, sat down, crossed her legs, and placed her purse on her lap.

She was happy she had stood her ground. Sometimes you had to "show your ass" to get things done.

They should be out here any minute now, Stephanie thought with a self-congratulatory smile.

Two and half hours later, a couple of detectives finally opened one of the doors near the front desk. Stephanie had just glanced at her watch for the umpteenth time when she saw them casually stroll toward her. They were sipping from coffee cups and chatting. She instantly recognized the slender one in the ill-fitting suit. When he grinned at her behind his thick mustache, her stomach plummeted.

Of all the damn people, she thought morosely.

"How ya doin', Steph?" he asked, still smiling, winking one of his blue eyes.

"Hi, Ted," she answered flatly.

"That's *Detective* Ted Monroe," he corrected, proudly hooking his thumb in his waistband.

Stephanie fought the urge to roll her eyes heavenward.

She had no idea Ted had been promoted from

patrol to detective at the Chesterton Sheriff's Office. If she had, she wouldn't have bothered coming here. She would have driven straight to the Virginia State Police barracks seven miles up the road.

She and Ted had dated briefly about a year ago. He had been all big talk and bravado, claiming at the time that he was a DEA agent/trust-fund baby and single with a two-bedroom condo and a hard-charging Mustang. He had taken her out to dinner a couple of times, but she quickly got bored with him. He was strictly of the "meet you at the door with a dozen roses, take you to Ruby Tuesday, then try to get into your pants" variety: *not* the caliber of man she was looking for. But Ted didn't take rejection well. He pursued her like she was a winning lottery ticket, and he showed up at her place one night, ready to convince her to go out with him again. Unfortunately, he hadn't realized that *his wife* had been tailing him the whole time.

When he climbed out of his Mustang and tried to plead with Stephanie as she opened her front door, his wife came leaping out of her Camry and charging across the parking lot screaming at the top of her lungs. That's when it all came out that Ted was a lowly patrol cop, not a DEA agent. He was married with three little ones at home, and if he had a trust fund, he certainly didn't spend it on his family. The poor woman's clothes were so threadbare, they seemed almost transparent.

Stephanie shut the door on them both as they argued. She could take drama over a man (she had her share of run-ins with crazy, jealous girlfriends and wives in the past), but she would not take drama for a man whose idea of fine dining was a platter of chicken quesadillas and sliders. Ted also proved her theory that married men were nothing but trouble.

She thought that night would be the last time she would ever see Ted again. Unfortunately, it looked like she had been wrong.

"So I hear you want to file charges," Ted said minutes later as he and his partner guided Stephanie down a long hall and past a series of doorways. He sipped again from his coffee cup. A few Sheriff's Office deputies passed them as they walked.

"Yes," she said, raising her chin. "Money was stolen from my bank accounts. I want the guy who did it arrested."

"Uh-huh," Ted murmured dispassionately as he waved her inside a room.

It was a stark white twelve-by-twelve foot space with four metal chairs with plastic bottoms. A wooden table sat in the center. There were no windows.

Stephanie assumed it was their "questioning" room. At least, that's what she believed they called it on those police television shows. She lowered herself into one of the chairs and crossed her legs.

"I guess you know who stole it then?" the other detective drawled as he plopped in the chair across from her.

This detective was as thin as Ted but a redhead with an aquiline nose. He cocked his eyebrow at Stephanie.

"I know *exactly* who stole it," Stephanie said vehemently, pointing her French manicured nail at the table in front of her. "My ex. His name's Isaac Beardan. That's B-E-A—"

"He sounds like a keeper," Ted muttered with a chuckle, leaning back in one of the chairs.

Stephanie glared at him. "Pardon me?"

Ted continued laughing. "Nothin'."

The redhead began to chuckle too.

She glared at them both. Shouldn't they be taking notes? Shouldn't they be recording this? How were they possibly documenting everything to press charges against Isaac with no notepad, pen, or digital recorder? She was about to ask that before they started asking her questions again.

"So why do you think *he* did it?" the redhead asked, sounding incredulous.

"He's the only one who could have done it! He's the only one who had access to my accounts! Then he just skipped down! It's so obvious!"

The redhead frowned. "How'd he get access to your accounts?"

"Well, I gave it to him . . ." She shrugged. " . . . Kind of."

The detective nodded. "I see. So these were accounts he was authorized to have access to."

"No! I gave him the password to my investment account and he used that to get access to the others."

"I see," the redhead said, nodding again. "But you can't prove for sure that he had access to those other accounts too, can you? You don't know for sure that he did it?"

"Well, no. Not for sure, but I told you that soon after the money disappeared, he skipped town! I could only assume that—"

"Did you have access to his?" Ted asked suddenly, finally putting down his coffee cup.

"His what?"

"To . . . his . . . *accounts*," Ted said loudly and slowly

as if she were the world's biggest simpleton. "Did you have access to any of his bank accounts?"

Stephanie paused. *What does that have to do with anything?* How did the questioning turn around so that *she* was now the focus?

She slowly shook her head. "No, he never gave me access to his accounts. I don't even know what bank he uses."

Ted raised his bushy eyebrows in comical astonishment. "Oh, come on, Steph! I don't believe that shit for one second! Are you honestly telling me you didn't have access to his bank accounts, his *credit cards?* Not even when you went shopping?" He laughed. "That doesn't sound like you, babe! Damn near every man in town knows how you operate! If a man won't hand over his Visa to you, you won't give him the time of day!"

Bitter much, Ted? She glowered at him and crossed her arms over her chest.

"Look, I'm not the one who . . . who committed a crime here! Even if I did use his credit card once or twice, I never would have—"

"Here's what I think happened," Ted said, cutting her off. "I think that boyfriend of yours spent a pretty penny on you. Knowing you," he murmured with an exaggerated roll of the eyes, "he probably dropped at least five figures between shopping trips, gifts, and such. I even bet he lent you some too. When you finally decided to dump him and move on to the next guy, he simply took back the money he was owed." He shrugged. "You said yourself you gave him access to your accounts."

"No, I didn't! I said I gave him access to my—"

"So he was just taking back what you owed him, that's all," Ted repeated, leaning back triumphantly in his chair, acting like Inspector Clouseau who had just explained how he had solved a murder mystery. "At least that's how *he* saw it. He was smarter than most of us."

Stephanie clenched her jaw, now furious all over again. "He stole my money! Whatever he gave me, he gave it to me freely! I didn't *take* anything from him! I didn't owe him a damn thing!"

"Steph, all you do is take, hon," Ted uttered with a slow shake of the head. "That's the type of girl you are."

At that, she balled her fists.

This is ridiculous! She had come to the cops to file charges against Isaac and instead she was getting a morality lecture from a married man who had tried to have an affair with her.

I may be a gold digger, but I am still a citizen, damn it, she thought indignantly. She still had rights!

She suddenly turned to Ted's redheaded partner, hoping that he was more level-headed, that he could see the error in all of this. But when she looked at him, all she saw in his green eyes wasn't sympathy, but cold contempt.

"All right," he drawled, giving a loud sigh, "enough with the theories, Monroe. As far as I'm concerned— based on what you've told us, ma'am—there isn't enough evidence to file charges against this guy. We'll take your complaint, Miss . . . uh . . . ."

"Gibbons," she said, feeling her heart pound fiercely in her chest. "My name is Stephanie Gibbons, and I won't be dismissed like—"

"Uh-huh, yes, Miss Gibbons," he responded blandly. "We'll take a formal complaint and include the stuff about your boyfriend in it. We'll see what we can do."

He then gave a condescending grin before raising his coffee cup back to his lips.

Stephanie seethed silently. She had as much confidence that he would "see what he could do" as she had that she would finally get her forty acres and a mule or that Sarah Palin would suddenly declare herself a Democrat. She had no confidence in him or Ted, whatsoever.

When Stephanie walked out of the Sheriff's Office fifteen minutes later, she was almost trembling with anger. The sun had disappeared and was now obscured by a heavy overcast, matching her dark mood. It started to drizzle as she walked to her car, wetting her hair, causing tendrils to cling to her forehead. Normally, she would rush to cover her locks but all vanity was pushed aside today.

Her vision blurred. Suddenly, she felt warm tears spill onto her cheeks as she opened her car door and climbed inside.

Isaac had taken almost all her savings. He had humiliated her and made her look like a fool, and now it looked like he was going to get away with it.

Chapter 7

"Damn," Keith muttered as he turned away from Isaac's front door. He hunched down and pulled the collar of his jacket around his ears as the rain fell overhead.

This was his second time checking Isaac's house today, confirming his suspicions. The worst-case scenario had indeed happened. The con artist he had been staking out for weeks was on the run again. Isaac had picked up stakes and moved on with the efficiency of Ringling Bros. Circus.

When had Isaac had the time to pack, let alone get his stuff into a moving van? Keith had been watching him almost sixteen hours a day. The only time he *hadn't* been watching Isaac was when he was asleep.

Keith wondered if, like Stephanie Gibbons, Isaac had suspected he had been following him this whole time. Maybe he had gotten wind of his impending arrest and had decided to skip town quietly.

"Or maybe she told him about you," the familiar voice in his head argued as he walked toward his SUV. "Maybe they were in cahoots this whole time."

Keith stood with his hand on the car's door handle. He paused.

In addition to finding out more about Isaac, he also had done a thorough investigation of his girlfriend. He knew from his research that she and her family had a bit of a reputation around town. But he hadn't been sure if he should take that little tidbit with a grain of salt and just dismiss it as town gossip— or whether he should take it more seriously. Now he was starting to wonder about a conversation he had almost a week ago with one of the townsfolk. Maybe he had let important information slip through the cracks.

Two days ago, Keith had been stealthily watching Isaac as he left Stephanie's real estate office when the rain swept in. It was one of those spring showers that came out of nowhere, much like it would in the tropics, except Keith was on a busy street in Virginia, not on a tourist beach in the Caribbean.

Keith's car was parked two blocks down. If he tried to make a run for it, the monsoon would drench him within seconds. To avoid the downpour, he turned and opened the door behind him, darting inside a flower shop. As he wiped his wet-sneakered feet on the doormat, he was instantly hit with the pungent mix of hyacinth, lavender, lilies, and lilac. He gazed around him.

The room was a splash of color in every hue imaginable with an array of bouquets in glass and ceramic vases of all shapes and sizes. A thin black woman stood on the opposite side of the shop behind a wide wooden desk and in front of a wall of glass-front refrigerators. She wore her salt and pepper hair in a sensible bun, a green apron, and reading glasses on the tip of her nose. She held garden shears in her gloved hand. It looked like he had caught her in the middle of her work. She was cutting off the stems and leaves from a pile of yellow roses splayed in front of her.

"Well, good morning," she said merrily, grinning. "Can I help you? You lookin' to buy some flowers?" she asked, raising her eyebrows expectantly. "Anything in particular?"

He shook his head. "No, sorry. I'm not here to buy any flowers. Just got stuck in the storm without an umbrella." He brushed the drops off his jacket shoulders and smiled. "I wanted to get out of the rain."

"Oh," she said, looking slightly crestfallen. "Well . . . stay as long as you like. It's not like I'm busy today."

"Thanks." He slowly walked toward a bouquet of red tulips and blue irises. He considered them before moving on to another bouquet as he waited for the storm to abate.

"You new in town?" she asked, lowering her shears to her wooden desk. "I haven't seen you around here before."

"I guess you could say I'm new. I came in a few days ago."

"You visiting someone in Chesterton? Maybe I know them."

"No, I . . . I was thinking about buying property around here," he lied.

"Well," she said, pushing her glasses to the crown of her head, "Chesterton is a lovely place to live. If you buy property here, it'll be a good investment.

What real estate agent are you working with?" She stepped from behind the counter. "I sure hope it's Mr. Lucas. He has an office on Cedar Brook Lane. He helped my daughter buy her first condo. He's a lovely, lovely man. I bet he could get you a good deal too."

Keith gazed at her slyly. He was stuck here for awhile; may as well do some detective work while he was at it.

"I don't have a real estate agent yet," Keith confessed. He glanced through the storefront window to Stephanie's office across the street. "I see you have a real estate agent over there though. Would you recommend her? Is she any good?"

The woman's cheery demeanor instantly disappeared. "No, I would not," she answered snippily.

Her response piqued his interest.

"Why?" He took a step toward the shopkeeper, tilting his head. "What's wrong with her?"

"Honey, you don't ever, *ever* want to get involved with one of those Gibbons girls. Not for business . . . and certainly not for pleasure!"

Keith noticed how her mouth screwed up when she said the name "Gibbons" and how her nose wrinkled with disgust. It intrigued him.

"What do you mean?"

"Those girls are nothin' but trouble! Everybody around here knows they're a bunch of gold-digging, thieving hussies! Every man they get their hooks in, they rob him blind and leave him with nothin' but his socks and his underwear!"

Normally Keith would have found a line like that amusing, but he was too shocked to laugh.

"They've been doing it for years and *years!*" the shopkeeper continued. "Their grandmama had three husbands. She probably would have had three more if the good Lord didn't decide to give the world a break and put her in a grave! Their mama kept having babies by rich men until it made her rich." She pointed toward the shop window. "That one that runs the restaurant on Main Street, almost a year ago she married an ex-football player. He owns the biggest mansion in Chesterton. He's worth I don't know how many millions. I don't think it's just a coincidence that she hooked up with him too," the shopkeeper sniffed. "I'm tellin' you, honey, they're *all* alike; sewn from the same cloth. All money hungry! All *evil!*"

Stephanie Gibbons might very well be a gold digger, but that didn't necessarily mean that, like Isaac, she was a con artist too. But still, the suspicion nagged Keith. As he drove away from Isaac's townhouse, he muddled over it.

He had been too distracted by her good looks, allowing it to blur his judgment.

"Fine, you're attracted to her," the voice in his head argued. "But you can't let that cause you to make mistakes like this."

He had let Isaac slip through his fingers and he was on the chase again with no leads so far. But Stephanie was still here in town probably. He had to see whether she had any idea where Isaac had gone next. He could continue to follow her around, but he had a feeling that would only waste more precious time. Another day wasted trailing Stephanie would mean even more distance put between him and Isaac.

No choice now, he thought as he drove away. *I've just got to talk to her.*

Fifteen minutes later, Keith hesitated as he stood in the light rain, took a deep breath, then pounded on Stephanie Gibbons's front door with his open palm.

This was against normal detective procedure, but he figured he had nothing to lose at this point. He couldn't make her talk, but he had to try.

He paused and waited, then pounded again. Within seconds, he could see a light turn on in the foyer window. The porch light came on next. A shadowy figure walked past the linen window curtains. He knew it had to be her from the curvy silhouette. The door swung open and Stephanie stood in front of him with a wineglass in her hand and a shocked expression on her face. The foyer light created a halo around her, giving her almost an ethereal glow.

"You!" Stephanie shouted with a hand on her hip. "You're that . . . that stalker guy! What the hell are you doing here?"

Standing here alone with her, Keith felt again the budding attraction he had felt since the first day he saw her. He quickly pushed those carnal thoughts aside and focused on the task at hand.

"Where is he?" Keith asked through clenched teeth.

"*What?*"

"Where the hell is he?" Keith asked again. He forced his way inside, making her sputter. He looked around her foyer, searching for any signs of Isaac. "I know you know where he is, so don't give me any bullshit!"

She lowered her glass to the mirrored foyer table and followed him into her living room.

"Look, I don't know who you are or what the hell you're talking about, but you better get out of my house now and I mean *right goddamn now!*" she yelled. "Get out before I call the cops!"

He looked around her living room. It was filled with feminine furniture: a small sofa with off-white silk cushions, two intricately embroidered armchairs with off-white pillows, and two delicate mirrored side tables. Several vases of fresh roses were throughout the room. But Isaac was nowhere to be found.

Which isn't a surprise, Keith thought morosely. He didn't really expect to find him hiding here. Isaac was long gone by now.

"Where's Isaac?" He turned around to face her. "Tell me now and make it easy on yourself!"

"*Isaac?*" She blinked, gazing at him dumbfounded. "You mean Isaac . . . my . . . my ex?"

"What other Isaac would I be talking about?" he snapped. "Look, one day you spot me and the next day he sprints out of town like his feet are on fire. That's not just a coincidence! He's facing some serious allegations, baby. You don't want to get yourself mixed up in this shit! Tell me where he is now and—"

"If I knew where Isaac was, I would be chasing him down myself," she said, crossing her arms over her chest.

The gesture tugged the cowl neck of her emerald green dress several inches lower, revealing more of her cleavage, drawing Keith's gaze. Realizing what he was doing, he snapped his eyes back to her face. He didn't need that distraction right now.

"Then when I found Isaac," she continued, "I'd beat him until he begged for mercy. Believe me!"

"Huh?"

"He stole my money!" she shouted, throwing up her hands. "He took almost all my savings! You think if I knew where he was I'd be here, drowning myself in a bottle of pinot noir, crying my eyes out?"

He looked at her more carefully. Her eyes were red and slightly puffy. Her nose was a little swollen. She *did* look like she had been crying.

"And the cops won't do anything! Not a goddamn thing! No one believes me! They act like *I* did something wrong!"

She sniffed and her eyes started to get misty again. Keith frowned as he watched her walk across the living room with hips swaying. She gathered a wad of tissues from a Kleenex box sitting on one of the end tables, blew her nose, and dabbed at the corner of her eyes with the tissue.

"So why are you so interested in Isaac?" She sniffed again. "What did he do to you?"

Keith cleared his throat. "It's not what he did to me. It's what he did to my client."

"*Your client?*" Now it was her turn to look confused. "What are you talking about?"

"I'm a private investigator. A woman in Maryland—a nice retiree—hired me to find Isaac... though when she knew him, he wasn't calling himself that. His name was Reggie Butler. He claimed to be a lawyer based in Virginia. He stole more than thirty thousand dollars worth of jewels from her by sweet-talking his way into her good graces and into her bed. I tracked him down here in Chesterton, but now I've lost him again."

Stephanie gaped. "So *that's* why you were following me around? Because of Isaac? He's who you wanted."

Keith nodded.

"Wait." She paused. "So you knew this whole time that Isaac was a conman? You knew what he planned to do to me? You knew he had planned to steal my money?"

Keith shook his head. "No. No, I didn't know that."

"But you had an idea though, right?" she argued, taking a step toward him, filling his nose with her alluring perfume. "You knew what he did to that woman in Maryland!" She clenched her fists at her sides. "Instead of following me around, why the hell didn't you warn me? Who lets someone walk into a trap like that?"

Keith was at a loss for words. He didn't want to tell her that he hadn't revealed the truth about Isaac to her because he had suspected that she and Isaac may be working together. She had an unsavory reputation, after all. What was he supposed to think?

"I'm a private investigator . . . the operative word being 'private,' " he said feebly. "I watch and document. I don't interfere."

"You don't interfere? *You don't interfere?*" She glared up at him. "Well, sorry, Mr. PI, but what the hell's the point of tracking him down if you're only going to let him commit a crime all over again? Thanks for all your hard work!"

Keith ignored her jab. He looked around the

room, absently scratching his chin. Too engrossed with the case, he hadn't shaved in four days and his newly grown beard was starting to itch. He had been wearing the same two pairs of jeans for almost a week now too.

I'd love to put on a set of clean clothes, he thought.

It was obvious he was at a dead end. He should probably go back home and get some sleep. In the morning, he'd take a shower, have a badly needed shave, go to his office, and talk to his partner, Mike Stokowski. He would show Mike all his files and notes. He desperately needed Mike's opinion on this. Maybe Mike had an idea of what to do next.

"Look, it's obvious you don't know where Isaac is," Keith said, returning his gaze to Stephanie. "I didn't mean to barge in like this, but I had to follow any possible lead. Here." He reached into one of the back pockets of his jeans and took out his wallet. "Take my card."

He pulled one of his business cards from the wallet's pocket and handed it to her. She hesitated before taking it from him.

"Stokowski and Hendricks Private Investigators," she said, furrowing her brows as she read the embossed letters.

"Yeah, my office number and more importantly, my cell number is on there. If anything comes to mind about Isaac, give me a call. Doesn't matter what time of day it is. Call me whenever." He turned to head back toward her front door. "I'll leave you now. Remember to call me."

"Wait!"

He didn't respond, but continued his long strides. "Wait!"

She raced ahead of him and held up her hands, pressing firmly against his chest, catching him by surprise.

Suddenly, the stirring Keith had been trying to keep at bay the whole time, came on full throttle. She hesitated and took a step back. He gazed at her, taking her in completely now.

Once again, she was wearing an impossibly short dress. She seemed to be fond of them. The dress revealed the long legs that were as familiar to him now as his home address thanks to the hours he had spent watching her. The imprint of pert nipples was visible through its silk fabric. It didn't look like she was wearing a bra. Her moist pink lips were parted. She looked like she was begging to be kissed.

Stephanie frowned, as if feeling the radiating heat of his charged gaze. She took another uncertain step back from him.

"You can't . . . You can't walk out like this," she murmured. "Do you realize the bomb you just dropped on me? You're following Isaac because he's done this before. If you're still looking for him, I want updates. I want to know where he is so I can deal with the bastard myself!"

Keith pursed his lips. "Look, when I find him, I'll contact the police and tell them that he stole from you as well. But I can't—"

"I'll hire you," she said hurriedly. "If you're tracking him down for that woman in Maryland, why can't you track him down for me too?" She tilted her head. "I could get the money together. What's your fee?"

Keith wavered. They could use a new client, but he wasn't too keen on the idea of working for Stephanie. The woman in Maryland had been in her early sixties. She was comely for her age, but matronly. In fact, Keith could see how a younger, suave guy like Isaac had won her over and conned her. She hadn't stood a chance. But Stephanie didn't look like the woman in Maryland. There was nothing matronly about her. She was dangerously attractive and she knew it. She was a gold digger who seemed well attuned to the powers of seduction. Now that Isaac had moved on from Chesterton, Keith planned to put as much distance between himself and Stephanie Gibbons as possible. A woman like her could cause him to do irrational things and get him into a lot of trouble.

"You can't . . . You can't hire me," he said slowly, shaking his head. "I work for one client at a time," he lied.

Her face fell. "But—"

"Look, I gotta get going." He started backing toward her foyer. "I'll tell the police. Don't worry. I'll give them all my supporting documents." He opened the front door. "When they arrest Isaac, I'll give you a call. You can give them your written statement."

He stepped through the doorway and shut the front door behind him, not giving her the chance to ask him to take on her case again. As he walked back to his SUV in the rain, the overpowering heat inside him slowly began to dissipate. He felt like an unbearable weight had been lifted.

Chapter 8

Stephanie took the steaming hot cup of coffee in her hands and blew on it to cool it down.

"Wait. Back up," Lauren said, making her glance up from her coffee cup. Her little sister pulled up a stool to the granite kitchen island and sat beside her. "Are you telling me Isaac was being followed by a *detective*?"

Stephanie sighed and nodded, gazing out her sister's kitchen window at the tennis court in Lauren's backyard. She then began the story about yesterday's encounter with Keith Hendricks, PI.

Today was a beautiful Saturday morning, but last night had been anything but beautiful. It had been long and restless for Stephanie. Each time she closed her eyes, she replayed the events of the past few days and tossed and turned in bed, unable to get any sleep.

She needed to talk to her family to help sort through this mess. But she didn't want to confide in her mother.

"You know the rules, Steph," she knew her mother, Yolanda, would say. "Never let a man hold the reins, and certainly never let a man hold all the keys to your financial future. All of this could have been avoided if you had simply followed the rules!"

No, I don't need a lecture, Stephanie thought. *I need advice.*

Lauren was a bit of a know-it-all. She had been since they were kids. Stephanie could remember pint-size Lauren lecturing Stephanie and the rest of the sisters in her high squeaky voice even back when she was five years old. But Stephanie had to admit that Lauren was also the most practical and resourceful of all her sisters, so she seemed like the best choice to talk to about something like this. Stephanie knew Lauren had a few hours before she had to be at her restaurant, so maybe she could spare some time to talk to Stephanie. After taking a quick shower, throwing on some makeup and clothes, Stephanie drove straight to the Weaver mansion to seek her little sister's advice.

Lauren now slowly shook her head and nibbled on crackers. She said they helped with her morning sickness.

"That is *so* crazy, Steph!" Lauren said between munches after Stephanie finished her story.

"I know." Stephanie's shoulders slumped. "The worst part is the detective has no idea where Isaac's gone. He thought *I* knew."

Lauren looked taken aback. "Why would you know?"

"That's what I said! Isaac stole from me just like he stole from that other woman. He wouldn't exactly give me a heads-up if he planned to skip town!"

Lauren pushed her box of crackers aside on the kitchen island, wiped the crumbs from her hands, and cleared her throat. "Well, if the detective found

Isaac once, I don't see why he can't find him again.
Don't worry. He said he would give you a call when
he found him and let you know, right?"

"Yeah," Stephanie answered, "but how do I know
he isn't just blowing me off like Ted and that other
detective did? I mean . . . I thought they were going
to help me and they were absolutely useless."

"Steph, you know damn well why they blew you
off! There was no way in hell they were going to help
you! The cops didn't help me when *I* needed them
either. Need I remind you of what happened with
my ex?"

Lauren was of course referring to her relationship
with her ex-boyfriend, James Sayers, who once had
been the richest and most powerful man in Chesterton. Lauren had agreed to be James's trophy girlfriend for a few years . . . that is until he became both
mentally and physically abusive. One night after James
had beaten her badly, she had run from his house
with just her car keys, purse, and nothing but the
clothes on her back. She drove straight to the local
Sheriff's Office to try to press charges against James.
But she said the sheriff had urged her not to do it.
He said her family could face some serious conse-
quences if she chose to go toe-to-toe with an influen-
tial man like James.

For months after that, James stalked her and tried
to intimidate her and her family in order to get her
to come back to him, but she had refused to allow
him to bully her. Lauren said the threats only stopped
when James and her then-boyfriend and now-husband,
Crisanto Weaver, finally had it out one night. After
that, James never bothered her again.

James had since pulled up stakes. He moved out

of Chesterton soon after Lauren and Cris married. Stephanie had heard that he had taken up permanent residence at his brownstone in New York. His mansion in Chesterton on Great Oak Drive had been up for sale for months. Rumor had it among local real estate agents that James may have to sell it at a loss.

Lauren was happy to see James gone for good, but she said that she would never forgive how she had been treated by the local police and many of the people in Chesterton during her whole ordeal. Being the wife of a former Dallas Cowboy had caused many people in their small town to act nice to her again to try to get in Cris's good graces, but Lauren said she would never be fooled. She knew deep down how some of them really felt about her.

"As far as a lot of people in this town are concerned, we're all the same and all of us are just getting what we deserve," Lauren now said, her old bitterness rising to the surface.

Lauren paused when her husband, Cris, entered the kitchen. Cris had returned from his morning jog around his property and was covered with a fine layer of sweat. His white tank top was nearly glued to his nutmeg brown skin. His numerous tattoos were on full display.

"Who thinks you're all the same?" Cris asked as he walked across the kitchen toward Lauren and Stephanie. He leaned down and kissed his wife. He then smiled and waved at his sister-in-law.

"The people in town, honey," Lauren said to Cris with a chuckle. "You know they think we're all the same."

Cris stared quizzically at them as he walked around

the kitchen island and opened one of the double doors of their industrial-sized stainless steel refrigerator. He then pulled out a bottle of Gatorade.

Watching him, Stephanie wondered if when Lauren had her baby, whether he or she would look more like Lauren or Cris. Maybe the baby would inherit Cris's Asian features: the dark, almond-shaped eyes and the high cheekbones that came from the Filipino side of his family. Or would the baby get Lauren's big doe eyes and small button nose and mouth? Whatever the baby looked like, any combination from such attractive parents Stephanie was sure would be beautiful.

"Look," Lauren said, returning her attention to her sister, "you can't judge everyone in the world based on those guys at the Sheriff's Office or this town, Steph. This Hendricks guy isn't from Chesterton. He's from out of town so I'm sure his feelings toward you are more . . . more . . . unbiased."

Stephanie pursed her lips. She shook her head. "That's not the vibe I was getting from him."

"What do you mean?"

"I don't know he just . . . he just . . ." Stephanie shrugged and placed her coffee cup back on the granite island. "He just made me feel . . . uncomfortable."

"*Uncomfortable?* Uncomfortable in what way?"

Stephanie shrugged again. "I don't know. It's hard to put into words, Laurie. When he was talking to me, it was like he . . . I felt like he was . . . well . . ."

"You felt like he was attracted to you?" she asked, finishing Stephanie's sentence for her.

Stephanie's gaze drifted to the kitchen's tiled floor and she slowly nodded.

Lauren laughed. "Well, what's wrong with *that*? So what if he's attracted to you? Many men are, Steph! He's human. So what? You've never had a problem with men being attracted to you before. Hell, I thought you relished it!"

"I do, but . . ."

Stephanie paused. She glanced at Cris who was avidly watching them and listening to their conversation. She didn't want to make this admission in front of him. There was still a strong part of her that believed in the family rules. One of those rules clearly stated that you didn't show your true emotions in front of men.

Yes, Cris was her brother-in-law, a member of the family—but he was still *a man*.

Lauren followed Stephanie's gaze. She found her husband leaning against the refrigerator, still drinking from his Gatorade bottle. She loudly cleared her throat and leaned her head toward the kitchen entryway. Then she gave him a wink.

"Well, uh," he announced, pushing himself away from the fridge after taking his wife's hint, "I'll . . . uh . . . go take a shower now. Gotta get out of these sweaty clothes. See you later, Steph."

"Bye, Cris," she said to his back as he made a hasty retreat out of the cavernous kitchen.

Lauren grinned. "You were saying?"

Stephanie took a deep breath. "I don't mind men being attracted to me, but this guy is different. Something feels off about it."

Lauren's grin abruptly disappeared. "Why? Is he creepy? Are you picking up serial-rapist vibes from him?"

"No," Stephanie said adamantly, shaking her head. "No, nothing like that! It's just . . . I feel like . . . I feel like I'm . . ." She took a deep breath. "I'm attracted to him too."

Her sister raised her eyebrows. "*So?*"

"I mean *really* attracted to him, Laurie!" She whimpered. "I've never felt like this about a man before."

It was true.

Stephanie wasn't a lesbian by any stretch of the imagination; she was attracted to men. But she had never *ever* experienced anything like what she felt when PI Keith Hendricks was in her living room last night. The moment had been so sexually charged it was almost electric. She felt her heartbeat accelerate and her palms sweat. When she pressed against him, her nipples started to swell and she started to feel a light tingle in her nether regions. She wanted to hop up, wrap her arms around his neck and her legs around his waist, and kiss him senseless.

She had always been taught that the goal was to make men tingle. The goal was to get *their* heartbeats to quicken. This wasn't supposed to happen the other way around!

Lauren regarded her sister. "So you like him, huh?"

"I don't know if *I* like him, but my vajayjay certainly does."

At that, Lauren burst into laughter.

"I think I can handle it though." Stephanie hesitated and contemplated those words. "Yeah, I'm pretty sure I can keep it under control. I'll need to if I'm going to get him to take my case."

Lauren stopped laughing. "Wait, I thought you told me that he said you couldn't hire him."

"He did . . . but I'm not giving up that easily! I want to find Isaac and *nothing* is going to stop me from doing that."

"So how exactly do you plan to win this Keith guy over?"

"The way I usually do with most men," Stephanie said with a shrug. "I've already established that he's attracted to me. I'll use that to my advantage."

"Steph," Lauren began quietly, "are you sure you want to do that?"

"Sure. Why shouldn't I?"

"Well . . ." Lauren hestitated, looking as if she was trying to choose her words carefully. "Don't you think . . . Don't you think your overconfidence in your abilities . . . in that area . . . is what got you into this trouble in the first place?"

"What do you mean?"

"She means exactly what you think she means," the annoying new voice in her head muttered. "By trying to trick men out of their money for years, you brought this one on yourself! It's justice due! Those Sheriff's Office detectives were right!"

Stephanie closed her eyes. "You think I brought this on myself, Laurie? You think that I deserved this?"

"No! No, honey, that's not what I meant!" Lauren argued earnestly. Stephanie opened her eyes. "I meant that because you were trying so hard to seduce Isaac, you didn't realize he was trying to do the same to you. It blindsided you. Besides, there are better ways to approach this. Instead of trying to use your feminine wiles on this guy, why don't you just try reasoning with him?"

"*Reasoning with him?*"

Lauren chuckled. "Yeah, I know. In our family, reasoning with a man is a foreign concept, but believe me, it can be done. He gave you his business card, right?"

Stephanie dug into her purse and pulled out the card. She showed it to Lauren.

"See, Steph! It has his company address on it. Go to his office and talk to him." She raised her eyebrows. "And I mean exactly that, Steph. Don't show him any cleavage. Don't give him any winks. Don't fool him into thinking he stands a chance of getting into your pants. *Talk* to him. That's all. Talk to the Stokowski guy on his business card while you're at it. He's probably Keith's partner. Maybe *he* can be reasoned with."

"Reason with them," Stephanie repeated, sitting upright on her stool. She let the words sink in.

It *was* a foreign concept to her. She was supposed to approach a man straightforward, with no seduction, no guile?

"Interesting," she murmured.

"Isn't it?" Lauren asked with another chuckle.

"Well, if I do by some chance get him to agree to take my case, Isaac stole almost all my money, Laurie, so could you—"

"You're going to ask me to lend you some cash, aren't you?"

Stephanie nodded.

"OK," Lauren said hopping off her stool, "I think I can lend it to you, but I have to talk to Cris first."

"You think Cris will do it?"

"If I reason with him, more than likely," Lauren said. "And if that doesn't work, I'll just do it the Gibbons way. I don't think any of my nighties fit anymore though. You wouldn't believe how much weight I've put on in the past few months!"

Chapter 9

"Here comes my big cup of hot chocolate!" the almond-skinned, plump, middle-aged woman behind the counter exclaimed as the handsome, dark-skinned man opened the glass-paned front door and walked inside the small greasy spoon.

The stained and faded sign MARCO'S PIZZERIA AND BURGER JOINT hung on the wall two feet above the cashier's head. She dropped a hand to her wide hip, stuck out her bountiful chest, and gave a broad smile, revealing the front gap in her teeth.

"I was hoping I would see your fine ass today! I haven't seen you in a while! Where you been?"

"Hey, Retha," Keith Hendricks replied, giving a lopsided grin that showed off his trademark dimples. "I've been away for a couple of weeks handling a case."

As he walked toward the counter, he reached into his back jean pocket, pulling out his wallet.

She raised her eyebrows, pushing back the elastic band of her hairnet by an inch. "You sure you weren't caught up with some woman? You're not lying to me, are you?"

"Now how could you ask me a question like that?" Keith winked one of his dark bedroom eyes at her. "You know damn well no woman could ever compare to you."

She laughed. "Boy, you better stop playin' with me! I'll jump over this here counter," she said, pointing at the linoleum, "throw you on the floor, and show you what we big girls are workin' with! Don't test me!"

Keith laughed.

"So what'll you have, baby?" She ripped an old receipt from the spool on the cash register. "The usual?"

Keith scratched his neatly trimmed goatee thoughtfully as he gazed at the menu on the washable board near the counter. "No, not today, Retha. I think I'll switch it up, if you don't mind."

Keith had ordered lunch at this restaurant in Vienna, Virginia, almost every day for more than a year. Retha and the fry cook in the back practically knew his order by heart; it rarely varied.

The pizza at Marco's wasn't the best—cheap tomato sauce, undercooked dough, and runny cheese—and many of the burgers were more burnt than charbroiled, but convenience won over taste in this case. The office of Stokowski and Hendricks Private Investigators—his place of work—was only a block away, located on the second floor of a two-story walk-up. Their shingle hung above a busy dry cleaner owned by a nice Korean family.

Keith squinted at the curly script on Marco's Pizzeria's white board. "So what's with the new menu?"

Retha sucked her teeth. "The manager said we should try to bring in more healthy options," she muttered, wrinkling her nose. "Some fruit, some vegetables, and sandwiches that taste just as good as dirt to me. So far, you're the only person who's even asked about it."

"Healthy menu, huh?" Keith contemplated for several seconds. "Well, I'll have the usual meatball sub and curly fries." Keith then tilted his head. "And I think I'll try the turkey on wheat with the bean sprouts too."

Retha raised her eyebrows again in surprise. "You sure, baby?"

Keith nodded.

He wasn't just buying lunch for himself today. He was buying it for his partner Mike too, in order to butter up Mike. Mike wasn't too happy when Keith told him last night that he had lost track of Isaac and let the conman skip town without a trace.

"*You let him get away?* How'd the hell that happen?" the older man had lamented.

No point in crying over spilled milk, Keith had argued. But that didn't mean Mike would let him off easy. The old man was going to drag Keith through the mud a bit before he used his forty-plus years of police experience to help Keith get back on Isaac's trail.

Keith hoped giving him a free lunch would speed up the process.

Minutes later, Keith climbed the stairs to Stokowski and Hendricks Private Investigators with two lunch bags in tow.

There was a small black-and-white plaque adjacent

to the door that let visitors know this was the office of licensed private investigators. Mike had been lobbying the landlord for the past year to put up something bigger, but the ornery old woman said she didn't want her tenants "tackying up her hallway with that ugly crap."

Keith shifted the lunches to one arm and opened the office door. He walked inside, almost bumping into the water cooler as he stepped through the doorway.

"*Heeeeey*, you're back," Mike shouted, raising his hands in the air in triumph. "It's about damn time! I'm starvin'!"

"For some reason I don't believe that," Keith replied as he glanced at Mike's ample belly. He tossed a paper bag on the gray-haired man's desk and sat a bottle of grapefruit juice near Mike's opened laptop before heading to his side of the room.

It was a large space, painted a stark white with two windows facing a busy street. There were a few paintings on the walls, ones that looked like they could have been found at an old Motel 6 or in a doctor's office in hell. Mike insisted they made the place look cheery. Keith joked they would probably look better in the Dumpster out back.

Beside the water cooler were two small chairs and a coffee table. That was supposed to be their "waiting area." Across the room was a door that led to a small dinette with a sink, microwave, and mini refrigerator. In the center of the room were their desks, which faced one another.

Keith's side was orderly and tidy, with a file cabinet filled with color-coded folders, pens and pencils arranged in an old coffee cup on his desk, and papers and books neatly stacked by his laptop. Mike's side was a complete mess. His desk was covered with a blizzard of paper, a discarded bag of potato chips, and a half-eaten box of powdered doughnuts. His trash can was filled to the brim and brown circles indicating old coffee stains decorated his desk calendar.

"What did you get me?" Mike asked Keith as he slid forward, rubbing his pale, hairy hands eagerly.

"Open it up and see for yourself," Keith muttered, throwing his jacket over the back of his desk chair.

Mike opened his bag, tucked a paper napkin into the collar of his shirt, and pulled out a cellophane-wrapped sandwich, small bag of baked potato chips, and an apple. With great trepidation, he unwrapped the sandwich. He frowned as he lifted one piece of whole wheat bread and examined the sandwich's contents.

"What the . . . *What the hell is this?*"

Keith fell back into his chair, twisting off the cap to his soda bottle. "What the hell does it look like?"

Mike's gray eyes widened comically, nearly bulging from the sockets. "It looks like a piece of shit!"

"I would have bought you a piece of shit, but they didn't have it on the menu." Keith chuckled, taking a bite from his foot-long meatball sub.

"Don't be a smart-ass!" Mike bellowed. "Come on, what *is* this?" He inspected the sandwich and poked it like it was some science experiment gone wrong. "It looks like grass or somethin'."

"It's a whole wheat sandwich with turkey, Dijon mustard, and bean sprouts. It's supposed to be good for you. One of the new healthy offerings on Marco's menu."

"So you got me this bean sprout crap . . ." He then gestured toward the sandwich Keith held. ". . . And you get meatballs and curly fries?"

"You're damn right I do!" Keith argued with a vigorous nod. "I'm not sixty-two, overweight, with high blood pressure and high cholesterol. Didn't the doctor tell you to go on a diet?"

Mike glared at the younger man. "You should be kissing my big hairy ass right now considering that you need *my* help! I thought you wanted me to help you figure out how to find this Isaac guy again."

Keith sighed. "I do."

"So you give *me* the meatball sub and you can have this rabbit food. Maybe then, I'll think it over."

"Are you serious?"

Mike raised his bushy eyebrows. "Does it look like I'm serious?"

Keith rose from his desk and carried his sub and soda across the room. He dropped both on Mike's cluttered desk. "Fine. It's you're funeral, man," he said, taking the bean sprout sandwich, grapefruit juice, apple, and baked chips from Mike.

Mike grinned, grabbed the sub, took a big chomp out of it, and closed his eyes in sheer ecstasy. "And what a way to go!"

Keith laughed and slowly shook his head. He then carried his lunch back to his desk.

He could never really get mad at Mike. The old guy was like a father to him. His life wouldn't be what it was today if it wasn't for the grizzly retired cop. In fact, he'd probably be dead by now with the way his life had been going all those years ago when the two first met.

When Keith met Mike, he had been ten years old, wearing a backward baseball cap, sporting Nike Air Jordans, and a satin bomber jacket that was two sizes too big for him. Back then, in the Baltimore projects where he and his mother found themselves, Keith had been the prized lookout for a few neighborhood drug dealers, letting out an ear-piercing whistle whenever he saw a police car drive by while his employers were "doin' business." He was barely five feet tall and weighed eighty pounds "soaking wet," as his mother liked to say, but he had a cocky attitude that the dealers liked. They called him Li'l Man and would toss him hundred dollar bills every now and then. He used the money to buy new shoes, a Nintendo game system, and a fake gold chain.

The other kids in the neighborhood admired Keith, watching in awe as he consorted with some of the roughest, toughest thugs in their neighborhood. Keith's mother was none the wiser. He hid his clandestine purchases from her and she was too tired from working two jobs to pay attention to what her son did on a daily basis. Every night she would arrive home with an aching back and dark circles under her eyes. She'd ask him halfheartedly if he made himself dinner and if he finished his homework. He'd nod "yes" and she'd smile before heading to her bedroom and collapsing into bed.

Keith started to skip school after a while. His lookout duties were more important. Whenever he stood on the street corner or hung out near the mouth of the alleyway, he kept a vigilant eye for cops. Pretty soon he started to notice the same police car driving by every day. It raised his suspicions. Having a detective's instinct even then, he wondered if the cops were starting to catch on to him, but he was too scared to tell the dealers that. He didn't want them to give his job away to someone else. After all, he had more things he wanted to buy. There was a bike in the pawn shop window two blocks from his home that had his name on it.

But one day, after doing his whistle routine, he saw the same cop car pull over, screeching to a halt near a broken bench tagged with spray paint. Two white beat cops—a short one who looked to be in his late thirties, and a tall, younger one with blond hair—opened the car doors.

Keith stood frozen in place, licking his lips nervously, watching as they walked toward him.

The older one held up his badge. "We'd like to speak to you, son."

That was the trigger Keith needed to wake up from his stupor. He did the only thing he could think to do: he turned and ran like hell. His little feet carried him a good eight blocks, through alleyways and behind Dumpsters, through playgrounds and around parked cars. The younger one finally caught him, grabbing him by the collar of his jacket. After doing all that running, the cop was angry and out of breath. He pinned Keith to the ground and put him in handcuffs, digging his knee into the boy's back.

"That's right! I got ya, you little piece of shit! You thought you would get away, but I got your ass!"

"Man, fuck you!" Keith screamed. "Suck my dick!"

"Goddamnit, get up! You're gonna crush his fuck-ing ribs!" the older one shouted, finally catching up with them. His face was red and slick with sweat. He pulled at the other cop's shoulder. "He's just a kid! Let him up!"

"Oh, come on, we've been watching this piece of shit for weeks! You and I both know he's been help-ing them peddle that shit!" He returned his angry gaze to Keith, shoving him into the concrete again. "I don't care how fucking old he is!"

"Get off of me! You hurtin' my arm!" Keith shouted, feeling saliva clog in his throat.

"I said let him up, Harris!" the older one ordered through clenched teeth.

"Or what?" the younger one named Harris spat.

"Or I'm reporting your ass to internal affairs."

"*Internal affairs?*" Harris paused a beat then he laughed coldly. "You'd really do that for this kid, wouldn't you? More of your bleeding heart bullshit! You—"

"Let . . . him . . . *up*. You got five seconds," the other cop repeated slowly.

Something in his voice said that he wasn't making an idle threat.

At the time, Keith didn't know what "internal af-fairs" was, but he was profoundly grateful it existed. Harris let go of him, but only after giving one final shove that jarred his scrawny shoulder. The cop then leaned against a park yard fence and wiped his sweaty brow. The older one shot him a look before walking toward Keith.

"Hey," the older one said, the anger now gone from his voice. He dragged Keith to the sitting position and kneeled beside him, gazing at him with watery gray eyes. Keith could barely see his lips behind his bristly mustache. "You all right?"

Keith didn't respond. The rule was that you never, *ever* talked to cops, not even if you wanted their help, not even if your life depended on it. He was covered in dirt and sweat. The front of his new jeans now showed a tear at the knee. His body ached all over, but he would never tell the cop that.

"Why'd you run?" the older one persisted. "We weren't going to arrest you. We were just going to ask you a few questions."

Keith shrugged, playing stupid. He kept his gaze on a broken seesaw on the other side of the yard.

"You know you don't have any business being out here doing what you're doing. You understand what those guys are selling, what they're doing to your neighborhood? You don't wanna get mixed up with that shit, son." He shook his head. "Does your mother know what you're doing out here? Does she know how close you are from disappearing for a long time?"

Keith turned his face into a block of granite, mimicking the hard, often intimidating expressions he saw on the faces of the neighborhood dealers. It was an expression that said he wasn't a snitch and he wasn't a punk. He wasn't afraid of going to jail either. But the hot tears coming from his eyes, searing his cheeks, gave him away. So did his sniffing.

The truth was that he *was* afraid. He wasn't a hardened criminal looking to make a fast grand selling crack on a street corner. He was a lonely ten-year-old boy who really, *really* wanted a ten-speed bike and was doing what he had to do to get it. He didn't want to go to jail and never see his mom again.

"Yeah, I didn't think so," the older cop said. He let out a heavy sigh. "Look, we're gonna let you go. I don't—"

"*What?*" Harris shouted, pushing himself away from the chain-link fence. "No, we're not fucking letting him go! I just sprinted a goddamn mile so we could bring him in. We're not—"

"We're going to let you go," the older one began again. He was talking to Keith but he turned his gaze to Harris. His gray eyes suddenly became hard as steel. "We're going to take off these handcuffs and we're going to send you on your way."

Harris gritted his teeth. His pink nostrils flared with anger. The blue veins stood along his forehead.

Keith, relieved beyond belief, fought back a smile.

"But I don't ever want to see you standing on some street corner helping those bastards again, all right?" the older cop ordered, returning his full attention to Keith. "Because if I *do* catch you doing it again, I *am* going to arrest you. You get me? I'm not bullshitting you here!"

Keith sniffed again and quickly nodded. The nod was as good as a solemn promise. A minute later he was out of the handcuffs, flexing his wrists, and nursing a sore shoulder. He glanced at the name tag on the older officer's chest.

Sgt. Stokowski, he sounded out slowly in his head. He had never seen a name like that before.

"Like I said," the officer repeated, "I don't want to see you out here ever again. But I want you to take my card." He handed Keith a business card. "You're gonna be the odd man out for a while. If some shit goes down, I want you to call me, son. You hear me?"

Keith grunted in reply. He watched as the two cops slowly walked off. Harris gave him one final menacing stare as he followed his partner. Keith fought the urge to give him the middle finger, deciding not to press his luck.

He was thankful to see their backs disappear behind the corner of a building and felt like he had aged twenty years in ten minutes. He silently vowed never to get caught in this type of mess again and stayed good to that vow.

He wished with the exit of the officers that would have been the end of it, but of course it wasn't. Word spread throughout the projects that Keith had been chased by the police, caught, and questioned. The many windows of their brick and concrete complex had eyes after all, but the eyes weren't always accurate. Some said that Keith—scared and intimidated—had given the police the names of drug dealers and information about where they hung out. The fact that he didn't want to work for the dealers anymore didn't help either. It made them even more suspicious.

The cop had been right. Suddenly, the industrious ten-year-old *was* the odd man out and had a lot fewer friends than he had before. He began to fear the hostile stares that followed him around his neighborhood when he arrived home from school. He watched his back whenever his mother sent him to the corner store for a pack of Slims. One night when gunshots went through the second-floor window of his and his mother's one-bedroom apartment, Keith knew it wasn't an accident. He took it as a warning.

You never, *ever* talked to cops, not even if you

wanted their help, not even if your life depended on it. But this time, Keith did. Unsure of whom else he could turn to, he told his mother everything and she called Sgt. Mike Stokowski. Mike met Keith and his mom at a diner by the Baltimore waterfront, over-looking the wharf. He paid for their meal of hamburgers, milk shakes, and French fries and listened to Keith's story. This time Keith did give names, but reluctantly. He had respected these neighborhood drug dealers. They were the closest thing he knew to celebrities. They had doted on him like he was a little brother, showering him with money, tossing him their castoff gold chains. But all that had changed now.

Half a dozen of them were arrested a month later based partially on information Keith gave, but by then, Keith and his mom were no longer living in the projects. Stokowski had helped them move to a small duplex in the Baltimore County suburbs. The land-lord—an old white lady who smelled like mothballs and seemed permanently coated with a layer of cat hair—let them live there at a steep discount thanks to a Section 8 subsidy and a good word from the Baltimore City cop. Keith transferred to the mostly white elementary school in his new neighborhood during the middle of the school year.

Keith felt like he had just been dropped into another world, full of strange people and odd customs. The streets were so clean that he was scared to spit bubble gum on the ground, and so quiet that he could hear crickets at night. They sounded as loud as police sirens. The kids at school didn't wear Air Jordans and satin bomber jackets, but polo shirts and acid-washed jeans. No one listened to Bell Biv DeVoe and LL Cool J, but U2 and this new band called Nirvana.

It was a hard adjustment in the beginning, but Mike told him it would happen over time. The cop checked up on him regularly to see how he was doing, to see if he was sliding back to his old ways.

After a while Mike became a permanent fixture in Keith's life. When Keith joined the basketball varsity team at his junior high, Mike cheered him on at games. When Keith graduated high school with a 3.0 grade point average, Stokowski stood in the crowd with Keith's mother, filming with a video camera as Keith proudly walked across the auditorium stage.

For years, Keith never understood why Mike had chosen him to watch over. The single man with no children wasn't exactly Santa Claus. He was a bit of a curmudgeon and could be gruff at times. But he always was there with open ears when Keith needed him. He gave money from his own wallet when household emergencies arose and Keith's mom was short on cash. Was Mike the bleeding heart his old partner had accused him of being, or some crazy white guy who felt the need to save all the poor black people from the ghetto?

Finally, when Keith was a sophomore in college studying criminal justice, Mike confessed that he had shown Keith so much attention because he had seen himself in him.

"Don't look so damned surprised," Mike said with a chuckle when Keith stared at him with wide-eyed disbelief. "We don't look a damn thing alike, but we're not that different you and me. I grew up in the Bronx. I was a smart-ass, smart-mouth kid just like you. I thought I could hustle and make my way in the world without help from anybody, but I figured out quick that wasn't true. When I wised up, I realized I needed help. I needed a guide, a mentor . . . just like you needed one. That's all."

But that wasn't all. Mike had long ago surpassed the role of mentor for Keith. The portly, foul-mouthed man was the paternal figure he never had and Keith was eternally grateful to him. He had taken Keith and his mom out of the projects. He had taught him about honor, respect, and how to be a real man who stuck to his word. He had changed the course of Keith's life. He had *saved* him. For that, he loved the old man with all his heart, despite Mike's many faults. He loved him like a father.

So when Mike retired after thirty-five years on the Baltimore police force, announced that he wanted to become a private detective, and asked if Keith would join him, Keith found it nearly impossible to say no. This was despite the fact that Keith had become an ATF agent only three years earlier after making several attempts to join their ranks. This was despite the fact that Keith wasn't sure if he was cut out for the life of a licensed private investigator. But, after a few weeks of reflection, he turned in his resignation to the feds and joined Mike at his new agency. He figured the old man had taken a chance on him long ago. It only seemed right that he return the favor.

Keith finished the last of his bean sprout sandwich. Mike had been right. It had tasted like crap. He looked across the room at Mike who was sucking the last of the marinara sauce from his plump fingers—

gloating like a five-year-old. Mike then let out a loud belch, making Keith shake his head in exasperation and chuckle.

"So," Keith said, leaning forward, "you happy now? Ready to help a brothah out?"

Mike slowly folded the sub's wax paper wrapping. He tossed it and his soda bottle into his already over-flowing trash can.

"Well," Mike said, "I was looking at your notes, and the only thing that jumped out at me was the part about his newest con victim, that real estate agent . . . the Stephanie woman."

"Yeah? What about her? I went to her place and talked to her. She said she didn't know where Isaac went." He paused. "Do you think she's lying?"

Mike slowly shook his head and looked down at the notes in front of him. "No, but you didn't ask her much else. You could've asked her for a few more de-tails, like if anything stood out the last day she saw him. Did Isaac say anything particular about where he was going? You know . . . stuff like that."

Keith shrugged. "Yeah, I guess I could have."

"But you didn't," Mike said, pointing down at the sheet of paper in front of him. "You said you stayed for ten minutes then high-tailed it out of there."

"I wouldn't call it 'high-tailing out of there.' "

"Well, you left in a hurry. Any reason why?"

"I don't know. I guess I just thought I got all the information I could get out of her," he said, starting to feel uncomfortable with Mike's questioning. He shifted his gaze to his desk. "And it was late. She looked tired. I didn't see the point in drilling her if she couldn't tell me anything."

Mike stared at Keith for several seconds. He narrowed his gray eyes. "What are you not telling me?"

"What do you mean?"

"The con artist who you've been tracking down for more than a month, who've you've been following almost nonstop for about a week suddenly jets out of town. You go to the house of the last woman who saw him and she agrees to talk to you. But you hardly ask her any questions because she '*looked tired.*' You don't even go back the next morning to talk to her or follow up with a phone call." Mike tilted his head. His bushy eyebrows were raised. "That doesn't make sense, Keith. Somethin's up."

Keith sighed. "Mike, what's with the third degree? If you want me to call her back, I'll call her back."

"Hey, it's just I've been in this business long enough to know when someone's bullshitting me. That's all. And a lot of stink is drifting off you right now, my friend. I just wanna know what's up? What are you not telling me?"

Keith didn't know how to explain to Mike that he had left Stephanie Gibbons's home and hadn't asked her more questions because he felt uncomfortable around her. He knew if he stayed any longer he was going to do something he regretted—like kissing her—and it seemed best for them both for him to just leave. But Mike was right. He definitely should follow up to question her more thoroughly. She certainly seemed more than willing to help him find Isaac again and she could offer a potential lead he hadn't considered. But he'd be damned if he did it in a room alone with that woman. That would just lead to all kinds of trouble.

"Look, I admit, I messed up," he said quietly. "I should have followed up with her. How about I give her a call and invite her up here to talk? That way we *both* can question her this time."

Mike nodded. "All right, that doesn't sound like a bad idea."

Good, Keith thought, as he looked through his copy of his notes to find the number to her real estate office. At least there would be a chaperone of sorts with Mike there. That way, Keith stood less of a chance of trying to kiss the small-town temptress senseless.

Chapter 10

I'm nervous, Stephanie thought, as she drove her silver BMW down the busy street. Her grip on the steering wheel tightened. *Why am I nervous?*

She was on her way to the detectives' office for a scheduled appointment. Stephanie wasn't sure what to expect when she got there. Her experience at the Chesterton Sheriff's Office had left her badly shaken and questioning herself. That look of contempt in the detective's eyes still haunted her. She sincerely hoped the meeting with these private investigators would go better.

She had been shocked when PI Keith Hendricks suddenly called her out of the blue and asked her to come to his Vienna, Va., office about 40 minutes away for an interview. She had planned to track him down and ask him if they could talk again, but he had beaten her to the punch. Maybe Lauren had been right after all. Maybe this guy was willing to take her seriously.

Stephanie decelerated and parallel-parked along the curb in front of a two-story, red-bricked walk-up that looked a lot like a townhouse. She pulled her key from the ignition and unbuckled her seatbelt.

She squinted at the building, staring at the English sign saying QUICKIE DRYCLEANER with Korean script beneath it in the first-floor window. She remembered the PI mentioning the last time she spoke to him that their detectives' office was located above this establishment.

Stephanie lowered the visor to look at her reflection in the mirror. A cursory glance showed every curl in place and no lipstick on her teeth, but she paused to do a more critical examination.

For the first time in her life, she had agonized over her usually sexy appearance, not wanting it to work against her. Initially, she had chosen to dress today as she always did when she wasn't working. She had put on a V-neck, ruby red Herve Leger bandage dress that hugged every curve of her body, and towering platform stilettos that complemented her long legs. It was a little breezy outside, so she threw on a suede bolero for the chill. But just as she was about to walk out her front door, she paused and glanced at herself in her living-room mirror. She wondered if maybe—just maybe—her attire gave the wrong impression about her.

Isaac had done her wrong. *She* knew that. But Stephanie also realized that with the reputation she had, some people would see what Isaac had done to her as justice due. Detective Ted Monroe certainly had. She would bet a million dollars that 80 percent of the residents in Chesterton thought the same. She didn't want to go through the whole spiel of explaining her story to Hendricks and his partner, only to have them take one look at her tight dress and bountiful cleavage and think what everyone else thought about her. She figured that the detectives would be less likely to jump to the wrong conclusions about her if she dressed more demurely.

So Stephanie quickly changed clothes, deciding to wear the most conservative outfit she had, which was a white silk blouse with a high, frilly collar and tight-fitting black slacks. It still wasn't exactly demure, but it certainly wasn't quite as sexy as the other ensemble. She examined her reflection one more time and gave it the nod of approval. With that, she felt ready for her meeting.

She now flipped up the visor and with great trepidation, took off her seatbelt, and opened her car door. A minute later, she climbed the hallway stairs to the detectives' office on the second floor. Stephanie nervously gnawed her bottom lip as she stepped on the final riser. Her heart pounded violently in her chest as she turned the doorknob and pushed the door open.

When she stepped inside the office, she found an older white guy sitting at his desk, reading the sports section of a newspaper. PI Keith Hendricks was standing near a printer across the room.

When Stephanie thought of detectives, a few archetypes came to mind: Sherlock Holmes with his pipe and traveling cape; Humphrey Bogart wearing a tan trench coat and a gray fedora, with a burning cigarette at his fingertip; and Columbo with his bushy eyebrows and enigmatic squint. But the two men in front of her didn't fit any those archetypes.

The older white guy could have been a high school principal. He was balding and fat and looked to be in his late fifties or early sixties with a fluffy, salt-and-pepper mustache and hairy, thick forearms. He wore a short-sleeved dress shirt and diagonally striped blue-and-gray tie. He was sipping from a coffee mug but stopped when she opened the door.

Keith was just as handsome as she remembered. The beard stubble was gone and was now replaced with a neatly trimmed goatee. He was wearing jeans again today and a gray T-shirt that showed off the ripples of muscles along his toned arms. His bedroom eyes locked with hers and she felt butterflies flutter in the pit of her stomach.

Stop that, she ordered the butterflies. She had no idea why she kept reacting this way to him but she would have to bring her emotions under control if she was going to reason with him and his partner like Lauren had suggested. She couldn't be nervous or flustered. She wanted them to take her seriously.

"Hello," Stephanie said, walking toward the man sitting at the desk. She extended her hand. "Let me guess. You're Mr. Stokowski?"

The old man stood from his chair. "That's me! And you can just call me Mike," he said, giving her hand a hearty shake. "Pleased to meet you, Miss Gibbons."

"Please, call me Stephanie," she said.

"Thanks for coming today, Stephanie." He pointed to Keith. "And you already know that crazy guy over there."

Stephanie nodded as Keith walked toward them. She swallowed and decided to handle this situation like she would handle an open house or a private showing with a potential buyer—as professionally as possible. She extended her hand to Keith and forced a smile. "Good to see you again, Mr. Hendricks. Thanks for inviting me."

He looked down at her hand in surprise, like he hadn't expected her to offer it. But he took it anyway and shook it. When he did, the butterflies started to flutter wildly again, trying to beat their way out of her stomach. They only quieted once the handshake ended.

"Thanks for coming down," Keith said quietly.

"No problem. I was . . . I was happy to come." She cleared her throat and looked away from him, choosing to concentrate on the older detective instead. Maybe that would help calm her overwrought nerves. "I want Isaac found just as badly as you guys want to find him. Trust me."

"Yeah, Keith told me that he stole money from you too," Mike muttered, shaking his head. "That's a damn shame. I'm sorry he preyed on you like that."

Stephanie lowered her eyes. "I'm sorry he did too."

"Well, we'll find him and make sure he pays for what he did. Don't worry." He then gestured to a nearby group of chairs. "You can have a seat over here, Stephanie," Mike said. "We'll get right down to business and start the interview now, if that's ok."

"Sure. That's what I came here for."

Stephanie sat down in one of the poorly padded seats and within minutes the two men sat in the chairs facing her with notepads and tape recorders in hand.

They were an odd pair—Keith and this Mike guy. She wondered how the two men had become partners. They seemed so different.

"So tell us how you met Isaac," Mike began.

For the next hour, Stephanie shared all that she knew about Isaac, trying to include as many minute details as she could remember. Mike asked a lot of questions, pausing to scribble notes, nodding his head attentively as she spoke. Meanwhile, Keith seemed to be barely paying attention to her. He kept getting up from his chair to go to the microwave, to the bathroom, or to answer the phone. His constant hopping up and down was starting to become distracting, not to mention that she found it incredibly rude. He didn't make eye contact with her either. Every time she looked at him, his gaze would shift away.

It was so odd. The last time they met, the attraction between them had seemed almost electric. Now he acted as if he didn't want to give her the time of day.

"So you say he gave you a Mercedes roadster and it was towed away?" Mike asked. His gray eyes fixed with concentration as he wrote.

Stephanie nodded. "Yes, Isaac said it was a gift for me. The next day some big guy with tattoos came and took it for nonpayment though."

"*Big guy with tattoos?*" Mike turned to Keith. "Do you remember Isaac ever driving a roadster or one being registered to any of his aliases?"

Keith slowly shook his head. "Nope, this is the first I'm hearing about it. He had a few cars that he drove around, but that wasn't one of them."

"That was the only time I ever saw him with this car," she quickly interjected. "He said he'd been keeping it at his place in South Carolina. The tags were from South Carolina so I guess he wasn't lying about that . . . at least."

"*South Carolina?*" Mike looked at Keith. "That's interesting."

The two men exchanged a look that Stephanie could not read.

"Would you happen to remember the license number?" Mike asked.

"No . . . not off the top of my head. Why?"

"If we had the license number, we could track down the name and the address of the owner," Keith said, finally speaking. "That could be a lead."

"Well, I don't remember that, but I do remember the name and number of the towing company."

Both men leaned forward. "You do?" they asked in unison.

"Yeah, it was pretty hard to forget it."

"What was it then?" Keith asked, pulling out his notepad again.

Stephanie opened her mouth to blurt out 1-800-TRUK-YOU but stopped herself. Judging by how eager both detectives seemed right now, she knew this information she had could be very valuable to them. Maybe she could use it to her advantage and get what she wanted out of this.

"I'll give you the name and number . . . if . . . if you do something for me first."

Keith furrowed his brows. "What would you like for us to do for you?"

"I want you to make an exception to your rule of not taking on more than one client at a time and let me hire you to track down Isaac."

Mike blinked. "Huh?"

"I said that I want to hire you to—"

"Yeah, I got that part," Mike said, holding up his

plump hand. "But what's this deal about us not taking on more than one client at a time?"

Stephanie's eyes instantly shifted to Keith. She pointed at him. "Well, the last time he and I spoke, he said . . . He said that you didn't do that sort of thing."

Keith loudly cleared his throat. He shifted uncomfortably in his chair. "Uh, I think you're a little confused, Miss Gibbons. What I said was—"

"No, I wasn't confused," she countered tightly. "That's *exactly* what you said."

Mike stared at them both in bewilderment. Keith looked away.

Her cheeks flushed with heat. He had lied to her! He had blown her off just like she had suspected. But she wouldn't stand for it. Not if they were the ones who needed *her* help this time. If they wanted her help, they would have to take her seriously.

"Mr. Hendricks, do you have a problem with me?"

Mike looked like he was holding back a smile behind his fluffy mustache. He glanced at Keith.

"Uh, no. No, of course not," Keith answered anxiously, clearing his throat again. "Why would . . . Why would you think I have a problem with you?"

"So I can assume you'd be more than happy to work for me then? Since I was previously *misinformed* about your ability to take on more than one client at a time, I guess you'll gladly accept my offer to hire you now?"

Keith grimaced a little. But he quickly regained control of his face. "Of course," he muttered.

"Good," she snapped.

The interview continued but there was obvious

tension in the room. By the time Stephanie left, she had given them all the information they needed—including the tow truck company's name and number—but she was livid. She was tired of being patronized and patted on the head. She was tired of men discounting her. First Isaac, then those two bozos at the Sheriff's Office, and now the PI Keith Hendricks was pulling the same crap! She had to take charge from now on. She was going to stay in control of this one.

Chapter 11

Keith climbed inside his SUV and pulled off seconds later, feeling triumphant.

His wallet was one hundred dollars lighter, but at least he had gotten the information he needed. Stephanie Gibbons hadn't been joking. That guy at Henry's Tow had been a tough nut to crack. The tattooed badass had refused not only to tell Keith the license number of the Mercedes roadster, but also to admit that he had even towed a Mercedes out of Chesterton a week ago. But once Keith stepped into the tow truck driver's office and spotted a picture on the wood-paneled wall, Keith knew he had him. It was a framed photo of the heavily built man standing on a dock, proudly holding up a giant bass. The man's grin had been so big that day that he looked like his cheeks hurt from smiling so much.

"So you fish, huh?" Keith had asked while pointing at the photo.

"Yeah," the tow truck driver had said, tossing a clipboard on his desk. "Why?"

"I fish too."

In fact, Mike had taken Keith fishing quite a few times when Keith was younger so Keith knew a thing or two about the rod and reel. The tow truck driver started talking about his best catches, and about the freedom he felt when it was just him, his boat, and a can of beer as he sat on the open water, waiting for a nip on his line. After awhile, his cold glare had softened. He no longer kept his arms crossed over his chest as he spoke to Keith. After an hour, the guy was more willing to answer questions. In the end, not only did he give Keith the license number to the roadster, but also the name, address, and last known phone number of the woman who had owned it. Keith gave him a hundred bucks to thank him for his time and cooperation. It was a small price to pay considering how much the man had told him.

As Keith now drove down the highway, he quickly punched into his cell phone the number that the tow truck driver had given him. He waited with bated breath as the phone rang, hoping to God that the number was still good.

"Hello? This is the Beaumont residence," a woman drawled on the other end. She sounded older, but she had a sultry air in her voice.

"Hello, ma'am, can I please speak to Ms. Beaumont?"

"Speaking, honey," she sang. "May I ask who is callin'?"

"My name is Keith Hendricks, ma'am. I'm a private investigator with Stokowski and Hendricks. I'm based out of Vienna, Virginia."

The woman grew silent. "Yes," she said. Her voice

sounded markedly colder now. "How may I help you, detective?"

"Ma'am, I understand that you own a Mercedes roadster that was recently towed here in Virginia. I wonder if you could—"

"Is this phone call related to Mason?" she asked, cutting him off.

Keith hesitated. "Excuse me? Related to who?"

"*Mason* . . . or Tony . . . or Reggie . . . or whatever name he's using now. Is that why you're callin' me? So they finally repossessed the car." She chuckled. "Good! I hope they left him stranded on the side of the road while they were at it!"

"So you do know why I'm calling?" Keith asked.

"Of course, I know why you're calling, honey! What trouble has he gotten himself into now? If it's anything illegal, I had absolutely nothing to do with it."

"He swindled two women," Keith explained. "He stole sixty thousand dollars from one, and thirty thousand dollars worth of jewels from the other."

Ms. Beaumont laughed again. "Oh, somebody has been a busy bee," she murmured. "So I guess you called me because you're looking for him. You want to track him down and bring him to justice?"

He wasn't sure if she was mocking him or asking a serious question. Either way, Keith nodded. "That's right, ma'am. That's exactly what I'm trying to do."

"Well . . ." She hesitated. "Under normal circumstances, I would tell you to go right to hell, Mr. Hendricks. I don't like talking to cops or private investigators, for that matter. But these aren't normal circumstances. You see, the man you are seeking . . .

He and I are currently on the outs. That's why I had the car repossessed. He and I go far back, but I refuse to be taken advantage of by him any longer. If you would like help finding him, I'll help any way I can."

Keith looked for a break in traffic. When he spotted one, he shifted to another lane and hastily pulled over to the side of the road. He flipped open his glove compartment, causing old papers and cellophane wrappers to spill onto the SUV's floor. He frantically dug in the glove compartment until he found a pen and notepad.

"Well, I'm glad you're agreeing to help me, Ms. Beaumont," he said, after yanking off the cap to his ballpoint pen with his teeth. He shifted his cell phone to the crook of his shoulder. "If you could just give me some background about this guy . . . that would be great. You say that you—"

"Oh, no, no, no, Mr. Hendricks!" She clucked her tongue. "This isn't the type of conversation a lady has over the phone. If you wish to speak to me, you will do it like a gentleman. You will do it in person."

He paused and lowered his pen. "In . . . *in person?*"

"Yes!" she exclaimed. "I am available next week if you are."

He pulled to a stop in front of the brick walk-up in Vienna less than half an hour later. He would have to talk to Mike about this one. If he was going to keep following Isaac's trail, it looked like he would have to take a trip to South Carolina, something that he hadn't planned on doing. He waved as he passed the window of the dry cleaner downstairs. The shop owner waved in return.

When he opened the entrance door, Keith heard his cell phone ringing. He looked down at it and saw that Stephanie was calling him—*again*. He gritted his teeth, grabbed the bundle of mail that sat on the WELCOME mat by the stairs, and climbed to the second floor of the walk-up where their office was. Stephanie had called him four times in the last three days. That woman would not let up!

When he stepped inside, he found Mike sitting at his desk, eating a bear claw and doing a crossword puzzle. Mike glanced up at him. His gray eyebrows raised in surprise.

"Hey! Back already?"

"Yeah, talked to the tow truck company and got the contact info for the woman who owned Isaac's Mercedes."

Mike's pale, wrinkled face broke into a grin. "Good job! So you're finally makin' some headway. That's great!" He then held up a Post-it note and waved it in the air. A name and number were scribbled on the neon-yellow piece of paper. "You can call Gibbons then and give her an update. She's called here twice today already *and* left messages. She wants to know how the investigation is going?"

Keith's shoulders slumped. "You're kidding me! She called here too?"

Mike's smile disappeared. "Yeah. What's wrong with her calling? Is something the matter?"

"Jesus, Mike, this chick has been blowing up my phone for the past *three days*! She's left voice mail messages, sent me a few texts and sent e-mails." He tossed his jacket onto his chair. "We should have never agreed to work for her! I *knew* this would happen!"

"Why's she been on your ass so much? Did you call her back and tell her you've got it covered . . . that she doesn't have to worry?"

Keith paused. "Well . . . no."

"What do you mean 'no'?"

"I mean I was going to call her back at the end of the week when I had some new info! But she hasn't given me the chance!"

Mike squinted. "So you haven't been returning her phone calls at all?"

"Did you just hear what I said? I was going to call her at the end of the week!" Keith snapped.

"So you're avoiding her and you wonder why she's blowing up your phone."

"I'm not avoiding her!"

Mike gazed at him for a long time, not saying a word. He shook his head and let out a deep breath.

"Have a seat," he said, gesturing to Keith's desk.

"I don't feel like sitting down," Keith grumbled.

"Son, plant your ass in that chair," Mike said, pointing at Keith's desk again. "Because you need a talking to and I want you to sit down while I'm doing it. You'll take it better this way."

Keith balled his fists at his sides. If any other man had talked to him like that, he'd punch him in the face, but this was Mike so he would never do that. Besides, the old man was probably still capable of whipping his ass anyway. He could be a dirty fighter when he needed to be. It was probably the Bronx in him.

Dejected, Keith walked across their office before sullenly plopping into his desk chair.

"You want some coffee?" Mike asked as he stood up and walked across the room to their coffee maker. It sat next to the microwave. They kept it around for clients but so far, Mike seemed to be the only one draining their coffee supply lately.

Keith shook his head. "No, and you shouldn't have any either. It's not healthy for you."

"Since when did you become an M.D.?" Mike asked, pouring himself a cup into a large blue ceramic mug.

"I didn't. But your doctor has one, and he said that you've got high blood pressure, so lay off the caffeine. He said it wasn't good for you."

Mike walked back toward his desk. "The doc told me to *cut back* on the caffeine. There's a difference."

Keith rolled his eyes heavenward. He had heard these arguments before.

"The doc knows I can't go cold turkey anyway. When I was a cop, I was practically shooting this stuff into my veins to keep going. I had long hours and some really tough shifts, if you remember."

Keith nodded thoughtfully, thinking back to the old days. "I remember."

He watched as Mike slouched down in the chair at his desk. The old man slid the chair forward. It creaked under his weight.

"But even with those long hours, I still managed to make it to all your basketball games and all your track meets."

"I remember that too."

"Good, then try to keep remembering it when I tell you what I'm about to tell you."

And here comes the lecture, Keith thought tiredly.

"If caffeine is the monkey I can't get off my back,

you've got a few monkeys of your own, my friend. You've developed those habits over the years to help you, but they hold you back sometimes too."

Keith stared at him with an incredulous expression on his face. "What do you mean?"

"I'm gettin' there! I'm gettin' there! Hold your horses." Mike waved his hand. He took a sip of coffee. "Even back when I met you on that shitty street corner in East Baltimore, I knew you were a good kid." He paused. "A good kid with a *good* heart . . . a really good heart. I could see it in you. You got yourself together. Started going to school again and got good grades. You went to college. I was and *am* very proud of you, Keith," Mike said with a firm nod. "I want you to know that. I consider you like a son and no son I could have made myself could have made me any prouder."

"And I consider you like a father, Mike," he answered softly, deeply touched by his mentor's words.

"You think I was the one who got you and your mother out of the projects, but that's not true. *You* did it. I just showed you the way, but whether you succeeded or failed, all depended on you."

"Thanks." Keith cleared his throat, feeling overwhelming emotions welling in his chest. "Thanks, Mike."

"You don't have to thank me," Mike said. "The past isn't something that you're proud of, but you should be. You've done good! You've got chutzpah, kid. You're very focused. You always have been. You don't let yourself get sidetracked by anything—be it life . . . obstacles . . . women . . ."

Keith raised his eyebrows in surprise. "Huh?"

Mike lowered his coffee mug to his desk. He clasped his hands in front of him. "I'm going to be honest with you, Keith. There are only a few times in your life where I've seen you act squirrelly . . . or out of character. The first was the time I found out you had been smoking that pot with your friends after school. You've never been good at lying to me. I could see the lie on your face right away, the very moment I asked you. The few other times when you were acting strange were when some girl or woman was involved. Women mess with your circuits, son. You're not good at dealing with them."

"Are . . . Are you trying to say that Stephanie is 'messing with my circuits'?"

"Seems that way to me! That's the only reason why I could think you'd be acting this way. Since when do you ignore a client's phone calls? Hell, you're god-damn Mr. Customer Service! I'm supposed to be the surly one. That's why you never let me answer the phone." Mike shrugged. "You said I sound too gruff."

"Because you *do*. I don't want you scaring off potential clients."

"And I don't want you messing up a case because you have the hots for a client!" He paused to sip his coffee again. "Look, I understand you're attracted to her. She's a nice-looking lady. That one is all legs!" he exclaimed with a grin and a wink. "But you can't keep dodging her like this. It's not professional, Keith. She's still a client. And frankly, it makes you look like a coward . . . a pussy!"

"I'm not dodging her . . . and I am not *a pussy!*"

"My friend," Mike said, taking another sip from his coffee mug, "you are runnin' scared, and if you were any more of a pussy, you'd be wearing a flea collar."

Keith sighed. Maybe Mike was right. He was avoiding her. There were several times the past few days when he saw her phone number on his cell phone screen and the alarm bells went off in his head. Only trouble came with a woman like her. But she was still a client. He had to talk to her.

"You know," Mike said, "if you actually dated women instead of sticking to those one-night stands of yours, you'd be happily married with kids by now and not running away from a client with legs that won't quit."

"Whatever, Mike," Keith said with a laugh, shaking his head.

"I'm serious! I've never seen you with any girl longer than two months. What was that one that worked at the hair salon?"

"Candy," Keith murmured with a smile. She had been a total basket case, but amazing in bed.

"Candy! Yeah! She was a real piece of work. No more dim bulbs like that one, please. It's time to meet a nice woman. Have some babies! You're thirty-six now! I know your mother isn't happy about you still being single either. She tells me all the time that she thinks you should settle down."

"This from a man who's still single at sixty-two?"

"Hey, I'm a lone wolf!" Mike shouted, making Keith throw his head back and laugh. "No woman can leash this animal, but you my friend have 'domesticated' written all over you."

"Yeah, yeah, yeah," Keith muttered. "So enough of this talk about babies and marriage. Can we get back to the case now?"

Mike nodded and returned his attention to his bear claw. "Sure," he said between chews. "Shoot."

"So I made a call to the woman who owned Isaac's car."

"Yeah? What'd she say?"

"She said she knew him . . . very well, actually."

Mike sat forward again in his chair. "You don't say. So did she give you any info on him? Did she tell you anything we don't already know?"

"That's the catch. She's willing to talk, but she doesn't want to do it over the phone. 'Ladies don't do such things, Mr. Hendricks,' " Keith said, imitating her Southern drawl.

Mike stared at him, confused.

"She wants us to meet in person," Keith further explained.

"Oh, is that all?" Mike set down his coffee cup and bear claw and threw up his hands. "I thought it was something serious. I guess that means you gotta go meet her then. The clients are paying for the gas mileage. What's the problem?"

"She's in South Carolina, Mike."

Mike's face instantly fell. "Oh."

" 'Oh,' exactly." Keith leaned back in his chair. "I'm not licensed for South Carolina. Neither of us is. Do you know of any PI's down there that could help us?"

"Off the top of my head . . . No, not really."

Keith closed his eyes, feeling defeated.

"But . . . that doesn't mean you can't keep investigating down there."

"It'll be tricky though with no license," Keith admitted, opening his eyes again. "I can't use my gun or show my badge."

"But you can pull it off. If anyone can, I know you will."

Keith opened his laptop computer. He clicked the ON button and watched as the boot-up screen appeared. "I guess I better start making travel plans then."

"I guess so," Mike said, finishing the last of his bear claw.

Chapter 12

"Steph, honey, are you sure this is a good idea?" her sister Lauren asked as she sat on the velvet stool at the end of Stephanie's four-poster bed.

Stephanie stood in front of the gilded-edged, full-length mirror in her bedroom, gazing at her reflection. She held an ice-blue sundress in front of her. She shook her head and tossed the dress aside. It landed on her settee. She then headed back to her walk-in closet to find another ensemble. She was only wearing a bra, panties, and high heels for the occasion.

"I don't know if it's a good idea," their sister Dawn answered drolly from her perch on Stephanie's bed, "but she looks like she's going to do it anyway." Dawn laughed and took a sip from her wineglass. "Just give up talking her out of it, Laurie. Her mind is set. She's going!"

Stephanie had finally gotten an update from the elusive PI Keith Hendricks. He told her that he had a possible lead on Isaac and he was heading down south this week to follow up on it. She had told her sisters the good news about the woman in South Carolina who had known Isaac. She also informed them that she would be headed to South Carolina with Keith to meet this woman. The only wrinkle in her plan was that Keith didn't know she intended to be his traveling companion.

But he'll get used to the idea, she thought as she eyed a silk tiger-print maxi dress on its padded hanger. She then took it out of her closet.

"I bet the weather is going to be warmer down there. I wanted to pack clothes that are light. So what do you think?" she asked as she turned around to face her sisters. She held the dress in front of her and tilted her head. "I want to look good, but it has to be comfortable enough for a road trip."

Dawn nodded thoughtfully. "It looks cute."

"Then I'll put it with the rest of the selections," Stephanie said, beaming.

"Seriously, Steph?" Lauren exclaimed. "*More* clothes?"

"My thoughts exactly. I mean . . . how long are you planning this trip to be?" Dawn asked as she reached for the chilled bottle of pinot grigio sitting on Stephanie's night table. She then poured a little more into her glass and lowered the bottle back to the table. "You're only going to South Carolina, right? Isn't that just a trip that'll take a couple of days at the most?" She eyed the growing pile of dresses, shorts, shoes, and purses on Stephanie's bed. "You've got enough clothes here to last you for a tour through Europe!"

Stephanie smirked. "A woman has to come prepared."

"A woman also should think things through," Lauren argued. "Steph, why are you going to South Carolina? I'm sure the detectives have this covered. They don't *need* you there to find Isaac."

"I'm going to South Carolina to protect my interests, Laurie, and *your* husband's money," Stephanie said as she sat down on the bench facing her mahogany vanity table. She then began to try on a pair of black stilettos. "Cris is paying a pretty penny for this. It only seems right that I make sure Keith is doing his job. You know what Mama always says. If you want something important done, don't leave it to a man to do it. You have to do it yourself."

Dawn nodded in agreement while Lauren fumed.

"But you don't think the private investigator is going to be annoyed having you hanging over his shoulder like this?" Lauren asked.

"Maybe. But frankly, I don't care!"

Stephanie examined her feet. *I should probably get a pedicure before heading to South Carolina*, she thought. Her toes were starting to look a little shoddy.

"But what about your work, Steph? Don't you have showings scheduled? Are you trying to tell me that none of your clients are buying houses?" Lauren asked. "Are they going to be OK with you just disappearing like this?"

"Even a real estate agent is allowed to take a break every now and then, sweetheart." Stephanie rose to her feet. "I'll only be gone for a few days. My assistant, Carrie, can handle everything. She's totally competent. If anything big comes up, she knows how to reach me."

"But, Steph—"

"No buts!" Stephanie shouted, stomping her foot

on the carpeted floor. She was getting tired of Lauren's constant questioning. "Why are you trying so hard to talk me out of this? I know what I'm doing!"

"Because I don't think you've considered everything before deciding to go on this trip," Lauren insisted.

"Yes, I have!"

"Oh, is that so?" Lauren tilted her head and gazed up at her older sister. "Have you considered, for instance, what's it going to be like to be in close quarters for days with a man you're attracted to?"

Dawn's brown eyes widened. She set down her wineglass. "Well, this is the first I'm hearing about this one! Stephanie's attracted to the detective? Ooooo, *spicy!*"

Stephanie glared at Lauren. "Thanks a lot, big mouth!"

"Well, I didn't know I wasn't supposed to tell anyone!"

Stephanie returned to her closet, muttering to herself.

"Why keep something like this secret?" Dawn called after her. "You don't want anyone to know you like him?"

"She doesn't just like him. She's *extremely* attracted to him," Lauren continued, undeterred. "In fact, she's so attracted to him that it makes her uncomfortable to be around him—and she thinks he's attracted to her too."

"You don't say. Well, if the spark is there then the spark is there. Why deny it?" Dawn paused. "Wait, how much do detectives make anyway?"

"Not enough for any one of you," Lauren mumbled petulantly.

"Does he have a side job?" Dawn asked Stephanie. "A trust fund, maybe?"

"I don't think so." Stephanie stepped out of the closet, clutching another dress. "He doesn't seem like he has a lot of money. His car is pretty old and his office was kind of *blah*."

Dawn made a face like she had just smelled dog poop. "Hmmm, I don't know, Steph. That sounds very blue collar to me."

Stephanie nodded in agreement. "He seems very blue collar."

Though she had to admit that since meeting Keith she had contemplated what it would be like to be with a blue-collar guy with a body and a face like his. Just closing her eyes now, she could visualize his sensual mouth, his muscular frame, and those sexy dark eyes. Oh, just thinking about him made her quiver! What would it be like to share a home and bed with a man who didn't make six figures and didn't drive a sports car, but could keep her in the passionate throes of sexual delight? But those thoughts came and went like the evening tide. She knew she could never be happy or have a future with a blue-collar guy like Keith Hendricks. They could share a nice roll in the sack, maybe, but that was about it.

"So are you going to do it?" Dawn asked.

"Do what?"

"Are you going to be the first Gibbons girl to hook up with a man with no money?"

"Ewww! No!" Stephanie answered with disgust. "Are you out of your mind?"

"Hey, I'm just asking! Because you know if you did, Mama would lose it," Dawn insisted. "You already told us she wasn't too happy to hear about what happened with Isaac. If she finds out you're hooking up with a detective with no money too, she wouldn't know what to do with herself. She'd probably drop dead right there."

Dawn was right. Yolanda Gibbons considered nothing more abhorrent than a man with no money, and she was a woman who practiced what she preached. She encouraged her daughters to date and marry rich men, and she did the same. In fact, she was already well on her way to locking down her *sixth* husband—a rich widower she had met several months ago. The widower wasn't the handsomest man, but he was giving Yolanda money and gifts, and helping her settle past debts. As far as she was concerned, that made him perfect for her.

"Well, Mama doesn't have to worry because I'm *not* hooking up with Keith and I am taking care of the situation with Isaac!" Stephanie said. "Nothing is going to happen between me and Keith. We're only going on a trip to South Carolina together. It's not like we're getting engaged!"

Lauren held up her hand. "Steph, you say that now, but trust me—when you're *really* attracted to a man, all bets are off. I kept telling myself I wasn't going to fall for Cris either, and look at what happened," she said, pointing down to her stomach. "Now we are married and we have *a baby* on the way!"

"That's different! You fell in love with Cris. I'm just attracted to this guy! Honey, I know how to control myself." Stephanie eyed one of her night-table drawers. "And if all else fails I have . . . you know . . . toys that can take care of that. I'll take one with me if you're really that worried."

Lauren narrowed her eyes. "So you aren't going to sleep with him?"

"No, I am not going to sleep with him!"

"Are you sure about that?" a voice in Stephanie's head asked, but she ignored it.

So what if Keith sent her pulse racing. Just because she was attracted to the man, didn't mean she had to sleep with him.

"My relationship with Keith Hendricks is and will remain *strictly* professional. Don't worry."

Lauren still eyed her warily. "OK, Steph, but just understand that I keep talking to you about this because I don't want you to get hurt. You just went through a very traumatic experience with Isaac. I don't want you to fall for another guy too quickly. I mean, if you really, *really* like the guy then—"

"Oh, for God's sake, Laurie," Stephanie shouted, "for the umpteenth time, you have nothing to worry about! I'm not falling for anyone. Stephanie Gibbons doesn't do love, honey!"

"All right, ladies, stop arguing," Dawn intervened as she strolled toward Stephanie's closet and pushed a line of outfits aside. "Steph said she's going to keep her legs closed and stay out of trouble, Laurie. You're just going to have to take her word for it. Now let's switch to another more important topic." Dawn eyed one of Stephanie's cocktail dresses. "Specifically . . . what the hell am I going to wear tonight?"

"Wear to what?" Lauren asked.

Dawn removed the dress from its hanger and held it in front of her. "I have to go to a party in Brooklyn. My boss wants me to win over some artist who's supposed to be at the party. He wants him to show his work at our gallery."

"Is this the same boss that's been trying to get into your pants for the past year?" Stephanie asked, crossing her arms over her chest.

"Pretty much."

"And what's the reason again that you won't have sex with him?" Stephanie paused and curled her lip in disgust. "Is he really gross?"

"Well, he's not my cup of tea, quite frankly, but it's not just that. He's my boss! You know what Mama always says, 'Don't eat where you sleep.'"

"I think that's, 'Don't poop where you eat,'" Lauren corrected.

"Either way, what he's asking me to do this time is actually work related and doesn't involve me getting naked, so I figured I should try to accommodate him."

"And you have to go all the way to New York to do it? *Tonight?*" Lauren asked.

"Looks like it. I'm taking the Acela to Penn Station at six-thirty." Dawn walked out of the closet and turned toward her sisters. "So what do you think?" She cocked her hip and gazed at Stephanie and Lauren expectantly. "Is this appropriate for a studio full of New York hipsters? I wanna look a little sexy . . . stand out a bit from the rest of the crowd without looking completely desperate, but I couldn't find anything in my closet that fit the bill. Will you let me borrow it, Steph? I promise I'll get it dry-cleaned when I'm done."

Stephanie nodded eagerly. "Sure, you can borrow a dress, but not that boring ol' thing! The New York art scene deserves a dress that's a lot more . . . adventurous."

Dawn wrinkled her nose and lowered the cocktail dress she was holding. "What do you mean by 'adventurous'? I'm not sure if I like the sound of that."

Lauren giggled. "Leave it up to Steph and she'll have you walking around New York with Band-Aids on your nipples and a G-string up your butt."

Dawn scowled.

"*Whatever!*" Stephanie strutted back across her bedroom. "Don't listen to her! She's a boring old married lady. What does she know?"

"*Old?*" Lauren shouted with outrage. "Excuse me! The last time I checked, I was younger than you, honey!"

Stephanie ignored Lauren and wrapped her arm around Dawn's shoulder before guiding her back into her closet. "Don't worry, girl. I can hook you up! Just leave it up to me. You're going to be the most sexy and fabulous chick in that room!"

Chapter 13

Dawn climbed out of the yellow taxi cab and slammed the car door closed behind her. She then tugged down the front of her incredibly short cocktail dress, cursing Stephanie under her breath as she did it. She never should have let her sister talk her into wearing this getup. The silver metallic dress was made out of some chainmail-like fabric that swayed and shimmered when she walked. She felt like a sparkling disco ball. It hit her just above mid-thigh, had a low back, and showed a great deal of boobage in the front. She couldn't bend down or lean forward without displaying all her goodies to the world.

Dawn had asked not to blend in, but she certainly hadn't expected to stand out *this* much. She'd be lucky if she didn't get stopped by the NYPD for street-walking when she tried to flag down a taxi later that night on her way back to her hotel.

She opened the clasp on her purse and pulled out the sheet of paper on which she had scribbled the address of Razor's studio. Thankfully, it was only half a block away. Dawn began to walk in that direction, pulling her leather jacket tighter around her to ward off the evening chill as she trudged along. She heard music as she drew closer to the building—a renovated warehouse. A guitar riff sailed toward her, along with the heavy beat of a snare drum. A few seconds later, she spotted a crowd standing on concrete steps, gathered around an open doorway. The boisterous group snapped Polaroid pictures of each other. Dawn climbed the stairs.

"Excuse me," she said, making her way through the throng. "Just heading inside, guys. Cutting through."

"Oh, for Christ's sake!" one of the young women exclaimed with a groan, making Dawn pause. "Not another one of *you!*"

Dawn stared at her, confused. "Pardon me."

"Pardon me?" the young woman repeated back mockingly, making Dawn frown.

The young Brooklynite eyed Dawn from behind her thick glasses. Her glare lingered on Dawn's silver minidress, making Dawn self-consciously tug down the hem again. In contrast, the young woman was in full hipster gear, in a bleach-stained black tank top, plaid skirt, and skinny jeans.

"You're like the fourth one tonight! I swear you guys are stupider than you look! Get a clue! We . . . don't . . . shoot . . . models . . . here," she said to Dawn in a patronizingly slow voice. She then tossed her cigarette to the ground before stomping it under one of her dirty Converse sneakers. "This is an art studio, *not* a photography studio. Razor may screw models, but he won't take pictures for your portfolio so . . . bye-bye!"

She then waved Dawn away like she was shooing off a fly. Dawn's frown now shifted into a scowl.

Just who the hell is this little girl, and does she know she is five seconds away from getting cursed out?

"God, Katy," lamented one of the young woman's male companions. "Why do you have to be such a bitch?"

He was more eccentrically dressed than Katy with his bowtie, cargo shorts, and a beard that was entwined with several rubber bands and colorful beads. He lowered his beer bottle and turned to Dawn, giving her a sympathetic smile.

"Sorry, she's just saying that Razor isn't a photographer. A lot of models make that mistake. But that just isn't his thing."

"Yeah, I got that," Dawn snapped, now more than just a little irritated.

She wasn't sure if she should be flattered or pissed that she was now being mistaken for a model, especially since present company seemed to have such a low opinion of those who made their money on the runway.

"Look, I'm not here to get Razor to take my picture," Dawn explained. "I'm here to see his work. I'm a gallery director."

The group fell silent.

"So if all of you could just step the hell aside, I'd really appreciate it."

Katy's brown eyes went wide as quarters. She cleared her throat and her face visibly paled under the dim streetlight. "Shit, I'm sorry! I . . . I just thought you were . . . well, because of the dress . . ."

Dawn ignored her and continued to climb the stairs.

The crowd parted, making a path for the angry black woman in stilettos.

"Hey!" Katy shouted. "If you're looking for stuff . . . umm, I'm an artist too! I've got some paintings if you're interested. I've—"

"Not really," Dawn replied bluntly before strolling through the open doorway.

She must be drawing close to the party. The music was getting louder. She climbed another flight of stairs and pushed through another crowd.

"Heads-up!" someone yelled as soon as she entered the doorway, making her hop aside. She just barely dodged a partygoer who stumbled toward her, holding his mouth as he ran for the door. He made it to the hall just before losing his lunch all over the black linoleum-tiled floor, drawing a series of shouts and groans from those who were smoking and lingering in the stairwell.

Dawn cringed.

"Sorry," his friend said with a shrug as he passed her. "Carl's a real pussy when it comes to Jägermeister."

"That's . . . quite all right," Dawn said.

She was just glad that none of it had splattered on her Alexander McQueens.

Dawn gave his nauseated friend a wide berth, turned back around, and gazed at the jam-packed studio.

The music from the live band on the other side of the room was almost deafening, but the rowdy attendees managed to rival the noise. Those who weren't shouting, laughing, and dancing were lip-locked in corners. One amorous couple hadn't even bothered to find a secluded spot and were making out in the middle of the makeshift dance floor.

Standing there, watching the scene around her, Dawn felt all her thirty-six years. She felt like a geezer among teenagers. She hadn't seen partying this hard since college.

"Well, no use in just standing here," a voice in her head egged on. "Go and find Razor so you can get the hell out of here and go back to the hotel."

Dawn sighed resignedly. She just hoped Percy appreciated how much she did for this damn job.

She began to make her way across the room, spotting Razor in the distance. The photographs in the newspaper and online hadn't done him justice. He was even more handsome in person—and just as smug looking. The artist was holding court by the band, surrounded by a gaggle of young women who were fawning over him. Dawn excused herself as she went, though few heard her over the noise.

"*Dawn?*" someone shouted behind her. "Dawn, is that you?"

She hadn't expected to run into anyone she knew tonight, especially not in a place like this. She turned and smiled, relieved to have someone at the party who wasn't high, wasn't a decade younger than her, and didn't vomit Jägermeister. But her friendly smile withered when she realized who it was.

"Oh," she said flatly. "Hello, Sasha."

Sasha Duncan grinned and embraced Dawn, kissing her on the cheek, making Dawn flinch.

"I thought that was you! What on earth are you doing here?" The fifty-something blonde stood back and looked Dawn up and down, still holding her shoulders. "And what *on earth* are you wearing, dear?"

Dawn shrugged out of Sasha's grasp and scanned her eyes over Sasha's short, blue, sequined dress with its fringed bottom. "I could ask you the same thing!" she shouted in return.

Sasha was the director of Sawyer Gallery in downtown DC—one of the major competitors to Templeton Gallery. But that wasn't why Dawn disliked her. She disliked Sasha—in short—because the botox-laden, St. John-wearing woman was a sneaky, conniving, two-faced bitch!

When Dawn got the job as gallery director at Templeton, Sasha was one of the first to welcome her to the DC art community, introducing her to the movers and shakers in town. They ate lunch together on occasion and had even attended a benefit or two together. Dawn thought that in Sasha she had found a mentor and a friend. She had even consulted Sasha when she found out that a whisper campaign about her had started around town. Rumors had circulated within the art community that Dawn was a talentless hack who came from a family of brazen gold diggers. Some whispered that she hadn't gotten the position at Templeton on merit, but because she was sleeping with Percy. Worse, there were rumors that Dawn was robbing the gallery's artists blind, and no one would be wise to work with her.

Sasha had counseled Dawn to simply ignore the gossip.

"What's that old saying? 'Sticks and stones may break my bones, but words would never hurt me,'" Sasha had advised one day. "You should just rise above it, dear."

Dawn took Sasha's suggestion, until word got back to her that the orchestrator of all the dirty gossip had been the very woman she had considered a confidante and friend: Sasha. When Dawn confronted Sasha, the woman vehemently denied the accusations . . . at first. But when Dawn gave her name after name of each person who had finger-pointed Sasha as the gossipmonger, Sasha finally relented and showed herself for the Brutus she really was.

"You should be grateful that I gave you entrée into some of the best social circles in town, Dawn," Sasha had said snidely. "It's not my job to be your cheerleader too. And it's not like what they claim I said was a lie. You *have* gotten around, dear, and you *do* love men with money."

The last dig made Dawn particularly angry, considering that everyone in town knew that Sasha—in her day—had "gotten around" quite a great deal herself. But the prim and proper married woman now looked down her nose at others who had done the same.

And there is nothing I hate more than a sanctimonious ho, Dawn thought. She had run into many in her life: women who looked down on her and her family in public, but would hop from bed to bed when no one was looking.

Also, Dawn had caught Sasha more than once being rather touchy-feely with Sawyer Gallery director, Martin Sawyer. Dawn highly doubted from the way those two carried on that Sasha's and Martin's relationship was strictly platonic and professional.

Since her discovery of Sasha's betrayal, Dawn had cut off their friendship and hadn't trusted the woman as far as she could throw her. But for some reason, Sasha insisted on pretending that they were still on pleasant terms.

"So what are you doing here?" Sasha shouted. "Don't tell me you came to see Razor!"

The live band had benevolently decided to take a short break so Dawn didn't have to shout her reply.

"Actually, I *did* come here to see him . . . not that it's any of your business."

Sasha's grin disappeared. "Well, frankly you're wasting your time, dear. Razor would never be interested in showing his work in the DC market. Not when he has the chance to show in some of the best galleries in Manhattan. Any gallery director worth her pay would know that!"

"*Oh, really?* If that's the case, then why are *you* here? This doesn't exactly look like your type of crowd. Was there a 'bring one fifty-year-old, get a beer free' deal at the bar that I wasn't aware of?"

"Very funny. No, I simply came tonight to meet a friend." Sasha tossed her hair over her shoulder and raised her nose into the air. "Unlike you, I do have contacts in New York. Not all of us are limited to the Washington cultural wasteland."

I'm sure your patrons would love to hear you refer to their hometown as a "cultural wasteland," Dawn thought. And she didn't believe for a second that Sasha hadn't tried to get Razor to show his artwork at Sawyer Gallery. More than likely, the young, up-and-coming artist had rejected Sasha's offer outright.

"Well, ta-ta," Sasha said, waving her fingers. "Good luck with your little endeavor, though I highly doubt it will work."

Dawn laughed. "Just because Razor turned you down doesn't mean he'll do the same for me, *dear.*"

Sasha hadn't been trained in the ways of charm and seduction like all the Gibbons girls had. Dawn believed she could use those skills to convince Razor to do what Sasha could not.

"But hey," Dawn continued, "maybe I can even squeeze you onto the invite list when his exhibit opens at Templeton Gallery . . . You know, a little favor for old time's sake."

Sasha clenched her jaw. Her face turned a bright crimson.

"Ta-ta!" Dawn then turned around and continued on her path toward Razor.

She paused to strip off her jacket. If she had to walk around in this sparkling minidress then she might as well use it to her advantage.

Razor isn't going to know what hit him!

Dawn could tell from the double-takes some of the men gave her as she passed that the dress was working. One hapless guy almost dropped his beer-filled plastic cup because he was gawking so much. He managed to catch it before it fell to the floor, only to spill half of it on his T-shirt.

"Razor," Dawn called out as she drew near the artist. He was regaling the group around him with some bawdy story that had them cackling. "Razor!"

"What?" he snapped, rolling his eyes and annoyed at being interrupted. He turned away from his adoring fans and tore the blunt that he had been smoking from his lips. But when his eyes settled on Dawn, the look of irritation instantly disappeared. His face broke into an impish grin.

"Well, hello!"

Two women who stood beside him glared at Dawn. One pouted while the other walked off.

"Hi, Razor," Dawn said, extending her hand. "Dawn Gibbons. Pleased to meet you."

He hesitated for a beat and looked her up and down. His bloodshot eyes lingered on her long dark legs, then her breasts, before finally settling on her face. He shook her hand. "Good to meet you too. But no need to be so formal, babe. We're pretty chill around here." He then extended his blunt toward her. "Want a hit?"

She blinked in shock, momentarily knocked off guard by his offer. But she hastily recovered.

Play it cool, she reminded herself. *Be charming.*

"No, I'm good. Thanks though."

He shrugged and smoked a bit more himself. "So what can I do for you? You're smokin' hot, but I hate to disappoint you. I don't shoot models."

"So I've heard." Dawn took a step toward him. "No, I'm not here to ask what you can do for me, Razor. I want to know what *I* can do for *you*."

He lowered the blunt from his mouth again and licked his lips. He leaned toward her so that they were almost nose to nose. "Well, what exactly did you have in mind, babe?"

She opened her purse, pulled out one of her business cards, and handed it to him. "You already have the acclaim and the money, but I'd love to extend your reach. Let me help you, Razor."

His shoulders slumped. Obviously, she wasn't offering what he had expected. He glanced down at her card and took it. "Oh, you work for a gallery?"

"Indeed, I do."

He shoved his fingers through his dark, shoulder-length hair. "Look, babe, I'm not really into that business stuff. I couldn't give a shit about 'extending my reach.' I just wanna make art, make love, and chill. You know?"

"And who says you can't do all that and more?"

"Yeah, but I—"

He was stopped midsentence by a finger she placed on his lips. He stared at her in shock.

Dawn shook her head. "Don't say no yet," she ordered seductively. "OK? Just think about it. Keep my card and think it over. Take your time and then get back to me." She lowered her finger. "Enjoy your party," she whispered against his lips.

She then turned and began to walk away, but halted when he grabbed her arm and tugged her back toward him, catching her by surprise. She landed hard against his chest. He linked an arm around her waist while his other hand cupped her bottom.

"Hey, where you going?" he asked, licking his lips again. "You don't want to stay? Have a drink with me?"

Her seduction plan was working. A lot of lust lingered in those green eyes. But she wanted his work in her gallery, not to end up in his bed. She obviously had underestimated the twenty-something libido.

Time to put on the brakes, Dawn thought.

She slowly peeled his arm from around her and his hand from her ass. "I'm afraid not, Razor. I've got to get back to DC early tomorrow."

"But it's not even midnight!" He grimaced. "Come on! Let's—"

"You've got my business card. You know where to find me."

He opened his mouth to argue, but she lightly kissed his cheek, turned again, and walked off.

Dawn grinned as she made her way through the crowded studio.

She could be wrong, but she suspected she would hear from Razor again and maybe she'd hear from him soon.

Chapter 14

Keith jotted down on a piece of notepaper the address of the woman in South Carolina whom he was supposed to track down. He then gave a quick goodbye to Mike before grabbing his duffel bag and heading to the office door.

"Give me an update once you get there?" Mike called out.

Keith nodded. "Will do. And lay off the bear claws while I'm gone, OK?"

Mike waved his hand dismissively. "Go! You're worse than an old lady with all your naggin'!"

Keith laughed and let the door fall shut behind him.

It would be a long car ride, but he hoped it would also be a fruitful one. He wasn't crazy about leaving the state. His PI license was limited to the state of Virginia, but he felt like he had royally screwed up this investigation. He had let Isaac slip out of his hands because he had allowed himself to be distracted. Keith took a foul-up like that personally, and the only way to rectify it was to find Isaac again. He would be operating like an average citizen now though, and not a PI during his search. But Mike was right, it could still be done. He just had to tread carefully.

He walked down the flight of stairs to the street below. He pushed open the door and looked up at the sky. It was a sunny day. Not a hint of a cloud was on the horizon, meaning he stood a chance of making good time at least during the first part of his journey if the rain held back and the traffic was good. He threw on his sunglasses as he strolled to his Ford Explorer. He loaded in his gear then slammed his hatchback closed. He walked toward the driver's-side door and was just about to climb behind the steering wheel, when he paused. He caught sight of something in the corner of his eye that made him stop and look more closely. He then did a double-take.

What the hell is she doing here?

Miss Pain-in-the-Ass also known as Stephanie Gibbons was standing by her BMW on the opposite side of the street. She had her python purse draped over one arm and a Louis Vuitton luggage bag in her other hand. She wore a tight-fitting, low-cut red dress and red stilettos. She smiled and waved at him.

He didn't wave back, but only glared in return.

"So I guess we're finally leaving now?" she called.

His eyebrows rose in surprise as she crossed the street and walked toward him. "*We?*"

"Yes, *we,* Keith."

She stopped in front of him and once again, he was overwhelmed by her scent. He wondered what perfume she wore because every time he smelled it, it made his mouth water.

Her ample cleavage was on full display today. When she tossed her long hair over her shoulder, her breasts jiggled, drawing Keith's attention despite his noble efforts to concentrate on what she was saying and why she was here.

You're going to fall out of that top, honey, Keith thought with amusement. He hoped she used double-sided tape.

"Uh, Keith," she said. She loudly cleared her throat. His eyes left her cleavage and snapped back to her face.

"I spoke with Mike and he said you're heading to South Carolina today to try to find Isaac," she explained. "I made sure to clear my schedule for the next few days so that I could come with you."

"You're . . . You're kidding, right?"

"I most certainly am not!" She dropped a hand to her hip. "You're working for me now, and I want to make sure my money . . . well, my brother-in-law's money . . . is being put to good use. So I'm coming with you."

"No, you're not."

"Oh, yes I am!"

"Lady, I said that you're not!"

"And *I* said that I am!"

Keith gritted his teeth. That was it. He had had enough of this! He ripped off his sunglasses and glared at her. "Do I look like I'm driving a school bus to you? This isn't a field trip! This is an investigation! I'm tracking down a con artist. You don't get to just tag along!"

"I'm well aware of who you're tracking down," she said firmly, raising her button nose into the air. "I'm also aware that if it wasn't for the information that *I* gave you, your trail on Isaac would be dead as a doornail right now. Am I right?"

His eyes narrowed.

"Look," she said, tilting her head. She placed her hand on his arm and leaned toward him. "Let's be reasonable about this," she cooed, batting her eyes. "I'm not going to get in your way. I'll hang back and let you do your little detective thing. I just want to see what—"

Little detective thing? "No!" he barked, swinging open the driver door. "Hell no!"

"But why can't I just—"

"I said no!" He climbed behind the wheel. "You're staying here and that's it! I'm driving to South Carolina. I'll send updates to Mike. Call him if you have any questions."

He then slammed his door in her face, leaving her gaping and fuming on the sidewalk.

Keith plugged the address in South Carolina into his SUV's dashboard navigation system. He then put his key in the ignition and watched in his rearview mirror as Stephanie scampered back across the street to her BMW, almost getting hit by a Mazda Miata as she ran across the roadway. She hastily threw open her car door and tossed her luggage and handbag inside.

When he turned on the engine and pulled off, she pulled off after him. When he made a left onto a side street, she did the same. When he made a right at the stoplight, she also made a right. Ten minutes later, when he jumped onto another roadway, she was right at his bumper. He watched in amazement as her BMW took the exit onto I-95, then pulled in behind him in the center lane.

She's following me. This crazy chick is following me, he thought. *Fan-damn-tastic!*

He was going to strangle her. If his head didn't explode first, he was going to kill her. What in the world had he gotten himself into?

Keith rubbed his neck and yawned. He had been driving for hours and was finally drawing close to the North Carolina border. He had stopped at a rest stop to use the bathroom and grab a drink from a vending machine, but hadn't stopped for gas yet. He didn't need to. He would in another hour though. He glanced in his rearview mirror and wondered if Stephanie was faring as well.

She hadn't pulled over to get gas either. He assumed that she hadn't because she didn't want to lose him. She only had a vague idea of where he was headed, after all. If she put any distance between her and his Explorer, she may end up lost.

A half an hour later, Keith adjusted his rearview mirror and watched in the reflection as Stephanie's car dropped back.

What the hell is she doing now, he thought in bewilderment.

She slowly steered her BMW to the highway shoulder. Smoke seeped from the sides of her car hood, creating a heavy, turbulent fog around the vehicle. The last thing he saw as he accelerated down the highway was her angrily throwing open her BMW's door and marching around her car to the hood. Stephanie's image became smaller and smaller and then disappeared.

So she stalled, he thought, slowly shaking his head as he drove. *That didn't take long.*

He had wondered if she had checked to see if her

car was up to snuff for the long journey. Her BMW was immaculate. Even the tires didn't seem to have a speck of dust on them. She probably hadn't driven the thing more than forty miles at any given time since she purchased it.

Not my problem, Keith thought as he signaled and moved to another lane on the highway. He had told her not to come. If she didn't bother to prepare herself for this trip, that was on her. At least now he wouldn't have to worry about her tailing him anymore. He could head to South Carolina and get some work done without having to worry about dragging her around.

"But what if she ends up stranded?" a voice inside his head asked him guiltily. "Shouldn't you go back and help her?"

Why did *he* have to go back to help her? That's what the AAA was for! And he had told her not to come!

"Yes, she didn't listen. Yes, she's pigheaded. So what?" the voice chided. "That doesn't mean she deserves to be stuck on the side of the road, waiting for a tow truck. Did you see what she was wearing? Do you really want her alone out there?"

Keith let out a deflating breath. He glanced at the sign over the roadway. If he was going to turn around and go back to get Stephanie, the exit ramp was coming up soon. He would have to make a decision pretty quickly.

So much for reaching South Carolina by the end of today, he thought as he threw on his turn signal and took the exit.

* * *

"Oh, don't do this to me now!" Stephanie shouted as she popped the hood of her BMW and threw it open.

She jumped back as soon as the smoke came billowing out, burning her eyes and nose. She waved her hand in front of her face frantically and coughed.

What on earth was wrong with her car? *Her baby?* When the smoke finally cleared a little she stared at the engine in confusion. The only thing she knew about her BMW was how to a) fill it with gas, and b) take it to a mechanic whenever she had any problems. She didn't even put in her own windshield wiper fluid! And now Keith was gone! He had deserted her. How in the world was she supposed to fix this herself?

"Damn it! Damn it! Damn it!" she yelled, stomping her high-heeled feet on the asphalt.

She looked up at the sound of a revving car engine. Stephanie whipped her head around, only to find a beat-up, blue pickup truck pulling off to the shoulder in front of her. When the driver killed the engine and opened his car door and hopped to the ground, she got a better look at him. What she saw didn't exactly make her feel like the cavalry had arrived to rescue her.

He was a large guy with huge muscles and a pot belly. He had a receding hairline but the rest of his dirty blond, stringy hair was pulled back into a ponytail. He slowly walked toward her and tucked his sunglasses into the front of his stained, black T-shirt. He smiled, revealing crooked and missing teeth.

"You need some help, honey?" he asked.

Yes, she needed help, but she didn't know if a guy like him was likely to provide it. She looked around her, watching as cars streamed up and down the busy roadway. Well, she doubted that he would try anything with all these people around. There were plenty of witnesses. Maybe she would be OK.

"Something's . . . Something's wrong with my car," she muttered hesitantly, tucking her hair behind her ear. She waved her hand toward the open hood. "I don't know what it is though."

He nodded. "Well, let's have a looksie."

He walked toward her car. As he drew closer she got the heavy smell of sweat, dirt, and gasoline. He braced his hands on the open hood and peered inside the engine.

"Could be a crack in your radiator or an oil leak," he said. "Could be anything."

She took a step toward him and gazed over his shoulder. "Well, what do you think it is? My BMW is only a couple of years old. I haven't had any problems with it before."

He turned to her. "Some cars can go to shit whenever they take a notion," he muttered with a chuckle. "Especially if you push 'em too hard."

"I don't think I pushed it *that* hard. I've only been driving for a few hours."

"*Few hours?*" He squinted. "You goin' on a trip somewhere?"

"Sort of." She gazed back at the engine, hoping to return the conversation back to her car. "So do you think it's the—"

"Where you headed?"

She hesitated. "To South Carolina." She pointed at her car again. "So can you—"

"South Carolina, huh? That's quite a ways." He was still smiling but the smile didn't reach his eyes.

Instead, they were analyzing her shrewdly like a hawk would his potential prey. "What's a pretty lady like you doing driving all the way to South Carolina by herself?"

She hesitated, not liking the look on his face or his questions. "I'm not . . . I'm not by myself," she answered shakily.

"You aren't?" He peered around the hood at her car's windshield. Her purse was in the front seat. Some of her luggage was in the back. He then gazed at her again. "Your car looks empty to me. Where's your friend?"

"He . . . He walked farther up the road to see if he could find a gas station."

"He left you alone with the car to find a gas station? Well,"—he laughed softly—"that don't sound very gentlemanly. Why didn't he just call a tow?"

"His legs were . . . were tired and he wanted to go for a . . . a w-w-walk."

"Uh-huh." His gaze dropped to her cleavage and lingered there.

"He should . . . He should be back soon," she said quietly. Her voice cracked. She took a step back.

And he's a really, really big guy, so don't try anything, she wanted to add.

"Well, why don't I give you a drive to the gas station where he walked to and we can meet him there?" the man asked.

Stephanie shook her head. "No, that's quite all right. I can just . . . I can just wait for him to come back."

"You sure?" He then jabbed his thumb over his shoulder. "My truck is right there." He hooked his thumbs in the front of his jeans. "It wouldn't be a problem."

"No, we've got it covered. Thanks," Keith said.

Stephanie suddenly turned to find Keith striding toward them. He had parked his SUV several feet away, farther down the shoulder.

She inwardly breathed a sigh of relief. She hadn't expected to see him again. She thought he'd be halfway to Charlotte by now.

The driver stared at Keith. "You with this lady?"

"Yeah," Keith said as he stood in front of him, "and I can take it from here."

The two men glared at one another, sizing each other up. Stephanie glanced nervously between them both. The silence between them seemed to drag on forever, but finally, it broke. Either the driver found Keith too intimidating or he figured Stephanie wasn't worth the battle. Whatever the reason, he backed down.

"Well, if that's the case . . . I'll be on my way then," the driver finally uttered curtly.

"You do that," Keith muttered in return.

"Th-thank you for your help," Stephanie called after him. The man didn't respond. She watched as he walked back to his truck. The truck pulled off a minute later, sending up a spew of exhaust in its wake, making her cough again.

Stephanie turned back around to face Keith. She found him focusing his steely glare on her, narrowing those dark bedroom eyes.

That man has no right to look this good when he's this pissed, she thought.

"Why were you following me?" he asked.

"You know why I was following you! Because you wouldn't let me come with you. I had no choice!"

"You did have a choice . . . and I made it! I wouldn't

let you come along for a good reason," he said as he turned to look at her BMW. "I thought you would slow me down and now you have!" He slowly shook his head and then leaned under the hood. "Shit, I *knew* this was going to happen!"

"You didn't have to come back and get me," she snapped. "I could have taken care of myself!"

"Yeah, right . . . and when I came up just now, you looked like you were doing a fine job of it. You were fifteen minutes away from being kidnapped by some toothless mountain man!" He scanned his eyes at the engine and exhaled a long breath. "We're going to have to get someone to look at this."

"Someone? *What?*" She waved at the engine. "You can't figure it out?"

He raised his eyebrows at her. "No . . . Can *you?*"

"No, but . . ." She shrugged. "I thought that's what guys do. Stick their head over the engine and say, 'Yep, there's your problem right there.' "

"Not quite," he muttered drolly and closed the hood with a loud bang, making her jump. "I'll stay with you until the tow truck comes and I'll see that your car is being taken care of before I move on, but after that I'm heading on to South Carolina. All right?"

She crossed her arms over her chest and pouted.

Keith made good on his word. He stayed until her BMW was towed to a beat-up-looking, small auto-body shop adjoining an old gas station just outside of Wilson, NC. But as soon as the wiry-looking mechanic raised the hood, Keith headed back to his Explorer.

"Wait!" she shouted, dragging her expensive luggage cases behind her. "*Wait!*"

"I'm not waiting," Keith mumbled as he threw

open his car door. "I've got a lot of time to make up. I've gotta get back on the road!"

"But the guy said the fix could take days! He may not even have the car part! I could be *stranded* here, Keith!"

"Stay at a motel. Sleep at a bed and breakfast. Make a weekend of it. Go exploring. I don't care!" Keith called back, climbing inside his SUV. "I've gotta go!"

He started to put his key in the ignition but stopped and stared at her in exasperation when she tugged open the passenger-side door and climbed inside.

"Stephanie, what the hell do you think you're doing?"

She quickly tossed her bags onto the backseat and plunked her bottom on the leather seat beside his. She then gazed out the windshield.

"I'm going with you," she answered obstinately.

He closed his eyes and silently told himself to count to ten. He then opened his eyes again. "Woman, you are *severely* testing my patience. We've been through this I don't know how many times. I'm not—"

"You're right! We have already been through this!" She leaned toward him. "Keith, do you realize what Isaac did to me? He stole my money! He humiliated me! I can't go back to Chesterton and just sit around in my office or in my living room waiting to see if someone finally catches him. Just sitting around, twiddling my thumbs, is going to drive me crazy! I *have* to do this! I told you that I won't get in the way. I'll stand back! You can do your work."

He opened his mouth to argue, but she cut him off before he could.

"I know how to be quiet . . . really! You won't hear

anything from me! Not a peep! You won't even know I'm there! But I can't wait around in Virginia. I can't sit on my hands waiting to hear whether you found him, Keith. I can't. I have to *do* something! Please?" she asked, clasping her hands together dramatically. "Please?"

His expression softened. He leaned back in his seat and gazed at her. She could see he was weighing her words, but she didn't know if she had swayed him.

"Do you promise," he began quietly, "that if I let you come with me to South Carolina, you won't get in the way, that you'll do what I say, and that you'll let me do my job?"

She eagerly nodded. "I promise! I swear!"

"If you don't hold up your end of this bargain, Stephanie, then the deal is off. You go home. No arguments. No complaints. Understood?"

She nodded again.

He stared at her a long time, making her wonder if he was going to send her back to Virginia anyway.

"Fine," he finally conceded, "then you can come with me to South Carolina."

"Yay!" she exclaimed, clapping her hands. "Thank you! Thank you! Thank you, Keith!"

She then threw her arms around his neck and gave him a hug, catching him off guard. She planted a warm kiss on his lips too, though she didn't know why the impulse had come over her—the heady smell of his cologne, perhaps, or even though he was acting like a real jerk, she still found him sexy as hell. Instead of tensing up when she kissed him, he instantly relaxed against her. His lips were full and strong—

made for nibbling. She did just that, taking his bottom lip into her mouth and running her tongue over it.

The instant she did, Keith jumped back as if she had stung him. Stephanie pulled away, only to find him staring at her like she was stark-raving mad.

Well, that wasn't quite the reaction she expected.

"Sorry," she muttered, settling back into her car seat and adjusting the front of her dress. "I just . . . I wasn't trying to . . ." Her words trailed off.

They gazed at one another. The silence in the Explorer seemed to stretch on endlessly.

Keith turned back around to face the windshield and put on his sunglasses. He cleared his throat. "Let's get going. We've got a lot of ground to cover and not a lot of time to do it."

She nodded and buckled her seatbelt.

Chapter 15

Dawn walked across the gallery toward her assistant, Kevin, while quickly scanning her messages on her iPhone.

"Just arrived in SC," Stephanie's message read. She had sent it to all her sisters more than an hour ago. "Staying @ shitty no-tell motel. Detective is a real ass! Will update you later."

Dawn shook her head and laughed at her sister. *Well, at least she got safely to South Carolina,* Dawn thought, though she also wondered what had happened to make Stephanie want to jump the detective's bones a few days ago, and now call him a "real ass." She was sure she'd get the details when Stephanie returned from her trip.

Dawn glanced up at Kevin expectantly and tucked her phone into the pocket of her flared skirt. "So how's everything going? Better I hope."

"I can't believe I'm saying this," Kevin muttered before turning to face her, "but I think everything is under control."

Dawn patted him on his shoulder. "Thank God!"

They had to put out a few fires—one, literally—before tonight's exhibition opening. In addition to a painting falling off the wall, a brief power outage thanks to a blown circuit breaker, and tonight's featured artist getting stranded in traffic, one of the placards had caught fire on the candlelit buffet table where they were serving wine and cheese. A fast-thinking waiter had managed to grab an ice pitcher and put out the blaze before the entire tablecloth caught aflame.

Thank goodness, no one was the wiser of those little catastrophes . . . well, no one except a few patrons who wrinkled their noses at the lingering burnt smell near the buffet table.

Hopefully, they'll just think it's the Limburger cheese, Dawn thought flippantly.

Now people were milling about the gallery, admiring the Japanese anime-inspired artwork on display. The gallery had even made a few sales so far.

"Everyone's in awe, Dawn," Percy said as he strolled toward her and Kevin. "You did a wonderful job, darling."

"Thanks, but I can't take the credit. Kevin handled most of the logistics tonight," she said proudly, patting her assistant on the shoulder again. "And the artist painted the artwork. I'm just standing back and enjoying everything tonight."

"Nevertheless, you've all done well." Percy wrapped an arm around her shoulder. "Darling, can I speak with you privately for a second? You don't mind, do you, Kevin?"

Dawn's smile disappeared. *Oh, hell, what now?*

Kevin hesitated then nodded. "Umm, sure . . . yeah. No problem. I'll let you know if anything comes up, Dawn."

"Thanks, Kev," Dawn mumbled.

She and Percy then began to walk across the room. Percy gave a polite nod in greeting to a couple he passed before returning his attention to Dawn.

"So how was your trip to New York a few days ago?" Percy asked, squeezing her shoulder.

"Good. Good," Dawn answered breezily.

She knew he was fishing. He had been raving about Razor's work since he saw that article in the *Times* almost two weeks ago. He was probably eager to hear about whether she had won over Razor and gotten him to agree to show his pieces in Templeton Gallery. She was surprised Percy hadn't asked sooner.

"So you met you know who?" Percy asked.

"Yes, I did," she replied.

"And you asked him you know what?"

"Yes, I did."

"And what did he say?"

"Not much," she answered honestly, sipping from her glass. "He didn't say yes. He didn't say no. I told him before he turned down my offer to think about it for a while."

"*A while?*" Percy exclaimed, dropping his arm from around her shoulder. He stared at her, aghast. "Darling, 'a while' could be a very long time! I'd like to have him in my gallery before the next decade! Why on earth didn't you give him a more concrete time period to respond?"

Dawn shook her head. "Percy, I couldn't exactly play hardball with him. You read yourself how every gallery in New York wants to show his work. He's the belle of the ball, and we're one of plenty standing around trying to get a dance with him. But don't worry. He'll get back to us before the next decade. Trust me. We'll hear from him soon."

"How . . . How can you be so sure?"

"Because I'm a woman who knows when a guy is going to call, and when he isn't? I'm not an optimist. I'm a realist. And Razor *is* going to call."

Percy continued to regard her with an incredulous gaze. "Well, I hope for the gallery's sake . . . for *your* sake, you're right, Dawn. I'd hate to be disappointed."

He then turned and scanned the room. His face brightened when he noticed someone. "Charles, hello! I didn't expect to see you here tonight!" he shouted before abruptly walking off.

When he disappeared from view, Dawn sipped from her glass and sucked her teeth.

She really wished Percy would leave her alone and let her do her work. She didn't need him hanging over her like this. She did a damn good job in running this gallery, and even if the great and wonderful Razor decided to show his art somewhere else, it wouldn't be the end of the world.

After she finished the last of her wine, she set it aside on a nearby table. She then turned to survey the room and raised her eyebrows in surprise when she spotted a familiar handsome face in the crowd.

Well, speak of the devil! He responded sooner than I thought. Take that, Sasha and Percy!

She strolled across the gallery toward Razor. The young artist stood in front of one of the floor-to-ceiling canvases with a wineglass in his hand. From the bored expression on his face, she guessed he wasn't very impressed with the art piece.

Though everyone else was smartly dressed for tonight's opening, Razor had shown up in a stained T-shirt, jeans, leather jacket, and scuffed black combat boots, like he had wandered into the gallery from a nearby construction site. A lit cigarette hung limply from his mouth, drawing stares from annoyed gallery patrons.

"You know, you aren't supposed to smoke in here," she said when she drew close to him, making him turn to face her.

He grinned sheepishly and yanked the cigarette out of his mouth. "Yeah, I saw the sign. Just thought I could sneak one in before anyone noticed."

She glanced at a couple who glared at Razor. They gawked in horror as they watched him drop the cigarette and extinguish it under the heel of his boot on the glossy hardwood floors.

"Oh, trust me. They noticed," Dawn said. "So to what do I owe the honor of this visit, Razor? Did you decide to take an impromptu trip to DC to check out the Smithsonian, or did you come here to tell me that you're taking me up on my offer?"

He gulped down the rest of his white wine. She expected him to toss the glass to the floor. Thankfully, he set it aside on a Lucite tray. "I'm still thinking about your offer actually. I was hoping you could help me make up my mind."

"*Really?* Now how could I do that?"

"Well, for example . . ." he said, taking several steps toward her. They stood so close that she could

smell cigarette smoke, his shampoo, and the lingering smell of another woman's perfume on his clothes.
"You haven't told me what you're offering me, babe."

She didn't like the sound of that or the look he
was giving her. And if he continued to call her "babe,"
she may have to punch him.

"You mean what the gallery is offering as far as
promotion, or how much commission we plan to take
from each sale?" Dawn asked, playing stupid. Maybe
if she steered the conversation back to business, he'd
stop leering at her. "I can assure you we'll have ads
placed in every major newspaper and arts magazine
in the DC region. We'll even run them in the New
York market. I've got good connections in the press
too and a strong contact list. As so far as commission,
traditionally we take 50 percent from retail sales, but
we're willing to negotiate if you don't find that equi-
table."

"No, babe, I told you I don't care about any of that
shit." His grin widened as he looped an arm around
her waist. He drew her toward him. "I mean what are
you offering me? Not what the gallery is offering."

Why does it always have to come to this?

She swore men had one-track minds. It wasn't
enough that she was willing to offer him better contract terms than she had offered any other artist who
had their work appear at Templeton Gallery. It wasn't
enough that she had trekked to Brooklyn, shown up
at the hipster equivalent of a frat party, and wooed
him personally. No, he felt he had to get into her
pants too!

And she wasn't going to sleep with him. No way,
no how! Razor was an artist she'd have to work with,

and she never blurred the lines between work and sex. It was an old family rule.

You don't eat where you sleep.

"You mean 'Don't poop where you eat,' " Lauren's voice corrected in her head.

But Dawn felt like she was in between a rock and a hard place, and she didn't know how to get out of it. Her mother had taught her well how to seduce men. Unfortunately, Yolanda Gibbons hadn't done quite as good of a job showing her daughters how to fend men off.

"I'm afraid I don't know what you mean, Razor," Dawn said flatly, removing his arm from around her waist. "What exactly are you asking me?"

"Look, there's this awesome Moroccan restaurant that I go to in Brooklyn . . . on Leonard Street. Why don't you come back up to New York next week and we can have dinner there together?" His eyes dipped to the swell of her breasts that peeked over her V-neck top. "Then I could tell you *exactly* what I'm asking for."

Dawn pursed her lips, summoning up all her patience. "Look, Razor, I can't—"

"She'd love to!" Percy shouted.

Dawn turned in surprise to find her boss standing behind her.

Where the hell did he come from?

"She'd love to go to dinner with you!" Percy extended his hand to Razor. "Percy Templeton . . . I'm the owner of this gallery, and it's a *pleasure* to meet you, Razor! I adore your work!"

Razor frowned down at Percy's hand before taking it and giving it a half-hearted shake. "Thanks, dude."

"I'm sure Dawn would be willing to clear her schedule this week to meet you," Percy assured before turning to her. "I believe she's even open tomorrow night! Aren't you, darling?"

She opened her mouth to say, no, in fact she was busy tomorrow night. She had important things to do like laundry and, uh . . . closets to clean. But she could tell from the expression on Percy's face that it would be a poor decision to disagree with him.

"Sure, I'm free," she said through clenched teeth.

Percy clapped his hands. "It's settled then! You and Razor will enjoy a lovely dinner and iron out the details of his work appearing in our gallery. I'm sure you'll both have a wonderful time!"

Dawn turned back to Razor who was smiling again. The lusty look was back in his eyes.

"Oh, I'm sure," she said dryly.

Chapter 16

"Where can a guy grab a bite to eat around here?" Keith asked as he stood at the motel counter.

The scrawny clerk stared up at him. "You didn't like our complimentary continental breakfast?"

Complimentary continental breakfast?

Keith glanced across the vacant lobby at the white buffet table sitting in the corner. It was covered with platters of rock-hard muffins and biscuits, squishy grapes and slices of pineapple, and jars of jelly with a freshness date that was highly questionable. Only the coffee had seemed vaguely acceptable . . . until Keith had poured himself a cup, that is. He had set the coffee aside too after he sampled some.

"No offense, but I've had better," Keith muttered.

"Well, there's a diner up the road," the clerk drawled, handing him back his credit card and receipt. He pointed toward the window. "It's about five miles from here. They sell flapjacks, bacon, and eggs for three dollars and fifty cents."

"Three-fifty, huh?" Keith tucked his credit card

back into his wallet. "Maybe I'll go check it out. Thanks."

The clerk nodded.

Keith turned and walked toward the glass door then let it slowly swing shut behind him. He strode across Starlight Motel's parking lot toward his Ford Explorer and glanced at his watch. It was ten minutes after. Stephanie should be here by now. He had covered his hotel bill and told her to meet him at the car at 9 a.m.

Where the hell is she?

"Typical," he muttered. "Just typical."

He should have known the pampered princess would have an issue with punctuality. She seemed to have an issue with everything else.

Stephanie had been in full diva mode since they arrived in South Carolina late last night. First, she had been appalled when she saw the state of their motel rooms.

"Oh my God," she had sneered with a curl in her lip, "it's like I stepped into a time machine and got dumped back to 1973! Is that *shag carpet?*"

Then she complained about the lack of room service and other amenities. "What decent hotel doesn't have turn-down service? Will I have to wash my own towels and sheets too?"

Then she squawked about them having to leave bright and early at 9 a.m.

"How am I supposed to get my beauty sleep? I'm exhausted, Keith!"

But worse than her whining and complaining was the fact that Stephanie had kissed him. And heaven help him, he had almost kissed her back before he quickly got his wits about him. That woman was a temptress . . . a treacherous one! The longer she was around, the more and more he felt like he had made the wrong decision letting her come here with him. But he had been swept by her pleas and sad brown eyes. Now he knew for sure that if she was going to keep tagging along, he had to be sterner with her. He had to lay down the law. He couldn't have her messing up his schedule anymore or messing with his head and libido.

He tossed his duffel bag inside the car and glanced at his watch once more. He shook his head again, slammed his car door shut, and stalked across the parking lot to her motel room.

It was a small motel that sat on a hill not far from the highway. The yellow-and-black sign facing the roadway advertised hot tubs and new wireless access in all rooms. Keith admitted that the bland brown décor and cheap particle-board furniture left much to be desired as far as accommodations, but the motel had served its purpose while they were here. Now they were moving on and headed to meet Ms. Beaumont to find out more about Isaac.

That is if Stephanie ever manages to leave her damn room, he thought with exasperation.

Her room was three doors down from his. He pounded on the door several times with his closed fist. He paused and waited for an answer. When he didn't hear one, he pounded again. After a couple of minutes, the door swung open.

"I heard you! I heard you!" she shouted. "Geez! Did you used to be a cop?"

He paused then nodded. "Yeah, why?"

"Because you've developed the art of banging on

doors like one," she muttered peevishly with her hand on her hip as she glowered at him. "I thought I was in a drug raid and someone was about to cart me off to jail!"

"I was banging on the door because you were supposed to meet me at the car at nine a.m. You were supposed to be ready to leave at that time." He pointed down at his wristwatch then gazed at her. She was standing in the doorway in a pink satin robe and her hair was partially in curlers. "It is now nine-fifteen and you are obviously nowhere close to being ready."

"Well aren't you just a big bottle of sunshine in the morning," she muttered then waved her hand at him dismissively. She turned around. "It'll only take a few minutes to get ready."

She sashayed across her motel room to the bathroom, pulling curlers from her hair as she went.

Keith told himself for the umpteenth time to count to ten. He then took a calming breath, stepped inside her room, and shut the door behind him.

He looked around and saw that piles of clothes were thrown all over her bed. The lid of her suitcase was open. Makeup and bottles of lotion were still on her dresser top. He closed his eyes.

"Stephanie, you are *not* going to be ready to go in a few minutes."

"Yes, I am," she sang through the cracked bathroom door. "You'll see!"

"It's impossible!" He opened his eyes and thought for a bit. "Look, why don't I do this? I'll head to breakfast and then come back to—"

"*Oh, no!* You think I'm going to let you leave me here alone? How do I know you won't do your interview without me?"

"I wouldn't do that," he answered tersely. "I promised that you could come along and I meant it. I'm a man of my word."

"So take me at *my* word, Keith!" she yelled through the door crack. "I swear that all I need is another ten minutes. I'm almost done anyway. Stop being such a slave driver," she mumbled under her breath.

Enough of this crap, Keith thought with frustration. He strode toward the bathroom doorway. "Damn it! Why don't you just . . ."

His words faded.

He caught a glimpse of her reflection through the cracked doorway. She was standing in front of the bathroom mirror, furiously running her fingers through her long hair, trying to comb out her nest of curls. She had taken off her satin robe and was now topless, revealing beautiful brown breasts that were a perfect handful and pointed dark areolas—little Hershey's Kisses that any man would be happy to nibble on. She also wore a black lace thong. She turned slightly and bent over, giving him a delectable view of her curvy bottom and sculpted thighs.

Keith's eyes raked over her. His mouth literally watered. He instantly became rock hard.

"Why don't I just what?" she snapped, completely oblivious to the fact that he was now ogling her naked body.

"Uh . . ." He loudly cleared his throat. "Uh, never . . . never mind. I'll . . . I'll wait for you at the car."

She furrowed her brows. "Huh?"

He abruptly turned, walked across the room and out her doorway, shutting the door behind him.

He took several deep breaths as he walked across

the mostly deserted parking lot toward his SUV. When he opened his car door and plopped onto the leather seat, his craving for Stephanie still hadn't subsided. His jean zipper felt like it was straining to hold in Mt. Kilimanjaro.

This woman was pushing him closer and closer to the edge and if he wasn't careful, she would push him right over. He could make a big mistake if he wasn't careful, like giving in to his desire for her. Even now, he was finding it hard to control the urge to go back to her motel room, push her against the bathroom wall, and show her just how much of a "slave driver" he really could be. If she let him, he could do things to her body that would leave her quivering in ecstasy and begging him not to stop. He'd make love to her until both of their bodies were sapped and spent.

But I'm not going to do that, he resolved.

He was going to stay focused on this case and not get distracted by her, yet again. He decided then and there that after they spoke to Ms. Beaumont, he was sending Stephanie back to Virginia. If the trail following Isaac continued to another county or another state, it didn't matter. He was following the trail alone. He didn't care how much Stephanie pled or whined or argued this time. She had to go.

Chapter 17

Stephanie glanced at Keith as he drove, wondering why he was so quiet all of a sudden. He had barely spoken to her as they ate breakfast at the small diner that morning. He hadn't looked up from his plate of pancakes and bacon, even when she tried to talk to him about the case, even when she waved her hands in front of his face and asked him, "Cat got your tongue?" He had only shaken his head and mumbled something in response, irritating her even more. He had paid the bill, left a tip for the waitress, and silently got up and walked back to his car, leaving her sitting alone in the diner booth.

She was starting to wonder if his silence was supposed to be some kind of a punishment. So she was a little late getting ready this morning. *Big deal!* It didn't mean she deserved the silent treatment.

She stubbornly crossed her arms over her chest and glared out of the windshield, deciding to ignore him if he insisted on acting this way. Minutes later, they turned onto a long, winding road and finally pulled onto a gravel driveway bordered by cypress trees. When Stephanie saw the house sitting on the crest of the hill, she gaped in amazement.

Stephanie was accustomed to opulence. Her mother's mansion was one of the largest and most finely decorated in Chesterton and was only eclipsed in size by a few others, including the property owned by Stephanie's brother-in-law Crisanto Weaver. But the house in front of her looked like something straight out of *Gone with the Wind*. She was sure she had stepped out of the present day and landed smack into the antebellum South. Pretty soon Scarlett O'Hara was going to come rushing out the door to battle with the Yankees.

It was a plantation style house with six ionic columns holding up a white veranda. Green shutters were on every window. Brick steps led to the green French doors. The front porch was flanked by flowering rose bushes, and ivy climbed up the latticework along the sides of the mansion to the roof.

Two women stood on the front porch. Both were smiling. One was a middle-aged white woman in a gray maid's uniform, wearing a lace-edged apron. In her hands was a silver tray covered with a few glasses and a sweating pitcher of lemonade. Beside her was a white-haired, sepia-toned black woman who looked to be in her mid to late sixties, but she had the physique of someone much younger. Her flowing white hair was held back on one side by a black hair comb. She reminded Stephanie of her own deceased grandmother Althea. She was certainly wearing a dress that Althea would have worn herself, were she still alive. It was red and slightly low cut. The bodice was form-fitting, showing her small waist, but the skirt flared, ending at her brown calves. Her bare legs were nicely sculpted.

When the SUV pulled to a stop near the house's entrance, the black woman's smile instantly widened. She walked down the brick steps toward the Explorer with round hips swaying.

"Mr. Hendricks, I presume," she drawled as Keith threw open his car door. She extended her slender, well-manicured hand.

"Ms. Beaumont." He nodded and took her hand in his own. He shook it.

"Please," she said, giving him a wink, "call me Myra. Any time someone calls me 'Ms. Beaumont,' I feel like an old schoolmarm." She laughed and placed her hand over his and squeezed. She then let her dark eyes trail over him slowly. She licked her red-painted lips. "My, my, my! I didn't expect you to be quite so handsome, Mr. Hendricks! I was expecting a—"

She paused when Stephanie opened the car's passenger-side door and climbed out of the SUV.

"Well, who is this?" Myra released Keith's hand. She narrowed her eyes at the younger woman, looking annoyed. "I don't remember you saying you were bringing a guest with you, Mr. Hendricks."

He sighed. "I didn't."

Myra cocked an eyebrow in confusion. "I'm sorry. So who is she?"

Stephanie shut the car door and quickly stepped forward. She extended her hand. "Hello, Ms. Beaumont. My name is Stephanie Gibbons. It's a pleasure to meet you, ma'am."

Myra stared at Stephanie's hand warily for several seconds before finally taking it. When she did shake it, she did it as if it pained her. "Pleased to meet you too, Miss Gibbons," she said flatly. "Welcome to my home."

"Thank you. You have a very beautiful home, ma'am."

"Nice of you to say." Myra pursed her lips. "So you are Mr. Hendricks's companion. Are you also a detective?"

Stephanie shook her head. "No, I'm—"

"She's my assistant," Keith interjected. "She's just . . . tagging along."

"Oh, how nice!" the older woman exclaimed, eyeing Stephanie again. "Isn't that charming? Does your assistant always 'tag along' with you, Mr. Hendricks?"

"Only when she refuses to be left behind," he muttered, making the older woman throw back her head and laugh.

Stephanie put her hands on her hips, not amused at being the butt of his joke. She knew why Keith was irritated with her, but she had done nothing to earn this woman's disdain. Obviously, this hot-to-trot old biddy thought she would have Keith—a strapping young buck—all to herself.

Hate to disappoint, lady, but I'm not going anywhere, she thought.

"Well, come on inside," Myra said, waving them forward. She walked back up the stairs to the French doors, but paused to stand in front of the maid. "Would you like some lemonade?" She held up the ice-cold pitcher and gazed at Keith adoringly.

"Yes, I would love some," Stephanie said politely.

Myra dropped the pitcher back to the tray with a *clink*. "Then Helda can pour you some."

Stephanie quietly seethed in frustration and

glanced up at Keith. She could see him fighting back a smile. The maid handed each of them glasses of lemonade and a minute later they walked through the French doors into the foyer that smelled like hyacinth and lemons.

Stephanie gazed around her in wonder. A winding mahogany staircase led to the second floor. A sitting room with French country wallpaper and Queen Anne furniture was to her right and the dining room with a table that looked like it could seat a dozen people was to her left. An awe-inspiring glass chandelier hung overhead in the center of the foyer. There were several paintings on the wall, mostly in rococo style.

This lady certainly doesn't believe in skimping, she thought grudgingly.

"So," Myra began as she ushered them into her brightly-lit sitting room, "you wish to find out about Isaac." She turned and waved her hand toward a pale yellow satin sofa, gesturing for them to take a seat. "Or at least that's what he's calling himself now."

"Yes," Keith said, sitting down. "You said you two knew each other."

Stephanie took the seat beside him.

"Oh, we knew each other *very* well!" Myra gave a thoughtful nod. "I've known him since he was nineteen years old. I was the one who taught him everything he knows."

Keith leaned forward. "What do you mean?"

Myra paused. She crossed her brown legs and tilted her head. "How candid can I be with you, Mr. Hendricks?"

"As candid as you'd like."

"I mean, sir, that I want to know whether I have to

worry about you blabbing to the authorities and telling them what I am about to tell you. If that is the case, then we can end this conversation right now."

Stephanie raised her eyebrows, taking a sip from her glass. She wondered how Keith would handle this one.

"If it's anything pertaining to the case I'm now investigating, I have to tell them," Keith said. "But if it's anything related to any other crimes, I will use my own discretion."

"Uh-huh," Myra said. "That's a very diplomatic but honest answer, Mr. Hendricks."

"You don't want me to lie to you, do you?"

"I suppose not." She waved her slender hand. "Well, what I'm about to say doesn't paint me in the best light. Thank God for the statute of limitations or I could face jail time for half the things I've done in my life!" She cleared her throat. "But I will tell you anyway."

"Why?" Stephanie asked.

Myra turned her gaze to her. "Because Isaac betrayed me, and the first rule I've ever taught him is that you do not betray your teacher. Now he has to pay the price for what he's done and the price he pays could be a hefty one, but so be it. He brought it on himself." She sat back in her chair. "When I met Isaac, he was a little street thug from a small town in Florida. He was what you young men call today a booster, I believe."

Keith nodded. "He stole cars."

"Yes, indeed, honey! He was working for some backwater kingpin named Big Red." She pinched her lips. "He was still wet behind the ears back then. He thought he knew more about the world than he

really did, but I could see that young man had potential. He was good lookin'—*very* good lookin'—and
he had a natural charm to him. I decided to take him
under my wing. I refined him. I taught him how to
seduce and how to turn up the charm. I taught him
how to run a con. He excelled at every lesson that I
threw at him. He took to being a conman like a fish
would take to water."

"Why'd you go out of your way to teach him these
things?" Keith asked, taking a drink of lemonade.
"You didn't do it out of the kindness of your heart."

"Of course not! Honey, I was forty-five and Isaac
was nineteen. I've always liked my men young and
virile. They're the only ones that can keep up with
me! And that boy was as good in bed as he was pretty!
He certainly had no problem with stamina." She gave
Keith another long, assessing gaze. "You know, you
remind me a lot of what Isaac was like back then—
very tough, very manly. You grew up in a rough neighborhood too, didn't you?"

Keith glanced at Stephanie and nodded. "East
Baltimore."

When their eyes met, he looked away again. Stephanie suddenly wondered what the childhood version
of Keith was like. Did he put up the same walls that
the adult Keith often did?

"Uh-huh," Myra said with a nod. "I thought so. It's
just something about you boys. The hardness doesn't
go away. I like a tough man though, honey! Oh, the
things I could have taught you . . ." She slowly shook
her head and clucked her tongue. ". . . You couldn't
imagine."

Stephanie nearly choked on her lemonade. She
started to cough. Keith bit back his laughter.

"Well," Myra said, getting back to the subject at hand, "every bird leaves the nest eventually. Isaac started to work his own cons, but he would always come back to visit every once and a while. He'd spend a few nights with me, then head on his way."

"When was the last time you saw him?" Keith asked.

"About three months ago, before he headed to Virginia. That's when I found out he had stolen money from me." She slowly shook her head. "*Me!* Of all people! How could he do that? I was practically like a mother to him!"

Stephanie raised an eyebrow. *I'm pretty sure most men don't get lessons in the bedroom from their mothers,* she thought dryly, but kept that opinion to herself.

"I swear the old saying holds true . . . there is no honor among thieves!" Myra continued. "If he comes back this time, he is not welcome. I told him never to darken my doorstep again."

"When was the last time you spoke to him?" Keith asked.

"Oh, a few weeks ago." She tilted her head. "He tried to smooth talk his way into my good graces. Whenever he finishes a con, he has to go into hiding for a while. He wanted to come here but I told him no. He told me he had just swindled some silly real estate agent who thought he was going to marry her." She chuckled. "Marry her! *Can you believe that?* Honestly, I swear some of these women are so gullible! They make cons so easy!"

Stephanie instantly stiffened. Her hold around her glass of lemonade tightened to the point that she thought it would shatter in her hand.

Keith glanced at her anxiously and cleared his throat. He then returned his attention to Myra. "Did

Isaac say where he was going? Where else does he go when he wants to lie low for awhile?"

Myra took a deep breath and thought for a bit. "If he doesn't come here, he usually goes to his hometown in Florida. Something with the word 'swamp' in it. It's not far from Pensacola." She sneered. "I tried my best to get him to leave that Podunk town behind. I especially wanted him to lose contact with that fat thug Big Red because that man is nothing by a liability, but it didn't work. Old roots run deep, I guess."

Keith nodded. "So if I want to find Isaac, I need to head to Florida then."

"I guess so, Mr. Hendricks."

"Can I count on your silence, Myra?" Keith asked, gazing into the older woman's eyes. "You aren't going to suddenly forgive Isaac and give him the heads-up . . . tell him that we're looking for him?"

She rose from her chair. "Trust me. You don't have to worry about me telling him anything. He crossed me and I'm not one to forgive and forget. He knows that." Her face suddenly brightened. "How long do you plan to stay in our fair town before you leave for Florida, Mr. Hendricks?"

He shrugged and stood from the sofa. "Not long."

Stephanie followed suit and stood with the rest of them. She guessed that was the end of the interview.

"Hopefully, for one more night, at least. You know, you're welcome to stay here, if you wish. My home has plenty of rooms!"

Stephanie noticed that she hadn't been offered a similar invitation. She watched as Myra took a step toward Keith. The older woman lowered her thick, dark lashes.

"You have an open invitation to one room in particular, Mr. Hendricks ... if you're interested," she said to him with a saucy wink.

Stephanie closed her eyes and slowly shook her head.

"Actually, we're staying at a local motel, but thanks for the offer, Myra," Keith said.

"Oh, well." Myra shrugged. "I tried. Like I said ... I've got a weakness for young men."

Chapter 18

"God, someone give that woman a cold shower!" Stephanie exclaimed as they walked down the brick front steps and the length of Myra Beaumont's gravel driveway back to his Explorer. "I thought your sex drive went down after menopause! If she's like that now, what the hell was she like at forty-five?"

"Too much for any one man to handle, I'm sure," Keith muttered as he walked beside her.

The temperature had increased since they had gone inside and it was now so sweltering hot and humid that their clothes instantly stuck to their skin. Stephanie fanned herself with her hands though it did little to cool her off.

"So it looks like we're headed to Florida now," she said with a smile. "I'm glad I packed a sundress. I wish I had taken one of my bikinis with me too though." She snapped her fingers. "You know what? Maybe I can buy one while we're—"

"I wouldn't plan your wardrobe just yet," he murmured, catching her off guard.

"Why not?"

"Because *I'm* going to Florida. You aren't."

Stephanie came to a stop. She yanked off her sunglasses and stared at him. "What do you mean I'm not going?"

"I meant exactly what I said." He opened his car door and climbed inside. "Our deal was that you got to come to South Carolina. That's it. You didn't mention anything about tagging along after that."

"Because I didn't know there would be anything after South Carolina!" Stephanie argued, climbing in after him.

"Well, that's tough luck for you, ain't it?" He stuck his key into the ignition. They pulled off seconds later, kicking up gravel as they went.

"Look, what is the big deal about having me here? I asked you before if you had a problem with me. You said that you didn't!"

"Well, I lied," he said as he drove down the highway. "I'm tired of your complaining. I'm tired of your whining. I've met toddlers that were less huffy."

"*Excuse me?*" She was absolutely shocked at what she was hearing. "Did you just call me 'huffy'?"

"Stephanie, I don't have time for the spoiled princess . . . prima donna routine. I've got a job to do! I suggest you go back home and let me do it."

"And what if I refuse to go back home?" she challenged, crossing her arms over her chest. "What are you going to do? Toss me on the side of the road?" She glared at him, raising her nose into her air.

"No, I'll quit the case," he answered succinctly. "I'll give you back your money. Your contract with Stokowski and Hendricks will become null and void. We end it at that."

She stared at him in outrage. "You wouldn't!"

"Yes, I would. Just try me, lady!" He tore his gaze from the roadway to glare at her. "Listen, I take my job very seriously. This isn't just fun and games for me."

"This isn't fun and games for me either!"

"I need to be able to do my work. I don't need any distractions."

She pointed at her chest. "And I'm a distraction?"

"Yes . . . a big one," he mumbled.

He looked away then, and she wondered what she had done to make this guy dislike her so much. Men usually adored her. This was the first guy she had ever met who seemed to find her outright repugnant. She found it hard to believe that this was the same man who seemed so attracted to her less than a month ago that his desire for her was almost palpable.

"So that's where we stand, huh? Either I leave or you quit?"

"Exactly."

Stephanie balled her fists in her lap. She was so angry, she couldn't see straight. He wasn't dumping her on the side of the road, but he might as well with the way he was treating her.

The rest of the drive was carried out in silence with Keith focused on the road and Stephanie obstinately staring out the passenger-side window with her back to him. They arrived back at the Starlight Motel to find that the rooms they had checked out of earlier that day were no longer vacant.

"A church group came through at around two o'clock and booked almost every room we had available," the clerk explained while popping his gum. He scratched his oily head and glanced up from his computer screen. "We've got one room left if you want it though. It's a double. It can fit the both of you."

"*One room?*" Keith dropped his head into his hands and leaned his elbow on the counter. "Great. Just great!"

His reaction to the news of having to share a room with her made her feel even more unwanted. *Who the hell does he think he is?*

"I'll sleep in the car if it's that big of a problem!" she snarled as they stood in front of the checkout desk.

The clerk's eyes widened and his gaze shifted between the two. He stopped snapping his gum.

"Like hell you would." Keith then returned his attention to the clerk. He pulled out his wallet. "We'll take the room. Thanks."

Their room was at the very end of the motel lot, next to the soda and ice machine. They trudged there and entered it in silence. Stephanie stalked over the shag carpet to one of the double beds and threw her luggage on top. Keith quietly unpacked his things on the other bed and loaded some of his clothes into one of the dresser drawers.

She spent most of her time also unpacking and trying her best to ignore the fact that he was in the room with her.

It didn't seem right to be this attracted to a man who wanted nothing to do with her, but she was attracted all the same. She could feel his presence and sense his body heat. Having him this close made her tense.

"I'll be back in a few," he said quietly an hour later. He then grabbed his jacket and his wallet. He opened the motel room door.

Stephanie didn't respond. She busied herself with arranging her clothes in the motel closet and only looked over her shoulder when he shut the door behind him.

"Asshole," she muttered. She then sat on the bed and angrily stomped her foot in frustration.

Keith couldn't do it. There was no way in hell he was sleeping in a bedroom with her sober. He had to get out of there. He drove for almost a half an hour before finally spotting a small bar on the side of the road. It was a hole in the wall with a flickering sign in front and posters of Miller Lite and tequila bottles in the windows. Two beat-up pickup trucks were parked in the few empty spaces in front of the bar.

Two minutes later, Keith pushed the barroom door open with a slow creak and saw that it was mostly deserted. Country music played on the glowing jukebox in the far-off corner. A silent baseball game played on the television overhead. Two trucker-looking types sat at the bar counter with a bowl of peanuts in between them. A plump older white woman wearing a black tank top with an eagle tattooed on her arm looked up as Keith stepped through the door. Her brown, pencil-thin, drawn-on eyebrows raised in surprise at seeing him.

For a split second Keith wondered if maybe he had made a bad decision by choosing to stop for a drink at a no-name bar in the middle of a small town in the Deep South, but when the bartender's wrinkled face broke into a smile, his wariness quickly subsided.

"Well, hello, stranger," she said with a hearty drawl, leaning against the counter. "What can I get you, hon?"

"Just a beer for now," Keith said as he sat on one of

the stools and pulled up to the bar. He nodded his head at the man sitting directly next to him. The bearded man nodded in return and then raised his beer in greeting.

"For now?" The bartender chuckled. "Oh, that doesn't sound good! You plannin' on drinking more than that?"

"I'll drink enough to get close to drunk," Keith said, "but I don't want to get drunk enough that I can't get home."

"I hear that one!" She laughed again and handed him a Bud Light. "All right, so what is it? Animal, vegetable, or mineral, hon?"

He tipped the beer bottle to his lips. "I'm not following you. What do you mean?" he asked after taking a gulp.

"What ails you?" She tilted her blond head. "You want to get drunk for a reason." She squinted her blue eyes and thought for a second. "I'm guessin' it's animal . . . one of the female persuasion. You have the look of a man who's not too happy with his old lady."

"I don't have an old lady."

The bartender looked taken aback by that.

"But I . . . I am dealing with a few things with one woman, in particular," he admitted.

"See! I called it!" She slapped her palm on the counter victoriously. "I knew it was a woman! So what happened? Did you guys fight? She in love with somebody else?"

"No, it's nothing like that. She's a client of mine." He gazed down at his bottle, picking at the label with his thumbnail. "And I'm . . . I'm having a hard time keeping her at a distance."

"Oh," she said, raising her pencil eyebrows again, "don't wanna mix business with pleasure, as you Yankees would say."

"Exactly."

"Is she having a hard time doin' the same thing . . . not mixin' business with pleasure?"

Keith considered her question for a bit.

There were moments when he got the impression that Stephanie was just as attracted to him as he was to her, but he knew those impressions couldn't be trusted. She was a woman who was good at throwing up a façade, making men believe what she wanted them to believe. According to the town gossip, her whole family was gifted with those skills. In fact, that was the part about Stephanie that bothered him the most. He couldn't trust his feelings for her because essentially, he couldn't trust *her*. Even if he was willing to look past her diva moments, how could he possibly get involved with a woman who was, on some level, no better than Isaac? She was no better than the man who had conned her.

"I don't know how she feels," he answered quietly.

The bartender gazed at him with sympathetic eyes. "You can't just ask her? You know it may help if you tell her how you feel."

"Not this woman," he said, shaking his head and downing more of his beer. "She'd smell blood in the water and go in for the kill."

She laughed again. "She's that bad, huh?"

He nodded. "Very."

"Well, I don't know of any man that can put up a fight for too long when he's really got it bad for a woman. It's just not in your nature."

"You think so?"

"I know so, hon! That's how I met my second husband. He was burnin' for me hotter than a coal on a fire! He didn't stand a chance!"

"I don't think I do either," Keith murmured drearily.

"Well, finish your drink. Sit here and talk about it all you want. Cuz it sounds like you don't have much of a chance with this one. Sorry, but you're in a pickle, hon."

Keith nodded. He was in a pickle, indeed.

Chapter 19

Dawn took a steadying breath before finally opening the front door and striding into the dimly lit restaurant.

Middle Eastern music played in the background and laughter and conversations buzzed around her. Elaborate colored tapestries with fanciful patterns hung on the gold-inlaid walls and couples sat on low seats, surrounded by silk pillows as they ate their meals of b'stella and beef shish kebabs. An adventurous few smoked from hookah pipes.

I don't know why I'm so nervous. It isn't like I haven't done something like this before, Dawn thought as she drew toward the back of the restaurant where Razor had texted he was sitting.

But she knew deep down that this time was different. It wasn't like in the past where she had manipulated men for her own gain. This time she wasn't calling the shots, and she wasn't sure if she would really benefit in the end.

Percy wanted Razor to show his work at Templeton Gallery—no matter what—and she didn't want to disappoint Percy. That meant taking the Acela train yet again to New York. She had to do everything possible to win Razor over tonight and that could easily mean ending up in bed with the young artist before sunrise—a prospect she truly hated. It wasn't that she didn't find Razor attractive. Yes, he was hot . . . in a grubby, bad boy sort of way. But he seemed more like a spoiled little brat than a grown man, and Dawn didn't have sex with children. And sleeping with him meant breaking one of the family's prime rules, something she just didn't do.

Well, I didn't do . . . up until now, she silently corrected.

Dawn found Razor sitting alone, leaning casually against a stack of pillows as he munched on dates. He watched a lithe belly dancer gyrate in front of him to the music. He was completely entranced by the woman's undulating body.

Dawn waited for him to notice her standing there. He didn't. After waiting for several seconds, she loudly cleared her throat. Razor finally looked up at her.

"Please . . . Don't let me interrupt," she said wryly.

Razor's handsome face curled into an impish grin. "You aren't interrupting, babe. You're *exactly* who I was waiting for."

No longer the center of attention, the belly dancer wandered off to sway her hips for a couple at another table. Razor held out his hand to Dawn.

She took it and began to sit down, intending to take the seat beside him, but she yelped in surprise when she felt him roughly tug her toward him. She tumbled face first into his lap. Razor cackled like a hyena and Dawn grimaced, muttering to herself. She rolled onto her side and sat upright. She shoved her skirt back down, which had flown up around her waist when she fell.

Great, she thought. *Now about half of the restaurant knows what color panties I'm wearing.*

"You thought that was funny?" she asked tersely, glaring at him.

"Oh, come on! Lighten the fuck up, babe! Life's a party. Enjoy it!" He held a date toward her. "Want one?"

"No thank you," she grumbled before adjusting in her seat.

"More for me then." He tossed the date high into the air and caught it in his mouth. He turned to her, grinning again like he had just kicked a winning field goal.

Dawn fought the urge to roll her eyes. *This is going to be a long damn night.*

"Just suck it up," a voice in her head urged. "Suck it up so that he'll agree to show at the gallery and you can be done with this."

She took another deep breath, trying her best to regain her composure. "So . . . thanks for inviting me to dinner."

"No prob." He leaned toward her. His green eyes twinkled. "I wanted to see you again. I couldn't get you out of my head since that night you showed up at my studio. Damn, you were hot!" He reached for his glass of red wine and gulped down what was left. "If I could have stripped you down and fucked you right there I would have."

Lord, give me strength!

"Uh . . ." She tucked her hair behind her ear and loudly cleared her throat again, deciding to pretend that she hadn't heard that last part. "Well, I've had a hard time forgetting about you too, Razor. I think you're very talented and I'd love to have your work at my gallery. I'm a big fan of yours."

"Big fan, huh?" He tilted his head. "So that's the only reason?"

"The only reason what?"

She tried to shift away from him slightly though he drew even closer.

"That's the only reason you couldn't forget about me?" he asked before trailing a finger along her chin, then her throat. His finger drifted lower, past the collar of her blouse. "I hope you're interested in more than just my art."

"Well, I . . . I . . . like you," she lied, reaching for one of the dates from the gold-plated dish in front of her, making him pull his hand away from her. She chewed. "Of course, I do. But you're an artist. I'm a gallery director. It only makes sense that we work together for our mutual gain. I mean . . . I acknowledge that DC isn't New York by a long shot, but it's an emerging market with plenty of wealthy people who are willing to pay—"

Her words drifted off when Razor loudly huffed. He lowered his wineglass back to the table in front of him and shook his head. "Babe, let's not talk about that shit tonight, all right? Business . . . money . . . dude, it just brings me down! It brings the world down!" He smirked. "Let's talk about us instead. Or better yet, let's not talk at all."

When Razor leaned forward and she felt his wet tongue flick across her earlobe, her first instinct was to push him away, but she fought it. This is what she came for, after all. This is what she knew she had to do to get this kid to agree to show his work at Templeton Gallery. Razor's lips left her earlobe and sucked at the skin along her neck.

"Damn, you're tasty," he murmured, before reaching for one of her breasts. He then roughly turned her face toward his and kissed her. His tongue dove inside her mouth like it was wearing scuba gear, making her cringe.

Dawn closed her eyes and told herself to just bear it. She was doing it for her job. She was doing it for the gallery. But none of those thoughts were working. Instead, she was silently cursing Percy, calling him just about every name in the book. Then she started to curse herself. Here she was a grown woman of thirty-six, sucking face with a twenty-two-year-old in the middle of a Moroccan restaurant in some Brooklyn neighborhood. Is this really what her life had come to?

"Hello, Razor. Sorry, I'm late. I—"

Dawn tore her mouth away and looked up. When she saw who was standing in front of their table, her eyes widened.

"*Sasha?*"

Sasha Duncan, Sawyer Gallery director and all-around bitch, stared at Dawn, looking equally shocked. "Dawn, what . . . What the hell are you doing here?"

"What do you mean, 'What the hell am I doing here?' What the hell are *you* doing here?"

Razor leaned back. "Sasha! Hey, glad you could make it!"

Dawn turned to glare at Razor. "Wait . . . wait, you invited her *too?*"

"Sure, I did. Why not?" He pet the open seat on the opposite side of him. "Thanks for coming, babe.

Don't worry about being a little late. We haven't started any of the dinner courses yet."

Sasha's face twisted with confusion then outrage, but she quickly recovered. The bottle blonde pasted on a smile and adjusted the front of her very short leather skirt. A skirt that looked better fit for someone about thirty years younger.

"Well . . . thanks for waiting," she gushed before lowering herself to sit beside Razor.

He draped his arm around her and Sasha giggled. This time Dawn did roll her eyes.

Dawn had known that Sasha was full of crap when Sasha said she had no interest in having Razor's work at Sawyer Gallery, but Dawn had underestimated the lengths that Sasha would go to get the job done. As the evening wore on, Dawn gradually realized how much she had underestimated Razor too. Not only was Razor a spoiled brat, but he was also a manipulative little bastard. He knew exactly what he was doing when he invited both her and Sasha to dinner. He also knew what both women wanted out of him—and he was going to make them work for it, playing one desperate gallery director off the other. There were several times when Dawn wanted to get up and walk out of the restaurant, but she fought down the urge. Not only did she have Percy to worry about, but now she also had her pride to consider. She wasn't going to lose this contest to the likes of Sasha Duncan.

No way, no how, Dawn thought stubbornly as she chewed her lamb.

When the trio finished the last of their mint tea and Razor wolfed down the last Moroccan pastry (*Such a gentleman,* Dawn thought flippantly), he stretched and wrapped his arms around each woman.

"So what do you babes say we take this back to my place?" He looked back and forth between the two.

Oh, hell no! He has got to be kidding! He doesn't actually think he's going to have sex with both *of us tonight, does he?*

"Absolutely," Sasha said, ruffling his beard.

Razor lowered his mouth to Sasha's and the two shared a sloppy, wet kiss that made Dawn cringe. To any bystander, Razor looked like he could have easily been kissing his mother.

Razor licked his lips and turned back to Dawn. "How about you, babe? You game?"

No! No, I'm not game, you greedy little asshole!

"But think about the *gallery*," the voice in her head pleaded.

Dawn hesitated.

"Hey, if it's not your thing, that's OK," he said, removing his arm from around her.

Sasha grinned arrogantly, pissing Dawn off even more.

"I just thought you were open to stuff . . . like me," Razor continued. "But if you don't—"

"Sure, I'll go," Dawn said quickly, forcing out the words before she had a chance to think any further. "Let's . . . Let's do this."

What the hell am I doing, Dawn thought for the umpteenth time as they climbed the stairs to Razor's East Williamsburg condo. *I can't believe I talked myself into this!*

Razor climbed the last step and walked toward his front door. He unlocked it and threw it open with a flourish. "Make yourselves at home." He gestured the two women inside.

Sasha entered first, taking off her shawl and revealing the leather bustier that matched her skirt. Dawn slowly walked in after her and looked around.

"Oh, my God! I love your digs, Razor!" Sasha exclaimed. "It's so . . . so awesome!"

At that, Dawn almost snorted, but managed to hold in her laughter.

Awesome, indeed.

The condo resembled more of a frat house than the upscale apartment it was supposed to be. The décor was expensive, befitting the rich kid that Razor a.k.a. Trent Horowitz really was. The furniture and paintings on the walls were easily worth a quarter of a million dollars, but the tables and floor were littered with empty bottles of wine and liquor as well as dirty glasses and several turned over plastic cups. Ashtrays piled high with used cigarette butts also dotted the condo's landscape and the living room smelled like a heavy mix of weed and whiskey. Dawn wouldn't be surprised if she stuck her hand underneath one of the couch cushions, she'd pull out a bra or a thong.

"Can I get you babes a drink?" Razor asked before strolling across the living room and into his state-of-the art kitchen.

"Scotch on the rocks for me!" Sasha shouted.

"No thanks. I'm good," Dawn answered as she shrugged out of her jacket and tossed it over the back of one of Razor's club chairs.

"You sure?" he called out, opening one of the overhead cabinets.

On second thought, if she was actually going to go

through with this whole fiasco, she should probably fortify herself with a drink or two.

Dawn shrugged. "I guess you can make me a scotch too."

He poured two glasses and returned seconds later. He handed a drink to each woman.

Dawn sipped from her glass while Sasha guzzled her scotch down in two gulps.

"So," Razor said, slapping his hands together, "you babes ready to have some fun?"

"Sure. What are you up for?" Sasha asked seductively, licking her ruby red lips.

"Whatever you're into." Razor grinned.

I'm into walking out that front door, getting a cab, and going back to my damn hotel, Dawn thought.

"Let me uh . . . tidy up some shit first, and I'll meet you babes back here in a couple of minutes, OK?"

"Sure," Sasha said.

Dawn nodded.

Razor walked off, disappearing down a hall. When he closed a door behind him, Sasha turned to Dawn.

"I don't know why you're pretending," Sasha whispered. "It's not like you're going to actually go through with this!"

Dawn set her drink on one of the end tables and crossed her arms over her chest. "Trying to psyche me out, Sasha? Can't take the competition?"

"No, just stating an obvious truth. You don't want to do it! It's written all over your face."

"Oh, like *you're* that eager to have a *ménage á trois* with a kindergartener? Isn't your son his age?"

"How old Razor is doesn't make a difference to me. I want him at my gallery and I'll do *whatever* I have to do to get him there! If that means me being part of a *ménage á trois*... hell! If that means me crawling around on all fours naked, I'll do it!"

Dawn raised her chin in defiance. "Well, maybe I will too."

Except the crawling part, she silently corrected.

"Bullshit! You don't have what it takes, sweetheart. So you can—"

"Babes!" Razor shouted, stopping Sasha mid-sentence. "I'm ready to go if you are."

Dawn turned and faced the hallway. When she saw Razor, her mouth fell open in shock.

He was buck naked, wearing only a watch and a smile. He wasn't lying about being "ready to go" either. His hard-on stood at full attention, showing that his artistic skill wasn't the only thing he could be proud of.

He doesn't waste any time, does he?

"Be right there, Razor," Sasha called back.

Dawn watched—stunned—as Sasha began to disrobe. Sasha lowered the zipper on her bustier before letting the garment fall to the hardwood floor. Despite her continual insistence that she had never been to a plastic surgeon in her life, Sasha had obviously had *some* work done. Her boobs were perky, but rock hard and her nipples looked as if they could poke someone's eye out. She tugged off her skirt next and kicked it aside. The gallery director stood in Razor's living room in nothing but her red lace panties and kitten heels. She slowly walked toward him. When she drew near, they shared another slobbery kiss. Sasha grinded her pelvis against his erection and Razor cupped her saggy, dimpled bottom, pulling her closer.

Despite her disgust, Dawn couldn't look away. She

suddenly sympathized with people who slowed down to look at car accidents. Something this disturbing was hard to peel your eyes away from.

The couple finally came up for air long enough for Razor to look over Sasha's shoulder at Dawn.

"You coming?" he asked breathlessly.

Dawn blinked, snapping out of her malaise. "Uh . . . yeah, I'm . . . I'm coming. You guys . . . go ahead and start. I'll meet you in the bedroom in a couple of minutes."

Razor nodded before kissing Sasha again. The woman looped her bony arms around his neck and he lifted her and carried her into his bedroom, making her squeal.

Dawn lowered her eyes. She looked down at her hands. They were shaking.

What am I doing? What the hell am I doing?

She rushed toward the end table where she had left her drink and grabbed her glass. She finished what was left of her scotch, coughing when the hot liquid burned her throat, hoping the alcohol would calm her nerves, but the feeling of unease didn't go away. Neither did her trembling.

"This doesn't mean anything!" the voice in her head argued. "It's just sex! You've done it plenty of times before with men you've felt nothing for. This isn't any different! You can't let Sasha win."

"Right. It's just sex," she muttered, unbuttoning her blouse. "It's just sex. It's just sex," she repeated over and over again as she walked toward the bedroom.

When Dawn neared the doorway, she heard Razor moan and Sasha whimper. She paused.

But it's not just sex, she thought.

This was about her *and* her body and if she used it to get something . . . then damn it, she wanted to use it on *her* terms for what *she* wanted! Not because she was being bullied by her boss. Not because some rich little asshole was trying to manipulate her. Dawn Gibbons didn't go out like that.

"To hell with this," she whispered.

She then turned around, walked back toward the living room, and grabbed her jacket. Dawn heard Sasha's cries of orgasmic delight just as she walked out. She ignored them and shut the front door behind her with a slam.

Chapter 20

Stephanie gazed listlessly at the television screen. She had changed into one of her silk teddies and a pair of shorts and was now under the stiff motel bed-sheets with her knees to her chest and her arms wrapped around her legs. She was huddled against the headboard. It was well after ten o'clock and Keith still wasn't back yet.

"Asshole," she muttered yet again.

Stephanie reached for her cell phone and began to call her sisters, hoping that a conversation with one of them would be a good distraction. She tried dialing Lauren first and of course got her voice mail. In retrospect, that wasn't much of a surprise since Lauren usually worked late at her restaurant on week-days. That would probably end soon as her pregnancy got further along. Stephanie tried Cynthia next and finally hung up when she was sent to her voicemail too. Knowing Cynthia, she was probably on a date. Then she tried Dawn's cell.

"Hello," her older sister answered tiredly after the third ring.

"Hey, sis!" Stephanie said, instantly perking up. "How are you? What are you up to?"

"Hey, Steph. I'm fine, just . . . exhausted."

"*Exhausted?* Why? What's wrong?"

"Don't get me started. It's just been a rough night. I'll share all the gory details another day. For now, I just want to put on my facial mask, close my eyes, and go to sleep."

"Oh." Stephanie's shoulders slumped. "Well, maybe I'll talk to you in the morning then."

"Sure." Dawn yawned on the other end of the line. "Talk to you in the morning. Good night."

Dawn hung up and Stephanie followed suit before placing her cell phone back on her adjacent night table. Stephanie stared at her phone, wondering what gory details Dawn was talking about.

Guess she'll tell me later like she said, Stephanie thought with a shrug. She grabbed the television remote again and started to flip channels. She finally settled on watching the eleven o'clock news. She glanced at the digital alarm clock on the night table in between the double beds, telling herself that she wasn't checking the time yet again because she was waiting for Keith. He obviously couldn't care less about her. Why should she have any concern for him?

But still, she thought, staring at the neon numbers, *it is getting late.*

Keith had disappeared hours ago and he still hadn't come back yet. It was a small town. There weren't too many places where he could go.

Where the hell could he be?

At around midnight, she turned off the television and turned off the lights. She tugged the sheets up to her chin, closed her eyes, and tried to fall asleep, but failed miserably. Instead, she opened her eyes again and gazed at the closed motel-room door, waiting to see when Keith would finally return.

Why hadn't he come back yet? Would he honestly let her drift off to sleep without giving her an apology?

"Maybe he doesn't feel he needs to apologize," a voice in her head countered.

But he had hurt her feelings. Surely, he could see that! His words had cut deeper than she would have thought. She still couldn't get them out of her mind. He thought she was a spoiled princess. He said she was a prima donna.

"Nothing you haven't heard before," the voice argued. "Your family tells you that all the time."

That was true, but coming from Keith, she took those insults very personally.

He crept into the bedroom less than an hour later, smelling like beer and cigarettes. The instant the door opened, she sat bolt upright in the bed. She turned on one of the brass lamps on the night table.

"Where were you? Where the hell did you go?" she asked, unable to hide her anxiousness in her voice.

He stiffened instantly. She watched as he walked toward his bed. He took off his jacket and tossed it on the worn, brown paisley comforter. "I just went to a bar and had a few drinks. That's all. I was coming back. You didn't have to worry."

Easier said than done, she thought angrily.

She hesitated and watched as he sat down on the edge of his bed with his back to her. He tugged off his shoes then his socks. She wanted tell him the thoughts she had been muddling over all night. She wanted to have a conversation with him. It would be a *real* conversation with a man—something that was virtually unheard of in her family, but she had some stuff she wanted to get off her chest. She opened her mouth to speak.

"We should get some rest," he said and then yawned. "We both need to get up early. We'll head back to the garage near Wilson to see how your car is faring. Maybe it'll be finished by tomorrow." He turned to her. "If it's ready, you could even be back in Virginia by tomorrow night."

"Keith," she said quietly. "I don't—"

"Good night, Stephanie."

He then turned off the light, summarily ending the conversation.

She slumped back into her bed and raised the sheets again. She watched him prepare for bed in the dim light of the motel room. He began to remove his clothes in the dark. When he had finally stripped down to his boxer briefs, he walked past her bed to the bathroom and turned on the bathroom light. She tried not to stare, but it was hard not to. He was a well-built man who seemed to be made almost entirely of hard muscle. His arms, broad back, and legs looked like they could have been chiseled out of black onyx.

She watched him brush his teeth then extinguish the bathroom light. He walked in the dark back to his bed. He pulled back his bedsheets, collapsed on the mattress, and closed his eyes. Within minutes, he was fast asleep.

But an hour later, Stephanie still lay silently in the dark, gazing up at the bedroom ceiling as he slept soundly. She could hear the steady drip of the faucet in the motel bathroom and the chug of the air con-

ditioning unit. She could feel the cheap bedsheets
scratching her delicate skin. An occasional kaleido-
scope of light would decorate the room when the
headlights from the cars on the roadway or the parking lot pierced the half-opened window blinds, revealing the water stains on the ceiling. When the car
drove farther down the road or the headlights were
turned off, the room would sink into murky darkness
again.

She glanced at the glowing alarm clock and saw
that it was already three a.m. She had been lying
awake for hours.

Stephanie turned on her side and faced the bathroom, closed her eyes, and tried yet again to get
some shut-eye. But minutes later she opened her
eyes. Her mind wouldn't let her sleep.

She flopped onto her back, grumbling to herself.
Another beam pierced the blinds. She turned her
head to look at Keith. He was on his side, facing the
window and he was still asleep. His shoulder and rib
cage went up and down with each breath he took.

He was the one who had hurt her feelings. *He* was
the one who dealt the blow. Why wasn't he agonizing
over this? Why was she the one tossing and turning in
bed?

Stephanie didn't know why she even cared what
Keith Hendricks thought about her. He was just
some detective, some cocky asshole her brother-in-
law was paying to find Isaac for her. He had no right
to judge her!

Stephanie blinked back tears and sniffed. She
couldn't believe it. She was actually crying over this
shit!

She hadn't used any of her usual tricks on him.

She had tried to rationalize with him, like Lauren had suggested. She had treated him like a human being. She had thought that eventually it would earn his respect and that he would see her as a *real* person—but she had thought wrong.

Stephanie wiped her eyes with the back of her hand and tossed back the threadbare covers. She walked into the bathroom and quietly shut the door behind her. She then turned on the lights and the faucet, grabbed one of the paper cups near the soap dish, and filled it with cold water. She drank and gazed at her reflection in the mirror, examining her tired face and her reddened eyes.

Admit it, Steph, she told herself. He wasn't just some cocky asshole. She was falling for him, just like Lauren had warned her that she would. That's why what Keith said had hurt her so badly. That's why she had been lying awake for hours. She paused at the realization, finding it scary and exciting all at the same time.

For years, Stephanie had chased men for their money and prestige. Keith had neither and yet she still wanted him and in more than just a carnal way. It didn't make sense, but she felt the attraction all the same—and she wanted him to feel it for her too. She had to talk to him, to finally get this stuff off her chest.

Stephanie turned off the bathroom light and opened the door. Another ray of light filled the room. She used it to find her way across the worn carpet to Keith's bed, creeping silently along the length of his mattress, stopping near his head. She hesitated, unsure of what to do next.

Shelly Ellis

Stephanie loudly cleared her throat, but he didn't budge.

"Keith?" she whispered. "Keith?"

Keith slowly opened his eyes. When he saw the outline of her body hovering over him, he jumped and stared at her in amazement.

"*Stephanie?* What's . . . What's wrong?" he croaked groggily, pushing himself up. He reclined on his elbows as another beam of light entered the room. The bedsheets fell from his shoulders, revealing his toned arms and chiseled stomach and chest. He squinted, wiping the sleep out of his eyes.

Stephanie sat on the edge of the bed. She hesitated again.

You've got me all wrong, Keith, she thought. *I'm more than just a spoiled princess. I'm not the person you think I am,* she wanted to say. But she was so nervous, too tongue-tied.

He gazed at her expectantly and she felt her temperature rise in the room. Her resolve was faltering. She felt cornered to say something, to *do* something. So she leaned forward and did what she really wanted to do: she kissed him. The light in the room faded again as their lips met.

He didn't respond to her kiss at first, keeping his lips firmly fixed like the onyx statue he resembled, keeping his arms stiffly at his sides.

He doesn't want me, she thought with alarm.

Desperate, Stephanie pressed her warm body against his and teased his full lips with her mouth and teeth. She slid her hands along his chest then wrapped her arms around his neck, clinging to him.

Keith began to respond then. He opened his mouth. He kissed her back tentatively then more voraciously. He shoved his fingers into her hair, tilting back her head so that the kiss could deepen. She moaned with relief.

The next thing she knew she was lying flat on her back against the bed and he was on top of her. He removed her silk top first, then her shorts with his deft hands. Her clothes went flying into some far-off corner of the motel room. Within seconds, they were both panting and naked.

Stephanie couldn't see Keith clearly in the dark, but she could feel him. His weight kept her pinned against the mattress. His fingers left electric tingles along her skin as he trailed his hands up and down the length of her body. His mouth was searing hot and wet, and she met it hungrily with kisses and responded to it with moans.

They both reached for each other blindly. She felt a phantom hand run along her neck, then her chest, before cradling one of her breasts. Keith then followed the path of his hand and lowered his mouth to one of her nipples. The hair of his goatee tickled her skin, making it gooseflesh. She started to giggle, but her laughter died in her throat when he licked the taut nub, took it between his teeth, and tugged it gently. She cried out in surprise and pleasure.

Stephanie could feel him easing her legs apart. She obeyed those phantom hands and wantonly spread her thighs wider, inviting his touch, feeling heady with anticipation. His fingers parted the slick wetness between her thighs and she breathed in sharply before biting down hard on her bottom lip. He began to massage her clit tenderly then more vigorously, coaxing her body to respond to him. He returned his mouth to her breasts, sharing equal attention between the two parts of her body that made her groan. He slid his fingers inside her wetness and Stephanie cried out again. Her thighs began to tremble. Her hips began to buck rhythmically, meeting each stroke of his sensual touch. She closed her eyes, enjoying luscious sensations that he was giving her. Her trembling only increased.

He continued to massage her between her thighs—making her wetter and hotter.

"Oh, God, Keith," she whimpered, fisting the bedsheets in her hands. "Don't stop. Please, don't stop!"

And she wasn't faking it. Keith wasn't getting one of the stellar performances that she often gave for other men. Her panting and moans were real . . . oh, so real. She bucked her hips even more, raising her pelvis from the mattress. She could feel her body quickly losing control. When the first spasms rocked her, she threw back her head and shouted in the dark. She grabbed his hand as her back and hips arched in a yoga-like pose, then she collapsed back to the bed. She had no idea how long she lay there trembling beneath him. But when she finally opened her eyes, she felt like she had just stepped off the world's wildest roller coaster.

Where's my souvenir picture, she thought with a laugh.

Now it was his turn. He reached blindly for her again, tracing the length of her arm. He then held her right hand and guided it downward. Her fingers rubbed the muscular contours of his stomach, then the telltale patch of rough curly hair, and stopped at his rigid manhood. He firmly wrapped her hand around it, urging her to stroke him. She smiled against his lips, figuring she could do one better.

Stephanie wiggled beneath him, shoving against

his chest. He hesitated, confused. After some seconds she felt him ease off of her slightly.

"I'm not stopping. Don't worry," Stephanie whispered in the dark. She wouldn't leave him hanging like that. After all, pleasuring men was her specialty.

She slowly guided him onto his back and straddled him. She then lowered her mouth to his and he enthusiastically kissed her back, cupping her bottom. She shifted her mouth to his neck then slowly descended to his chest. She left a weaving wet trail of kisses and taunting licks along his torso, making him breathe in sharply. When she finally reached his manhood and lowered her mouth to it, she felt the muscles in his stomach clench.

"Shit!" he cried out as she pleasured him in the pitch black of the room, savoring the taste of him. He fisted his hands in her hair. His breathing quickened with every saucy tongue flick and stroke of her hand. She was torturing him and pleasuring him all at the same time.

Minutes later, she could tell he was close. She stopped, pulling her mouth away, and straddled him again. Just as she centered her hips over his, she felt herself being abruptly pushed onto her back. She fell back against the mattress. Her head teetered dangerously close to the edge of the bed. Her hair cascaded to the carpeted floor like a black curtain.

Stephanie felt him shift and scramble toward the head of the bed. She heard the sound of spare change sliding across a wooden surface, a loud clatter of metal, and then a *thump.*

What the hell was that, she thought, raising her head and squinting in the dark.

"Shit!" he muttered again. "Knocked over the damn lamp."

"Keith, what are you doing?" she whispered.

He didn't answer her, but he didn't have to. She heard the tell-tale sound of a packet being ripped open. She guessed he had one in his wallet. She had a half dozen of them herself. She didn't know how he could manage to put on the condom in this pitch blackness, but when he returned to her less than a minute later, she guessed he had figured it out.

He climbed on top of her and Stephanie felt her thighs being spread wider again. He raised her hips and crouched between them. She reached blindly for him, grabbing his hips and bracing herself just as he slid inside her. She cried out. He grunted.

It was an odd sensation, being made love to in the dark, not seeing the person who was doing it, but the sensation was erotic all the same. He pumped rhythmically and her hips met his own. The squeak of the old motel bed was like a metronome, keeping the ardent tempo of their lovemaking.

Stephanie felt his hand on her breast again, rubbing the nipple between his thumb and forefinger. Another hand cradled her round bottom and squeezed it.

If Keith had been holding back before, he wasn't anymore. The pace suddenly increased and was almost rough in its abandonment of tenderness and control. But she liked it. Her body was responding to it.

He drove even deeper inside her, making her have to spread her legs even wider to accept him. Her thighs began to tremble again. She closed her eyes.

She felt it when he did. Their bodies jerked simultaneously, clenched in spasms of pleasure. Stephanie cried out again and her back arched once more as the waves crested over her. So did Keith. Then the sensation slowly dissipated. Her body went slack. His manhood gave one final jerk inside her. He then fell hard against her, taking several deep breaths before finally rolling off her and onto his side.

They lay there in the silent darkened room for what seemed like an eternity. Minutes later, another shaft of light entered the room as a car pulled into the motel lot. Keith abruptly stood up and used it to guide his way as he walked toward the bathroom. She crawled back to the head of the bed.

"Shit," he said seconds later. Then started mumbling to himself.

"What?" she called out, frowning in the dark.

"Nothing. Nothing," he murmured in reply.

He returned to the bed and lay down beside her. She faced him.

Stephanie suddenly realized that Keith hadn't said much this whole time—well, unless you counted moans and shouts. She wanted him to say something, *anything*. They had just made love. Shouldn't he say something in response?

"Keith?" she whispered. "*Keith?*"

When he didn't answer her, she began to wonder if maybe he had fallen asleep. She placed her hand on his shoulder and gently shook him. "Keith, are you—"

"Go to sleep, Stephanie," he murmured. "We should get some rest. Got an early day tomorrow."

Early day tomorrow? He was still expecting her to go home? He still didn't want her here? She closed her eyes, feeling rejected and humiliated. She started to rise from his bed and go back to her own on the other side of the motel room.

"We have to head out early if we're going to get to Florida by tomorrow tonight," he mumbled, turning onto his side.

Stephanie paused. Her eyes widened. "*To Florida?* You mean . . . You mean I can come with you?"

"That's what you wanted, isn't it?" he asked.

"Yes, but I didn't—"

"Go to sleep, Steph."

Stephanie listened as his breathing gradually deepened. Then he began to snore. There would be no more talking tonight.

She lay by his side again and snuggled closer to him. She closed her eyes. This time she fell asleep within seconds.

Chapter 21

You are one dumb man, Keith thought to himself in the wee hours of the morning as he lay in his motel bed. *And gullible. Don't forget to add really damn gullible.*

Though he was wide awake, his left arm was still asleep. Stephanie was slumbering on top of it, using it as a makeshift pillow. Her thigh was slung over his legs. One breast was pressed against his rib cage. She murmured as she dreamed. A content smile was on her face.

She had every reason to smile. She had won, after all. It looked like the princess was going to get what she wanted: she was going with him to Florida and he was still working for her.

Keith certainly had underestimated the lengths she was willing to go to get what she wanted. He had expected her to use a multitude of tactics: arguing, pouting, and stomping her feet—maybe even a guilt trip. But he hadn't expected her to wake him up in the middle of the night, climb into his bed, and throw herself at him.

I'm definitely not her type, Keith thought. He wasn't pulling a six-figure salary. He couldn't drape her in diamonds or add even more designer shoes and handbags to her collection. He had eight thousand dollars in his savings account, a lease on a small one-bedroom apartment, and a seven-year-old Ford Explorer. But none of that mattered to Stephanie last night. She had a goal and she went after it—full throttle!

And what had he done in return? Politely refused her advances?

Nope.

Gotten indignant and turned her away?

Hell no!

He had responded like a thirsty man would if he had suddenly stumbled upon a Deer Park water truck, like a starving man would if he was shoved in front of an all-you-can-eat buffet. Keith had responded so enthusiastically, in fact, that he had thought it a good idea to put on a condom in the dark while he was only half sober. He thought he had felt the damn thing slip off at some point. When he went to the bathroom later, the evidence only confirmed his suspicions.

"You better hope she's on the pill," a voice in his head warned.

Keith began to grumble again.

The bartender had warned him that he wouldn't be able to put up a fight much longer, but he had no idea he would capitulate this fast! Last night, he had let his dick do all the thinking for him, and his dick had just gotten him into a whole heap of trouble as he suspected it would. How he was going to clean up this mess, he did not know.

Keith flexed his fingers, trying to bring feeling back to his numb arm. When he felt sensation return and his arm began to tingle, he started to tug it gently, trying not to wake Stephanie. He wasn't in the mood to talk to her right now. He was too angry at her and pissed at himself for what had happened last night.

Keith shifted again and tried to ease her thigh off his legs. This time she did wake up, despite his efforts. She squinted against the sunlight coming through the window blinds, yawned, and smacked her lips.

"What . . . what time is it?" she whispered drowsily, wiping her eyes.

"Hell if I know," he muttered, shoving her off of him. He finally climbed out of bed and rose to his feet.

Stephanie didn't seem to notice his rudeness. She had a goofy smile on her face. Like a cat in a warm sunbeam, she stretched languidly and gazed up at him.

"Good morning," she said, pushing her rat's nest of hair over her shoulder and out of her eyes.

She was still naked from the night before. The body Keith had felt in the dark, he could now see plainly in the light of day. Unfortunately for him, her nakedness excited him all over again. He instantly hardened at the sight of her.

The breasts he had only glimpsed in the bathroom mirror were now on full display. Her flat stomach led to round hips and long, supple, brown legs. When she rolled onto her belly and stretched again, he saw that plump rear end. A birthmark in the shape of the state of Georgia was on the right cheek.

She gazed at his crotch, seeing the evidence of his growing arousal. Stephanie rose to her knees and slowly crawled across the bed toward him.

"You know . . . I can take care of that for you," she whispered seductively, wrapping one arm around his neck and her hand around his manhood. She began to stroke him. "Would you like me to take care of it for you?" She then raised her lips to his, closed her eyes, and kissed him eagerly.

"Push her away," a voice in his head commanded. "You know what game she's runnin'."

But with her warm naked body pressed against his, with her hand wrapped around him and kneading him gently, Keith could feel the same spell from last night descending over him again, making his heart pound and his blood surge.

His arms felt like they were being controlled by marionette strings as he wrapped one around her waist. He cupped her bottom. When she slipped her tongue between his teeth, instead of twisting his mouth away, he met her tongue with his own. His dick swelled and pressed urgently against her thigh, filling her hand.

Goddamnit, Keith thought in frustration as she began to stroke him more vigorously, as she pressed her breasts against his chest.

I'm not doing this shit again.

But it looked like that was exactly what he was doing.

This time, though, there would be no pretense of lovemaking, no foreplay. After all, she was getting what she wanted out of this. He might as well get his too, right? There was no crime in that. If this was what she was offering then . . . *fine.* He'd take it!

Stephanie stopped when he tugged her hand away and roughly grabbed her by the shoulders. She gazed at him in amazement just as he gave a hard shove and she landed sprawled on the mattress.

She yelped when Keith grabbed her calves, tugging her toward him until her legs dangled over the edge of the bed. He spread her thighs and climbed between them. She raised herself to her elbows and tried to kiss him again, but he shifted his mouth away and shoved her back down. She tried to wrap her arms around him, but he tugged her hands away and held her wrists, pressing them firmly against the mattress. She cried out when he entered her with no warning. He glided in smoothly. She was wet already or still wet from last night. With such a warm welcome, his body shuddered with pleasure as he filled her.

The pace of his thrusts was even faster than last night—and even rougher. He wasn't sure if she was getting anything out of this but, frankly, he didn't care. His body felt like an overloaded electric circuit, ready to burst at any second. His heart felt like it was trying to pound its way out of his chest. He was all sensation now, oblivious to the fact that a living, breathing human being was underneath him. All he felt was warmth, wetness, and a tight silkiness that enveloped him.

Keith began to groan then moan, and lowered his head into the crook of her shoulder. His hands tightened painfully around her wrists. His body began to jerk and quiver. He shouted with each spasm. Spent, he collapsed on top of her.

* * *

Twenty minutes later, Keith turned off the blast of hot water and stepped out of the shower into the muggy bathroom.

The complimentary motel soap had taken care of the sweat from last night and this morning; not a speck of its salty residue lingered on his skin. But the soap did not wash away his sense of self-loathing. He would need something a lot stronger than soap to make that go away!

When he had climbed off Stephanie, realizing just what he had done, he had expected anger from her. He had been so callous, so rough. He had treated her like he should toss a hundred dollars on the night table. But instead of cursing him out, she gazed up at him with that same goofy smile on her face from earlier. She wrapped her arms around him and tried to cuddle. Dumbfounded, he had stared at her, gaping.

"What does she care?" a cynical voice in his head mocked. "So what if you treated her like a blowup doll? As long as she gets what she wants in the end, she's happy!"

Stephanie could do what she wanted, but Keith knew he was a better man than this.

As he toweled himself off, he resolved that this would be the last time he gave in to his lust—period. He would resist the urge, no matter how much she tempted him and how much he wanted her. Like a recovering alcoholic, he was going cold turkey, getting her out of his system.

Keith wiped off the foggy mirror with his towel, braced his hands on opposite sides of the sink, and gazed at himself, making his silent promise. But the serious moment was ruined by Stephanie's loud chatter. He could hear her through the bathroom door talking on her cell phone.

Keith turned on the faucet and started to brush his teeth.

"Hey, Carrie, it looks like I'm going to be gone a few more days," Stephanie said. "Yeah, I'm headed to Florida . . . Yeah . . . I should definitely be back by the end of next week."

Keith paused from brushing. He closed his eyes. He didn't know how he was going to endure another week with this woman. What was he thinking getting involved with her in the first place?

"Hey, by the way, how did the open house on Wednesday go?" Stephanie asked.

Keith shut out the rest of the conversation. He finished brushing his teeth, wrapped his towel around his waist, and opened the bathroom door. He found Stephanie standing in the middle of the motel room with her cell phone cradled between her shoulder and her ear and a remote control in her hand. She had brushed her hair and was now wearing it in a ponytail. She was also wearing an oversized gray T-shirt—one of his own that he had been planning to wear today. She had probably gotten it out of his dresser drawer. The hem of the shirt skimmed just beneath her bottom, hinting at the shadow of a butt cheek and revealing her long bare legs.

He clenched his jaw. If she had worn a thong and bustier that would be less appealing. A woman in a man's T-shirt had always been one of his favorite turn-ons, only two steps below her being totally naked.

Resist temptation, he told himself as he averted his eyes and walked around her to his bed.

Stephanie glanced at Keith. "Hey, Carrie, can I call you back? Yeah, I'll update you in a few days." Stephanie sighed. "Thanks for taking care of everything. You're the best, Carrie . . . Talk to you later. Bye." She then hung up her phone and tossed it and the remote onto her bed.

"How was your shower?" she asked, strolling across the room toward him.

"Fine," he muttered, grabbing boxer briefs from his night-table drawer, still trying not to look at her.

"I would have joined you, but I knew I had to update my assistant that she's going to have to take over a bit longer," she said and plopped down on his bed, crossing her legs.

He didn't respond but instead grabbed a pair of wrinkled jeans and a button-down shirt from another drawer, draping both on the bed.

"So I was thinking," she said seductively, leaning back. Her T-shirt rose even higher, revealing the tantalizing triangle of hair underneath. "Whatever hotel we decide to stay at in Florida, we should make sure it has a big sunken tub . . . with Jacuzzi jets."

Ignoring her, Keith busied himself with getting dressed. He stepped into his boxer briefs and tugged them on before dropping his wet towel to the carpeted floor. "What do you think?" Stephanie asked expectantly.

"What do I think about what?"

"About the Jacuzzi jets!" Stephanie gushed. She sat up and crawled across the bed toward him. "We could draw a big bubble bath," she said, wrapping her arms around his waist, "and I can soap you down and—"

"Damn it, will you stop!" he shouted in frustration,

tugging Stephanie's arms from around him. He then shoved her away so that she landed on the mattress.

Stephanie's smile faded. "What's wrong?"

"Look, you don't have to keep doing this," Keith said irritably.

She sat up, looking crestfallen. "Keep doing what?"

"All the touching and kissing and . . ." He buttoned his shirt. "I told you that you can come to Florida. I'm not quitting. You don't have to keep trying to convince me. I'm good! OK?"

She looked absolutely staggered.

"You think . . ." She licked her lips and pointed at her chest. "You think I had sex with you because I wanted you to let me come with you to Florida? You think I did it to keep you from quitting?"

Keith opened his mouth then closed it. He shrugged. "Well . . . yeah."

In a matter of seconds, the expression on her face morphed from shock, to utter humiliation, to sheer anger.

"You son of a bitch," she muttered through clenched teeth, slowly shaking her head. "You *son of a bitch!*"

"Stephanie," he said tiredly, holding up his hands. "Look, I know you—"

In a flash, she turned, grabbed one of the bed pillows, and threw it at his head. He ducked and shifted to the other side of the motel room. She threw a second pillow, then reached down, grabbed one of her high heels, and lobbed it at him. He ducked again, narrowly missing getting blinded by a stiletto. She opened one of the night-table drawers and grabbed a phone book. She threw it at him too. This time it caught him squarely in the chest.

"Damn it, will you stop throwing shit at me?"

"*Why?* Why should I stop?" she shouted, grabbing for a pile of travel magazines. She hurled them at him too. They landed uselessly on the floor a foot in front of him in a cloud of fluttering glossy paper. "You think you can just keep saying whatever you want to me . . . You think you can keep making me feel like shit? You think you can act like I'm some . . . some *whore* and I'm just supposed to accept it?"

"I didn't say you were a whore," he began. "I just—"

"Just *what?* You just said I had sex with you to keep you on the case! I spread my legs and sucked your dick to get you to do what I wanted! What the hell is that if it isn't a whore?"

Keith shook his head, frustrated and bemused. "Come on, Stephanie, stop playing games, all right?"

"What?" she screeched.

"I'm a detective! I do my research! What did you expect?"

She glared at him. "*What research?* What the hell are you talking about?"

"I know about you. I know about you and your sisters, all right? I know what you guys do. I'm just telling you that you don't have to do it with me. You don't have to seduce me." He took a deep breath. "It's not . . . It's not necessary. That's all. That's all I meant."

"Oh, that's all!" she said with a cold laugh as she closed her eyes. "That's all he meant to say!" She turned away from him.

He watched as she sniffed, wiping at the few tears that spilled onto her cheeks.

"She's a helluva good actress," a voice in his head mocked. "A regular Academy Award winner."

But a nagging part of Keith questioned whether she was acting. Had he really hurt her feelings?

After a few seconds, Stephanie finally got herself under control. The tears stopped. She sniffed and opened her eyes. The room fell silent and for several minutes, time seemed to stand still.

"If we're . . . If we're going to make it to Florida by this evening," Keith began tentatively, "we better head out soon."

He had obviously said the wrong thing again. She gave him a look that could have frozen boiling water. He prepared for the next onslaught. What was she going to throw next? But he was surprised when she took a deep breath.

"Give me twenty minutes," she said brusquely.

He watched as she stomped across the motel room and slammed the bathroom door closed behind her.

Chapter 22

"I returned the key and paid the bill at the front desk," Keith called out. "Are you ready to go?"

Stephanie didn't answer him. Instead she concentrated on finishing the last of her packing. She opened and slammed shut dresser and night-table drawers, grabbing clothes and dropping them into her bags.

Her body looked tense. Her face was set in a deep frown. She shoved the last of her things into her Louis Vuitton luggage bag, closing it with a loud zip and then doing the clasp. She threw the strap over her shoulder and grabbed her other suitcase while Keith waited in the motel room doorway, leaning against the doorframe, staring at her.

He wanted to say something, anything to ease the tension in the room. But there was no going back from what he had done, and knowing that fact made him feel like absolute shit.

And damn it, I shouldn't, he thought with frustration. Stephanie was a woman who used men like they were disposable, who took advantage of their affections and money, who manipulated them to get what she wanted. He shouldn't feel guilty about what he said to her. He was only telling the truth. He thought he owed her enough to be honest with her, but obviously she hadn't felt the same way.

Stephanie's bag was so heavy that she had to shift her weight to stand upright. She walked across the motel room.

"I can carry that for you," he said, reaching for her luggage as she eased past him.

"I can carry my own damn bag," she snapped, still refusing to look at him.

She put on her designer sunglasses and marched across the parking lot toward his Explorer, taking long, angry strides. Her long ponytail swung wildly behind her. The hatchback was open so she threw her bags inside. He watched as Stephanie then prissily opened the passenger-side door before plopping onto the seat and slamming the door closed behind her.

Keith sighed wearily. He shut the motel room door behind him, letting it lock automatically. He then slowly walked toward the SUV, shut the hatchback, opened his car door, and climbed behind the steering wheel. Keith inserted his car key into the ignition, but before he turned on the engine, he paused. He sat back in his seat and turned to gaze at Stephanie.

She glared out the tinted passenger-side window, stubbornly refusing to meet his gaze.

"Stephanie," he began, clearing his throat. "Stephanie, look, I don't want us to—"

"Just drive," she said curtly, reaching into her

purse. She then took out her cell phone and ran her manicured nail over the glass screen.

Keith gritted his teeth, feeling his frustration build as he watched her pretend to be engrossed in her text messages.

He wasn't going to apologize. As far as he was concerned, there was nothing to apologize about. She was just angry he had called her on her scheming ways, but he hadn't exactly shown stellar behavior in the past twenty-four hours either. There had to be *some* way to make amends, but it didn't look like she was going to give him the chance to do that. She was giving off more of a chill than an arctic blizzard.

He took a calming, deep breath.

"OK," he murmured, shifting the SUV into reverse. "If that's the way you want it." He then backed the car out of the parking space. With one flash of his turn signal, they were on the open road.

Keith drove for a few hours before finally hitting the Georgia border. They didn't speak the entire way, but the silence between them felt different this time around. It weighed heavier on him.

Keith kept glancing at her as he drove, but she continued to stubbornly glare out the window and ignore him. He couldn't see her eyes. They were masked by her darkly tinted sunglasses. But he knew he would find anger and resentment there if he could see them.

Keith kept an eye out for a green sign demarking an upcoming rest stop. One popped up on the highway shoulder. Five minutes later, he pulled to a stop in one of the parking spaces outside the rest stop area. A group slowly ambled out of tour buses several feet away. He turned to Stephanie.

"You can take some time to stretch your legs for a bit," he murmured. "Maybe use the bathroom. Get something to drink."

She didn't respond. Instead, she opened the car door and slammed it closed behind her. She then strode toward the bathrooms.

He watched her disappear behind the maroon ladies' room door. When he did, he let out a pent-up breath. This trip was going to be painful if they continued like this. She couldn't stay angry at him forever, could she?

Keith unbuckled his seatbelt and pulled out his cell phone. He then dialed Mike's number. He had called Mike yesterday to share the information that Ms. Beaumont had given him about Isaac. He asked Mike to do a detailed search of all the small towns and counties near Pensacola, Florida, that had the name "swamp" in them. He wanted to find out what Mike had discovered.

After a few rings, the gruff detective picked up the phone.

"Stokowski and Hendricks Investigators," Mike mumbled between munches.

"Jesus," Keith lamented, "could you at least finish eating first before you answered the phone?"

"It's one o'clock! You caught me while I was downing lunch," Mike exclaimed. "What the hell did you expect?"

Keith shook his head. "From you—not much. So did you find anything?"

"Yeah," Mike answered, munching again, "about eight cities within a hundred-mile radius."

Keith grimaced. "*Eight,* huh? Shit."

"Yeah, I'll e-mail you the list. It's a lot of ground to cover, but it could be worse. I could've found twenty of them." A slurping sound suddenly filled the phone line. Keith guessed that Mike was finishing the rest of his Big Gulp. "You can winnow down eight to just one or two in the next week or so," Mike continued after a loud burp. "I don't doubt you can pull it off."

"Well, your vote of confidence is much appreciated," Keith said as he stared at the ladies' room door. "I could use it right now."

The munching continued on other end of the line. "Why? What happened?"

Keith hesitated. He wasn't sure if he really wanted to pour his heart out to Mike, especially knowing that Mike would be really angry that Keith had crossed a line with Stephanie that he should not have crossed. But it was eating away at him. He needed to talk to somebody and in the past Mike had always been the male figure he leaned on when he was filled with doubt.

"I fucked up," Keith finally said, dropping his head back against his seat. "I fucked up royally, Mike."

The munching on the other end of the line came to an abrupt stop. "What do you mean you 'fucked up'?"

Keith closed his eyes and gritted his teeth.

"What do you mean you fucked up, Keith?" Mike asked again, louder this time.

"I didn't want her to come here, Mike. I told her to go home! I didn't need the distraction. I knew if she stayed here that this would happen!"

"You screwed her, didn't you?" Mike breathed deeply on the other end of the line. "Ah, son," he said softly, "tell me you didn't."

"Of course, I did! If I didn't, I wouldn't be kicking myself right now!"

"Shit, Keith," Mike muttered.

"Look, I didn't expect it to happen. I would change what I did if I could, but I can't. And now it's blown up in my face and she's pissed off at me and . . ."

Keith stopped rambling when he heard Mike chuckling on the other end of the line.

"Why are you laughing? What's so goddamn funny?"

"*You!* You're so goddamn funny! You've been dodging this lady for more than a month and you get stuck with her for less than a week and you've already fallen in the sack with her!" He laughed again. "Don't get me wrong . . . She's a gorgeous broad, but talk about not having any willpower!"

Keith glowered. "Thanks for rubbing it in."

"Oh, come on, Keith! She's a client . . . I get that. Under normal circumstances, I would be ripping you a new one right now, but I'll make an exception this time. You've been acting squirrelly about her since you met her. You two falling in bed together was bound to happen at some point or another. I just didn't expect it to happen *this* soon!"

"I haven't been acting 'squirrelly.' "

Mike's full throaty laughter filled the phone line again. "Keith, didn't we already have this conversation a week ago? You can sell that load of bull to someone else, but not me. I've known you since you were ten years old! I know when you're acting buggy." He cleared his throat. "Look, why keep denying it to me and to yourself? For whatever reason, you feel something for this woman and that feeling ain't just in your pants!"

"No, I don't," Keith said firmly. "I was attracted to her. That's it! And I knew if I followed through with that attraction, it would end up like this. And I was right! We never should have slept together!"

"Why, because she's pissed at you?"

"Exactly!"

"So is she pissed because you screwed her, or pissed over what happened after you screwed her? I know you! You felt like shit for what you did and gave her the cold shoulder, didn't you?"

Keith fell silent. Mike began to chuckle again on the other end.

"Yeah, I thought so. Trust me, son, you'll be much better off once you stop bein' so goddamn stubborn and admit the truth to yourself."

"Which is?" Keith snapped.

". . . Which is that despite all your bobbing and weaving, you got caught. Keith Hendricks got hooked by a broad and now he's making things ten times worse by pretending that he didn't."

"So . . . So what am I supposed to do now?"

"First of all, tell her that you were an ass for how you treated her. You can start there. Then maybe, if she forgives you, you take her out on a real date when all this is over. And that date shouldn't involve a motel room and take-out Chinese, all right!"

"These are your great words of wisdom?"

"Hey, you got any better ideas?"

Keith closed his eyes. He didn't. He had no idea

how to handle this. He just knew that somehow, some way he had screwed up and he needed to fix it.

"OK, I'll . . ." He took a deep breath. "I'll apologize to her. But—"

"No buts, Keith. Just do it, you big pussy!"

Mike then hung up the phone.

Chapter 23

Stephanie took off her dark sunglasses and gazed at her reflection in the dingy rest-stop bathroom mirror. She took a paper towel and dabbed at the corners of her reddened eyes.

She had been crying off and on since this morning, since Keith told her that he had "done his research" about her. He said he knew her secrets. He knew what she really was.

She had never felt so much shame in her life, or so insulted. She felt like he had physically stabbed her in the chest. Yes, she had dated men for their money. She may have even done things for them sexually with the expectation of what she would get in return. But when she had sex with Keith last night, she hadn't expected anything out of him. She had sex with him because she wanted *him,* because she was falling in love with him. But he didn't believe someone like her was capable of falling in love.

Just thinking about it was making her emotional all over again. She sniffed as the tears welled in her eyes.

Her phone started tinkling. She opened her purse and pulled out her cell phone. She looked down at the number on the screen. It was Lauren's phone number.

Oh, God, not now, she thought with desperation.

She didn't want to talk to Lauren, especially in the state that she was in, but she knew she couldn't ignore this call. She hadn't spoken to Lauren in a couple of days and her overprotective little sister was bound to get worried if she didn't talk to her soon.

Stephanie took a deep breath and cleared her throat. She pasted on a smile before clicking the button on her screen to answer the call.

"Hey!" she cried, trying to sound as light as possible.

"Hey, Steph," Lauren answered chirpily. "How's it going?"

"Oh, good. Pretty good," Stephanie lied, blinking back tears. She sniffed.

"Wait, don't share any details yet! Let me put you on speakerphone first. Dawn and Cynthia are here. They want to hear everything too."

Stephanie took another deep breath. She didn't know if she had the strength to lie to all of her sisters at the same time.

"OK," Lauren said a few seconds later, "you can tell us everything now. So how's South Carolina?"

"Sorry, I couldn't talk last night, Steph. It was just some work-related drama I'd rather not get into now," Dawn shouted in the background. "Anyway . . . Did you find Isaac yet?"

Stephanie's bottom lip started to quiver. She sniffed again.

"I . . ." she said. "I . . . We haven't . . ."

"We can't hear you, Steph," Cynthia shouted. "Speak louder!"

Suddenly, Stephanie broke down into tears. Her sobs echoed off the bathroom's tiled ceiling and walls. A plump, white-haired woman wearing a matching peach tank top and shorts who was washing her hands at the sink next to Stephanie now gazed at the younger woman cagily.

"Good Lord, is it going that bad?" Cynthia asked drolly on the other end of the line.

"Steph, what's wrong?" Lauren called. "Honey, stop crying and tell us what's wrong!"

"I feel so stupid," Stephanie wept into the phone, wiping her eyes with the back of her hand. "*So* stupid! I put myself out there and he doesn't even care! Does he realize that I've never done anything like this before? This is the first time I've had feelings like this!"

"What the heck is she talking about?" Dawn murmured.

"I have no idea," Lauren said in response.

The woman beside Stephanie began to dry her hands with a paper towel, but still stared at Stephanie warily.

"I have never, *never* felt this way about a man before. I've never been this vulnerable and he thought I was pretending. He thinks I'm trying to manipulate him! Why does he think the worst about me? What the hell did I do to him?"

"Are we still talking about Isaac?" Cynthia asked.

"I don't think so," Dawn said.

"Steph, honey, who are you talking about?" Lauren inquired, hoping to bring the confusion to an end. "We're not following you."

"I'm talking about Keith! I slept with Keith!" Stephanie shouted. She dropped her face into her hand. "And now I feel so stupid . . . and . . . and cheap. He made me feel cheap!"

The woman beside her tossed her paper towel into a nearby trash can. She opened the bathroom door and let it fall closed behind her, slowly shaking her head.

"You *slept with Keith?* Oh, Steph . . . I thought we talked about this before you left, honey," Lauren said. "I knew you were falling for him! Didn't I tell you this would happen?"

"I guess the toys didn't work," Dawn muttered.

"Who the hell is Keith?" Cynthia inquired.

"The detective who's trying to find Isaac," Dawn answered.

"She slept *with a detective?*" Cynthia exclaimed. "Wait . . . How much do detectives make?"

"Not enough," Dawn said.

"I mean . . . What do I do? Damn it, I am so . . . so . . . so pissed off!" Stephanie shouted, stomping her foot on the tiled floor. "And so heartbroken and humiliated. How am I supposed to look him in the face day after day knowing what we did and how he really feels about me? I don't know for sure if it is, but if this is love, Lauren, damn it, I don't want it! I hate how it makes me feel! I just want to pack my things and go back home to—"

"Wait! *Wait!*" Cynthia said. "Are you seriously going to let some detective run you back to Chesterton?"

"Cindy," Lauren said softly, "Steph just said that she was heartbroken. I think this guy really hurt her. She only wants to leave because—"

"Gibbons girls don't get heartbroken, certainly

not by some *detective,*" Cynthia said contemptuously. "Look, Steph, this guy may be the finest man in the world and amazing in bed, but I would be damned if I let him run me back to Virginia! You came there for a reason, right? You wanted to make sure Isaac was found."

Stephanie sniffed. "Well . . . yes."

"Then stay there until it's done. Stay there until he finds Isaac," Cynthia said firmly. "Don't leave before that happens."

"But . . . But what do I do about how I feel about him? I think I'm . . . I think I'm in love with him."

"*So!*" Cynthia exclaimed.

"Cindy!" Lauren shouted. "What do you mean 'so'? How can you possibly be so callous? She's really hurting here!"

"I'm not being callous! I'm being practical," she snapped. "Damn it, somebody has to! All this talk about love and feelings is making me nauseous! Stephanie, you know the rules. Honey, you aren't the first or the last woman to fall in love with a man, but you can't let it deter you from what you're doing. So stay focused. The goal is to find Isaac, right?"

"R-r-right," Stephanie stuttered between sniffs.

"Then, honey, that's all that matters."

Stephanie nodded. "You're right. You're absolutely right, Cindy."

She didn't know what had come over her these past couple of days. She had been so caught up in the maelstrom known as Keith Hendricks that she had forgotten all about why she had followed him here in the first place. She didn't do it because she was in love with Keith. She did it because she wanted

Isaac to pay for conning her and stealing her damn money!

"So wipe away those tears, Steph. Fix your makeup and pull yourself together," Cynthia said. "Stay focused. You're a Gibbons girl. Remember that!"

"OK," Stephanie answered, nodding again. "OK, I'll get myself together."

"Call us in a few days, Steph," Lauren said softly. "Let us know that you're all right."

"I will. Talk to you guys later." She then hung up the phone.

Stephanie returned her gaze to her reflection and pushed back her shoulders. She dabbed at her reddened eyes one last time and gave one last sniff.

She wouldn't let Keith get the better of her. She had come here for a reason and she would stay until it was finished. She would stay until Isaac was found.

Chapter 24

Keith sat upright in his seat when he saw the bathroom door open and Stephanie step out of the doorway. She raised her head and strode toward him.

Since hanging up the phone with Mike, he had given a lot of thought to what his mentor said. Maybe Mike had a point. Maybe he had been too harsh with Stephanie. His wariness of entering a relationship with a woman like her—who he knew had the ability to wrap him around her finger, if she tried hard enough—had made him act colder to her than he intended. No woman deserved this type of treatment—even an opportunistic gold digger like Stephanie Gibbons. She was still a human being. He had to make amends.

He watched as Stephanie opened the car door. She looked a lot better now than she had when she walked into the bathroom fifteen minutes ago. She had touched up her makeup. Her sunglasses were now pushed to the crown of her head and he could see that her eyes were bright and cheerful. She was even smiling.

That's quite a transformation, he thought, a little bewildered. When he saw the state that she had been in when she left, he hadn't expected her to come back this way.

She sat in the leather seat beside him and he loudly cleared his throat.

"Uh, look, Stephanie . . . before . . . before we get back on the road, I think we need to talk."

She buckled her seatbelt. "Talk about what, Keith?"

What did she mean, 'Talk about what?'? It was pretty damn obvious what they needed to talk about!

"Stephanie, we need to discuss what happened back there at the motel." He closed his eyes. "Look, I think I came off harsher than I meant to. I shouldn't have said what I said. I didn't mean to hur—"

She shook her head. "Keith, it's all right. We don't need to talk about it."

"We *don't?*"

"No, we don't have to rehash what happened last night and this morning." She shrugged her shoulders. "We just had sex! No big deal. We're both adults. We had fun. We'll leave it at that."

He now gazed at her in amazement as if her body had been taken over by an alien life form. Was this the same woman who had screamed and cried and thrown things at him in the motel room? Was this the same woman who had refused to look at him for the past three hours?

"But . . . but I thought you—"

He stopped mid-sentence when she raised a hand to his lips, silencing him. She shook her head again.

"Keith, it's all right. Really. I'm OK. I've gotten over it."

"*In fifteen minutes?*" a voice in his head shouted. "Talk about a rebound!"

"Besides, I think we need to focus on the issue at hand here," she said.

He cocked an eyebrow. "Which is?"

"Finding Isaac." Her dark eyes narrowed. "What's gone on between us is irrelevant. I'm only here for one thing and that's to find that scheming son of a bitch. I don't want to be lovers. Hell, we don't even have to be friends! I just want you to do your job, which is to find him. Understood?"

He stared at her. Maybe this was how women like her operated. Maybe they could click some internal switch to turn off their emotions like some gold-digging Terminator. Either way, it left him totally befuddled.

"Understood," he mumbled behind her hand.

She dropped her hand from his mouth. "Good. So . . . where to next?"

"Well . . . Mike sent a list of towns we should go to. He said any one of them could be where Big Red is based."

"Great!" she exclaimed, dropping her sunglasses back to her nose. She rubbed her hands together eagerly. "Then let's get this show on the road!"

"Yeah . . . sure, Steph," Keith said, shifting the car into drive. He gave one last cagey glance at Stephanie before finally pulling off.

After about a week of searching for Big Red, each backwater town started to look like the next. They all had the same rundown look. All the neighborhoods were filled with old, beat-up looking houses with weed-infested front yards and chain-link fences. All of the towns had the tired-looking strip malls on the outskirts with the no-name restaurants and stores. Crime was rampant. Drug dealers were on every other street corner. Cars that had been stripped of everything but their steering wheels were on cinderblocks in empty alleyways. A few women stood on street corners in tight-fitting tops and ill-fitting skirts, ready to sell themselves to the next man who pulled up and offered them twenty dollars.

The towns reminded Keith of a slower, more country version of his old neighborhood in East Baltimore. In some ways, they were a lot like home.

Keith could see how an industrious and wayward man like Big Red could quickly take over towns like these, but unfortunately he had yet to find the particular town where Big Red reigned from his drug-dealing throne. They had been looking for days and at each place they went no one knew where they could find a guy named "Big Red," though a few had tried to point Keith in the right direction.

Keith now pulled to a stop in front of a small convenience store. He turned off the engine. "I'm going to go inside to grab something to drink. Do you want anything?"

Stephanie shook her head. She barely looked up from the magazine that was in her lap. He watched as she flipped to another glossy page.

She had been acting like this all week, not really giving him the outright cold shoulder, but she was aloof to the point that it was almost unnerving. They didn't argue anymore. They barely said anything to one another, actually. She would sit quietly in the car

while he staked out neighborhoods or hopped out of
the SUV to go somewhere and ask questions. He
would give her an update and she would nod her
head and return her attention to her magazine or
cell phone.

Her sudden behavior shift was throwing him off.
He felt like some undercurrent of anger and hurt
still lurked beneath the surface, but Stephanie refused to talk about it and he wasn't going to press the
issue anymore.

He shut the car door behind him and walked inside the convenience store, leaving her behind.

It was a small store with only a few shelves of goods
and one freezer in the back filled with beer, soda,
and ice-cream cones.

Keith noticed a group of black men standing near
the counter. They laughed and joked, slapping each
other's backs while they talked. But when he entered,
their conversation came to a sudden halt. Keith noticed a distinct chill enter the room.

He nodded to the four men and only the one in
the center of their throng nodded in return. The rest
gazed at him suspiciously. He wasn't surprised.
Again, this reminded him a lot of home. If a stranger
had walked into a store in his old neighborhood, all
the dudes standing around would stare at him cautiously too. Strangers couldn't always be trusted.

Keith slowly walked to the back of the store, slid
back the freezer door, and pulled out a bottle of
Coke. As he did, he glanced out the store window
and saw that Stephanie had gotten out of the SUV. She
must have gotten bored with reading her magazine.
She was now slumped against the hood, adjusting her
bra straps and the front of her tank top, gazing at noth-

ing in particular. Her brown legs glistened in the bright sun.

Keith walked back toward the front of the store and placed his soda on the counter. He noticed that all of the men were still silent, but now they were staring out the doorway at the parking lot. Stephanie seemed to be the object of their avid interest.

"What's up, man?" the one in the center called out to Keith.

He was rail thin and wearing a stained tank top and drooping jeans around his hips. The top of his boxer shorts was on full display. He also sported several gold chains and a Rolex watch. The young man nodded and raised his lips, revealing a mouth full of gold teeth.

Keith nodded. "What's up?"

"That your girl out there?" the young man asked, pointing out the door.

Keith raised his eyebrows in amusement. He followed the path of the guy's finger and watched as Stephanie grimaced and lazily fanned herself in the scorching sun and sweltering Florida heat. She raised her hair from her shoulders and twisted it into a knot at the crown of her head.

He had to admit, she did look pretty damn good standing out there. He understood why the men couldn't take their eyes off her.

"Yeah, I guess you can say that," he finally answered.

"Well, you one lucky nigga! She a dime, man!" the young man exclaimed with a smile. He turned to one of the men beside him. "Ain't she? She even better lookin' than Renee!"

One of his companions slowly shook his head. "Oh, nigga, don't let Big Red hear you say that . . . talkin' about his chick that way."

Keith was handing his money to the cashier, but paused at the mention of Big Red's name.

"Why?" the skinny one argued. "It's the truth! Tell me she ain't finer than Renee . . . and Renee's one bad bitch!"

"I don't know, man!" one of them protested, glancing at Stephanie again. "I'd have to see those bitches side by side to really say. You can't really judge this way."

"Man, you full of shit! You know damn well—"

"Who's Big Red?" Keith asked, feigning ignorance.

The group of men abruptly stopped arguing. They turned around to face Keith again. The skinny one narrowed his eyes with distrust. "Why you wanna know?"

Keith shrugged casually. "Just because. You said he has a chick that's finer than mine. I want to know who the dude is."

The skinny one sucked his teeth. "Man, Big Red's chick ain't finer than yours! This nigga just talking shit! You can see her yourself at the Hangar Club on Fridays. She works the center stage. Sometimes, she's with Big Red down at the bar on 15th too. He's there all the time."

Keith nodded, paid the cashier, and grabbed his soda. He then walked back toward the convenience store entrance.

"Hey!" the skinny one shouted. "Yo! Your lady got a sister, man?"

"Several of them!" Keith assured.

"Well, tell them to roll up down here and pay me a visit. Monty knows how to take care of a bitch," he said, holding up his gold chain as evidence.

Keith nodded. "I'll do that."

He walked out of the convenience store and made a beeline to where Stephanie was standing. She was still slumped against the car, fanning herself. She frowned despite the fact that he was now smiling ear to ear.

"Well, that was a long errand," she muttered testily, crossing her arms over her chest. "You took the car keys with you! I was frying in there. What the hell took you so long?"

He didn't respond. Instead, he cupped her face, leaned down and gave her the hottest, wettest kiss he could muster. Her eyes widened in surprise, but quickly drifted closed. She wrapped her arms around his neck and he wrapped his around her waist, lifting her off the ground as they kissed hungrily. It was a heady reminder of the passion they had shared a week ago, a passion that he desperately wished he could sample again. When he finally lowered her back to the asphalt and she gazed up at him, her eyes were dazed and her lips were swollen.

"What . . . What was that about?" she whispered, staring up at him dully.

"That's me thanking you for sticking around," he said, licking his lips.

He grinned again then walked around the SUV's hood and opened the driver's-side door. She climbed in after him.

"What?" she asked.

"Thanks to you, we now know where we can find Big Red."

"*What?* Really? You better not be joking, Keith!"

"I'm not joking. He's at a bar on 15th Street and we're headed there tonight!"

Chapter 25

Stephanie and Keith watched as three men slowly strolled across the parking lot toward the bar. She leaned forward and was practically sitting in Keith's lap to get a better view.

A morbidly obese one was in the middle. He wore a black tracksuit with white piping and a black visor with the bill turned toward the back of his head. His curly red hair was in cornrows that hung down his back. He waddled and wheezed as the group made their way toward the doors.

He was flanked on both sides by two hulking dark-skinned dudes covered in tattoos. One had cornrows, the other had dreads. They looked like club bouncers or college linebackers who had missed the NFL draft.

As the three walked toward the entrance, the crowd lingering near the doors separated, giving them ample room. Stephanie noticed how one guy practically ran to get out of the way. A few seconds later the three men disappeared behind the barroom doors.

"Do you think that was Big Red?" she whispered.

"How many fat black guys with red hair could there be around here?" Keith muttered. "Of course, it was him."

"Well . . . Are we going in then? Why are we just sitting here? Aren't you going to go in there to talk to him?"

"Steph, a guy like that isn't someone who you just roll up on, asking questions. He's a drug dealer and a crime kingpin around here. He's probably had several bad run-ins with the local cops. I doubt he's likely to start rambling to me just because I buy him a beer and tell him I'm a private investigator."

"But I thought that's why we came tonight! I thought we came here so that you could talk to him! We certainly didn't come here to take his picture!"

Keith turned to her. "No," he said tensely, "but I can't go charging in there without a plan. Just give me a damn second to think about how I should approach this. You only get one chance with a thing like this. I don't want to mess it up."

"And while you're thinking about it, Isaac could be getting away!"

He narrowed his eyes at her. "Fine, if you're in such a damn hurry, then what's your bright idea on how to handle this?"

She glared back at him, knowing that he was trying to cow her, but she wouldn't be cowed by him this time. "Yes, actually I do have an idea on how to handle this," she lied.

"Oh, and what would that be?"

He leaned back in his seat and tilted his head, gazing at her expectantly.

Actually, she had no idea on how to handle this, but she had had just about enough of Keith and his condescension. His smugness was really starting to irritate her. Suddenly, an idea popped into her head. Even she knew it was crazy, but still, she had to take a chance.

"I'll go talk to him myself," she said firmly, raising her nose into the air.

He laughed, making her scowl.

"What's so goddamn funny? You don't think I can do it?"

"Oh, I *know* you'll do it. You'll do it just to prove me wrong and in the process, royally screw up whatever chance we have of finding Isaac again." He closed his eyes. "Stephanie, look, I know you're still angry at me because of what happened between us back in South Carolina."

She gazed at him, completely stunned. He was actually making this about him . . . about their having sex? What an ego this guy had!

"This has nothing to do with that, Keith!"

"Yes, it does. And I want you to know that you don't have to try to get back at me for what I did. I know I was wrong for the way I handled it."

"You really think that I'm going in there to get back at you?"

"Yes, I do, and you're only putting yourself at risk by doing it. Look, I've tried repeatedly to make amends and start all over again with you, but—"

"Keith, this isn't about us, damn it!" she snarled. "I'm not going in there to get back at you. I'm going in there to talk to the one man who might know where we can find Isaac! We've been to every shitty town within fifty miles trying to find this guy, and I'm not going to let him get away because you want to sit here twiddling your thumbs or talking about where we went wrong!" She flipped down the visor in front of her and opened her purse. She then pulled out her lipstick and a compact and gazed into the visor mirror. "You may have years of experience as a police officer and the ATF . . . You may even have experience being a detective, but *I* have experience at being a woman." She pointed at her chest. "You say that you can't just 'roll up in there' asking him questions, and you're probably right. *You* can't do it. But *I* can."

"You really think that Big Red is going to be swayed by a pretty face and nice legs?"

She applied her lipstick and puckered her lips. She then opened her blush compact. She began to apply some to her cheeks. "Maybe. It wouldn't hurt to try."

"Stephanie, no woman is that gorgeous that a hardened criminal is going to just start spilling his guts because she winked at him. It doesn't work that way. This isn't the goddamn movies!"

She ran her fingers through her hair, admiring her reflection. "I know that, Keith, but what else have I got to lose?"

"Your life," he said steadfastly, grabbing her wrist, catching her by surprise. His dark eyes gazed intensely into hers. "You could lose *your life* if you keep messing around, Steph. Or if not that, something else could happen to you in there. Don't do this. It's not worth it!"

She pulled her wrist out of his grasp and stared at him. "You're just . . . just trying to scare me," she said shakily. "I can take care of myself. I'll be fine."

"If I say I'm sorry, will that get you to stay? Will you give up this crazy idea of going in there alone, and let me handle this instead?"

She lowered her eyes. Her heart ached a little at his words.

But even if Keith said he was sorry, she knew he didn't mean it. She could tell. He still thought she was some small-town floozy, a gold digger who had tried to use her body to win him over. He didn't care about her welfare. He only cared that she was an unnecessary burden, some frustration that he had been lugging around with him since Virginia that he hadn't been able to offload. He didn't want her to go into the bar because he was worried about the drama she would unleash, but he didn't have to be concerned. Like she told him, she was fully capable of taking care of herself. She could do this.

Stephanie gave her reflection one final glance before she flipped up the visor. She then dropped her lipstick and compact back into her purse and closed the zipper. She opened the car door.

"Steph!" Keith yelled. "Damn it, Stephanie!"

She stepped onto the wet asphalt and shut the door behind her, ignoring Keith's calls. She then adjusted her denim skirt and jacket, pushed back her shoulders, and walked across the parking lot.

"Are you sure you know what you're doing?" a small voice in her head asked as she walked toward the bar.

Not really, but I'm not going back there now, she replied. She wouldn't give Keith the satisfaction.

With each step she took she felt a growing mix of dread and excitement. A few men in the crowd near the door glanced her way and smiled. She smiled in return.

"Hey, baby," one drawled to her. "Wanna dance?"

"Maybe later," she said.

She was a Gibbons girl, after all. She had been trained her whole life for a moment like this. Big Red wouldn't know what hit him by the time she was finished with him.

Chapter 26

Keith sat in the driver's seat of his Ford Explorer, drumming his fingers on the steering wheel as he waited for Stephanie. He glared down at the green digital numbers on the dashboard, then at the bar's neon-lit doorway and grumbled loudly. She had been in the bar for almost two hours now.

What the hell is happening in there?

Of course, she wouldn't text him or give him a call if she was having any problems. She was too proud to do something like that. But the least she could have done was send him a message to let him know she was OK.

He perked up when he saw the bar door open finally and he relaxed when a woman in a denim skirt stepped outside. It looked like Stephanie . . . but he couldn't be sure. He squinted, trying to see her face as she walked out of the shadows and across the sparsely lit parking lot. His shoulders slumped when he saw her take a pack of cigarettes from her skirt pocket.

That definitely wasn't Stephanie. She didn't smoke.

In the glow of a street lamp, he could see the woman more clearly: the wrinkles that etched her brown, haggard face; the dark semicircles under her eyes; and her pinched lips. The jean skirt also looked about two sizes too small under closer inspection and her flowing dark hair was really a cheap wig.

The woman lit her cigarette and unceremoniously plopped on the hood of an old gray Cadillac parked in the row of cars facing his. He watched as she hunched over, tugging her jacket tighter around her to ward off the evening chill. Sensing his eyes on her, she suddenly looked up. Seeing Keith, she beamed.

"Hey, honey," she called in her grainy smoker's voice, tossing her fake hair over her shoulder. She stuck out her chest. "Lookin' for a good time? Want some company tonight?"

Keith shook his head and shifted his gaze back to the barroom doors.

"Come on, baby," she begged, taking a few steps toward his SUV, teetering slightly in her well-worn heels. "It won't cost much. A good lookin' man like you, I'll even give a discount. Fifteen bucks for a hand job. Forty for a blow."

No, he mouthed sternly, glowering at her.

She sucked her teeth and rolled her eyes before plopping back onto the Cadillac's hood. "Your loss," she mumbled, before smoking her cigarette again.

Fifteen bucks for a hand job. Forty for a blow, Keith thought with disgust.

That was what Stephanie was competing with in there!

"Shouldn't have let her go alone," he mumbled to himself.

But what was he supposed to do, *wrestle her to the ground?* She was a grown woman and he had warned her, but she was so sure of herself, so hell-bent on proving she could do what Keith could not: squeeze information out of Big Red. She thought she could just bat her eyes, show some cleavage and some leg, and find out what they needed to know, but Keith knew better. If Stephanie wasn't careful, she could easily get in over her head in there. Flirting and throwing on the charm may work with small-town millionaires, but men like Big Red were a lot rougher and dirtier. They would expect a lot more than a smile and an ass rub if you wanted to get something from them.

"And who says she wouldn't be willing to do it," a voice in Keith's head mocked. "She did it with you."

Oh, come on, he thought in reply. *Even she has standards—and limits.*

But Keith wasn't so sure. He glanced at the dashboard again, resolving if Stephanie didn't leave the bar in the next thirty minutes, he was going in after her. *Thirty minutes.* That's how long he would wait. No longer. If he had to save her from herself, so be it!

With that declaration, he closed his eyes and leaned his head back against the headrest, trying to calm his nerves. He took several deep breaths. It was an exercise he had learned while in the ATF—how to focus, how to center himself before intense situations. It had seemed like mumbo jumbo when he first learned it, but it actually worked most times. He was supposed to visualize something serene. Keith focused until slowly, a vision came to mind. It was a crowded bar filled with people.

Not very serene, he thought.

He saw Stephanie holding Big Red's chubby hand,

guiding the gargantuan man through the throng of
people in the bar into one of the back rooms. It
looked like a utility closet filled with brooms, mops,
and liquid detergents. He saw Big Red step inside first,
then Stephanie squeeze in after him. It was a tight fit,
but she managed. She winked and Big Red gave a big
toothy grin, revealing his gold tooth. She then fell to
her knees. Big Red licked his lips and leaned his
head back against the wall. Stephanie lowered the
zipper of his pants, stuck her hand inside, and . . .

"That's it," Keith thought, opening his eyes.

He threw open his car door and jumped down to
the wet asphalt.

He wasn't waiting another thirty minutes. He was
going in there and dragging her ass out *now!*

Keith threw open the barroom door and was instantly hit by the smell of cigarette smoke and the heavy
undercurrent of weed. The pungent haze burned his
eyes, making them water.

He winced as he passed a wall speaker. The feedback nearly blew out his eardrum.

The blues band was playing at full throttle with a
heavy bass and a driving rhythm that had several in
the crowd screaming and shouting with delight. A
few couples were grinding on the dance floor. One
woman in a miniskirt and halter top who was nursing
a bottle of beer did a lazy, drunken shimmy alone
with her rolling eyes half-closed. A few people stood
off to the side, pointing and laughing at her before
one man grabbed her hand and roughly yanked her
to one of the booths along the wall.

Keith's eyes scanned the cavernous room. He looked

at the bar, which was fifteen feet away. All of the bar stools were occupied, but none by Stephanie. The bartender—a rail-thin, dark-skinned man who stood in front of a glowing "Miller Lite" sign—simultaneously poured shots, smoked a cigarette, and watched Keith as Keith walked across the room. In his jaundiced eyes was a mix of mild curiosity and suspicion. Keith instantly stopped frowning. He relaxed his shoulders and loosened his fists. He didn't want to raise any red flags this early—not until he found Stephanie, anyway. He nodded to the bartender. Though the old man still seemed wary, he nodded back at Keith.

Keith moved farther into the room, passing a few pool tables where men loudly talked trash and badly played pool. One bumped Keith's shoulder as he passed.

"Watch where da fuck you goin', man!" the surly player shouted over the music, glaring at Keith. His two front teeth were missing. So was his right eye. Keith decided that life had done enough to this man to let this one offense slide. He kept walking.

Keith drew closer to the back of the barroom and finally found Stephanie. She was sitting with Big Red at a table where the backwoods hustler held court with several other men. Two were the bodyguards who had come in with him.

Well, sitting *with* Big Red wasn't an accurate description. It was more like Stephanie was sitting *on* him. She was perched on his ample lap, holding a perspiring beer bottle in her hand, throwing back her head as she laughed.

Keith was incensed. He watched as one of Big Red's plump hands cupped Stephanie's bottom while the other casually cradled her thigh. Keith instantly charged toward the table and when Stephanie saw him coming, her laughter died in her throat. She lowered her bottle and gazed at him quizzically.

Big Red noticed Stephanie had stopped laughing. He followed her gaze and stared up at Keith. He tilted his round head.

"Can I help you, brah?" he asked, revealing his 24-karat smile.

"No," Keith answered succinctly. He then returned his attention to Stephanie. "Get up. It's time to go," he said firmly.

Stephanie blinked in amazement.

Big Red chuckled. "I don't know. Don't look like she's fittin' to go—least don't look like it to me. Are you ready to go, baby?"

Stephanie hesitantly glanced at Keith's stern face before looking back at Big Red. She laughed nervously and shook her head. "No, baby. I'm fine right here."

"See that," Big Red said, now gloating. He tightened his arm possessively around her waist. "She ain't ready. So I think you need to move the hell along."

"I wasn't talking to you!" Keith barked, making Big Red's smile disappear. "I was talking to her!" He suddenly returned his focus to Stephanie. "I said get up! It's time to go!"

Stephanie gazed at Keith like she wasn't sure if he was doing some great performance or if he was serious. Her eyes silently pled with him. "What the hell are you doing?" they asked.

"Baby, is this your man?" Big Red drawled.

"Uh . . ." Stephanie uttered anxiously. "Well, kinda yes . . . kinda no."

"Then you better tell him to back the hell up, because he 'bout to get hurt!" Big Red sneered. He glared up at Keith. "You don't know who you fuckin' with!"

Suddenly, the two very large men who Keith had seen walking into the club with Big Red earlier now rose from the round table and slowly walked around it toward Keith.

Stephanie's eyes widened with alarm. "Look, OK," she said, putting down her bottle on the wooden table. She held up her hands and rose to her feet. "Really there's no need for all of this. I'll go! I just—"

Big Red roughly tugged her back down to his lap, catching her by surprise. She cringed after landing hard on his massive thigh.

"Nuh-uh, baby," he said, pointing at her chest, "where the hell you think you goin'? No bitch walks out on Big Red. You go when *I* tell you that you can go!" With that taken care of, he suddenly glared up at Keith. "Look here," he sneered, "I'm gonna—"

It was a split-second decision that Keith was sure he would later regret, but he did it anyway. The two bodyguards were drawing closer and Stephanie looked like she couldn't get out of this situation even if she tried. So Keith did the only thing he could think of doing: he drew his gun.

Keith had contemplated leaving the Glock 22 back in his glove compartment before he came inside. He only had a license to carry in Virginia, not here in Florida. He could easily face a charge for gun possession carrying it around. Plus, he knew guns could make a bad situation twenty times worse in the wrong hands. He preferred for guns to be the last resort in a tight situation, not the first. But sometimes they couldn't be avoided. You get backed into a corner and a gun could be the ultimate equalizer.

Before he pulled it out of the back of his waistband, he had glanced at the two men's jackets and shirts as they approached to see if there was a telltale bulge to let him know they were carrying. He didn't see any, but he knew that didn't prove anything. Their guns could be tucked somewhere a lot more inconspicuous, but maybe not. Either way, it would take the guys some time to get to them. Thankfully, Big Red was too preoccupied with Stephanie to pull out his gun. So Keith took a chance—a massive one.

Everyone at the table gaped at him.

"What the . . . What the fuck?" Big Red murmured, loosening his grip on Stephanie. "Did this nigga just pull a gun on me?"

"Shit, she ain't all that, man!" one of the bodyguards muttered, making Stephanie angrily furrow her brows.

Keith used the small window of surprise to his advantage. He grabbed Stephanie's hand and yanked her toward him. He then wrapped his arm around her waist.

"Look over my shoulder and tell me if anyone's coming toward me," he said into her ear, keeping his gaze focused on Big Red and his bodyguards, keeping his Glock pointed at them.

"*What?*" she squeaked.

"Look over my damn shoulder and tell me if anyone is creeping up on me," he whispered harshly.

She did as he ordered and slowly shook her head. "Uh, n-n-no . . . No one's coming."

"I want you to keep lookin'," he said. "I want you to walk quickly with me toward the door. Understood?"

Stephanie blankly nodded.

"OK, go!" he said, abruptly backing out of the room.

Stephanie didn't have time to argue. Before she knew it, she was being hauled off her feet.

Chapter 27

"Would you ... put ... me ... *down!*" Stephanie shouted as Keith carried her toward his Ford Explorer.

One minute she was walking quickly out of the bar, trying to match his long strides; the next minute, her feet were dangling a good two inches off the ground.

She twisted and gave him a hard shove. Keith finally released her, dropping her like a heavy sack he was happy to be rid of. He tucked his gun back into his waistband.

Stephanie glared up at him. He glared back at her.

"Why did you do that?" she shouted in the parking lot, throwing up her hands. "He was telling me about Isaac! I had just found out where he was!"

"So why the hell were you still in there, huh? Were you hanging around for the *ambiance?*"

"I was gonna leave, Keith!"

"Then why hadn't you left yet? You were in there for more than two goddamn hours! Why'd I have to come in after you?"

"You didn't have to come in after me! I didn't need you to come chasing me down like some psycho jealous boyfriend! What was that about?"

"I was saving you from yourself!"

Stephanie paused and screwed up her face in confusion. "*What?*"

"And it's good I came in when I did! That slimy piece of shit had his hands *all* over you," Keith yelled, curling his lip in revulsion, "and you were sitting on his lap like he was goddamn Santa Claus!"

She gazed at him, stunned. Keith threw open the driver's-side door to his SUV and climbed inside. She opened the passenger-side door and climbed in beside him.

"What the hell are you talking about?" she asked, facing him. "Damn it! I *told* you that was what I was going in there to do! What did you expect?"

He didn't answer her. She watched as he scowled at the steering wheel. He put his key into the ignition.

"Put on your seatbelt," he murmured.

"*What?*"

Had she heard him correctly? He had just drawn a gun on someone in a bar, dragged her like some caveman across the parking lot, and gotten into a shouting match with her, and he actually was worried about whether she wore a seatbelt.

"You are *not* serious."

"Yes, I am serious! Put on your goddamn seatbelt! I'm not getting a ticket over you!"

Stephanie rolled her eyes. She reached for the seat harness and buckled it with a loud click. "It's on. You happy now?"

"Not really," he muttered, suddenly shifting the

car into drive and flooring the accelerator. Stephanie grabbed the dashboard as the car leapt forward, bouncing slightly on its shocks. The SUV went reeling through the parking lot with tires screeching. Keith then made a hard right and they were on the road. She watched in alarm as the needle on the speedometer climbed to eighty miles per hour.

"If you're so damn worried about getting a ticket, why are you driving so fast?"

"Thanks to you, those assholes back there could be following us."

"*Thanks to me?* How the hell did this become my fault? *I* wasn't the one who pulled the gun!"

He didn't respond. Instead, he squinted at the two-lane roadway.

A pickup truck loaded down with a big-screen TV and mattresses was in front of them, slowly chugging along, sending up a mucky cloud of exhaust. Keith crossed the double yellow line—not dropping speed—to get around them. The headlights of a sports car going southbound suddenly came into view. The driver of the sports car beeped his horn.

"Keith, you should . . . You should get over now."

The sports car horn beeped again, frantically this time. Keith stubbornly stayed in the southbound lane. Stephanie gripped the dashboard so hard her fingernails were digging into the upholstery.

"What are you doing? You're going to hit them!" she shouted.

He has lost his damn mind!

Stephanie closed her eyes, prepared for a head-on collision. Keith whipped the wheel to get back in the northbound lane only seconds before his Ford Explorer and the sports car would have slammed into one another. The driver angrily beeped his horn again. The blaring sound echoed in the night.

Stephanie opened her eyes seconds later, happy to find that she wasn't being greeted at the pearly gates, but was still on some back road in Florida. She nervously licked her lips. "No one is following us. You can slow down."

The needle crept up to ninety miles per hour.

"Damn it, Keith! Slow the hell down!"

She saw his grip relax on the steering wheel. Finally, the Ford Explorer began to decelerate. When the red needle dropped back to forty miles per hour, she exhaled slowly, slumping back against her seat.

"You can't keep doing this," he muttered.

She stared in puzzlement. "Keep doing what?"

"Keep handing yourself over to those guys! You barter with your body to get what you want! It's pathetic . . . and it'll age you fast. And trust me, you're no spring chicken! I don't think you wanna speed up the clock."

"*No spring chicken?* No spring chicken?" she screeched.

She was only thirty-four years old!

"Oh, you can go to hell," Stephanie said. "In fact, you can go to hell but make sure you kiss my ass before you go there, Keith Hendricks!"

"You're going to be just like that old hooker I saw in the parking lot tonight," he continued, undeterred by her outrage, "battered and used up. Then what? Who the hell is going to want you then?"

"Wait, are you seriously comparing me to some sad old hooker you met in the parking lot? Is that how it is?" She angrily pointed at him. "It must be really nice to think you know everything, but I tell you something: You don't! You don't know what I've done in my life! You just know what you've *heard!* So some old bitches in Chesterton gossiped about me! So what? They gossip about all of us—the whole damn family! If I slept with half the men they *claim* I've slept with, I'd be in the *Guinness Book of World Records* by now!"

"I don't have to listen to gossip!" he yelled back, turning onto the road that led to their hotel. "I know what I've seen with my own damn eyes!"

"And what exactly did you see? I was just having a *drink with him!* I was sitting on his lap! I wasn't having sex with him!"

"This time! But what about next time? What about when you had sex with me, huh?" he snapped. "Don't sit here and lie and tell me you weren't trying to get something out of that!"

At those words, all the fight drained out of her and all witty retorts died on her lips. The car fell silent as Stephanie felt hurt curdle in the pit of her stomach again.

No spring chicken . . . pathetic . . . She had taken those attacks better than she could ever take this. She swallowed the lump clogging her throat, fighting back tears.

"Huh?" he prodded again. "Got nothin' to say to that, do you?"

"Actually, I do," she said quietly. "Because I want to set the record straight. Yes, I did have sex with you, Keith . . . something I now regret. Believe me. And I had an ulterior motive, but I wasn't bartering my damn body! I wasn't doing it to get anything from you! I did it because I liked you, which was my mistake! I thought . . . I thought I was . . . I was going to lose you. I thought you were going to send me back to Virginia, and I . . . I'd never see you again. I'd just be the client that you e-mailed a final report to when all this was over.

"I did it for the same dumb reasons that every other woman in the world does this stuff. But that doesn't make me a damn prostitute! That makes me human." She furiously shook her head. "But don't worry. I won't make that mistake again. I'm over it!"

He finally tore his gaze away from the roadway and looked at her. She didn't meet his eyes.

Wounded, Stephanie turned around in her seat and stared out the passenger-side window. She could feel tears stinging her eyes again, begging to spill onto her cheeks, but she stubbornly held them back.

Why do I let him do this to me?

Stephanie could pretend like she was hurt, pout her lips and get misty-eyed when the occasion called for it, but she had never really considered herself "thin-skinned." When it came to Keith though, she felt like she didn't have any armor. Every putdown left her ego bruised. Every unkind word left her frustrated and bewildered.

They rode in silence before arriving at the hotel five minutes later. When the car came to a stop, she threw open her car door.

"Stephanie!" Keith called after her. "Stephanie!"

She didn't look back. Instead she walked swiftly to her hotel room at the end of the courtyard, digging in her purse, searching for her key. It took some effort. Her vision was blurred now, obscured by tears.

Cynthia had told her to suck it up, to get over it. But Stephanie didn't think she could do it, not this time.

She just wanted to get inside her hotel room so she could cry in private. Maybe sample some of the complimentary bottles of Jim Beam and Jack Daniels in the hotel mini-refrigerator to drown her sorrows. In the morning, she would put on a good face, get the old Stephanie back, but tonight she would let the mascara run.

Stephanie finally found her hotel key card in the bottom of her bag. With shaky hands, she shoved the card into the lock, opened her door, and stepped inside, but felt someone looming behind her. She looked over her shoulder in alarm, expecting to find Big Red or one of his thugs. Instead, she saw Keith standing there.

"Stephanie, I—"

She tried to slam the hotel door before he could finish. He was faster than her though—and stronger. He grabbed the door and shoved his way inside, despite her trying to lean against it, despite her shoving back with all her might. He then closed it behind him, locking the deadbolt with a *click*.

"Get out of my room!" she shouted.

"Not until we talk," he said calmly, taking a step toward her.

"*Talk?* I don't want to talk! Get out of my goddamn room!" She shoved at his chest, though he didn't move an inch. "You have your own room five doors down! I suggest you go there!"

"Look, I . . ." He took a deep breath. "I owe you an apology."

"Save your damn apologies! The *old hooker* doesn't want to hear it!"

He slowly shook his head. "I don't think you're

old . . . and I don't think you're a hooker either," he hastily added.

"Yes, you do! You've made it pretty damn clear what you think about me! That speech in the car explained more than enough."

"I know what I said in the car! I was angry! Goddamn it, I'm *still* angry! I hate watching you do this to yourself, Steph! " He closed his eyes and clenched his jaw. "Look, I'm not trying to hurt you! I'm just trying to—"

"*Hurt me?* You can't hurt me!" she lied, sneering with contempt, trying her best to wound him like he had wounded her.

He opened his eyes.

"How the hell could you hurt me? I don't give a shit about you! Why would I?" she choked, feeling the saliva lodge in her throat. "I've dated men who make more in a year than . . . than you'll make in your entire lifetime!"

"And that's what counts? How much a man makes? How much he can give you? That's all that matters to you?"

"No!" she shouted. "I mean, yes! I mean . . . I mean . . ." She angrily balled her fists. "Damn it, stop psychoanalyzing me! I'm not listening to your shit anymore!"

"So they wine and dine you and buy you gifts," he continued quietly. "A gold watch? New shoes?" He pointed at her feet. "That's worth trading yourself for?"

"No, it's not! I'm not trading myself! Stop calling it that! I'm doing it for . . . for . . ."

He looked at her expectantly. "For what?"

She blinked. *What am I doing it for?*

A sense of security? Maybe, but it never stayed for long. Sugar daddies went through playthings like they went through cars. They were always looking for the newer, better model. But at least she had something to show for it in the end, right? Stephanie thought back to her jewelry box of trinkets her ex-boyfriends had given her over the years. In total, they were probably worth forty thousand dollars, give or take a few hundred, but with one year of work she could have made more in commissions. Her ex-husband's alimony checks had petered out over the years to less than two hundred dollars a month since he had lost his car dealerships thanks to the recession. Had what those men given her really been worth all the time and effort?

Her shoulders slumped.

No, it wasn't, she concluded sorrowfully. She had spent almost all of her youth chasing after men who would readily trade her in for something better, who had never truly *loved* her. And while examining her life in the past few weeks, she wondered sometimes what was there to love about her? She had always been a taker, not a giver. She had manipulated and used them. Besides her mother and her sisters, she had never truly loved anyone.

But she was in love now. She had fallen for Keith and he refused to believe it! Here was someone who she wasn't trying to manipulate, who she didn't want anything from but love and affection in return, and he thought it was a trick. He still thought she had run some con on him, much like the one Isaac had run on her. It hurt that he felt that way about her. It was so painful it tightened her chest, twisting its grip like a vise.

Keith looked at her intently, still waiting for her reply. With those dark eyes on her, she could feel her armor melting away. He could see it. He could see through her angry protests and her taunts. He could see her, and she was ashamed of what he saw.

"Stephanie," he said softly, "you have to want more. You're *worth* more."

"I . . ." She choked. "I . . ." Her eyes stung. She was unable to hold back the tears any longer. She turned away in frustration, not wanting to cry in front of him again.

He reached out for her and she frantically shook her head and waved him away. She tried to seek refuge in the hotel room bathroom, but Keith stopped her. He tugged her back toward him and wrapped her in his arms.

"Don't touch me, damn it!" she hiccuped as she buried her face against his shoulder, linking her arms around his neck as she sniffed. She left black streaks of mascara on his T-shirt as she wept.

"I'm not touching you," he murmured, rubbing her back.

"I don't need anything from you. I don't even *like* you!" she argued between sniffs, clinging to him, not wanting to let him go.

"So you keep telling me," he said with a wry smile before lifting her head from his shoulder and lowering his mouth to hers.

Stephanie didn't fight him. To the contrary, she stood on the balls of her feet and passionately kissed him back. When she felt herself being lifted from her feet and carried across the room to the hotel bed seconds later, she docilely let Keith do it. She wanted his hands on her. She wanted to ease the throbbing between her legs and the ache in her heart. She didn't care if he would mistake her affection for manipulation, or if he would turn cold as soon as it was over. At this moment, all she wanted was him.

They continued to kiss even as they undressed, standing by the edge of the bed. She felt the familiar warm tingle on her skin as his hands trailed over her body while he opened buttons, lowered the zipper of her denim skirt and pulled away her shirt. The vibrating heat snaked its way up her limbs as his teeth toyed with her lips, as his tongue delved into her mouth.

Her breathing deepened. Her lashes lowered. Her nipples hardened and she pressed herself eagerly against his chest. When she felt her denim skirt being roughly pushed over her hips and down her legs, she was almost dizzy with desire. She staggered drunkenly on her heels and fell back against the mattress. He lowered himself on top of her and she spread her legs wide in willing invitation. She cupped his face and dragged his mouth back to hers.

He didn't pull his lips away, even as he slowly peeled her bra straps from her shoulders and pushed the bra cups to her waist. He took a breast in each hand and kneaded them lovingly before lowering his mouth to one of the nipples. She moaned and arched her back. She bit down hard on her lower lip just as he lowered one of his hands. He pushed past the elastic band of her thong and his fingers crept between her legs. He massaged her, teased her, making her moist, making her groan. She closed her eyes again and twisted and bucked underneath his touch.

He hadn't known her body very long, yet he seemed to know instinctively what it wanted and what it needed.

He removed the thong completely and slowly shifted to the end of the bed, leaving a trail of kisses all over her body that made her whimper and moan. He eased her legs over his broad shoulders and lowered his mouth to the wetness between her thighs, lashing her clit with his tongue. The torturous teasing became even worse. Her twisting and bucking only increased. She clenched the bedsheets in her fists, dug her nails into his shoulders. She fought to take shallow breaths, feeling her chest rapidly rise and fall. When she felt that she could endure it no longer, the sensation reached its peak. The trembling and shaking started. Her back arched and her toes curled. She shouted his name over and over again as the spasms washed over her body.

She wished the sensation would never end, but she knew she would die if it didn't.

"Oh, God," she moaned breathlessly minutes later when her body finally went slack. "Oh, God."

She wasn't given much time to recover. He slowly flipped her over. She prostrated beneath him on all fours, naked save for her high heels.

Unlike last time when they had given away completely to abandonment, this time he did pause to use a condom. She shuddered with anticipation while she waited for him to put it on.

When he steadied her hips and entered her from behind, she accepted him almost with relief. Her body finally had gotten what it had been yearning for. His pounding had her clutching the sheets again, but this time to steady herself. She closed her eyes and suddenly the room became only noise and sensation: the feel of his hands on her, the mattress digging into her knees and elbows, the sound of his groans, the creak of the bedsprings, and the rapid beat of her own heart in her ears. Then there was the familiar throbbing at her center that grew wider and wider until even the tips of her fingers seemed to quiver.

She only opened her eyes when she came again, feeling as if she was just given an electric shock. She shouted his name for the umpteenth time as she felt the tremors crest over her body and her thighs began to quake. She felt Keith jerk inside her with his own release and heard him shout her name a second later. Her arms no longer seemed able to bear her weight and she slumped forward tiredly, barely able to see because of the tendrils of hair that had fallen into her eyes. He slowly lowered himself on top of her. He lay half on her back and half on the mattress, breathing deeply.

They lay in silence for several minutes, both trying to catch their breaths. He pulled himself from her and slumped on the bed beside her. He trailed his hand along her bare spine and then the roundness of her behind. When her breathing and her heartbeat finally slowed, Stephanie turned her face away from his. She gazed at the headboard.

She was resigned to what she was about to say, but knew she wouldn't have the courage to say it if she had to look at him in the face. She was about to break the biggest Gibbons family rule. By this admission, she was giving Keith—a man—all the power, but she had to get it off her chest.

"I love you, Keith," she murmured.

The hand that had been caressing her stilled.

"I know you don't believe me when I say it, that you think someone like me couldn't mean it, but I do. I love you and I don't want anything from you, all right?"

She felt him shift at her side but he still didn't speak a word.

"I'm not trying to get anything out of you. I'm not saying that you . . . that you have to love me back," she continued. "I just . . . I just wanted you to know that I love you."

She slowly turned around to face him. She was terrified at what she might find when she looked at his face. Was he horrified by her confession? Would he doubt her again?

Instead, she found understanding in his eyes. He reached out and pushed a lock of hair out of her eyes.

"It took a lot for you to say that, didn't it?"

She lowered her gaze to the crumpled bedsheets. "You have no idea how much. The women in my family don't fall in love. We certainly don't admit that we did."

"Well, if it makes you feel any better, I think I'm in love with you too."

Her eyes leapt back to his face in surprise.

"I don't know when it happened. I don't know *how* it happened. We haven't even known each other that long, but it's what I feel." He slowly shook his head in bafflement. "I came charging into that bar ready to beat the hell out of any man who put his hands on you. I went in there to get you and bring you back, because you belong with *me*, Stephanie Gibbons."

He trailed a finger along her cheek. They both

climbed to the top of the bed and lay silently for several minutes, holding one another.

Stephanie felt as if she could stay this way forever wrapped in his arms. She raised her head and watched as Keith's eyes started to drift closed. She shook his shoulder and smirked. "Oh, no, you don't. Don't go to sleep on me," she whispered. "Not yet."

His eyes popped back open. He gave a tired smile. "It's your fault I'm falling asleep. You wore me out, lady."

She trailed her fingers along his chiseled chest, then his stomach. Her eyes lingered on a jagged one-inch scar that marred his torso. She felt the callused skin underneath her fingertips. "How'd you get this?"

He raised his head and leaned forward to get a better look at where she was pointing. He cocked an eyebrow. "*That* is a stab wound."

She sat up from his chest and gazed at him in amazement. "Are you joking?"

He laughed. "Believe me. I wouldn't joke about something like that."

"When did you get stabbed?"

"Back when I was a cop. Before I joined the ATF," he said, fingering the scar. "That little souvenir was from a perp who didn't want to go to jail quietly."

"Good God, Keith!" she exclaimed. She cringed in anguish as if *she* was the one who had been stabbed. "You must have been terrified."

He linked his hands behind his head. "No, not really. I didn't even realize that I was stabbed until about a half an hour later, when my partner pointed out that I was bleeding all over my uniform. I was more pissed that the guy got away from me when I tried to get him in handcuffs. I chased him for a good half a mile before I could tackle him to the ground and get those handcuffs back on."

Her gaze returned to his body. She wondered what other tales lay on his dark, smooth skin. Her eyes stopped when she noticed a brand on his right arm, just beneath his shoulder. It was about the size of a silver dollar and it looked like the number nine but the branding was so crude, she couldn't really tell what it was.

"So what's this?" she said, pointing at it. "How'd you get this one? It definitely doesn't look like someone stabbed you there."

He slowly shook his head. "No, no one stabbed me. I did that one myself."

"How?"

"I took a coat hanger and used a pair of pliers to make a 9. Then I put it over the kitchen stove and burned it into my skin."

She cringed all over again. "Why on earth would you do that?"

"To fit in," he answered bluntly. "All the guys I looked up to had one. It was the symbol of the 9th Street Crew and I wanted a brand just like theirs."

Stephanie fell silent. She rested her chin back on his chest and gazed into his eyes. "Was this back when you were in East Baltimore?" she asked, remembering what he had told Myra Beaumont more than a week ago.

He nodded.

"And that's what you had to do to belong?"

He pursed his lips. "Among other things," he said cryptically.

She trailed her fingers along his chest again. "Among other things?"

"Yep."

She looked at him expectantly, waiting for details. When he continued to gaze at her and not say a word, she hesitated.

"It doesn't . . . It doesn't sound like you want to talk about it."

"It wasn't a high point in my life, Steph. Who *would* want to talk about it?"

She didn't want to pry, but part of her ached to know more about him. The more she found out about Keith Hendricks, the more complex he seemed, and she wanted to know every facet of him. She was in love with a man whom, admittedly, she barely knew anything about. She felt like she was playing a game of catch-up. What food did he like? What books did he read? What did he do to relax? Where and how did he grow up?

"But you were young, Keith," she persisted, tilting her head, trying to draw him out. "A lot of people do crazy things when they're kids, honey."

"Yeah, well, when most people talk about the crazy things they did when they were younger, they're talking about the candy bar they stole from the drugstore. Or they're talking about the time they broke into their parents' liquor cabinet and took a sip from their dad's bottle of schnapps. They aren't talking about the time they got chased down by police, or when they skipped school to be a drug dealer's lookout. They won't tell you the story about when someone shot through their window and almost killed their mother because all the dealers in the neighborhood had marked them as a snitch." He gritted his teeth. "I'm pretty sure that's not what they mean when they say, 'I had a wild youth.' "

He was right. When she thought of most people's crazy childhoods, none of those stories came to mind. Stephanie had been wild and rebellious in her youth. She had been the spoiled little rich girl who would climb out of her bedroom window and shimmy over the balcony railing of her mother's terrace to sneak to a party with friends. She had bowed to a dare and skinny-dipped in a lake not far from Chesterton. She had partied and got drunk with the rest of them, but she had never experienced anything remotely close to what Keith had experienced in his life.

"All of those things happened to you?" she asked softly.

"Yeah, and none of it I'm proud of. Some people like having street cred. Frankly, I don't." He closed his eyes. "If Mike hadn't found me on that corner twenty-five years ago, who knows where I would be right now." He opened his eyes and shook his head. "No, I know *exactly* where I would be: I would either be serving twenty-five years to life in prison, or lying six feet deep in a cemetery."

"You had it hard, didn't you?"

"More than you know. But other people had it worse." He shrugged. "At least I got out. A lot of my friends didn't. I bet most of them are dead or in jail now."

She let the gravity of what he had just said sink in, now at a loss for words.

He tilted his head. "So . . . why don't I ask you a few questions?"

She hesitated, wary of what he might ask. But she had made him discuss his painful old wounds. It only seemed fair that she do the same. She swallowed. "Oh . . . OK. Go . . . go right ahead."

"Have you ever been married?"

Stephanie licked her lips and shifted uncomfortably on top of him. She had expected this question to come eventually—just not this soon. "Yes, I've been married."

"When . . . and how long?"

"Well, I married my ex seven years ago. We were married for four of them."

"Who wanted the divorce, him or you?"

"I did," she answered honestly. "I knew the marriage only had a short shelf life anyway. Besides, I knew I wasn't in love with him . . . and he had already moved on to someone else."

Keith squinted. "What do you mean he had moved on to someone else?"

"I mean he had a mistress, Keith . . . a couple of them actually. When I married him, I was still in my twenties. I figured my expiration date was drawing close once I turned thirty. He'd have to move on eventually."

He traced his finger along her jawline again. "You think men see you like that . . . as something with an expiration date?"

Stephanie nodded. "Of course, they do! That's just a fact of life."

She could tell from the look on his face that he was confused by her response.

"Look, Keith, I learned at an early age that beauty can get you lots of things. It can give you money. It can get you power. But your beauty won't last forever. You only have a short time frame to use your looks and your charm to your advantage. Mama always says that a man who's head over heels in love with you now, may not be when you're covered in wrinkles. He'll also be more than happy to forget about you if a better, younger model comes along."

Keith's finger shifted from her cheeks to her lips. He traced their circumference with his fingertips. Her eyes drifted closed as she enjoyed the sensation of his touch. He leaned in for a kiss and she eagerly kissed him back. Gradually, he pulled his mouth away, but not before taking one last nibble at her lips. He gazed down at her.

"Do you think I'd fall out of love with you once you got wrinkles or if I found a better model?"

Her eyes fluttered open at his words. She had accepted her ex-husband leaving her to run to the waiting arms of another woman as par for the course, but she didn't know how she would react if Keith did the same. "Maybe you will."

"You really think that?"

"I . . . I don't know, Keith. All I could do is to try to prepare myself for that day if you did," she answered softly, feeling her heart break a little at the future prospect.

"You don't give men a lot of credit do you, Steph?" he whispered.

"I've been taught not to."

"Well," he said, staring into her eyes, "then you've been taught wrong. You don't have a shelf life with me. I'm not some millionaire who wants to buy you like he would a house or a car then trade you in for a new one. I don't want to add you to my collections." He tilted his head. "Now I admit that I don't have a lot of money. I certainly can't buy you lots of things— at least not the things that you're accustomed to, but

I could love you and respect you . . . and treasure you. I could offer you more than any of those millionaires could."

Stephanie felt the tears flowing again, except this time they were happy tears. She reached for the hand that lingered near her cheek and held it. She kissed the inside of his palm tenderly then leaned over to kiss him. It didn't take long for the kiss to deepen. Stephanie closed her eyes and Keith eased her back onto the bed. He slowly climbed on top of her.

That night they made love several more times until the wee hours of the morning. They expressed with their bodies and with words what they felt in their hearts. When they finally drifted off to sleep, Stephanie was delirious with love and with happiness. She snuggled against Keith, feeling a greater sense of peace than she had felt in quite a long time.

Chapter 28

Stephanie slowly opened her eyes to the sun-dappled hotel room. She stretched, turned, and looked at the pillow beside her. She saw that it was empty. She slowly pushed herself to her elbows and looked around the room. Keith was nowhere in sight.

For one fleeting moment, she feared that last night had been only a dream. None of it had really happened: their making love, their confessions, and falling asleep in each other's arms. But she turned when she heard the bathroom door open. Keith walked out of the door and into the hotel room with a towel wrapped around his waist. His muscular chest was bare and covered with droplets of water from the shower. He smiled and relief washed over her face.

"So you're finally up then?"

She returned his smile and yawned. "Yeah, did I sleep late?"

"I would say so. It's almost noon."

"*Noon?*" She glanced at the alarm clock on the night table.

Keith was right. It was 11:53 a.m.

"Yep, and you were snoring too. You have a very cute snore."

She wiped her eyes with the back of her hands, remembering roughly when they had finally fallen asleep, which was sometime around dawn. "I was just tired, I guess."

"I figured." He leaned against the doorframe. "My lovin' tends to have that effect on women."

"Oh, please!" She rolled her eyes heavenward and laughed.

"I remember you shouting that a few times last night too."

She made a face, grabbed one of the pillows on the bed, and playfully tossed it at him. It landed near his bare feet.

"Throwing stuff at me again, huh?" He reached down, grabbed the pillow, and walked toward the bed. "That's kind of a bad habit of yours."

He tossed the pillow back beside her. He then flopped on the bed and stretched across her legs. She leaned forward and gave him a languid kiss. He absently rubbed her thighs.

"So now that you're awake," he said, "I suggest we order breakfast. Then talk about what we should do next about Isaac."

She nodded. "Big Red gave me an idea of where he might be. He thinks Miami."

Keith stilled. "Why Miami?"

"Something about it being his old stomping ground. Big Red said he used to run a lot of cons down there. Rich lovers were ripe for the picking, and it's a big enough city for him to stay inconspicuous."

"And also big enough that it may be hard for people like us to find him," Keith said.

"But it's worth a try."

He nodded. "You're right. We'll go anyway. Might as well." His smile returned. "In the meantime, let's order breakfast."

"Good, because I'm *starving!*" she exclaimed, holding her stomach. To illustrate that point, her stomach growled loudly.

She watched as Keith walked across the hotel room, opened the cardboard menu on the dresser, and dialed room service. He made the orders and returned to the bed.

"They said it's a twenty-five-minute wait."

She nodded and pulled back the bedsheets and tossed her legs over the edge of the mattress. "Well, that's plenty of time for me to take a shower and do something with my hair."

Her hair was still tussled and matted from the night before. She hadn't seen herself in the mirror yet, but she was sure she looked a fright.

Just as she was about to rise to her feet, Keith stopped her by firmly wrapping his arm around her waist, catching her by surprise. She yelped when he pulled her back to the bed. She fell back naked beside him.

"Hold on for a second there," he whispered. "Twenty-five minutes may be plenty of time for a shower, but only just enough time for something else."

His hand shifted from her waist to one of her breasts. He caressed it, tantalizingly running his hand over the nipple until it hardened. He circled his thumb around its peak then squeezed it gently. Her eyelashes fluttered closed. She bit down hard on her bottom lip.

His hand drifted from her breast to the soft skin of her stomach then glided lower. "Want to shout 'oh, please' a couple more times, sweetheart?"

When his hand rested between her thighs, she spread her legs slightly, inviting his touch. "I take that as a 'yes,' " he whispered with a chuckle before lowering his mouth to hers.

Under his skillful hands, her legs went slack and he took advantage of the opportunity. While one hand toyed with her nipples, the other slowly massaged her clit, making her moist, making her moan. She threw back her head and she began to slowly rock her hips, meeting each of his languid strokes. When he slipped his fingers in her, Stephanie cried out. The rocking only increased. She closed her eyes and enjoyed the delicious thrill of sensations cresting over her body.

Minutes later, he pulled his hand away and she whimpered. She opened her glassy eyes and looked almost drunk.

"Why'd you stop?" she moaned.

He reached for one of the condom packets left on the hotel night table and lowered his mouth back to hers.

This time she kissed him with a hunger that was almost overwhelming. She began to explore his body with her hands, her mouth, and her tongue, making him shudder. They rolled around on her bed, seeking better access to one another, enjoying each sensation. Finally, Keith couldn't take it anymore. He put on the condom, eased her legs apart, and raised her hips. When he entered her, she whimpered his name against his ear and he groaned as the warm wetness enveloped him.

He slowly rocked and grinded on top of her with both hands cupped beneath her bottom. She wrapped her arms around him and brought her mouth back to his and their tongues danced, becoming almost entangled. Minutes later, he suddenly picked up the pace of their lovemaking.

That's when she felt it. Not just the tingles starting to surge over her body like mini-electric shocks, but she could feel her heart becoming lighter and lighter. *So this is what it is like to be in love,* she thought, *and to be loved in return.*

Stephanie cried out his name again. Her muscles tightened and so did his grip around her, to the point that she wasn't sure if he was going to hurt her. Keith clenched his teeth and let out a slow guttural groan. It sounded like sheer agony but she knew that it wasn't. It was the exact opposite.

The final spasm shook his entire body. Suddenly, he loosened his grip. His hands fell away. He slumped on top of her, like a heavyweight after a knockout punch. He took a long, deep, shuddering breath.

Stephanie was pretty sure the waiter from room service heard her cries of ecstasy when he finally arrived with their waffles and pancakes exactly twenty-five minutes later, but she was too happy to care. She bashfully sat in her robe on the edge of the bed with her hair still wild and matted and a silly grin on her face while Keith paid the bill.

"You enjoying breakfast?" he asked as they shared a plate of pancakes.

"Immensely!"

That's when they heard the pounding a few doors down.

"Open up, motherfucka!" someone yelled. "I know you're in there! Open the goddamn door!"

The voice sounded eerily familiar.

Stephanie stopped mid-bite.

Keith rose from the bed and cautiously walked across the hotel room. He gradually opened up the dusty blinds just a smidge. He did it just enough for him to see outside but not enough for someone else to see inside the room. He peered through the window at the parking lot.

"Shit," he whispered.

Stephanie's heart began to thud faster in her chest. She slowly lowered her fork back to her plate. "*What? What's wrong?*"

"Looks like they found us," Keith said.

Stephanie climbed off the bed and crossed the room to stand beside him. She looked through the parted blinds. What she saw made her bite down hard on her bottom lip.

Big Red was a few doors down in front of Keith's hotel room, with his two bodyguards in tow. The guy from the hotel front desk was also there, looking nervously around him.

Judging from the angry look on Big Red's and his bodyguards' faces, she guessed that the three men were there to do a lot more than talk. They must have either followed the Explorer last night or had somehow spotted Keith's car from the highway. Either way, it looked like she and Keith were trapped.

"Damn it," she muttered. "What the hell do we do now?"

Keith let the blinds fall closed. "Don't know yet. I will say though that it's lucky for me that I slept here tonight. At least I'm not in that room right now."

"But all your clothes are in there," she said, looking worried.

"Honey, all I need are my car keys, my wallet, and my cell phone. Shit, I can buy new clothes!"

Stephanie walked back to the bed. She sat down and started to nervously wring her hands. "So what do we do? Make a run for it? Should I . . . Should I wear a disguise?"

He gazed at her and cocked an eyebrow. His mouth curved in amusement. "Again, this isn't the movies, baby. We're not making any 'run for it' without calling the cops first. That poor guy down there could get the shit beat out of him if we just walked out right now."

Stephanie watched Keith pick up the hotel phone and begin to dial 9-1-1. She was a little crestfallen to hear that's how Keith planned to end this confrontation. After the excitement from yesterday, she had imagined their escape from Big Red and his goons would be a lot more dramatic. A big car chase . . . dodging in and out of traffic . . . firing guns out of windows . . .

On second thought, she contemplated, *maybe that isn't the best idea.*

Keith glanced at her. "You can take your shower and get dressed while we wait."

The cops arrived about half an hour later.

Stephanie watched from the doorway as the police officer stood in front of Big Red and his bodyguards, looking bored.

"There goes the motherfucka right there!" Big Red shouted as she and Keith casually walked back to their SUV, acting as if they had nothing to do with the scene around them. Stephanie bit back a smile as

Big Red pointed frantically. "He's over there! That's the same dude that pulled a gun on me!"

They both climbed inside the Explorer and shut the doors behind them. Keith then threw on his sunglasses.

"So I guess we're off to Miami then," he said.

"Looks like it," she replied.

"Try not to get me into any more trouble while we're down there, please?" He put his key into the ignition and turned on the engine.

"Well, try not to pull out a gun next time!"

He laughed. "All right, you got me there."

Chapter 29

"*Now* you're heading to Miami?" Dawn asked, furrowing her brows.

"Yep!" Stephanie giggled on the other end of the phone line. "We're heading there now. We're hoping to get there by this evening if we can make the miles. This is one of our few pit stops. I wanted to get lunch."

Dawn leaned back in her office chair. The search for conman Isaac seemed to be forever ongoing. Dawn wondered where the journey would take her sister next.

To Mexico, maybe, she thought glibly. *Antarctica?*

"So . . . Is your assistant OK covering everything for you while you're gone?"

"Uh-huh, I told her it would only be a couple more weeks. If we don't find Isaac by then, then I have to head back to Chesterton. I trust Keith to continue looking for him without me."

"Well, are you OK with being alone with Keith for another week or so? I thought he really pissed you off. It doesn't bother you to be around him?"

"Of course, it doesn't bother me. Dawn, I'm . . . I'm in love with him."

At those words, Dawn's phone slipped from her fingers. She almost dropped it to her desk, but she quickly recovered before bringing the receiver back to her ear.

"Wait, say that again, Steph. I don't think I heard you right the first time, because it sounded like you said you were in love with him."

"Actually, that's *exactly* what I said. I am hopelessly in love with him, girl."

Dawn was tempted to ask if her sister was currently under the influence of some illegal substance, but she bit her tongue. Dawn could tell by the sound of Stephanie's voice that she was sober and more importantly, truly happy. But . . . *in love?* Stephanie Gibbons—of all people—was in love? How the hell was this possible? Stephanie had mentioned during their last phone conversation that she thought she was falling in love, but Dawn had just mistaken it for wild rambling.

"Look, I know it sounds crazy," Stephanie rushed. "And I'll admit, it's . . . It's a little scary to own up to my feelings like this, but I really do love him, Dawn. And he loves me too. I think we really have a chance to be happy together. I definitely want to give it a chance anyway."

"But Steph . . . He's a detective. He drives a shitty Ford Explorer, for God's sake! You said that it doesn't seem like he has a lot of money. Are you sure you want to hook up with—"

"Yes, I'm sure. I couldn't walk away from this even if I wanted to. It would eat me up inside."

"Maybe you're going through some weird Stockholm syndrome—you know, forced to be around someone you hate, like you're his hostage. I get that you find him attractive. The man's hotter than a chili pepper. Understood! But maybe being stuck with him all this time is messing with your head and—"

"No one's messing with my head. I *know* what I feel."

"But what about the *rules?*" Dawn asked earnestly, hoping to talk some badly needed sense into her sister's head. "What about—"

"Some rules are made to be broken."

Dawn sighed. Stephanie had broken a great deal of rules lately. Dawn wasn't convinced that breaking yet another one wouldn't lead to more frustration and heartache. But Stephanie was an adult. She had a right to make her own decisions.

"OK," Dawn mumbled. "You're in love. I won't say anything else about it. Con . . . congratulations."

"Thanks, Dawn. I know you don't understand where I'm coming from, but I appreciate you trying to be supportive."

"Hey, I'm your sister," Dawn said with a shrug. "That's what I'm here for."

The tender moment was abruptly interrupted when Percy burst into Dawn's office. Kevin trailed after him.

"Sorry, Dawn," Kevin apologized, doing a little hop to peer at her over Percy's broad shoulder. The alarm was evident on her assistant's tanned face. "As I told you, Mr. Templeton, Dawn is taking a phone call at the moment. She—"

"Well, then she can end her little chat, because I need to speak with her *now,*" Percy said icily.

What the hell is this about?

"Hey, Steph, let me call you back," Dawn whispered, gazing up into Percy's cold blue eyes.

"Oh, sure, talk to you later!" her sister chirped on the other end.

"Bye." Dawn lowered her phone receiver back into its cradle. "What's wrong, Percy?"

She jumped in surprise when he slapped a gilded envelope on her desk. Kevin, realizing the situation was about to get ten times uglier, made a quick exit, shutting the office door behind him.

"You said it couldn't be done." Percy spoke slowly through his tight, thin lips as he paced in front of her desk. "*You* said he wasn't interested in showing his work in the DC market! Well then what the bloody hell is this?"

Dawn reached for the envelope and opened it. Inside was an engraved invitation.

"A preview of the phenomenal work of artist and genius, Razor, to take place at Sawyer Gallery," Dawn read aloud.

The preview was slated for eight o'clock that evening.

"Shit," Dawn muttered. So Sasha had won over Razor after all, and all it took was one night in the sack.

" 'Shit' indeed, darling!" Percy boomed. "How could you let this happen?"

"Percy, I tried. Really, I did. There was no way—"

"Well, obviously, you didn't try hard enough! If you did, he'd be showing his preview at *my* gallery and not that . . . that tasteless amphitheater Martin Sawyer tries to pass off as an exhibition space!" Percy stopped pacing. He shook his head and took a deep breath. "You've deeply disappointed me, Dawn . . .

deeply. I thought you were a woman who could deliver. That's why I hired you, isn't it?"

She didn't say anything in response. What was there to say? If she had to do it all over again, she still wouldn't have done a threesome with Razor and Sasha. She had to draw the line somewhere. But it did anger her that Sasha had managed to get Razor in the end. To lose to a woman like that made her stomach turn.

"*Well?*" Percy persisted. "What do you have to say for yourself?"

"I'm . . . I'm sorry I disappointed you, Percy," she said quietly.

Percy cleared his throat and Dawn lowered her eyes, prepared for the worst.

"*You're fired, darling,*" was the next thing she expected to hear.

"Martin is a lout of the worst kind but . . . He and I run in the same social circles." Percy adjusted the lapels of his jacket. "My absence tonight would look like a case of sour grapes. So I suppose I shall have to attend the preview . . . and you, darling, will attend with me."

Dawn's eyes shot up. Did she hear him correctly? "You . . . you want me to go to the preview tonight?"

"Yes, I do. If I have to . . . What is it that you Americans say? . . . 'Eat shit with a grin,' then you'll have to do it also. I'll pick you up here at seven-thirty." He turned toward her office door and swung it open. "Make sure you're ready when I arrive. We wouldn't want to be late, now would we?"

He then stepped into the hallway, slamming the door closed behind him.

Dawn slumped low in her chair and dropped her

head into her hands. How she would make it through tonight without punching either Sasha or Razor in the nose, she did not know.

"Dawn! Percy! Glad you could make it!"

Dawn almost choked on her champagne at the sound of Sasha's voice, but she managed to swallow it down. She also managed to morph her grimace into a pained smile by the time she turned around and faced her foe.

Sasha was wearing a red suit today: the same shade of red as the panties she wore that night during her clandestine tryst with Razor, Dawn noted. But she wasn't with Razor tonight. Instead, Sasha was linked arm and arm with her lover and gallery owner, Martin Sawyer, and her husband, Teddy.

Martin was a large, balding man with a stomach that hung over the front of his pin-striped slacks. His barrel chest was barely contained in his suit jacket. In contrast, Teddy was a much smaller, skinnier fellow. He had shaggy hair and wore wire-framed bifocals that made his brown eyes look several sizes smaller. He always had a slightly sour look on his face, like he had sucked on a lemon.

"How you doin', Percy?" Martin boomed, extending his plump hand.

At the sight of his frenemy, Percy's body instantly stiffened, but he accepted Martin's handshake. "I'm well, Martin. Very well. Thank you."

"No, thank *you* for coming here tonight! I know things are busy for you guys over at Templeton. I appreciate you taking the time out to visit us."

"Oh, please! I told you everyone is eager to see

Razor's work, Martin! I'm sure they wouldn't miss this for the world," Sasha gushed before turning her saccharine-sweet grin toward Dawn. "Right, Dawn?"

Dawn knew that Sasha was gloating. The woman had all the subtlety of a barreling metro bus. Choosing to ignore Sasha and her baiting, Dawn turned her attention toward Martin instead. "Kudos to you guys for getting this together so quickly, Martin. In just a couple of weeks! That's quite a feat. Have you even had a chance to see the finished work yet?"

Martin lowered his champagne glass from his mouth and shook his head. "No, I haven't. But Sasha tells me this Razor kid is the real deal. I trust her." He glanced around the crowded room, taking in the hundred or so people who had come for the preview. It was standing-room only. "And judging from the turnout, I think she made the right call."

"So are you saying you aren't even giving us a *hint* of what we're going to see tonight?" Percy asked.

Sasha removed her arms from Martin and Teddy. She wagged her finger at Percy and clucked her tongue. "No, we will not, my dear. It will be a surprise for all of us! You'll just have to wait and see."

"Wait . . ." Dawn squinted, now staring in disbelief at Sasha. "Even *you* haven't seen the piece yet?"

Sasha fixed Dawn with a scornful glare. "No, I have not. Razor wanted it to be a surprise. I know he's brilliant. I don't need to see his work in advance to know that it will be superb," she said haughtily, making Dawn grit her teeth. Sasha then glanced down at her watch and adjusted her suit jacket. "Well, Martin, we should probably start now. My people tell me that Razor has arrived. I guess we can begin."

"Good!" Martin shouted. "Wait any longer and only

more people will show up. The fire marshal will make us turn them away if this place gets any more crowded!"

Dawn watched as Martin and Sasha walked toward the back of the room with Teddy bringing up the rear.

Whereas Templeton Gallery chose more subtle décor with brick and white plaster walls so that the artwork was the focus, Sawyer Gallery believed in making a star of its exhibition space. The room was filled with glass panels, rusted copper pipes, stainless steel beams, and very expensive blond hardwood floors and custom overhead lighting. It was obvious that Martin had invested a pretty penny in the space.

Sasha grabbed a mike that one of her assistants handed to her before shooing the young woman away. She then climbed a few stairs to the raised stage.

Dawn and Percy gradually moved forward with the rest of the throng that gathered in the gallery. They were all eager to see what was behind the glossy curtain.

"Hello! Hello, everyone!" Sasha called over the microphone feedback. A few in the crowd grabbed their ears. "We're ready to begin. If you all could . . . just settle down . . . we can begin! I know you're all excited, as am I. But really . . . You must settle down."

The crowd finally fell silent.

"Thank you so much for coming. We're happy to see all of you here at Sawyer Gallery, *the* premiere gallery in our nation's capital!"

A few in the crowd clapped politely while Dawn bit back a grumble.

Another hour or so and I can head home, she silently told herself.

"Many of you have heard of the artist known as

Razor." Sasha grinned. "He was recently featured in the *New York Times* as one of the top artists of 2013 to watch. I can vouch for the fact that his creative mind knows no limits. His work is a sensual experience that cannot be replicated. That is why we are happy to announce that several of Razor's pieces will appear at our gallery during an exhibition in six months. But until then, he has benevolently agreed to give us a preview. Something to whet the appetite!"

Sasha gave a throaty chuckle and others in the crowd laughed, making Dawn shake her head in disgust.

"I'm going to hand the mike to Razor. Come up here, Razor, dear, and tell us about your work."

The crowd parted slightly and Razor strode toward the stage. He was wearing his signature stained white T-shirt and wrinkled jeans today. His shoulder-length hair was mussed. He looked like he had just crawled out of bed.

He climbed the stage steps two at a time and grabbed the mike from Sasha before leaning down to give her a kiss. Sasha abruptly turned her head to the side. The wet kiss landed on her cheek. She smiled politely at him before awkwardly patting him on the back and walking off the stage. Sasha took her place beside her husband, Teddy, who still looked pretty sour-faced. She linked her arm through Teddy's.

Razor laughed. "Oh, it's like that, huh? I see how it is, babe." He then turned toward the audience. "Well, if you know me, you know I don't believe in bullshit. I like to turn a mirror to the world and show the good, the bad, and the ugly. Nothing embodies that more than sex and power, and that's what this piece is about. People will be shocked. People will get angry. It'll . . ." His words drifted off. He smirked. "Ah, fuck it! I'm gonna stop talking. Let the piece speak for itself." He then dropped the mike and hopped down from the stage. The lights in the room lowered and the glossy curtain was pulled back.

Suddenly, the room was filled with a spectrum of neon lights. Old-fashioned signs from strip joints from the '50s and '60s, showing half-naked women with large behinds, engorged breasts, and in seductive poses were stacked on top of one another creating a wall of nudity. Between several of the signs were television monitors that were filled with static. A woman's face suddenly flashed on all of the TVs.

"*Yeeeeees,* Razor!" she moaned, before the camera panned back, revealing Razor crouched behind her. The couple was obviously having sex.

Dawn cringed. She wasn't conservative by any means, but she wasn't sure how a porn show constituted art. She glanced up at Percy, watching his face in the flashing neon lights. He looked totally enraptured.

Why am I not surprised, she thought dryly.

The monitors flashed several more pornographic scenes starring Razor and more than one sad, misguided young woman, and Dawn drifted off, losing interest. She pulled back her jacket sleeve and glanced down at her watch. She wondered if she'd make it home in enough time to catch the black-and-white movie marathon she had planned to watch tonight.

Dawn heard Sasha's voice and looked up, assuming that Sasha was announcing the end of the presentation.

Thank God, Dawn thought.

Instead, Dawn saw Sasha's face on the video screens. The camera panned back and there was Sasha on all fours, crawling naked across the hardwood floors of Razor's bedroom. Dawn gawked.

"Holy shit," someone muttered behind Dawn.

"Umm, is this for real?" someone else whispered.

"Bark!" Razor shouted off camera. "Bark, bitch!"

"*Arrf! Arrf!*" Sasha barked like some demented Chihuahua, still crawling toward him. She wiggled her behind. "*Grrrrr! Arrf! Arrf!*"

At that, Dawn almost spit out her Moët.

"What the . . . What the hell is this?" Sasha's husband, Teddy, shouted in the darkened room. "What is the meaning of this?"

The murmurs in the crowd grew even louder.

And it only got worse. Razor had obviously taped everything he and Sasha had done together in his apartment that night and he hadn't spared any footage. Sasha should have gotten a nomination for the porn awards because she certainly went all out.

Dawn started to hear a ruckus near the stage.

"You . . . you *whore!*"

"Wait! Teddy! Teddy, it's a mistake!" Sasha yelled. "Honey, don't—"

"Get . . . off of me! Don't touch me!" he yelled back. "You'll be hearing from my lawyer!"

Teddy then stormed off, shoving his way through the crowd toward the gallery's front door.

Dawn stood wide-eyed, looking at the scene around her, absolutely stunned. And to just think, if she had sex with Razor that night, he would have taped her too.

Dodged a bullet on that one, girl!

Sasha, who hadn't been as lucky, stomped up the stage stairs and strode to the monitors. "Turn it off!" she shouted, over the sound of her recorded moans and high-pitched squeals. She turned toward the audience. Her normally cool demeanor was gone. She was practically frothing at the mouth. "Goddamn it, Razor! Turn this fucking thing off! Right now!"

"But it's art, babe!" he said with a chuckle. "It's the *truth!* Don't try to silence the truth."

"You little son of a bitch!" she screeched as Razor continued to laugh. "I will sue you! I will *ruin* you!"

"Now, Sasha, calm down," Martin called in a placating voice from the edge of the stage. He climbed the steps. "No one's suing anyone. Just . . . Just take a deep breath."

Meanwhile, the house lights came on and Sasha's assistant rushed toward the back of the room, trying frantically to find the button or the plug that would turn off the monitors. But Sasha didn't have patience for that. She let out another screech before shoving at one of the television screens. It pivoted slightly on its stand, but didn't topple over.

"Sasha!" Martin yelled, reaching for her. "Sasha, what the hell do you think you're doing? That's a *hundred-thousand-dollar* work!"

She ignored him and shoved at the television again. This time it did fall backward, landing with a thud and the sound of breaking glass. The crowd let out a collective gasp and stepped back from the stage as they watched the whole debacle. Sasha turned and shoved at another monitor, but Martin caught her this time. He held her tight around the waist but she bucked, screamed, and kicked. She clawed at him with her red nails.

"Security!" Martin yelled. "I could . . . I could use some help up here!"

The gallery's two blank-faced security guards finally stepped into action and rushed the stage. It took all three men to finally subdue Sasha and wrestle her to the ground. A minute later, Dawn watched as they carried her arch nemesis off the stage.

Razor was still standing off to the side, laughing like the jackass that he was. Rather than drinking from a glass of champagne, he took a swig from a bottle.

"Cheers!" he shouted before turning to an attractive young woman who tapped him on the shoulder. "Well, hello, babe," he leered.

Several in the audience looked absolutely horrified by what they had just witnessed. A few who Dawn knew to be journalists and bloggers rushed from the room, madly clicking away at their phone screens and keypads.

Dawn sighed contentedly.

If she guessed correctly, come tomorrow, Sasha Duncan's name would be infamous in not only the DC art circle, but also a few across the country. Sasha would finally get the attention from the New York scene that she craved—but for all the wrong reasons.

Dawn felt as if she had just received an early Christmas present all wrapped with a pretty bow.

"Well, that was . . . interesting," Percy said flatly.

"Wasn't it?" Dawn replied, giving a mischievous grin. "Damn, I love art!"

Chapter 30

Stephanie and Keith had arrived in Miami late in the afternoon, and Stephanie had made quick business of getting reacquainted with one of her favorite cities. She had visited Miami a few times with one of her ex-boyfriends, but didn't mention that to Keith. Instead, like Keith, she rolled down the windows and looked around wide-eyed at sultry downtown Miami with its palm trees and its riverwalk. She gazed up at the high-rises and scanned the high-end boutiques and beautiful tan pedestrians who strolled along the sidewalks. She loved the city's cosmopolitan Latin and Caribbean flavor. She always had. Too bad she wasn't here for fun, though she planned to enjoy steamy Miami and all it had to offer when their search for Isaac ended. For now, they were there to find the conman and, as Keith kept reminding her, "finding that S.O.B. in Miami will be as easy as finding a needle in a haystack."

Keith was struggling to figure out where they should start. "It's not like we can stand on some random street corner showing everyone his picture," he had muttered.

So Stephanie suggested that they instead focus on places where the victims Isaac usually targeted would frequent.

"How about ritzy day spas and hair salons?" she had suggested that evening as they sat at a small dinette table in a Cuban sandwich shop. They shared a plate of plantain chips between them. Stephanie took a sip of mango juice from her Styrofoam cup. "What do you think?" she asked.

"You know . . ." Keith tilted his head and shoved a forkful of rice and beans into his mouth. He chewed. "That's not a bad idea." He wiped his mouth with a paper napkin. "So you're as smart as you are beautiful."

She proudly raised her chin. "I try."

"I guess the plan then is for you to go into these spas and salons and start asking questions? See if anyone has run into Isaac?"

"I get to do it?" She grinned. "You mean like a *real* detective?"

She had gotten a taste of what Keith did for a living when she talked to Big Red, but doing something like this would mean going around with a picture of Isaac and asking strangers if they had seen him—like a real gumshoe. It sounded so exciting!

"I don't see why not," he said, eating more of his food. "You've been doing a pretty good job so far. There's no reason to hold you back now."

She paused and squinted. "Wait. Can I do this type of stuff? I mean . . . Is it legal? I'm not licensed."

"Well, technically, my license stopped working

once I crossed the Virginia border. In the state of Florida, neither of us is really considered a 'detective.' So hey, by all means, give it a try. Anyone's allowed to ask questions, right?"

She clapped her hands excitedly. "Private Investigator Stephanie Gibbons. I like the sound of that! I can't wait! It's going to be so much fun!"

He slowly shook his head and regarded her with amusement. "We'll see if you feel that way a few days from now, sweetheart."

Keith was right. Stephanie would soon regret her words. She quickly discovered that detective work wasn't as fun or as easy as it seemed. Though she went to great lengths to look the part of a wealthy woman of leisure with her dark-tinted glasses, high heels, a flouncy sunhat and expensive maxi dress, it didn't mean things ran smoothly when she walked into the snooty salons and spas around town. She didn't always get the chance to ask her questions, even when she attempted to do it inconspicuously. One salon threw her out for soliciting even though she had tried to explain that she wasn't selling anything. Another spa asked her to leave because she was upsetting the clients.

"Sorry, the oxygen infusion process doesn't work as well when the clients are distressed," one aesthetician had explained to Stephanie as she was escorted out of the facials area.

Another salon owner was a lot less polite. She threatened to call the police if Stephanie didn't leave the premises immediately. After a few days of footwork at more than two dozen high-end establishments spanning from South Beach to Coconut Grove, all Stephanie had to show for it was several manicures, a few pedicures, and newly highlighted hair. She still hadn't found any new information about Isaac.

Her ego was bruised and battered. She felt like a complete and utter failure.

"My feet are killing me!" Stephanie cried after flopping face first onto their king-sized hotel bed at the end of one particularly bad day of investigating.

They were back to sharing a room again. Their current hotel room was on the twenty-third floor of one of the high-rise hotels in downtown Miami near the convention center. They had a view of the river and at night they occasionally heard the thud of the drawbridge nearby as trucks passed over the steel grates.

Keith sat on the bed beside her and slowly pulled off her high-heeled sandals from her feet. "Rough day?" he asked, fighting back a smile.

"The worst," she mumbled into the comforter then raised her head. She gazed up at him with saddened eyes. "How do you do it?"

He started to massage her feet. "How do I do what?"

"How do you do this detective thing?" She paused to close her eyes, loving the feel of his strong hands on her worn soles. She then slowly opened her eyes again. "People are either paranoid about me asking them questions, or just plain rude! Some of them wouldn't even look at the picture of Isaac I was trying to show them! It would've taken only a few seconds of their time, but they acted like they couldn't be bothered."

"Well, it's not a job that's meant for everybody," he conceded as his healing hands shifted to her calves, raising the hem of her dress as he massaged her tense muscles. "But you just have to keep at it. It just takes time."

"I know," she grumbled. "But I feel like we've been at this for weeks. I thought we were at the finish line."

"We might not be, honey. Isaac might not even be in Miami. We could be searching for a man who's not even here."

"*Ugh,* don't say that!" she cried, dropping her head back to the bed. "Please!"

"You have to face that possibility, baby."

"I know! I know! But I don't want to," she said sullenly.

"Look, don't think about any of that tonight. Focus on tomorrow. Tomorrow's another day and another opportunity to find Isaac. Plus, we agreed to at least give it a week before we discussed giving up and moving on to somewhere else." He lowered her legs back to the bed and rose to his feet. "So come on. Get undressed."

She raised her head again, turned to look at him, and frowned quizzically at his abrupt subject change. "Huh?"

"You need to relax. Get undressed," he said again, pointing to her clothes. "I'll turn down the lights. Make a bubble bath then . . ." His smile broadened, revealing the dimples she so loved. ". . . We'll see where it goes."

"*We'll see where it goes?*" She snorted. "Keith, you know damn well where it will go! It'll end up with me bent over the edge of the bathtub. That's usually what happens anyway."

His eyes twinkled mischievously. "We can stay in the water, if you prefer."

"Why do men think everything can be solved with sex?"

He shrugged. "Because it usually can be."

She shook her head then pursed her lips. She contemplated his offer. If there was anything that could make her feel better, she knew that it was Keith's warm embrace. She seemed to forget everything when she was wrapped in his arms or moaning beneath him.

She slowly pushed herself to her elbows and stood. "All right," she said, raising her hands to the strings around her neck that were holding up her maxi dress, "but only because you insist."

Stephanie took a deep breath before tugging open one of the double glass doors of the Salon de la Agua. After a few days of doing this, each salon and spa started to blend into the next. They all had the same soothing techno muzak playing in the background. All the stylists and aestheticians were dressed head-to-toe in black. Everyone who worked in these establishments was so stylish and thin they looked like they had just stepped out of the pages of the fashion magazines their clients were browsing as the women waited to get their hair or nails done. But this particular salon had the distinction of having a floor-to-ceiling waterfall in the center of the room. Stephanie gaped in wonder as she stared at it.

"Hi, can I help you?" the perky blonde at the black-marble front desk asked.

Stephanie tore her eyes away from the waterfall and looked at the receptionist. "Uh, yes." She took off her sunglasses. "I don't have an appointment, but

I wondered if any of your stylists were open today. I just need a shampoo and a trim."

The blonde looked at her contemptuously. "Well, we usually don't do same-day appointments, ma'am. Many of our stylists are booked months in advance, but I'll see what I can do." The receptionist took her name and leaned her head toward their waiting area. "You can have a seat over there."

Stephanie nodded and walked across the room to the sleek Bauhaus chairs in the corner. Two other women were sitting in the waiting area: a busty Latina brunette with big, long hair and a tall, thin redhead with a blunt bob. Stephanie smiled at them politely.

"Hi," Stephanie said as she sat down.

The Latina nodded and grinned. The redhead ignored her, peering down instead at the cell phone in her hands.

"Do you two have appointments?"

"Yes, with Marisol," the Latina volunteered. "She's one of the best stylists they have in here, but I guess she's running a little late today."

The redhead only nodded.

"Yeah, I don't have one, unfortunately," Stephanie said. "I wish I did though. But I've been so busy lately I haven't been able to schedule anything." She reached into her purse and retrieved a three-by-five-inch picture. "You see I'm looking for someone . . . the guy in this photo. I wondered if either of you have seen him around."

The Latina leaned forward and peered at the picture of Isaac. "No, I haven't seen him. Sorry."

"Doesn't look familiar," the redhead said. She had finally looked up from her cell phone. "Are you a process server?"

Stephanie paused, taken aback by the question. "No. Why?"

"Uh-huh," the redhead said, looking as if she didn't believe Stephanie. "Look, if you *are* a process server and you're here to serve divorce papers, this is an incredibly tacky place to do it. My ex did that when I was getting a body wrap two years ago."

The Latina raised her hand to her bubble-gum pink lips in astonishment. "*Oh, no!* Are you kidding?"

"I most definitely am not! There I was wrapped in seaweed and some asshole comes walking up with a stack of papers in his hand."

Stephanie quickly shook her head. "No, really, I'm not serving divorce papers. It's nothing like that. I'm just—"

"All the women in the exfoliating room were staring at me," the redhead continued angrily. Her face turned as red as her hair. "I was so humiliated! I will *never* forgive my ex-husband for doing that to me! Never!"

"I wouldn't either," the Latina said.

"Miss Gibbons? Miss Gibbons?" the receptionist called.

Stephanie rolled her eyes, wondering if the receptionist had overheard their conversation and if she was about to be kicked out of yet another hair salon. She rose to her feet. She slowly walked back to the receptionist desk, ready to be escorted to the front door. But the blonde was smiling.

"You're in luck, Miss Gibbons," she said. "One of our stylists just came open. That rarely if ever happens around here."

"Great!" Stephanie exclaimed, relieved that she wasn't being shown the door for once.

Minutes later she was escorted across the salon to the chair of a young stylist with a spiked haircut. "So all you need is a wash and a trim, huh?" the young woman asked.

As Stephanie sipped the salon's complimentary green tea and sat in her styling chair discussing the layered hairstyle she wanted, she managed to show Isaac's picture to a few more people, including her stylist and the women sitting beside her, but none of them had seen him.

Soon after a cape was draped over her chest, she was escorted to the shampoo bowls where a bronze-skinned, dark-haired Adonis awaited.

"Hey," he said with an impossibly white smile. "I'm Rafael. I'll be shampooing you today."

He guided Stephanie to his shampoo bowl. She sat down and lowered her head. Rafael turned on the water and began to massage in the lavender-scented shampoo. She cooed as he kneaded and caressed her scalp. So he was cute *and* he knew how to pamper a girl. She knew plenty of women in Chesterton who would die to sit with their heads in his bowl—if you got her drift.

"You like that?" Rafael asked huskily as he ran the spray of hot water over her hair.

"*Mmmm hmmm,*" Stephanie moaned.

"I'm known as magic fingers around here."

"I bet you are!"

He continued to wash her hair and Stephanie continued to enjoy it.

"Can I ask you something?" he asked five minutes into the wash.

"Sure."

"Why do you have a picture of Manny's boyfriend?"

"I'm sorry. *Who?*"

"Manny's boyfriend, Devon. That's who's in the photo, right?"

Stephanie's eyes shot open. She suddenly raised her head out of the shampoo bowl. Soapsuds and water oozed down her temple and neck. It almost ran into her eyes, but she didn't care. She turned and gazed at Rafael in disbelief.

"You recognize the guy in this picture?" she asked Rafael, holding up the photo she was still clutching in her hand. She had hoped to inconspicuously show it to the woman getting her hair washed beside her. "You *know* this guy?"

Rafael nodded, looking confused as to why she was so surprised. "Sure, I see him with Manny at Coco Locos three days a week. They're usually hiding in the VIP section. I told you . . . They're an item."

Stephanie wanted to jump up and down with joy. Rafael had seen Isaac! After days of searching and going to so many salons and spas she had almost lost count, she had finally hit the jackpot!

"Devon's kind of a jerk though. Always walks around with his nose in the air," Rafael continued with a curl of disgust in his lip. "Personally, I think Manny's too good for him. Manny could do so much better."

"*Manny?* Who . . . Who's she?"

"Not *she*, honey. *He!*"

Stephanie's eyes bulged out of her head. Isaac was dating *a man?*

"His name is Manny. He's Manuel Alvarez."

She gazed at him blankly.

"You know . . . the famous developer." He paused. "You aren't from around here, are you?"

"No, I'm from Virginia."

"Well, Manny is a big guy here in Miami . . . owns lots of real estate around Miami Beach and South Beach. He and *mi novio* have worked together on a few deals. That's how I know him. He's also part owner of Coco Locos. I go there all the time. It's got a good vibe. It's one of the best gay clubs in town."

Isaac would do a lot of things to make a buck: lie, cheat, even get into the pants of sixty-year-old women. But she found it hard to believe that he also was willing to seduce men to thicken his wallet. He had seemed so . . . so straight.

"Yeah," a voice in her head chided, "well, he seemed to be a lot of things that he wasn't."

She held the picture toward Rafael.

"You're definitely sure it's him? *This* is Manny's boyfriend?"

Rafael didn't hesitate before nodding again. "Sure, it's him. Devon doesn't have the goatee anymore, but trade the suit for a low-cut tank top and Rock & Republic denim jeans and you've got that queen! There's no mistaking it."

Stephanie lowered her head back into the shampoo bowl, gazed blankly at the ceiling, and let the news about Isaac sink in. This was a plot twist she certainly hadn't anticipated. She bet Keith would be shocked to hear it too.

"So you never explained why you have his picture," Rafael persisted, rinsing her hair again.

"Ummm, well, I've . . ." She hesitated. "I've been looking for him."

"Looking for him? Has Devon done something wrong?" He turned off the water and made a *tsk, tsk* sound. He grabbed one of the dark towels off the wooden shelf behind him. "I swear there's something about that guy that has always rubbed me the wrong way. When I met him, he seemed so shady."

"Well, don't tell anyone I told you this," she whispered, deciding to be honest with Rafael since he didn't seem particularly fond of Isaac either—or *Devon*, as he was calling himself now. "But he's wanted by the police in Virginia. I've been tracking him down for weeks."

"Wait. *You're a cop?*"

"No, I'm a private detective . . . sort of."

Rafael grinned as he dried her hair. "I didn't know they had detectives as cute as you."

She winked. "If you're angling to get a big tip, it's working."

"So I guess you want to know where you can find Devon."

"If you're willing to tell me . . ." She shrugged. "Sure!"

He wrapped the towel around her neck and patted her shoulder. "I will not only tell you where to find him, but I'll write down the address and give you directions. Wait right here."

Stephanie grinned as she watched Rafael walk across the salon. She clapped her hands triumphantly.

An hour and a half later, Stephanie rushed back to the hotel to tell Keith what she had learned that morning. She had gotten the address for Manuel's villa in South Beach from Rafael. She raced into the hotel room, making Keith look up from his lunch at her in surprise. She was so excited that all she could do was jump up and down.

Keith stood from his chair and held up his hand. "Calm down, baby. Take a deep breath."

She did what he said and slowly breathed in, then out. When she did, she felt a lot calmer.

"Now," he said slowly. "Tell me what happened."

When she finished telling Keith the story Rafael had told her, Keith stared at her. He looked absolutely stunned.

"His next mark is *a man?*"

She nodded and kicked off her high heels. "Looks like it. Rafael said they've been dating only a couple of weeks. He gave Manny and all his friends some cock and bull story about being an actor from California."

"But a man!" Keith exclaimed, still shaking his head. He slumped back into his chair. "*Seriously?*"

"Manny may be a man, but think about it, Keith! He fits the description of all the other victims Isaac targeted. Manny's unattached and supposed to be pretty wealthy." She tilted her head. "In fact, if Manny was straight, I probably would have tracked him down myself."

Keith chuckled. "He *does* sound like your type."

Stephanie leaned down and kissed him. She then sat in his lap and wrapped her arms around his neck. "Not anymore. I like average Joes who drive old, beat up SUVs and are really, *really* good in bed."

"Well, that's much appreciated." He laughed again then quickly grew somber. "All right, so we should probably plan on heading there tonight. Maybe we can finally get a glimpse of Isaac."

"You mean like a . . . a *real* stakeout?"

"Sure, we can call it a stakeout, if you want."

She untangled her arms from around his neck and instantly jumped to her feet. "Great! I have the perfect outfit!"

Keith raised an eyebrow. "Huh?"

"Just give me time to change!" she shouted before raising the hem of her dress and rushing toward their hotel bathroom. She then pulled her dress over her head and tossed it to the floor.

Chapter 31

"So is there any reason why you're wearing all black?" Keith asked as he glanced over at Stephanie. She could tell he was fighting back a smile.

She was sitting in the passenger seat beside him wearing a tight-fitting, black T-shirt, black Capris, and a black beret. She gazed at him quizzically.

"You said we were going on a stakeout," she said, tucking her hair behind her ear. "What's wrong? Did I wear the wrong outfit?"

He slowly shook his head in bemusement.

They were parked across the street behind a line of cars, not far from the wrought-iron gates of Manny's Moorish-style villa. They had been hunkered down for almost an hour, sitting in the dark, waiting for Isaac. Stephanie was starting to feel a little anxious. It was odd to know that after all this time and after all they had been through, their journey might be finally coming to an end.

"Did you ever think two months ago that you'd be doing something like this?" Keith asked quietly, reading her thoughts.

She shook her head and giggled as she gazed out the car's windshield. "Nope. I thought I was well on my way to seducing a rich financial consultant and becoming Mrs. Isaac Beardan." She turned to Keith. "But in some ways, I'm glad things didn't turn out the way that I planned."

"*Really?*" he asked, raising his brows.

"Yep. I mean . . . I still want my sixty thousand dollars back and for that bastard to rot in jail, but I don't think I would have been happy with Isaac, even if he turned out to be the real thing and not a conman. That life was . . ." She paused, searching for the right word. ". . . empty. *I* was empty. It had to end. You gotta grow up eventually."

Keith leaned back in his chair. A smile slowly crept to his lips. "What brought you to this conclusion?"

"I don't know. Maybe going through all this stuff helped me to figure it out." She shrugged. "I mean I've done more stuff in the past week than I ever thought I was capable of doing. Maybe falling in love did it too. It makes me see things differently now."

He trailed a finger along her cheek. "You're an amazing woman, Stephanie Gibbons."

She grinned and leaned toward him, gazing into his eyes. "It's about damn time you realized that."

"Oh, I realized it. I just tried really hard to deny it."

"Why?"

"Because just like you were set in your ways, so was I. It's been just me and only me for a very long time, Steph. Mike keeps ragging on me about it, but I admit that it's true. I was a single, independent guy and I liked it that way. No commitment . . . a few one-night stands . . ."

She frowned. *One night stands? OK, he's going to have to clarify that later.*

"I haven't been in a serious relationship with a woman in a very long time . . . probably not ever, if I really think about it. To let someone else wedge themselves into my life isn't something that I'm used to."

"So am I wedging into your life? And more importantly . . . Am I getting in?"

"More and more every day," he whispered before lowering his mouth to hers.

They kissed and she felt the familiar tingle that she always felt when he touched her lips. She hoped he would continue to let her into his life, because she didn't know what she would do with herself if she had to let go of this man.

The kiss deepened and she suddenly wished that they were back in their hotel room so they could go a lot further. Too bad they were stuck in some SUV staking out Manny's house, waiting for Isaac.

Isaac! Is that Isaac? Stephanie thought with alarm when she heard the sound of a car's engine. Her eyes fluttered open and she pushed herself away from Keith. She turned to see a black Bentley pulling up to the gate. The words TOO HOT were on the license plate.

"Oh, my God, Keith! I think it's him! I think we finally found him!"

She and Keith watched as the driver's-side window of the Bentley slowly lowered. And then it finally happened. After about a month on the road searching for him, she finally saw Isaac and she instantly saw red. The rage against him that had been bottled up for weeks and weeks suddenly burst to the surface.

She watched as he leaned out of the car window and punched a code into the gate's wall panel. The villa's automatic gates then began to slide open.

Stephanie didn't know what had taken over her, but the instant she saw Isaac drive his Bentley inside the property, she threw open the SUV's door and bolted.

"Stephanie!" Keith whispered shrilly after her. "Stephanie, what the hell are you doing?"

She didn't answer him. She didn't have time to respond.

She wasn't sure where she had found the strength or the ability to run that fast, but she did—making the distance from the SUV to the front gate in less than ten seconds. She made it inside the villa's grounds just as the gate slid closed behind her.

Keith was probably thinking she had lost her mind, but there was no turning back now. She was officially trespassing, but she was on a mission. Seeing Isaac wasn't enough. She *had* to confront him.

Stephanie bent forward with her hands on her knees and took several deep breaths. That run had taken a lot out of her. She rested her hand over her rapidly beating heart and closed her eyes. After a few seconds, her heart slowed its pace. She took her final deep breath and stood upright. She squinted and looked around her.

With the exception of a few floodlights near the double doors of the villa, it was pretty dark outside. The decorative foliage on the grounds created many shadows. It made it a challenge to see around her, but the darkness was the coverage she needed if she didn't want anyone to catch her.

She watched as Isaac threw open the driver's-side door of the Bentley and stepped out. Panicked that he would see her, Stephanie instantly shifted, squatted, and hid behind a hibiscus bush and a palm tree. She pushed a few leaves aside and gawked at him.

Isaac certainly looked different. His goatee was gone, just like the shampoo guy Rafael had said. Isaac also had given up the perfectly tailored suits she remembered him wearing back in Chesterton and was now sporting a white T-shirt with a deep V collar that showed off his pecs and waxed chest. His jeans were so tight you could almost see the imprint of his balls even from this distance. He wore a garish silver chain around his neck with a giant gothic cross that dangled near his navel and a leather cuff on his wrist with silver studs.

The man was certainly a chameleon. He barely resembled the Isaac she remembered from back home.

She watched as Isaac shut his car door behind him, locked it with a loud beep, and tossed a leather jacket over his shoulder. He then casually strolled to the villa's front doors.

Stephanie crept up the winding driveway, walking past the trickling water fountain then the Bentley. Just as Isaac inserted his key and pushed opened the villa's front door, she ran behind him, giving him a hard shove that sent him careening into the marble-tiled foyer.

"What the hell?" he shouted then suddenly whipped around to face her.

Before he could get his bearings, Stephanie balled her fist and gave him the hardest punch she could muster—a right hook to his jaw. It sent him stumbling backward again.

Her hand hurt like hell, but the punch had made her proud.

"Oww!" Isaac screamed, raising his hand to his mouth. He then raised his gaze and looked up at his assailant. Isaac's brown eyes almost popped out of his head when he saw her standing there.

"*Stephanie?*" he squeaked.

"You goddamn right it's me, you son of a bitch! Where the hell is my money? Where is it?"

"Stephanie, what . . . What are you doing here?" he asked, taking several hesitant steps back. "How did you find me?"

"That's all you have to say to me?" she yelled as she stalked toward him. "What the hell do you think I'm doing here, Isaac . . . or Devon . . . or Reggie . . . or whatever the fuck your name really is? I want my money!"

He shook his head. "I don't kn-know what you're talking about, Steph. What money?"

"Bullshit! You know damn well what I'm talking about! Your conman days are over! You have messed with the wrong chick! You stole sixty thousand dollars from me! So either you give me my damn money," she said, pointing her finger into his muscled chest, "or I'm taking it out of your hide!" She then balled her sore fist again and held it up menacingly.

Isaac's mouth fell open in astonishment.

"Why is this woman screaming at the top of her lungs in my home, *querido?*" a voice suddenly boomed from above them.

Stephanie and Isaac looked up.

A patrician-looking man who was in his late fifties or early sixties stood at the top of the double staircase with one hand perched casually on the wrought-iron banister and the other hand holding a wineglass. He slowly walked down the stairs toward them.

He was wearing a white linen shirt, tan drawstring pants, and brown leather sandals. His skin was wrinkled but he had a healthy tan. His white hair was cropped short. When he descended the last riser, Stephanie saw that he barely stood five feet tall.

"Why is this woman here?" he asked Isaac. He then glanced at Stephanie.

"I have no idea, darling," Isaac said, holding his mouth again.

Stephanie's brows furrowed angrily.

"She followed me inside. She just started hitting me for no reason."

"No reason?" Stephanie screeched. "You know damn well why I hit you, Isaac! You're lucky that's all I did!"

"Manny, you stay here with her, while I call the police," Isaac said as he took a few steps across the foyer. "I want her arrested."

"Yes, Isaac, call the damn police!" Stephanie shouted. "And while you're at it tell them about the money you stole from me, the diamonds you stole from that other woman in Maryland, and all the other women you seduced to get *their* money!"

Manny gazed at Stephanie, absolutely stunned. "Devon, what is she talking about?" He narrowed his eyes at Stephanie. "And why do you keep calling him Isaac?"

"I'm calling him Isaac because that's the name he gave me when we were dating. But that's not his real name. Devon isn't his real name either. He always changes his name when he's running a new con."

"What?" Isaac exclaimed, looking horrified by her

accusation. If she wasn't so angry she would have laughed at his shoddy performance. "She's delusional, baby!"

"Manny," Stephanie said, earnestly gazing at the short man, "he's conning you now just like he conned me a little more than a month ago. I know now that he's done this so many times that even he has probably lost count."

"Lies!" Isaac shouted. "All lies, Manny! This woman is insane!"

"It took weeks to track him down and trace him here," Stephanie continued. "He stole my money. He told me his name was Isaac Beardan and that he was a financial planner. He told me lie after lie after lie. He gained my trust and he stole my savings."

Manny seemed to study her, gauging whether she was telling the truth.

"Baby, you're not actually listening to this crap, are you?" Isaac yelled, pointing at her. "You wouldn't take her word over mine, would you?"

Manny stayed silent.

"I have no idea who this woman is or why she's saying these things!" Isaac insisted, feigning being hurt. "You have to believe me, baby! I've never seen her before in my entire life before today! She—"

"So why did you call her Stephanie?" Manny asked quietly, turning his penetrating gaze back to Isaac.

Isaac paused. "Wha-what?"

"Before I came downstairs, I overheard you call her Stephanie." He turned to look at Stephanie and pursed his lips. "That *is* your name, isn't it?"

She nodded. "Yes, Stephanie Gibbons."

Manny glared at Isaac. "How did you know her name, *querido,* if you two have never met before?"

Isaac's face clouded with alarm. "Umm, I . . . Well, I—"

"Don't lie to me," Manny said firmly, holding up an index finger in warning. "Just answer my question. Do you know this woman? Did you steal money from her?"

Isaac took a deep breath. He looked at Manny then looked at Stephanie then back at Manny again. He knew when he was cornered. His shoulders slumped. "Honey, let me explain."

Manny slowly closed his eyes. "That's all the explanation I need," he said, shaking his head. "Miss Gibbons, would you please follow me? *Querido,* you can come too."

Manny then slowly walked toward a room adjacent to the foyer. He took a sip from his glass as he went. The soft flap of his sandals echoed off the marble floor in the foyer.

Stephanie and Isaac glanced at one another in surprise. Manny seemed to be taking the news about Isaac being a conman pretty well. Stephanie hadn't expected him to start screaming and throwing things—which was definitely more her style—but she hadn't expected this subdued reaction either.

She followed Manny into the adjacent room, which turned out to be a home office. Isaac trailed behind her.

The space was opulently decorated with lush leather furniture and floor-to-ceiling wooden bookshelves filled with volumes upon volumes of books. All the books had antiqued leather and gold binding that made them look like they should be on the auction block at Christie's or Sotheby's. Several expensive-looking pieces of art hung on the walls and a few small sculptures decorated the room.

Stephanie understood now why Isaac had targeted Manny. The man obviously had a lot of bank.

She watched as Manny walked to the large desk in the center of the office.

"You don't have to explain anything to me," Manny said as he set down his glass and opened one of the desk drawers. "I've seen plenty of beautiful young men pushed into these situations before."

Stephanie frowned. *Huh?*

"The world can be cruel. It leaves you with little options. Some young men turn to these games in order to survive. They use their pretty faces to their advantage." He pulled out a gold pen and check-book. He then gazed at Isaac. "Believe me. I understand. I'm not judging you."

Stephanie's mouth fell open in shock. *You've got to be kidding me,* she thought with frustration.

"*Querido,* whatever you have done in the past means nothing to me. You will always have a place in my home and in my heart. You don't have to steal or play these games anymore. I will take care of you." He suddenly ripped off a check he had been writing and held it out to Stephanie. "Is this enough?"

She gazed down at the check and saw that it was written for one hundred thousand dollars. Her mouth dropped even lower to the point that her chin was almost on her chest. She gazed at Manny, utterly aghast.

"Why are you giving this to me?"

Manny cocked an eyebrow. "I'm giving this to you so that you have more than enough money to cover your loss . . . because I want you to take this check and leave us alone. My giving you this money is contingent upon that promise from you. You will not follow Devon anymore. You will leave him at peace."

"But didn't you hear what I said? He's conning you too! He's doing the same thing to you that he did to all of us! You're no different!"

"Sweetheart, what he did with you women was just a performance." Manny smirked and raised his nose triumphantly into the air. He then walked around the desk toward Isaac. He wrapped an arm possessively around the younger man's trim waist. "What he and I have is *real* passion . . . *true* love."

Stephanie then stared dumbfounded as the tiny man stood on the balls of his feet and kissed Isaac with the same passion he professed. To Isaac's credit, he didn't flinch. He leaned down and kissed Manny back just as earnestly.

Stephanie felt as if she had just stepped into the Twilight Zone.

Manny pulled his mouth away from Isaac and licked his lips. "Now if you would please take this check and leave," Manny said, holding it out to her again. "I had planned to have a quiet evening at home with my fiancé and you are ruining that prospect."

"*Fiancé?*" Stephanie squeaked.

Isaac proudly held up his left hand and smiled, showing a silver wedding band. "We're having the nuptials in New York next month."

Stephanie shook her head. Some people couldn't be helped. She had tried to save Isaac's next victim from a similar fate as her own, but he was hell-bent on the idea that he and Isaac were truly in love. She had been lulled by the same stupidity and the same hubris. She could sympathize—a little.

Pride goes before the fall, she thought. But that didn't mean *she* shouldn't be made whole in this crazy situation.

"Fine," Stephanie said, snatching the check out of Manny's hand. She then folded it and tucked it into her bosom. "But don't say I didn't warn you."

"You're a real piece of work," Stephanie mumbled.

Isaac gave a sly, self-congratulatory smirk as he held her arm and dragged her back to the villa's front gate. "Aren't I?"

Isaac was escorting her off the property per his fiancé's instruction. Manny stood silently in his study window, watching them as they went. Stephanie glared up at Isaac, wishing she could punch him in the jaw all over again.

"Oh, come on! Don't look so mad, Steph!" Isaac said. "You'll leave this whole nightmare forty thousand dollars richer! Now tell me that isn't a good thing."

"That's not the point! It's *his* money, not yours! He did this for you because he's in love with you, Isaac! This isn't just some game to him! Don't you feel like shit taking advantage of him like this? Have you ever felt bad for what you've done?"

Isaac sucked his teeth as they walked. "Oh, please, honey! *A lecture from you?* How many men have you taken advantage of in *your* life, Stephanie Gibbons? How many men did you pretend to love to get money from them? You're just as much of a con artist as I am. I knew what you were the minute I laid eyes on you."

"But I never stole from them!"

"No, you just lied, connived, and seduced." A smile crept back to his lips. "You know . . . you and I aren't much different, Steph."

She cringed in disgust.

"And out of all of my cons, I admit, you were one of my favorites. I had a lot of fun with you, gorgeous—in the bedroom and out." He ran his thumb gently along her forearm. "I could teach you a thing or two about how to run the hustle, how to do it properly. You're pretty good, but you still could use a few pointers in how to pleasure a man." He smirked. "Sometimes your performances were a little . . . uninspired, shall we say."

"Go to hell," she spat.

Isaac chuckled. "Oh, if you weren't so angry, you could see that there are real possibilities here, Steph! I'm offering you a great opportunity, gorgeous. Think about it . . . We could do these cons together. Play off of one another. We could be partners! We could be a team!"

She gazed up at him in bewilderment. *He's actually serious,* she thought. Did he conveniently forget that he had lied to her and stolen money from her, or did he just expect her to forget?

"You and me—*together!* Can you imagine the damage we could do? We'd be unstoppable, Steph! Come on, what do you say? You willing to put old offenses aside for an opportunity like this? You game, gorgeous?"

As they drew closer to the gate, she saw Keith standing on the other side. He was clutching the wrought iron in his fists and gazing at her worriedly.

"No, thanks," she said to Isaac. "I already have a partner."

"Steph, are you all right?" Keith shouted. "Did they hurt you?" He then glared at Isaac. "Open the god-damn gate, you son of a bitch!"

Isaac instantly paused. The unease and dismay showed on his handsome face. "What the hell is *he* doing here?"

"I couldn't do this alone. I had to hire a detective. It only made sense to hire the guy who was already tracking you down."

"Damn it," Isaac snarled.

"Yeah, so guess that means you'll be on the run again, huh?"

"Probably," he muttered.

The two men stood glowering at one another.

"Isaac," Stephanie said, nudging him, "open the gate."

He swallowed loudly before finally pressing a button along the driveway's stucco wall. The gate slowly slid open and Stephanie instantly yanked her arm out of Isaac's grasp. She ran toward Keith, but he was faster in closing the distance between them. He wrapped her in his arms and picked her up. He kissed her so hard it knocked the breath out of her. He then pulled his mouth away so he could examine her.

"Are you OK?" he asked.

She nodded.

"Why the hell did you do that, Steph? You just ran! You scared the shit out of me! You were gone for al-most a half an hour! I thought something was hap-pening to you in there!"

She demured. "Sorry, I didn't mean to make you worry."

He kissed her again. When he pulled his mouth

away a second time, she rested her head on his shoulder and let him embrace her.

"Well, isn't this touching," Isaac murmured sarcastically, crossing his arms over his chest.

Keith shifted Stephanie aside. "You're lucky she's OK. If something happened to her, I wouldn't have waited for the cops to make an appearance this time. I would have gone in there to kick your ass myself!"

Isaac grinned. "Come on, detective. You've been following me long enough that you know roughing up women isn't my style. I'm a lover not a fighter."

"Yeah, a lover of women *and* men, so I've heard," Keith said, tilting his head. "You just love everybody, as long as they have money!"

"*And?*" Isaac answered blandly. "Is that so bad?"

"You're a leech, a parasite," Keith continued through clenched teeth. "And I look forward to the day when the cops throw your ass in jail!"

"They'd have to catch me first."

"Oh, they will. I'll make sure of it this time! And the next time I see you, you'll be prostituting yourself for a pack of cigarettes instead of a Bentley and an ugly-ass silver chain."

"Platinum," Isaac clarified dryly before giving a lofty sigh. "Look, detective, I'd love to continue this banter, but my fiancé has dinner waiting. I should head back." He turned to Stephanie. "Remember my offer, gorgeous. It still stands if you're interested."

"No thanks. I'm not," she answered succinctly.

He shrugged his shoulders. "Your decision."

Stephanie watched as Isaac turned and strolled back up the driveway. She wondered how long it would take him to high-tail it out of Miami now that he knew Keith had found him. She wondered how long it would take him to find yet another victim.

Not very long, knowing Isaac, she thought.

The gate slowly slid closed behind him. She and Keith walked back to his Ford Explorer.

"So what did he offer you?" Keith asked. His arm was still wrapped around her shoulders protectively.

"He offered to become partners. He said he could teach me to become a proper con artist because I needed the training."

"He's a real piece of work," Keith murmured as they reached the SUV.

"Yeah, that's what I said."

Keith opened the driver's-side door and climbed inside. "So I guess you talked to his boyfriend, Manny, too? How'd that go down?"

Stephanie opened the passenger-side door and climbed inside. She then told the story of her encounter with Manny. When she finished, Keith sat gazing at her, dumbfounded.

"Wait, so he wasn't angry? He actually made excuses for him?" Keith asked.

"He insists that he and Isaac are in love. Isaac must have really worked his magic on him."

"I guess so."

"You should have seen it, Keith! Isaac really knows how to work it. He tongued that little shrimp down right in front of me. If I didn't know what a liar Isaac was, I would have believed he was really into him too."

"Uh-huh. Well, I'm glad I missed that one," Keith muttered as he inserted his key into the ignition. He turned on the engine. "I also suggest you cash that check as soon as possible. Manny's probably going to put a hold on it as soon as Isaac is arrested."

"That's *if* Isaac gets arrested. I bet he'll be out of town again by tomorrow night. The police in Virginia and Florida may not get things coordinated by then."

"Maybe not . . . but the FBI will," Keith said as they pulled off.

Stephanie frowned. *"The FBI?"*

"Yeah, while you were going to salons and spas, I wasn't just sitting on my hands all day. Mike suggested I get in touch with the FBI since it's an interstate deal now. I used one of my old contacts at the ATF and managed to get a meeting with one of the agents at the FBI's Miami field office. I explained the situation and how Isaac is wanted in Virginia, South Carolina, and it looked like now he's running a new con in Miami. The agent didn't promise me anything but he said he'd look into it." He glanced at Stephanie as he drove back to their hotel. "Once I saw you running inside, I knew the shit was about to hit the fan. Isaac would get hot feet and run out of town again. I gave the agent a quick call and said we found Isaac. Before the agent hung up the phone, he said he was on his way. I expect him, a few other FBI agents, and maybe some Miami-Dade police to be pulling up to Manny's villa any minute now."

"Well done!" Stephanie said, supremely proud of her man. "Why didn't you tell me you were doing all that stuff behind the scenes?"

"Because I *know* you! You'd get pissed enough at Isaac that you might blab to him that the FBI was on to him now too."

"I would not!" she yelled, feigning outrage.

OK, maybe I would, she thought.

"Besides," Keith said, giving her a side glance, "a man's allowed to have some secrets."

A woman is too, Stephanie thought.

That would explain why she hadn't told Keith that she should have gotten her period a week ago but as of today, she still hadn't gotten it. She'd let him bask in his victory now and drop that little bombshell later. Besides, maybe she was only late due to all the excitement in the past few weeks.

"So now that Isaac is taken care of and you're swimming in cash, what do you say we spend a couple of days just enjoying Miami?"

"That sounds wonderful," she gushed, gazing up at him lovingly.

"First order of business is a bubble bath though."

"Indeed."

"Maybe I can wrangle up some candles from room service."

"We have to stop and get some chocolate syrup too."

He did a double take. *"Chocolate syrup?"*

"For *before* the bubble bath," she clarified.

"Ahh! Chocolate syrup, it is."

Epilogue

Saturday brunch at Mama's was a Gibbons family tradition that had lasted as long as any of the girls could remember. Yolanda Gibbons didn't mandate that all her daughters attend brunch, but they knew they would be punished with her cold silence if they didn't.

It was a tradition that began with Althea, the family matriarch. She had started it after hearing about what the wealthy landowners in her small North Carolina town would do on the weekends to celebrate having all their family around them. When she became a wealthy woman herself several decades later and had a family of her own, she decided she would do the same.

In the past, brunch had consisted of the Gibbons girls and their mother plotting over French toast, sausage, and eggs Benedict how to chase men and take their money. But today, thanks to a few new interlopers—including Lauren's husband, Cris, and Stephanie's beau, Keith—talk of how to snag a wealthy man would have to be put on the back burner. Besides, this Saturday brunch wasn't an ordinary brunch, after all. They would be celebrating the birth of Lauren and Cris's newborn son, Crisanto Jr.

Keith pulled his Ford Explorer to a stop in the circular paved-stone driveway in front of Yolanda's mansion. He parked behind Cynthia's black Lexus SUV. The bushes of pink and white dahlias that were usually in bloom near the entrance had given way to December snow. The house looked like something found in a sketch on the front of a Christmas card. Icicles dangled underneath the portico and sparkled in the morning sun. There was a warm orange glow coming through the first-floor windows. A wreath of poinsettias and holly hung on each of the French doors.

Stephanie fussed with the bow on the baby blue, oversized, gift-wrapped package she balanced on her knees.

"I hope little Cris likes it," she murmured worriedly, fluffing the bow once more.

Keith turned off the car's ignition. "Sweetheart, he's six weeks old. The only thing he likes right now is eating, sleeping, and pooping his diapers."

She unbuckled her seatbelt. "Pardon me," she said, raising her button nose into the air haughtily. "But he is a *Gibbons,* honey. Even at a young age, we develop discerning tastes."

Keith chuckled and shook his head. "Oh, I don't doubt that you do."

Stephanie flipped down the visor in front of her and glanced at her reflection. Her makeup was flawless, but she noticed her face had been very puffy lately. Even Keith had developed the habit of calling her "Fat Cheeks" though she wasn't sure sometimes if he was referring to her face—or her derriere. It couldn't be helped though. She was now approaching the end of the seventh month of her pregnancy and she seemed to be gaining weight at a rapid pace. It seemed that every time she stepped on the scale in her bathroom nowadays, she had gained another pound. One would think that a woman as vain as herself who had once prized her perfect size 6 figure would be dismayed by her body's changes, that she would hate the swollen ankles and the stretch marks and seeing herself growing larger before her eyes. But Stephanie really didn't mind being fat and pregnant. She was happy with her baby and happy with Keith and every time the baby kicked, it was a reminder of the unexpected love and contentment she had found. This was a surprising gift and she was never one to turn away a surprise.

She had no idea a year ago that her life would turn out this way. But she knew now that life was filled with twists and turns.

She and Keith now lived in her townhome in Chesterton. Three days a week he made the commute to the Stokowski and Hendricks offices in Vienna, Virginia. The other days he worked from home. In a few weeks, he planned to work out of Chesterton permanently. He said he didn't want to be that far away from Stephanie now that their baby's birth was drawing closer. Mike didn't mind losing him. The grizzled ex-cop and private investigator had been walking around with his chest puffed out for the past several months, boasting to everyone who would listen that he was going to be a grandfather soon. Since Mike was the closest thing to a father that Keith had ever known, he would only smile and nod his head when the older man made that strange proclamation.

"Now if only you'd put a ring on that girl's damn finger, everything would be perfect," Mike had lectured Keith a week ago.

"I don't know if Stephanie and I are ready to get married quite yet," Keith had explained. "Maybe in a year or two."

Mike had grumbled in response. "Son, you're living with her and you're having a baby together. I hate to break it to you, but you *are* married. You just need to get pen to paper and make it legal."

Though the future was full of promise for Keith and Stephanie, she knew things weren't going quite as peachy for Isaac or "Lucas Edwards" according to his birth certificate, which the feds unearthed. The grand jury had met a month ago, examining the evidence in the case of *The United States of America v. Lucas Edwards*. FBI agents had unearthed a string of cons spanning from California to Puerto Rico that Lucas had committed. They dated as far back as the late '90s, back when Lucas was a teenager. The handsome conman now faced multiple counts of fraud and embezzlement for his various crimes.

Though his fiancé, Manny, had promised to stick by his side through the whole ordeal, Manny's promise didn't last for very long. The developer didn't like all the negative publicity that came with being engaged to a man who swindled more than thirty lovers out of more than a million dollars in the course of fifteen years. Manny broke off the engagement. He was now dating a nice strapping young man from Orlando whom the shampoo guy Rafael had introduced him to. By all accounts, Manny was happy with his new lover.

No longer having a wealthy benefactor, Lucas had turned to the one person he had always turned to when things got bad for him: his old flame and mentor, Myra Beaumont. But the older woman had meant what she said when she proclaimed that she wasn't the kind to forgive and forget. She refused all of Lucas's calls and letters from prison while he awaited trial. (The judge had deemed him a flight risk and he was now being held in a federal penitentiary somewhere in Florida.)

With all the charges he was facing and with so few friends, prospects did not look good for Lucas. Stephanie guessed Keith had been right all along. One day soon, Lucas would be prostituting himself in prison for a pack of cigarettes instead of a Bentley and an ugly-ass silver chain.

Stephanie flipped up the car's visor and turned to Keith.

"Ready to head inside?" Keith asked, tugging on his wool gloves.

She nodded.

Stephanie and Keith made their way through the foyer and then the corridor that led to the sunroom. On one side of the hallway was a row of windows that brightened the dark corridor with shafts of light. On the other side was a row of portraits of all the Gibbons women, or the "Gibbons family hall of fame," as they jokingly liked to refer to it. The paintings started with the saucy portrait of Grandma Althea reclined on a white satin chaise with her gray hair falling around her shoulders, and ended with the baby picture of Stephanie's niece, Clarissa. But spaces would have to be made on the wall now for more portraits since they were adding more members to their clan.

She and Keith stepped out of the corridor into the well-lit sunroom. A seven-foot-tall Christmas tree sat in a far-off corner while baby blue helium balloons dotted the room. A table covered with gift-wrapped packages sat not too far from the tree. Stephanie's sisters were standing throughout the space. Even Cynthia's daughter, Clarissa, was there thanks to her winter break from college. Clarissa was turning into quite the sophisticated young lady, and seemed to have inherited her mother's beauty.

Yolanda Gibbons held center court in the sun-room. The Diahann Carroll look-alike smiled at her family and proudly gazed down at her new grandson.

Yolanda hadn't been very happy when she heard the news about Keith and Stephanie. Her daughter had hooked up with a detective? A *blue-collar man*, no less! She didn't put up too much of a fight about it though. Lauren had already dismayed Yolanda by falling in love with Cris more than a year ago despite her mother's warnings that loving a man gave him the ultimate power, breaking one of the biggest Gibbons family rules. Yolanda knew now from experience that she faced an uphill battle if she tried to talk Stephanie out of her relationship with Keith.

"You girls and your *falling in love!*" the elegant older woman had exclaimed with mild exasperation. "Oh, well, at least he's giving me another grand-baby."

Though she didn't exactly welcome Keith with open arms, she tenuously accepted him into her family.

Yolanda was now tickling Crisanto Jr.'s slobbery chin. "That's Grandma's baby!" she exclaimed, smiling ear to ear. "Oh, isn't he just so handsome! You're going to break all the girls' hearts when you get older!"

Cris was holding his infant son in his big, strong arms. The petite Lauren stood at his side with a hand draped on his shoulder. The couple painted quite the fetching picture. Lauren looked toward the doorway. Her smile broadened when she saw Keith enter the room, holding Stephanie's hand. Keith guided the very pregnant woman down the short flight of steps to the sunroom's terracotta-tiled floor.

"There you guys are!" Lauren shouted as she walked toward them. She kissed Stephanie on both plump cheeks and gave Keith a warm hug. "I wondered when you guys would show up. *I'm* the one who's supposed to be late for Saturday brunch, Steph. Not you," she said with a wink.

Stephanie cupped her hands over her ample belly. "Well, I hate to break it to you, Laurie, but thanks to the extra cargo, I haven't been able to move very fast lately. It seems like I'm always late now."

"Yeah, she slows us down a lot," Keith joked then grimaced when Stephanie playfully slapped him on the shoulder and made a face.

"Well, well, well!" Yolanda said, looking up from her grandson. "You two have finally arrived! I guess we can eat brunch now." She clapped her hands then gestured toward the center of the room where a large round table sat. "All right, everyone! Quiet down! Quiet down! We're all here now. Let's have a seat."

The throng slowly made their way to the table. Keith held out a chair for Stephanie and she carefully lowered herself into the seat. When she landed, she let out a long breath.

"Are you good?" he asked.

She nodded. "Yeah, I'm good. I may need help getting up again though."

He took the chair beside her.

Minutes later, everyone was seated at the table, but it was a tight fit. More bodies had been added and Keith's and Cris's broad shoulders seemed to take up more than their share of space.

The walls echoed with the conversations that now filled the room. Yolanda waved to get one of her maids' attention and motioned for all the water glasses to be filled. Clarissa eagerly reached for the basket of croissants at the center of the table. Keith grabbed a platter of bacon and dropped a few slices on his plate and Stephanie's. Dawn and Cynthia sat with their heads huddled together, laughing over local town gossip. Cris poured himself a cup of coffee from a sterling silver pot while Lauren held their baby in her arms, whispering softly as she fed Cris Jr. his bottled breakfast.

Stephanie gazed around the table. Yolanda had warned all her girls against falling in love, but Stephanie knew now that love couldn't be *that* bad if it brought about something like this. Their brood was expanding and she had a feeling that it would expand even further in the near future. Stephanie wondered what other surprises were in store for the Gibbons girls. Knowing her family, they probably would be big ones.

"What are you smiling about?" Keith asked as he chewed a piece of bacon. He cocked an eyebrow.

Stephanie quickly shook her head. She raised her water glass to her lips. "Nothing. Nothing at all," she lied, holding in her laughter.

Don't miss the first book in the Chesterton Scandals series,

Best Kept Secrets

On sale in September 2015!

Chapter 1

Leila Hawkins paused as she mounted the last con-crete step in front of the double doors of the First Good Samaritan Baptist Church—one of the oldest and largest churches in Chesterton, Virginia, her hometown. Nestled on Broadleaf Avenue across the street from rustic Macon Park, the house of worship had hosted many a baptism, funeral, and nuptial in-side its brick walls in the one hundred and some odd years of its existence. And since 1968, a stark white sign had sat along its exterior, highlighting a Bible verse chosen by the honorable reverend, or the assis-tant pastor when the reverend was ill or on vacation. Leila stepped aside to let a couple pass as she squinted at that sign, which hung a foot away from the doors and several feet above her head.

A FOOL GIVES FULL VENT TO HIS ANGER, BUT A WISE MAN KEEPS HIMSELF UNDER CONTROL, the sign read in big bold letters. PROVERBS 29:11.

Her eyebrows furrowed.

What the hell . . .

Was someone reading her mind?

Who cares if they are?

She grabbed one of the church's stainless-steel door handles.

She was on a mission today and she wasn't going to be deterred from it. She was giving "full vent" to her anger, whether any celestial being liked it or not. Leila was crashing this hifalutin wedding, and only lightning bolts or locusts would keep her away!

She walked into the vestibule, then tugged a heavy wooden door open, preparing herself to be met by a hundred stares, finger pointing, and indignation the instant she stepped inside the sanctuary.

"Hey! You're not supposed to be here!" she waited for someone to shout at her.

Instead, she was greeted by a light melody played by a string quartet and the polite chatter of the two hundred and some odd guests who were taking their seats in the velvet-cushioned pews.

No one stared at her. Hell, they barely seemed to notice her!

The tenseness in her shoulders instantly relaxed. Her white-knuckled grip on her satin clutch loosened. She reminded herself that she was walking into a wedding, not a gladiator pit.

"You're here to talk to Evan," a voice in her head cautioned her. "Not to fight with him. Remember?"

That's right. I'm just here to talk to him, to have a conversation with an old friend.

And if Evan chose not to be polite or listen to her, then and *only then* would she go off on him.

She looked around her.

The sanctuary was filled with splashes of pink and lavender, which Leila remembered were the bride's favorite colors. Roses, hydrangeas, freesias, and lilacs decorated the pulpit and pews, filling the space with their alluring scent. Ribbons and ivy garland were draped over anything and everything, and free-standing candelabras were along each aisle and by the stained-glass windows.

Leila felt an overwhelming sense of déjà vu. She hadn't set foot in this church since her own wedding day ten years ago. As she gazed around her, all the memories of that day came rushing back like a tsunami: the anticipation and nervousness she had felt as she waited for the church doors to open, the happiness she had experienced when she'd seen her handsome groom waiting for her at the end of the aisle, and the overwhelming sadness that had washed over her when she had looked at the wedding guests and had not seen her then best friend, Evan, among their friendly faces.

But she had known Evan wouldn't come to her wedding. Stubborn Evan Murdoch had told her in the plainest way possible that there was no way he would stand by and pretend that he was happy about her nuptials.

"That son of bitch is going to break your heart," Evan had warned her over the phone all those years ago when she'd made one last-ditch effort to ask him to come to the wedding. "He's going to drag you down. And when he does, don't come crying to me."

Leila wasn't sure what had made her angrier: that Evan had given her that dire, bitter prediction on the eve of her wedding—or that his prediction had come true. But today she would have to put aside all that resentment and anger if she was going to get Evan to do what she needed him to do for her mother. Her mother . . . a proud woman who had juggled multiple jobs and saved every dime she had for decades to gather the money to put Leila through school and give her a reasonably happy life. Leila had tried to repay her by purchasing her a two-bedroom bungalow in a middle-class neighborhood where they still held summer block parties, where neighbors still waved and said hello. But now Leila's mother would lose her home in a few months without Evan's help.

Leila's grip on her purse tightened again.

She'd argue. She'd beg. She'd do what she had to do to get Evan to listen to her.

For Ma's sake, she thought.

"Bride or groom?" someone asked, yanking Leila from her thoughts.

"What?" Leila asked.

She turned to find an usher leaning toward her. An officious-looking woman stood behind him with the kind of pinched face reserved for those who waited at the counter at the DMV and dentists' offices. A clipboard covered with several stacks of paper was in her hands. The woman discreetly whispered something into her headset while the usher continued to gaze at Leila expectantly.

"Are you with the bride or groom?" He gestured toward the pews. "On which side would you like to be seated?"

That was a tricky question. The bride hadn't invited Leila to the wedding; neither had the groom. But Leila certainly knew the bride better. Paulette Murdoch, Evan's sister, was someone Leila had once considered a friend—almost a little sister.

"Umm . . . uh, bride . . . I-I guess," Leila finally answered.

They noticed her hesitation and exchanged a look that Leila couldn't decipher. The woman behind the usher whispered into her headset again and waited a beat.

What? Leila thought with panic. *What did I do wrong?*

The woman stepped forward, plastering on a smile that seemed more forced than friendly.

"I'm sorry. Would you mind giving me your name?"

"Uh . . . why?"

"I just want to make sure you're seated in the proper area." The woman then pulled out a pen and pointed down at the stack of papers. Leila could see several names listed along with check marks next to each of them.

You've gotta be kidding me, Leila thought.

They actually had a guest list for the church! What did they think? Someone was going to sneak into the wedding?

"You *are* sneaking into Paulette's wedding!" the voice in her head chastised.

But still, this was ridiculous! Leila wondered if the guest list had been Evan's idea.

Wouldn't want the unwashed masses to wander in off the street, would we? Leila thought sarcastically. *Wouldn't want the poor people to stink up the place! Only the best and the brightest for the M&Ms!*

M&Ms or Marvelous Murdochs . . . People had been muttering and snickering over that nickname for decades around Chesterton, using it to derogatorily refer to the Murdochs—one of the most wealthy, respected, and (some said) stuck-up families in town. Of course that was better than their old nickname, the "High Yella Murdochs." That name had faded once the Murdochs became more equal opportunity and let a few darker folks like Evan's mom into the family.

"Well, my . . ." Leila paused, wondering how she was going to get out of this one. She most certainly wasn't on the list. "My name is . . . my name is, uh—"

"Leila! Leila, over here!" someone called to her. Leila turned to find her childhood friend Colleen waving wildly. Colleen sat in one of the pews toward the front of the church.

Saved by the bell!

"Come on, girl!" Colleen shouted, still grinning. "Sit by me!"

"I guess my 'proper area' is up there, then?" Leila asked.

The usher laughed while the woman with the clipboard continued to scrutinize her, not looking remotely amused.

"Go right ahead," he said, waving Leila forward.

She walked down the center aisle to Colleen. As she did so, she ran her hands across the front of her pale yellow dress. It was an old ensemble that she had thrown on at the last minute after raiding her closet. She hadn't wore it in years, certainly not since she had given birth to her daughter. It felt a little tight and she worried that it wasn't very flattering. The ill-fitting dress only added to her already heightened anxiety.

"I haven't seen you in ages, girl! I didn't know you'd be at Paulette's wedding," Colleen cried, removing her heavy leather purse from the pew and plopping it onto her ample lap. She shifted over, causing an elderly woman beside her to glance at her annoyance. Colleen then adjusted the wide brim of her sequin- and feather-decorated royal purple hat. "I saw you come in, but you didn't notice me waving at you. What were you thinking about, staring off into space like that?"

Leila pursed her lips as she took the seat nearest to the center aisle. "Just took a little trip down memory lane, that's all."

"*Memory lane?*" Colleen frowned in confusion. Suddenly, her brown eyes widened. "Oh, I forgot! This was the church where you got married too, isn't it?"

Leila nodded.

"Ten years ago last month! Girl, I remember," Colleen continued. "It was a beautiful day, wasn't it? And you had looked so pretty in your gown." She patted Leila's hand in consolation. "I'm so sorry to hear about you and Brad, by the way."

"Don't be sorry," Leila assured.

I'm certainly not, she thought.

Not only had Brad broken her heart, like Evan had predicted, but that man also had put her through so much pain during the course of their marriage—between the lies, philandering, his get-rich-quick schemes, and his all-around bullshit—that he was lucky she hadn't thrown her wedding ring down the garbage disposal in outrage. Instead, she had pawned it to pay for a hatchback she'd purchased for her move from San Diego back to Chesterton. She'd had to get a new car after her Mercedes-Benz was repo'd thanks to Brad neglecting to mention that he hadn't made any payments in four months.

"So it *is* final then?" Colleen asked. "It's over between you two?"

"Almost. The divorce should be finalized in a few months, I guess."

Leila certainly hoped it would be. But frankly, it was no telling with Brad. He had been dragging his feet on the divorce proceedings, saying that his focus was instead on his criminal case. He faced charges for fraud and money laundering because he and his partners had bilked several wealthy clients in Southern California out of more than twenty million dollars with some elaborate Ponzi scheme.

Thanks to Brad, his lawyer, and the California court system, Leila's life was still in limbo. She felt like she was *still* swimming her way out the whirlpool Brad kept sucking her into.

"Well, I'm glad you came back here," Colleen said. "We missed you. I know I certainly did. I'm sorry your divorce is the reason why you came, but . . . you tried your best, right?"

Leila nodded then turned away to stare at the front of the church, wishing desperately that Colleen would drop the topic. She didn't want to think about Brad right now. She had enough on her plate today.

"You put up with more than most wives would," Colleen continued, oblivious to Leila's growing discomfort. "It's a wonder you lasted as long as you did. I know I wouldn't have!"

Leila's smile tightened.

"All that lying and cheating—and now that pyramid-scheme nonsense! That man has dragged you through the mud, Leila. Right on through it!" Colleen shook her head ruefully. "Girl, I would have taken a frying pan to the back of that man's head *years* ago!"

It was bad enough to have a wreck of a marriage, to find out that you were sharing a bed every night

with a liar and a hustler. But it was ten times worse knowing that everyone in town also knew—and Chesterton
was a town that loved its gossip. She was sure her failed
marriage and Brad's criminal charges had been gossip
du jour in every beauty salon, church gathering, and
coffee shop in Chesterton for months!

Of course, Evan had discovered the truth first, but
he hadn't needed the town gossips to tell him. He
had figured it out himself. He had seen through the
varnish and spotted the shoddy workmanship underneath. He had seen the *real* Brad back when she met
the smooth-talking Casanova her junior year in college. Though Brad had blinded Leila with his sweet
talk, worldliness, and charm, Evan had called him on
his bullshit. But she had been too naïve and lovesick
at the time to listen to her then best friend. She wished
now that she had. It could have spared her a lot of dis-
appointment, agony, and heartbreak in the long run.
It could have spared her from severing ties with Evan
and the humiliation she was suffering today.

"The flowers are beautiful," Leila said with a false
cheeriness, trying to change the subject from Brad.
She looked around her again, taking it all in.

Paulette Murdoch was probably deliriously happy
with how the decorations had turned out. The décor
fit her to a T.

"I knew everything would be this nice though,"
Leila said. "Paulette's dad never spared an expense,
especially when it came to his little girl. I've been away
for a while, but even I remember that much."

Colleen shook her head and leaned toward Leila's
ear. "Not her father, honey," she whispered. "All this
was arranged while he was sick in the hospital and
after he died seven months ago. It's Evan who dished

out the money for this wedding. He controls the purse strings now!"

Of course he does, Leila thought sullenly. Evan controlled everything. He held all the cards, which was why she was here today.

The last note of the melody the string quartet had been playing ended and the violins started to play *Canon in D Major.* The chatter in the sanctuary ceased as the church doors opened. The groom and his six groomsmen strolled toward the front of the church, near the pulpit, in single-breasted tuxedos with pink calla lilies pinned to their lapels.

The groom was a handsome man. He stood at six feet, had ebony-hued skin, and wide shoulders.

Just Paulette's type, Leila thought, remembering when Evan's little sister had described her ideal man more than a decade ago as Leila painted the teen girl's toenails.

Leila watched as the bridesmaids began the processional. They were all wearing satin gowns of various designs, but in the same shade of lavender. They clutched bouquets of hydrangea, freesias, and roses. The adorable ring bearer and the flower girl made their way down the center aisle next. The little girl reminded Leila of her own daughter, Isabel.

Suddenly, the music changed again. This time it was Vivaldi's *Spring.* Everyone took their cue and rose from the pews in anticipation of the bride's entrance.

Seconds later, Paulette stood in the church doorway, and she took Leila's breath away.

Leila couldn't believe this was the same unassuming teenager she had last seen ten years ago. This woman was beautiful and regal. Her long, dark glossy hair cascaded over her bare burnt-copper-toned shoulders. Her curvy figure was accentuated by the mermaid cut of her strapless wedding gown, which was decorated with Swarovski crystals and lace. A cathedral-length veil trailed behind her dramatically.

Paulette looked so beautiful, so stunning, so absolutely—

Perfect, Leila thought as she stared at her in awe.

And holding Paulette's satin-gloved hand was Evan. Being the new family patriarch, it only seemed right that Evan would give the bride away today. Judging from the grin on his strikingly handsome face, he seemed proud and happy to play the fatherly role.

Evan hadn't aged much in the past decade, but he certainly looked more handsome and distinguished than Leila remembered. He had the same coppery skin as his sister and was even taller than the groom. The glasses he'd often worn during childhood were gone. Leila was happy to see he had finally given them up for good. She had always thought he had the most soulful dark eyes that shouldn't be hidden behind thick, plastic lenses.

As the brother and sister walked down the center aisle toward the altar, a lump formed in Leila's throat. Her heart ached a little. This was the man whom she had once called her best friend. Once, they had been so close. She had been able to turn to Evan in her darkness moments, to confess to him her worst fears. Now he wouldn't even return her emails or phone calls. He hadn't met her daughter. He had gotten married five years ago and she had found out about it months later. She hadn't even met his wife!

Leila stared at the front pew, looking at the faces of the folks who sat there, wondering if his wife was among them.

She and Evan were practically strangers now. What the hell had happened to them?

Time . . . distance . . . silence, she thought.

But they could still make it right, she told herself, filling up with the warmth of the moment. They could put the past behind them. They could make amends. The guy standing in front of her didn't seem petty or angry. Maybe she had just misunderstood him. Maybe they just misunderstood each other. Once she told Evan why she needed his help, he would listen. She knew he would!

As Paulette and Evan drew closer, Leila grinned at the bride, whose loving gaze was focused solely on her husband-to-be.

Meanwhile, Evan's eyes drifted to the wedding guests. He nodded at a few in greeting. Finally, he noticed Leila standing in the pews near the center aisle.

"Hey, Magoo," she mouthed before giving him a timid wave.

Magoo. It was the nickname she had given him back when they were kids. Whenever he hadn't worn his glasses, he had squinted like the cartoon character, Mr. Magoo. His nickname for her had been "Bugs" after Bugs Bunny, thanks to her bucked rabbit teeth, which had thankfully been corrected over time by a good set of braces.

When Leila waved at him as he walked past, Evan did a double take. Leila watched, deflated, as his broad smile disappeared. His face abruptly hardened and his jaw tightened. The dark eyes that she had once admired now snapped back toward the front of the church. Evan looked more than irritated at seeing her standing there in the church pew. He looked downright furious.

The warm, mushy feeling that had swelled inside of her abruptly dissolved. Her cheeks flushed with heat. Her heart began to thud wildly in her chest again.

"There goes that fantasy," the voice in her head scoffed.

She should have known it wouldn't be easy. Evan was obviously still cross at her and even more so now that she had sneaked into his sister's wedding.

Fine, she thought angrily. *Be that way, Evan.*

But she wasn't giving up. She was still going to find a way to talk to him today—or yell at him or plead with him, whatever was required. She would find a way to plead her mother's case.

Grab the Hottest Fiction
from
Dafina Books

Grab These Novels by
Zuri Day

Available Wherever Books Are Sold!

All available as e-books, too!

Visit our website at **www.kensingtonbooks.com**

The Hottest African American Fiction
from
Dafina Books